(Reprinted from *Sunday News*, December 11, 1932)

HAS JUSTICE BEEN DONE IN THE LIBBY HOLMAN CASE?

Story of Libby Holman—Amazing Epic of the Age

Whirligig! Speed! Faster! Crazier!
Champagne Cocktails . . . Corn liquor straight . . . Pour it on . . . Step on the gas . . . Shoot the works . . . Speed! Gin, rye, bourbon, sex.

Dizzy dames. Dizzy house parties. A thousand-acre estate. Private golf course . . . tennis courts . . . swimming pool . . . lake. Moonlight dips. Dances. Joyrides. Airplanes. Yachts. High powered cars. Speed! Chasing a new thrill today. Tiring of it tomorrow. Nowhere to go but places. Nothing to do but things.

Speed, with youth at the throttle, millions to spend—and bored stiff. Life's blah. The world's a phony. The whirling spins on, and 20-year-old Zachary Smith Reynolds, son of Richard Joshua Reynolds, tobacco king, sleeps beside his father in the family plot in Winston-Salem Cemetery. He died of a bullet wound in the head early on the morning of Wednesday, July 6 last.

The whirligig spins on, and Libby Holman Reynolds, his 28-year-old bride, the toast of all Broadway playboys, and Albert (Ab) Walker, 22, his playmate since childhood, are accused of his murder . . .

Fred Pasley

Also by Milt Machlin:

STRANGERS IN THE LAND
ATLANTA
PIPE LINE
FRENCH CONNECTION II
THE SET-UP
FAMILY MAN
THE SEARCH FOR MICHAEL ROCKEFELLER
THE PRIVATE HELL OF ERNEST HEMINGWAY
NINTH LIFE: THE CARYL CHESSMAN STORY
THE GOSSIP WARS

LEISURE BOOKS NEW YORK CITY

A LEISURE BOOK®

AUGUST 1990

Published by

Dorchester Publishing Co., Inc.
276 Fifth Avenue
New York, NY 10001

Printed in the United States of America.

LIBBY

Contents

Part One

Elsbeth Holzman

1
The Legend

In 1932, when the world was stumbling through the greatest economic depression in modern times, Libby Holman was at the height of a fantastic career. No woman could have asked for more. The sultry, black-haired, torch singer was the biggest star on Broadway. For the nation as a whole, things were in a desperate condition. Coffee at the A&P was selling for 19 cents a pound; lettuce was 15 cents for two heads; there were 13 million unemployed and wages were 60 percent less than they had been at the peak of prosperity in 1929.

Only three years earlier, Libby Holman, then twenty-five, had received an ovation when she stopped the show with her rendition of "Moanin' Low," in *The Little Show*, a Broadway revue in which she co-starred with Clifton Webb and Fred Allen. Critics raved over her voice. Brooks Atkinson described it as a "dark purple flame." In those grim times, the theater was packed every night to hear Libby sing her sexy, torchy specialty in the manner of the Harlem blues singers she admired. Overnight Libby seemed to become a national sex symbol. By the end of 1930, Libby was earning more than $2,500 a week, in hard Depression dollars.

Though not a classic beauty, her long, shiny black hair, perfect olive complexion, exotic features and sexy, long-legged figure, accented by the clinging, low-cut golden gowns she favored, sent the public and critics alike into frenzies of adulation. Half the men in New York were in love with her and almost as many women. It was said that she liked both, but leaned more strongly toward the latter. Her taste in men inclined toward the young, pretty, and androgynous, as her long and tender relationship with Montgomery Clift would later show.

She already numbered among her female lovers such prominent personalities as Jeanne Eagels, the original "Sadie Thompson" in the Broadway play, *Rain*, Josephine Baker, the American Negro star of the *Folies Bergère* and Tallulah Bankhead. But her favorite friend was undoubtedly Louisa Carpenter du Pont Jenney, heiress to a considerable number of the du Pont millions.

Louisa and Libby, on their nighttime rounds of Manhattan, used to startle blasé Broadwayites by appearing regularly in men's clothes and identical bowler hats to eat spareribs and cole slaw at the Clam House in the early hours of the morning. They would be joined by their friends Bea Lillie and Tallulah Bankhead. On Saturdays, Libby liked to mock convention by lighting and ceremoniously smoking in public a huge Havana cigar.

Libby had a natural talent for attracting publicity. In any event, people of the smart set were quick to emulate the various fads she initiated. She was the first New York actress to paint her nails a vivid scarlet. "They are my only jewels," she told reporters. She was the first to own a Ford "flivver" with a liveried chauffeur. Along with Marlene Dietrich, she was one of the first to set the style of sporting brightly colored, high-fashion pajamas as casual wear, and one summer, while in Europe visiting her friend Josephine Baker, she was arrested on the beach at

Libby at 50 in 1954.

Deauville for indecent exposure.

These famous eccentricities soon became the rage with other actresses, chorus girls, society debs, and svelte Park Avenue matrons. Interviewed in the old New York *World*, she said, "I want to live to be a smart old witch who rules with an iron scepter. I want never to end, I want never to be dependent. At fifty, sixty, seventy, and eighty I want to have enough charm and fascination inside of myself to draw the admiration and love of men."

Certainly many men sought her favors, including some of the best names on Broadway, Wall Street, Bradstreet's and the Social Register. She was the center of attraction everywhere she went and received so many mash notes backstage that she never found time to read even a tenth of them. She'd make four or five dates for the same evening and then break them all to keep a sixth.

Meanwhile, her friend Louisa showered the attention on her that only the wealthiest can give. She chartered an eighty-foot yacht once, to fulfill a chance whim of Libby's to go on a cruise, and when Libby got tired of her flivver, bought her a sixteen-cylinder Rolls Royce convertible. Newspapers referred delicately to their association as a "beautiful friendship."

Though Libby frequented many of the New York Prohibition Era night spots, her favorite night dates were usually in Harlem where she would almost invariably be persuaded to climb on a table and give a rendition of her specialty, "Moanin' Low." The song itself swept the nation. Music publishers could not print enough copies to meet the demand. Libby was besieged with offers to make records. She recorded a song for one company and it instantly became what today would be called a gold record. No radio program seemed to be complete without a rendition of "Moanin' Low." Stenographers hummed it, newsboys whistled it. And the song's composers, Ralph Rainger and Howard Dietz, raked in a fortune in royalties.

Just when it seemed Libby's star could rise no higher, she was introduced to a slim, moody, seventeen-year-old

North Carolinian aviator named Zachary Smith Reynolds. Libby at first treated the boy with a motherly affection suitable to the eight-year gap between their ages. But Reynolds was so instantly taken by Libby's exotic charms, so unlike that of the cool Southern belles to which he was accustomed, that he threatened to commit suicide if she would not marry him instantly, a threat that Libby took as just another example of his Southern gift for hyperbole.

She had, in fact, met and gone out with the impassioned young man several times before she realized that her suitor, described around Broadway as "that rich kid from North Carolina," was actually one of the four children of R. J. Reynolds, the manufacturer of Camels cigarettes and founder of the great Reynolds Tobacco fortune. He had inherited some twenty million of those nicotine-stained dollars in trust when his father had died twelve years earlier.

Libby was always a woman of intrigue. People talked about her. They wanted to know the answers to innumerable questions. Was she really a lesbian, or did she like men as well? Perhaps her relationships with all those women really were simply "beautiful friendships." Certainly until Smith Reynolds came along, she was not known to spend much time with any one man in a serious way, although she dated many.

There were other questions people asked, too. Some people insisted that she was a heavy, almost pathological drinker; others said she drank moderately. She was subject to extreme changes of mood and bizarre behavior. Did she take drugs, people wondered, or was she simply a crazy, go-to-hell kid with a wild sense of humor and a taste for the *outré*?

Other things puzzled people also. Was she really born in 1906 as she claimed? And graduated from college at sixteen? Or had she been born in 1904, as some records seemed to indicate? Researchers who tried to find the answer to that question were stymied. Somewhere along the line, Libby's actual birth certificate had disappeared.

She was originally named Elsbeth Holzman. The family later Americanized the Germanic name during World War I, in a gesture of patriotism at a time when people were calling sauerkraut "Liberty Cabbage" and German Shepherds "Alsatians." Early in her career, she made contradictory statements to news people and there was considerable speculation about her origins. She told a writer from *Collier's* that her family was Huguenot German. Many people, hearing the peculiar husky timbre of her voice and the sure blues phrasing of her songs, were positive that she had at least what was then called "a touch of the tar brush." Or was she a plain Jewish girl from Cincinnati?

Howard Dietz, who wrote many of the sketches and most of the lyrics for her first hit show, *The Little Show*, said, "No one in theater was more discussable than Libby Holman, who came from Cincinnati and was game for anything. Though she had studied law, she was a frivolous personality who appeared in the nude in her dressing room and therefore had a lot of visitors." She was accused of being snooty when she walked past friends without so much as a nod, but Dietz points out that she was terribly nearsighted and almost certainly didn't recognize them. She was so myopic, Dietz said, that she couldn't see anything more than two inches away from her. "She somehow found her way out onto the stage, but she could only get off by clutching the curtain as it came down and going off with it."

Dietz, who started to see Libby socially after the *The Little Show* opened, remembers that she tended to do "outrageous things," even when she was with him. For example, one Friday she told him she was tired of "being nice" and she decided that on their weekend at the home of the Henri Souvaines, to which they both had been invited, that they would be disagreeable instead of their usual charming selves. Dietz didn't think much of the joke and was certain he couldn't carry it off. "Well, *try*," Libby said. Mrs. Mabel Souvaines showed them the garden and Libby said, "I hate flowers." Henri, a well-known composer, played one of his songs and Libby said, "I don't like what you're playing." Mabel, who was nothing if not sharp, caught on to the trick and turned to Libby with a big smile and said, 'I don't like *you*!" Dietz was astonished to find that this was the beginning of a great friendship between the two women.

As someone who had known and traveled in Libby's set for some time when she met Smith Reynolds, Dietz suspected, as did other friends of Libby's, that they wouldn't have long to wait before something disastrous happened. Libby and Smith Reynolds had little in common. The bulk of their conversations consisted of interminable spats over whether Libby would ever consent to marry the smitten heir. Smith, whose mother and father had died in his childhood, seemed extraordinarily dependent on Libby's affections. He was jealous of her many male and female friends and of the work that took so much of her time.

Smith's most ardent wish was that she would give up show business and the Broadway crowd with whom he felt so ill at ease, and move to Winston-Salem, where his dark moods were accepted and where he was treated as a young prince.

Ultimately, after Smith pursued her all over the country and across half of Europe, Libby consented to marry the young tobacco heir. Smith's feelings of insecurity persisted, and he still wanted Libby to give up her career and devote her time exclusively to him.

Finally these differences flared up into what became the greatest mystery in Libby's life. During a weekend party in Reynolda, the Reynolds family's thousand-acre estate on the outskirts of Winston-Salem, came the predicted disaster. It took place after days of drinking, quarreling, and intrigue which involved not only Libby, but Smith Reynolds' lifelong chum and recently appointed "secretary for life," Ab Walker, another wealthy Winston-Salem boy.

About one o'clock in the morning, when all of the guests had retired or departed, a muffled shot sounded in the room occupied by Libby and Smith Reynolds. Libby staggered out onto the second floor balcony, the front of her peach silk negligee soaked with blood, and screamed, "My God! Smith's shot himself!"

Ab Walker who later said he was downstairs cleaning up after the party raced up to the Reynolds' room where he found Smith Reynolds, face down on his bed with a bloody wound in his temple, an apparent suicide.

The coroner agreed that it was a case of self-administered death. A few days later, however, Sheriff Transou Scott announced that he felt otherwise. He informed the press that there were many clues indicating that suicide was unlikely. For instance, the wound was in the *right* temple and Smith, Scott said, was lefthanded. A hole made by the exiting bullet was found six feet up in the window screen of the sleeping porch in which Reynolds was found, in such a position that, if he had committed suicide, he would have had to twist in a bizarre fashion and fling himself across the bed. Furthermore, the gun was not found until the following day.

There were other things that bothered Sheriff Scott. Libby's slippers and sweater were found in Ab Walker's room. Witnesses said that she was seen in intimate positions with Walker earlier in the weekend and even on the night of her husband's death. Libby and Smith had quarreled openly before guests at the party. There were strange discrepancies in accounts of the time schedule required to take Reynolds to nearby Baptist Hospital, where he died several hours later. Libby, who took a private room in the hospital to be near her husband, had taken Walker into the room, perhaps to comfort her. A nurse reported that when she went to the room to report Smith's death, she found Libby and Walker on the floor flimsily dressed and in what could only be called a compromising situation. The nurse overheard Ab cautioning Libby not to say anything to the police or anyone else about the case.

Sheriff Scott felt that despite the coroner's verdict these assorted mysteries were important enough to bring before the grand jury. So he did. After listening to Scott's presentation and that of several other witnesses, the grand jury returned an indictment: Abner Walker and Libby Holman Reynolds "did on or about the sixth day of July A.D. 1932 in said (Forsyth) county, commit the following offense; to wit: Did unlawfully, willfully, feloniously, premeditatedly, and of their malice and forethought, kill and murder one Z. Smith Reynolds."

The news that America's greatest torch singer and her alleged lover were accused of murdering her husband, heir to one of America's greatest fortunes, made headlines across the world, and raised the curtain on what was to be the greatest drama in Libby Holman's tumultuous and enigmatic life.

2

In the Beginning

Elsbeth Holzman was born on May 23, 1904 in Cincinnati, Ohio. Her family, of German-Jewish origins on both sides, was one of the most distinguished Jewish families in America. Her mother, Ray Workum,had been a schoolteacher before marriage. She traced her ancestry back to Sir Ezekiel Workum, noted sculptor and leader of the Jewish intellectual aristocracy in this country. He came to America in the early nineteenth century. Disraeli and Supreme Court Justice Benjamin Cardozo were of this same Sephardic line. So was Sir Moses Ezekiel, knighted by the German Emperor, who created statues for the outside niches of the Corcoran Gallery in Washington, D.C. In Rome, where he went to work, he leased the Baths of Diocletian and transformed them into one of the most beautiful studios in Europe. It was believed that this Sephardic strain, originating in pre-Inquisition Spain, was responsible for Libby's much-discussed olive complexion.

The Workums were one of the pioneer families ol

Cincinnati. Levi Jay, one of Ray's forebears, was born in New York City, and settled in Cincinnati in 1925. He was a co-founder of the country's largest distilling firm, which made four or five leading brands of sour mash whiskey. But despite this background of wealth and power, Libby's branch of the family seemed to inherit only disaster. Her paternal great uncle George Holzman settled in Rochester, Indiana, in the 1870s. He opened a general merchandise store, and did what appeared to be a thriving business. He soon became one of the leading merchants in Rochester, so that the Ohio River city was astonished when one day he went into voluntary bankruptcy and disappeared before his creditors could catch up with him, leaving his wife in reasonably comfortable circumstances in the cottage they had occupied since coming to town. When the heat had died down, Uncle George Holzman appeared as suddenly as he had vanished and joined his wife to live in seclusion in the cottage until his death. He was never again seen on the street or even on the front porch, perhaps for fear that there were creditors still on his trail.

One of Holzman's four daughters, Bess, went to Cincinnati, where her parents had originally been married, to become a teacher in the public school. There she met her second cousin, Ross Holzman, the twin brother of Alfred, who was to become Libby's father. Bess and Ross were married in the little gray cottage in Indiana and Alfred was the best man. The couple returned to Cincinnati to live and the two brothers founded a stock brokerage and banking firm that prospered and developed branches in a number of Midwestern and Eastern cities. They were members of the New York Stock Exchange and the Chicago Board of Trade, among others. Brother Ross, with his genial personality and glib tongue, was the smooth-talking front man of the organization and Libby's father Alfred was considered the workhorse. Both were prominent in local society and in 1901 Ross was elected the treasurer of the Cincinnati Club, the town's most exclusive Jewish organization. By this time, Alfred had met, wooed and married Ray Workum and fathered Libby's oldest sister Marian, known as "Dilly" to the family. Just about the time of Libby's birth rumors began to circulate about her uncle Ross, who was suddenly given to long, unexplained absences. It was said that the Holzman firm made several bad investments and that the whole financial structure of the brokerage house was shaky. These rumors were heatedly denied by both brothers.

But in 1904, the year Libby was born, a petition of bankruptcy was filed in the local court by Libby's father, Alfred. It was the biggest business failure in the city's history. Investors' losses were said to total a million dollars. Exhibiting a handful of small change, Alfred, who stayed in Cincinnati and faced the bitter music, told friends, "This is all I have in the world." So Libby's chance to be born the heiress to a reasonable amount of wealth collapsed before she was even a year old. Meanwhile, her uncle, who adored the dark-haired infant, left, saying he was going to Ohio to raise money. He disappeared and a few weeks later, it was discovered that he was $7,000 short as the treasurer of the Cincinnati Club. There were rumors that he had been seen in South America, the West Indies, Japan, Germany, and Italy. In any event, he was never heard from again.

His wife, Bess Holzman, left penniless, returned to the little gray cottage in Rochester to live in seclusion, just as her father had. But the obscure little cottage continued to be a source of gossip and mystery to the people in the Indiana town. They believed that there was a secret basement vault, underneath trap doors of the gray cottage. Local talk intensified when townspeople reported the midnight arrival at the railroad station of a "dark, smooth-shaven stranger," who entered a hack and was driven to the cottage and let in through the rear door. Some people thought that it might have been the missing Ross. Newsmen from Cincinnati and investigators swarmed into Rochester and besieged the cottage but the inquiries were met with the explanation that the man was

Mrs. Holzman's brother from St. Louis. However, nobody was allowed to see him or even gain entry to the house. The newsmen's siege was intensified when Alfred Holzman was reported to have visited the cottage with baby Libby, to whom Ross was passionately devoted. Ross' wife stayed in the cottage for several years. Then she finally left, went to the East, obtained a divorce on grounds of desertion, and married a Westchester man.

Meanwhile, Libby's father Alfred settled down again to practice law and to rebuild his fortune and his reputation. Both he and his wife Ray expressed disappointment that Libby had not been a boy who could move into the family law firm and help rebuild the Holzman fortunes.

Household help in those pre-World War I days was cheap and even in their troubled circumstances, the Holzmans could afford a nurse for the children and a cook. According to Libby, it was her black nurse who first discovered her powerful voice when she let out an enormous bellow in response to a misapplied safety pin. Hoping that these early "musical" tones heralded an artistic future, her parents bought her a violin and paid for lessons, but they found her always skipping away on solitary picnics in the marshes and woods around her native suburb, only to return at night to assault the family's ears with vivid imitations of the noisier local fauna. Croaking bullfrogs were her specialty, but she could also imitate the lifelike groans and moans of lovesick bitterns. Libby told reporter John B. Kennedy of *Collier's* in 1929 that on one zero-degree night she had sent a learned neighbor, a biologist at the University of Cincinnati, into frenzied excitement when he capered into the faculty house with the astonishing news that he had positively heard a bullfrog booming in the campus snow! According to Libby, no one thought that man was "quite right" after that.

"My mother was afraid of my ambition to become a singer," Libby told Kennedy. "We were not a puritan family, but the theater was not for us."

She told Kennedy that the family was determined there would be no stage people in their household. "Let her take her musical feelings out on the violin," her father said. "Lots of people do, why shouldn't she?" However, the damage had already been done, when her father took her at the age of four, to see her first musical comedy.

Libby continually pestered her family to let her go into show business. When Libby was about eight years old, her mother decided to settle forever her doubts about Libby's talent.

Mischa Elman was performing in Cincinnati and had made Alfred's acquaintance. Would the great man listen to a possible prodigy and advise the family? He said he would. Libby was dressed in her best gingham skirt and Elman settled into an easy chair to listen to the performance of the youngster with an olive complexion and gazelle eyes. She raised her fiddle to her plump chin and played—not for very long but apparently long enough. "Mr. Elman," Mrs. Holzman asked anxiously after the brief performance, "what do you recommend for my daughter to develop her musical ears?"

"Washing them at least twice a day has its advantages," the distinguished violinist replied with a gentle smile. That evening, Libby told Kennedy, there was hell to pay in the Holzman household. Libby's youngest brother made some indiscreet wisecrack and wound up wearing the fiddle as a crown. Furious, Libby took the bow of the now hated violin and snapped it against her knee.

"All right," her father said, settling back into his Morris chair after the fracas, "now there will be no more nonsense. She'll go through high school and college and get her law degree. Girls can be lawyers, too. She will be useful surely, and ornamental, perhaps."

Libby meanwhile had retired to her room to soothe her battered ego. A few minutes later Papa Alfred heard, coming from her room, a tune, in a formless doggerel Libby had picked up in her childhood wanderings among the neighboring "nigger" shanties where she used to go to listen to the primitive, haunting blues melodies brought up the Mississippi River by migrating Southern blacks. "That's all I could do," she told *Collier's*, "with whatever music was in me. Let it go in blues."

But to her parents, these songs were not so much a gift as an eccentricity. Alfred Holzman said, "I don't care what you sing, as long as you go through college and get your law degree." One thing was certain; whatever her talents as a singer or musician, Libby had a good brain. "When I was fourteen," she told one reporter, "I found a volume of Nietzsche in the library of a friend's home and borrowed it. It wasn't altogether intelligible to me but I knew it was smart to read such things so I read and reread it from cover to cover. Then I stumbled on a copy of Oscar Wilde's epigrams in a public library and it so fascinated me that I never returned it.

"After that, I was a bug on psychology. Then I went in for sex in a big way—Freud, Janet, Schnitzler, and Eleanor Glyn." It was amusing, Libby told the reporter, to sit in her schoolgirl's sweater discussing in shocking, clinical detail, sexual case histories and psychology. She had absolutely no practical experience of these matters, for all through her early years, Libby was not known to have had any serious boyfriends, or even to associate much with the opposite sex. She was nonetheless considered extremely attractive and was very popular with men.

Even in grade school, Libby was marked as a girl apart and something of an enigma. Her early announcement that her ambition was to be a lawyer was considered in those days bizarre. Her family's Jewish background precluded them from socializing with the parents of other children in the school. In addition, the growing hatred of Germans, brought about by the fervor accompanying World War I, made the Holzman family name something of a drawback. Anyone who didn't know the Holzmans assumed they were German, and in any event German Jews were no better liked than other Germans. Finally, Daddy Alfred, seeing the writing on the wall, discreetly dropped the Teutonic-sounding "z" from the family name and from then on thus went by the name of "Holman."

On April 2, 1915, Alfred's brother, Wallace, superintendent of a wholesale liquor company, shot himself through the head in his office in downtown Cincinnati. Libby's father was doubly distressed, because the week before Wallace had confided his suicidal intention to Alfred who tried vainly to free his brother from his morbid obsession. Only Alfred and Wallace ever knew the motive for Wallace's suicide.

In September 1916, still in possession of some of her baby fat, plump but flat-chested Libby was just one of a thousand others who trooped up the steps of the Hughes High School. It was a red brick edifice with medieval towers and was perched on a hilltop overlooking the Ohio River and the blue grass country of Kentucky beyond. The entering students gazed in awe at the Winged Victory which dominated the entrance and then timidly entered the auditorium. Breathlessly they waited as their names were called, assigning them to their freshman classrooms.

Libby was excited about entering a school which would provide a much larger forum for her budding talents than the tiny public school she had previously attended. She soon proved herself an excellent student, as she had in grade school, and an active participant in many of the school's extracurricular activities. These included the Honor League, a girls' organization devoted to the promulgation of moral standards (its motto was "To do the thing I know is true, and should not be ashamed to do, to try to make some others see, the thing that so appeals to me.") She also joined the French Club and, of course, the Glee Club, as well as the staff of *Old Hughes*, the monthly humor magazine, and the Quills Club for would-be writers.

On *Old Hughes*, Libby, known all her life for her sharp wit and glib expressions, was quickly assigned to the humor department. She was also in charge, anonymously, of a gossip column called. "The Rambler," in which she gave a coy clue to her identity.

"I am tall and very slim,
Am I a she or am I a him?"

In the Quills she devoted her attentions to short stories. The ambition to write never left her, even when she became a star. One of her short story contributions to *Old Hughes* was called "What's a Girl Good For?" It told about an ill-clad youngster who, after falling in love, was inspired to sartorial splendor. But at the end the story, told in heartrending detail, the girl two-times the now dapper young man and leaves him to return to his original gear.

Throughout the years she attended Old Hughes, Libby showed little interest in boys. Once in a while she would go to parties at the homes of girl friends, but she would never participate in the giggling games of post office or other puppy-love shenanigans. When they started she would invariably put on her hat and leave without explanation or apology, clearly miffed at the goings-on. Some thought this was because of her proper Jewish upbringing; some had other ideas. But her rigid attitude toward sexual dalliance seemed not to impede her growing popularity with the boys; even then they thronged around her to the point where she soon acquired a reputation among jealous classmates as a vamp who would lead the boys on just so far, and then leave them flat.

In addition to her other extracurricular activities, Libby of course took a prominent part in all theatrical and musical events. In her sophomore year, the United States entered the war in Europe and the girls of the class spent the afternoons knitting socks and sweaters for overseas soldiers, while the boys participated in drives for Thrift Stamps, Liberty Loans, and the Red Cross.

Even during that period of feverish national excitement, Libby was an outstanding figure. In addition to taking the leading part in most of the school's amateur theatricals, she never failed to make the class honor roll. She also liked to swim and ride. In those days she wore her shiny black hair in a bun. She was flat-chested, long of limb, and plain-featured. Still she had a provocative lift to her shoulder, a sidewise tilt of the head, full, petulant, bee-stung lips, and an appealing, hurt look in her grave, green eyes.

By 1920, her high school graduation year, Libby's talent and versatility had so impressed her schoolmates that the class prophet wrote of her in the Old Hughes Annual: "Elsbeth is one of the most original girls in our class. Her contributions to Old Hughes have made her famous. She is a talented actress, too. We all expect to see Libby before the footlights someday. Indeed, she has already given us many manifestations of her art." This was followed by a bit of doggerel which ended with the line, "And she dances such a way."

Libby's popularity was not based on any extravagance in style or dress. She dressed sloppily, although she had a gift for accessorizing that always gave the impression of smartness. Even then, Libby was at her best before an audience, expecially if she got a good reception, which she did on making her first public speech at exercises just before her high school commencement. Her poise was impressive and she delivered all of her lines in a casual, off-hand, and slangy way that seemed completely spontaneous. She loved a crowd and she loved personal display. In school pictures, Libby invariably stood in front.

On Commencement Day, the sixteen-year-old girl mounted the platform smiling and unembarrassed. As her classmates recall, she wore a long blue skirt, the style for young girls that year, and the traditional white middy blouse. Her dazzling black hair was bound by a red ribbon. She stood beside the principal and he rested one hand on her shoulder as she beamed with pride.

"Elizabeth Lloyd Holman (she had apparently stopped calling herself Elsbeth somewhat earlier) is the most representative girl of the senior class," he said. "She is all that we want our students to be in scholarship, the social life of the school, in extracurricular activities, and in wholesome interests. We can expect her to go far."

Libby, called on to respond to this accolade, did so without a tremor. In a voice already rich, a deep contralto-baritone with an earthy undertone, she approached the podium. "Thank you, Mr. Merry," she said. "And I want to thank the faculty for making it possible for me to achieve the little success you have been kind enough to recognize, Mr. Merry. I hate to leave you, my teachers and the school."

For some reason, this simple speech brought down the house, and Libby loved it! She left the commencement exercises glowing with excitement, surrounded by admiring friends. Under her arm she had tucked the classbook, which listed her as "the nerviest girl in the class" and the "most original girl." It's rare that high school classbook prophecies come so close to the mark, but Libby, at sixteen, was just beginning her rise to fame—or notoriety.

3
College

At the University of Cincinnati, in the fall of 1920, Libby, then two months past sixteen and two years ahead of her class, tried to make up in her appearance what she lacked in maturity. She bobbed her hair during the first two weeks, getting rid of the two distinguishing curls which previously had dangled in front of her ears. Once it was cut short, her coiffure became even more ungovernable, but now she had a perfect windblown hairdo without even trying. Half her hair stood straight up from the crown of her head and on either side stuck out horizontally in a tangle that curled attractively into a wide swirl at the nape of her neck.

Libby was not exactly a beauty. Her hands were a little too big and they always seemed to be in her way, but she had a wonderful complexion, which remained remarkable through most of her life, deep olive and without a blemish. All this set up her sensuous cupid's bow mouth and exotic eyes which later, along with the sultry, low, tantalizing voice, were to make her famous.

The Holman family, which had never completely recovered from the financial shock of the Holman twins' bankruptcy more than ten years earlier, did not have a lot of money to give Libby for her clothing allowance, so she had no striking new clothes to dazzle her classmates with. Some say that the few, inexpensive things she had were worn carelessly, but others pointed out that Libby knew how to make the most of her accessories—a white collar or lace cuffs to set off an otherwise somber outfit, or a rare piece of costume jewelry which always seemed to have the right accent for the simple garments she wore. Even then Libby had the native intelligence and inborn taste to give an impression of being modish and ahead of the styles without spending a fortune to achieve the effect. During her first year at Cincinnati she became addicted to slipover sweaters in bright colors, short plaid skirts, tan wool knee-length stockings, and flat-heeled shoes. In general, she gave the impression of a good, wholesome freshman. But her sexuality soon attracted most of the eligible boys. Libby, somewhat consciously, set out to attract the most desirable of the fraternity men and to make one of the "good" sororities.

Here she ran into a problem she never really encountered before. There was at the University of Cincinnati, and at almost every other university in those days, a ruling excluding Jews from any except strictly Jewish organizations. No sororities for Libby. The rejection hurt her deeply, but Libby resolved to compensate for it by becoming an even greater vamp among the men, if only to show the bigoted sorority snobs that she could be a success without their support.

When she decided to become a vamp she went at it with her characteristic style and energy and quickly showed her rival coeds just what a real high-class worker could do. Soon the men were flocking around her in droves. A roster of their names looked like a page torn from the Social Register. Libby, never anxious to get involved with any one man, let them all hope for success. She would let all of her suitors dangle, never quite letting them down, never letting them go too far, and never allowing a rival to take one away from her, which did much to improve her popularity among the men, but very little to enhance her reputation among the women. Many of them, even in later years, continued to regard her with venom. Libby was simply the one and only Libby in her class. Other women on campus tried to emulate her, but always in vain.

One woman, interviewed almost ten years later, when Libby was at the peak of her success, commented bitterly, "She never cared whom she hurt. She never respected the wishes of anyone but herself. She was selfish and a menace to men and women alike, whenever she thought it to her advantage to exert her sensuous allure."

A strange, ambiguous statement to make after all those years, but of course, the coeds at the time did not take into account the hurt they inflicted on Libby by rejecting her because of her religion.

During her freshman year, Libby, among other activities, spent a lot of time swimming at the YMCA, and joined the Mummers, a campus dramatic organization. Most of her work outside of the classroom had something to do with drama or performing of one sort or another. She was never happier than when the eyes of a crowd were on her. Despite all of this extracurricular activity, Libby never got less than a B.

In her second year at the university, Libby increased her activities. She joined the French Club and the History Club. In her third year she directed the annual students "Junior Show," in which members of this class burlesqued the graduating seniors.

Libby was already beginning to have serious thoughts about going into show business, and was therefore excited by appointment to direct. Since she was an undergraduate, it was a considerable tribute to her talents. She set seriously about arranging the revue. It was more of a job for a politician than a producer, since so many girls had to be accommodated within the program space. When the lineup was complete, it was noticed that everyone in the

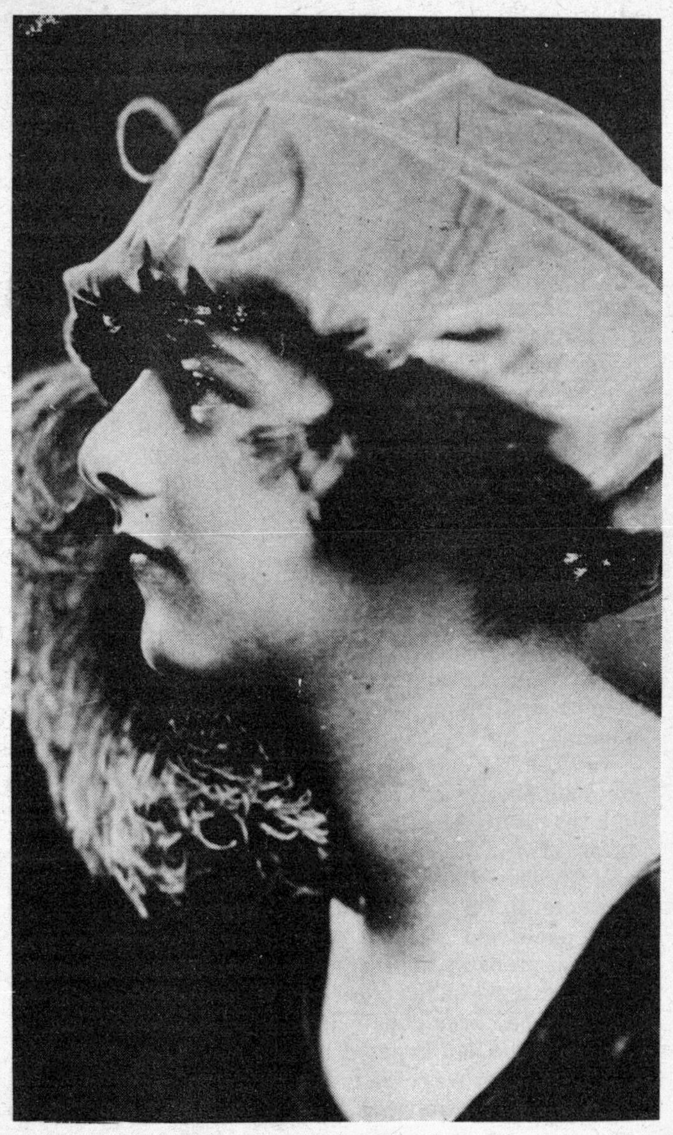

Libby in 1923, when she was a junior at the University of Cincinnati.

class had a part, except Libby. People were surprised but pleased by her modesty and her tact was admired.

"But," said someone, "the smartest thing that she's done was to break the fourteen scenes of the play up with songs, one following each scene."

"Yes," said Libby, joining the group discussing her remarkable achievement, "and I'm going to sing all the songs."

It worked out the way she had planned and the show was remembered as one of the most remarkable of the junior series.

During her last year of college, Libby took a dramatic course under the tutelage of Mrs. Carlyle Cunningham, who, as Virginia Loring, had been a star on Broadway at the turn of the century. Libby did a fair job of acting in one of her comedy productions called *Herrlinger's Son.* It was an original by Tupper Greenwald, another student. Libby also did passably well in *Dover Road* by A. A. Milne but she really hit her stride in a musical extravaganza called *Fresh Paint*, in which she sang an original composition by one of the troupe called "Bohemian Life." The rich, throaty, contralto-baritone that wowed them years later on Broadway got its first tryout before a sophisticated adult audience in that number and, to her delight, Libby brought down the house.

In 1924, only a few months before she was supposed to graduate, she did another drama by Milne called *Belinda.* In it she played the role that Ethel Barrymore had played on Broadway with great success. Nobody said that Libby was another Barrymore, but her performance was adequate. In her final musical show, *Lemme Alone,* she again got a wild, standing ovation.

It was probably this second success that decided Libby to seek a career on the musical stage, although up to that point she had been equally interested in straight drama. Now that she had exposed her special vocal attributes, however, Libby was even more popular on campus than ever and she certainly was not stingy with her particular red-hot type of entertainment. When she sang, she evoked the haunting, mournful quality of the Negro blues. Libby sang whenever she had an audience, which was frequently, and especially when there were a lot of men. Often at university functions, she would do an imitation of the famous torch singer Helen Morgan, and invariably she was almost mobbed by her male fans.

One of her campus rivals commented, bitchily, "All I can remember about these performances was that Libby always showed her leg clear up to the lingerie!"

Meanwhile, despite the success of her musical career, Libby and her sister Marian, who also had enrolled in Mrs. Cunningham's class, worked very hard in every spare moment, not only acting, but building sets, running errands, sweeping up, and all the various other activities to which young theater apprentices are assigned.

The first professional or at least off-campus theater that Libby ever acted in was an abandoned bank building, one hundred and ten years old, with cracked mortar in its walls, ceilings about to crash in, and absolutely no lighting facilities. It was a tiny place for a theater. Under Mrs. Cunningham's direction the two huge steel vaults which it contained were converted into women's dressing rooms. Throughout the transformation of the building, the girls and their boyfriends Mike Kahn (who later married Marian) and Sigmund Raab, who courted Libby, labored endless hours.

Despite all these efforts, however, Mrs. Cunningham was only modestly impressed by Libby's talent and almost forgot her in the years between her leaving Cincinnati and her later successes.

She did remember a few personal details about her former pupil.

"There certainly wasn't anything famous about the Elsbeth Holman who came to ask me to give her a chance," her teacher said in later years, recalling Libby's apprenticeship.

"Her eyes were popping out of her head with excitement when I told her we'd see what she could do.

She wasn't a genius. She was just a plump, unsophisticated little Jewish girl, with a lot of enthusiasm but not much talent, the same as dozens of others. She wasn't even pretty." Mrs. Cunningham said several times that she thought Libby's sister Marian was the prettier and more talented of the two. "But my goodness," she remarked, "she was a hard worker!

"She took many a scolding from me. Of course, I don't mean a real bawling out. I never had to correct her twice, however, for the same mistake. She learned fast. Nearly every day, after classes, Libby would come running, her books under her arm, puffing and hoping she wasn't late for rehearsal.

"Never once in the three years she was with me, did I know her to have a serious love affair. She had a flock of male admirers, of course. What attractive girl doesn't? But she was too wrapped up in her work to bother her head much about boys.

"Libby had insignificant parts at first, gradually going on to better and more important ones. Some of the finest work she did in our little theater group was that of the leading lady in *She Stoops To Conquer.*

"Libby is a finished legitimate actress. This torch singing that made her so famous in New York—I simply can't understand it. Libby never had a voice . . . She left me able to act. I next find her famous on Broadway for something she was never able to do. Isn't it amazing?"

Occasionally Broadway stars who were passing through Cincinnati on tour used to appear at Mrs. Cunningham's theater and it was on one of these occasions that Libby first made the acquaintanceship of Blanche Yurka, a famous actress and then the wife of Ian Keith, a youthful actor (eight years younger than Blanche, to be exact) who had a reputation as an alcoholic and a homosexual. The marriage dissolved shortly afterward.

When Libby left the Cincinnati art group, she didn't leave much of a gap.

"I vaguely remember when Libby and her sister

dropped in to say goodbye," Mrs. Cunningham told New York *Mirror* writer Arthur Mefford. "I scarcely had time to do more than wave at them and then go on with work that had to be done. I didn't realize that I was being told farewell by a future celebrity."

In spite of the pressure of all these activities, Libby, by taking extra courses during the summers, had managed to finish her four-year college stint in three. She tentatively agreed to enroll in law school as her father urged but decided to accelerate her program so that she would have at least one year to take a shot at success in the theater. She graduated at twenty, ninth in a class of two hundred, Law schools in those days would not admit students until they were twenty-one.

It wasn't until almost the end of her senior year that she had the nerve to approach her father, sitting quietly studying a law brief in the living room of the Holman homestead, with the dusk filtering through the haze on the Ohio River.

"Daddy," Libby said as quietly as possible, "I'm going on the stage."

"Well," said Mr. Holman, "there are New York trains both ways, five times a day. Leave your diploma behind while we frame it. It won't interest Ziegfeld or Charles Dillingham (another famous Broadway producer). Neither, I fear, will you."

4
A Foot on the Ladder

Alfred Holman's prediction proved to be, in the beginning, about half right, which is what lawyers are paid to be. Libby's early endeavors met with so little success that she enrolled in Columbia for a writing course. She wasn't sure even then whether she wanted to be a writer, an actress, or a singer. She knew, as her friend Howard Dietz later said, only that she wanted to be "great at something."

"I wanted to sing," Libby told interviewer Paul Yawitz later. "I wanted people to hear me sing. I wanted fame. It's a queer bug that stings you, but there is no antidote for the poison so I turned to the stage."

Fortunately Daddy, although not in accord with his daughter's ambitions, gave her enough of an allowance to pay for her tuition at Columbia and her rounds of the theaters. These turned out to be quite discouraging. So, for that matter, were her courses at Columbia, where she showed a modest talent for writing, but was not exactly star material in the opinion of the faculty. Certainly there appeared not to be a great future for her as a professional writer. As for being a professional in show business, the future at first seemed to be even bleaker. One casting director told Libby, "You're not pretty enough to be a chorus girl, you're entirely too big for a dancer, and as for your voice—well—that's simply terrible."

The fact was that while Libby's auditions were often impressive and magnetizing, she sometimes was terribly off-key and had not yet learned to be consistent in her delivery.

Even with her parents' contributions, Libby was often broke. There were many evenings when she remained in her little theatrical hotel room just west of Broadway, hungry but too tired to eat even if she had money. For more than a year Libby haunted the doors of producers, booking agents and the like without experiencing a glimmer of success. She tried hard to sell her voice, but only rebuffs came her way.

Throughout this period, though, she never lost faith that someday she would be a success "at something." At one point it looked as if she had it made when she applied to the famous Flo Ziegfeld for a job. Mr. Ziegfeld looked over the long-legged, dark-skinned girl with the sexy smile and said, laconically, "You'll do."

"I know," Libby said. "But what'll I do?"

"The usual thing," said Mr. Ziegfeld. "Drill hard, be a good girl, and furnish your own hosiery when needed."

But Libby was no shy, shrinking violet about her ambitions. "I want a specialty," she said to the surprised Ziegfeld. To demonstrate what she had in mind, Libby burst into song.

After a quarter-hour or so of listening, Ziegfeld became thoughtful. At that time, Helen Morgan, one of his established stars, was having trouble with the law because of her drinking and other problems. Ziegfeld was actually shopping for another mournful singer. He decided to hire Libby but, unfortunately, Libby never got to sing for Ziegfeld. *Show Boat*, in which she was to be an understudy, got hung up for a spell and Libby had to eat, so she went elsewhere to seek her fortune.

Finally, as it must in all theatrical biographies, the time came when her luck seemed to have completely run out. It was then that she got her first break. She had reached the point where she thought she might have to use her last resource, the ticket home tucked in her bosom. Since she was hungrier than she was homesick, she invested those last few dollars in food and with her new-found ambition, stormed a legitimate theater manager's office.

Channing Pollack, then one of Broadway's most noted playwrights, was present. Pollack always had a warm place in his heart for Cincinnati. His plays netted good royalties there. So when he overheard the sad-faced young woman with an eager and very hungry voice ask for a part in the road company of his play, *The Fool*, and give her home address as Cincinnati, he decided to okay her for her first job. She was so excited that, without thinking what was involved, she wired her parents to attend the opening night when the play reached Cincinnati. At the moment she didn't consider how Mama might react to her role, that of a streetwalker, and not a very classy one at that. But though she had little personal background to draw from for the part, Libby was quite convincing in it. So much so, that a leader of a local morality group marched determinedly into her dressing room and stormed the door with prayer when Libby refused to be preached at in person. Mama somehow survived the shock of seeing her daughter playing the part of a harlot and her other friends in Cincinnati weren't terribly surprised that she was cast in that role. Although her behavior had certainly been exemplary, the tone of Libby's voice and the songs she selected to sing around the campus always seemed to suggest sin and the seamy side of life.

Although Cincinnati was able to arouse a modicum of appreciation for the local girl made bad, *The Fool* bombed on tour. The South was apathetic and after eight weeks, two big trucks took the remains of the production to a theatrical warehouse.

But Libby's luck seemed to have turned. She got another engagement almost instantly in a piece of fluff from Vienna called *The Sapphire Ring*. At first she thought that she had avoided the typecasting that was already beginning to haunt her. She played a lady's maid, but by the time she read her side she realized that the maid was the mistress both of the butcher boy and the master. The play opened and closed at the Selwyn Theater in the same week.

The day before it closed Libby went with a friend named Stanley Lindahl to a Child's Restaurant for a cup of coffee and a snack. There they ran into two platinum-blonde girls who were friends of Lindahl's. The girls said that they were attending tryouts for a Junior Theater League revue to be called *Garrick Gaieties*. It was scheduled to run just one day but the girls argued it might be a good showcase. Perhaps some of the critics would catch their acts. Lindahl and Libby decided to give it a try. Neither was doing anything else at the time. Certainly their chances had doubled by the time they reached the Theater Guild's new playhouse on West 52nd Street, since the Guild had decided by then to extend the run to *two* nights, instead of one, largely because the Guild needed more money to buy costly drapes for the interior. This, in fact, was the basic reason for doing the show, which was to star new talent. The production budget was $5,000.

Libby, after a brief singing tryout, was given a job on the chorus line with the two blondes, largely on the basis of her legs, which everyone said were superb. Nobody seemed much impressed by her voice, not even the two young writers who had composed the songs for this new revue, a couple of songsters named Richard Rodgers and Lorenz Hart. Hart was a short, moody character who doubled as a comic in the revue. Also in the cast were Sterling Holloway, Harold Clurman, House Jamison, Philip Loeb, Sanford Miesner, Lee Strasberg, and Richard Rodgers himself. Morrie Ryskind contributed to the sketches and the sets were by the Mexican artist Miguel Covarrubias. The revue was smart and sophisticated with an emphasis on wit and humor. A similar revue had been produced the previous year by Andre Charlot and had been a huge success with Beatrice Lillie as the leading comedienne.

Two of the songs introduced in *Garrick Gaieties* by Rodgers and Hart impressed the critics. They were "Manhattan" and "Sentimental Me." True to the wishful expectations of Libby and her friends, the new revue did catch the critics' eye and subsequently ran for twenty-five weeks at the Guild Theater. Libby's star was rising.

Lindahl, later recalling this historic moment in her career, said, "Libby was actually hungry and I suppose if I hadn't helped her get that job when I did, she might have returned to Cincinnati and lived a pleasant, conventional life with her family, the same as countless other girls who have tried Broadway and failed." In that first show Libby had been given a small specialty number to do. It was a song called "Black and White," but at one of the rehearsals the director, Philip Loeb, listened to Libby on one of her off-key days and said, "My God, that gal can't sing!" He took the song away from her.

"So I had to yell in the chorus and step around while June Cochran did my song," Libby said. "Was I disgusted? was I downhearted? was I discouraged? Write your own ticket."

At least one other person agreed with Loeb's estimate of Libby's voice. While she was appearing in *Garrick Gaieties* in Cincinnati, Libby had a surprise visit backstage from her former drama teacher, Mrs. Cunningham. The encounter, the drama coach later recalled was embarrassing to both of them. Mrs. Cunningham, in a long and distinguished dramatic career, had had nothing to do with such frivolities as musical comedy and revues. She was shocked to see her former protege in a skimpy costume amply displaying those long tan legs for which Libby became famous—and Libby was embarrassed that her teacher had seen her in the chorus. Unfortunately, she had come on one of the nights when Libby was still trying out her specialty song, "Black and White."

"All Libby had to do in this show," Mrs. Cunningham said, "was to step out of the line once, and sing two verses of some silly little song. And I knew how that little girl *couldn't* sing. She piped out her verses just as I expected. The audience could scarcely hear her. It was quite discouraging to see the result of all my pains come to this. I left very sad."

With the summer doldrums came the eventual closing of the history-making little musical after a run of twenty-five weeks. Critics later said that the *Gaieties* furnished the mood and inspiration for the new type of intimate fast-paced revue that was to dominate the stage for the next decade or so, and Rodgers and Hart were established names in show business from this point on.

Summer also meant the end of Libby's classes at Columbia. She had a little money left over from the show and with what she had been able to save from her allowance, determined to cross to Europe, try a little singing, if possible, and see the continent. Things were cheap on the other side at that time, and prohibition made the crossing seem even more adventurous, though there is no record that Libby did any serious drinking as yet in those years. She crossed on the *Majestic* with a fairly glamorous crew.

The *Majestic* was the largest liner afloat at the time and perhaps the most luxurious. There were several people on the passenger list Libby already knew, and some she was slated to cross paths with in the near future. They included: the insouciant musical star, Clifton Webb, who was going over for a dancing engagement at the Jardin Des Messieurs; The Dolly Sisters, trailing identical long chiffon scarves around the promenade deck; Dwight Deere Wiman, heir to a Midwest fortune and a fledgling theatrical producer and millionaire-about-town; and Marilyn Miller, Ziegfeld Follies star and then the hottest thing on Broadway, with her husband Jack Pickford (whose sister was none other than America's sweetheart, Mary.)

Libby, still a mere showbusiness upstart, was overwhelmed by the wealth and power of these big names, but managed to hold her own socially with her native wit and good humor, and made a valuable contact for the future when she struck up a friendship with Clifton Webb.

Libby saw the sights of London, took in the opening of the London Company of *No, No, Nanette*, met Tallulah Bankhead, sang for free at parties and night-clubs, where the British and French were highly taken by the gutsy black-inspired blues songs which were her forte. But she couldn't seem to land even one paying job. In Paris she stayed long enough to catch the arrival of a new all-black show called the *Revue Negre* which featured the Claude Hopkins Band with Louis Armstrong, Sidney Bechet and a striking, lithe, tawny dancer named Josephine Baker. Armstrong and Baker danced the Charleston, which as Bechet remembers had not yet been seen in the City of Lights, and it brought down the house.

Libby, always interested in black music, managed to make the brief acquaintance of "La Bak-air" as Josephine was already known, and passed a delightful week with her until the revue went on a smash tour of Europe. Josephine was hired shortly after the tour by the *Folies Bergère* and didn't return to America for more than ten years.

Libby, unable to find work in the theater in Europe, and somewhat dazzled by all the big stars she had met, was discouraged and decided to go back to Ohio and return to her second love, journalism. She had heard there was an opening in the Midwest bureau of a new magazine being started up by some Yale men with money.

"Then one morning," Libby later told reporter Michael Mok, "out pretty early for some shopping, a fellow I didn't know from Adam talked to me in the street. What's this, I thought? A pickup in the pure provinces? 'Haven't I seen you in New York?' he asked."

"There are a lot of people in New York," Libby told him. "You may be mistaken."

"'Oh, no,' the man said. 'I know you very well; I saw you in the *Garrick Gaieties*.'"

That was different. The man introduced himself to

Libby, early in her career.

Libby as Stanley Rayburn, which didn't mean a thing to her. Rayburn was manager of a touring company of a revue called *The Greenwich Village Follies*. Libby told the man that he was too late. She was through with show business for good. She had gotten a job with a magazine called *Time* in their Midwest bureau, and was going to be a writer.

"Stop talking nonsense," Rayburn said. "You're going into *Greenwich Village Follies* and you're going to wow them."

The show was playing in Cincinnati and what Rayburn didn't say was that he was absolutely desperate for a replacement for Rosalie Claire, a featured singer who had suddenly quit the show. (Two weeks after Libby was hired Rosalie Claire died in an auto crash. In later years, this incident was recalled to give a somewhat sinister tone to Libby's career, but the fact is that she was hired weeks before the unfortunate occurrence.)

"So right then and there," Libby told the reporter, "I phoned my poor mother from the corner drugstore and told her to pack my trunks. The company was off the next day for Minneapolis.

"But now comes the payoff," Libby told Mok. "At this point the producers of *Greenwich Village Follies* had not been entirely happy with the music written for the show by another fairly new songwriter with a big future ahead of him, Cole Porter. His best song in the show, 'I'm in Love Again,' didn't seem to click, and neither did the others. So they approached the management of the defunct *Garrick Gaieties* and bought one of the unused numbers from the owners. Do you see it coming?" Libby asked the reporter.

"Of course. Among the numbers was 'Black and White.' The third night I was with the show, the girl who sang it got sick and went back to New York, and I was given back my old little number."

Supporting Libby's tiny efforts was the well-known Broadway comedy team of Moran and Mack and Vincent Lopez' famous band. Eventually the cast of the somewhat shaky and constantly revised revue was also beefed up by the addition of a young comic named Fred Allen and a chorus girl named Portland Hoffa, later Mrs. Fred Allen. On that tour, a brash young New Yorker named Leonard Sillman took over many of the important assignments. Sillman, who later gained fame as the producer of the *New Faces* revues, among other things, recalls that he had twenty-three numbers in the show, often following himself from one number to the next. To accomplish this, he would usually wear the costume for the next act under the one from the previous one.

"I wore so many layers of clothing in *Greenwich Village Follies*," Sillman recalls, "that I scared the customers. From opening curtain to finale every night I seemed to lose about thirty pounds."

Sillman soon became close friends with the exotic singer from Cincinnati and advised her that her name, Elsbeth, would never go in show business. "Libby" went better with Holman. "Under my gentle prodding, twenty-four hours a day, she changed it." The two young performers (Libby was actually three or four years older than Sillman, depending on whose age estimates you believe) soon became close friends.

"She was a large girl, with a fuzzy head of hair," Sillman recalls. Of course, since Sillman himself was barely five feet tall, it was natural that he would think of Libby as "large." In fact, Libby was 5′6½″, tall for those times.

"She had slits for eyes, and a bee-stung mouth, and a somewhat unreliable singing voice."

It was those slitted eyes that gave Libby much of her reputation for having a sensuous, sexual, come-on look, but this was more due to the fact that she was very near-sighted, and constantly squinted to get even the vaguest idea of where her place should be on the stage.

"When she felt good," Sillman remembers, "she was a fabulous singer. When she was not fabulous, she was flat. She went around in a ratty old beret and an overcoat made from pelts of one fox and several rabbits with rabies. From all this, I realize it may be difficult to conjure up an image of a rather fey, irresistible enchantress. But that's exactly what she was; she could exert a strange fascination. There was a boy in the show we all called 'Horseface.' He had such a lech for Libby that he followed her around like a puppy, which meant following *me* around, because by that time I was never far behind the witch myself. After the show each night the three of us would sit around until dawn, drinking milk, eating coleslaw, hating life. It was at one of these bull and beef sessions one night that Libby got up, walked to the writing desk, and proceeded to write a letter. She put it in an envelope and left the room. I picked up the envelope and saw that it had been addressed to—of all people—Miss Libby Holman. Naturally, I read the letter. It said: 'My divine Libby, How can you tolerate two such stupid people as Leonard and Horseface? They are without doubt the most dreadful, the most common and vulgar people I have ever seen. I love you, divine Libby, wonderful Libby, beautiful Libby. Love, love, Libby.'"

At another night, following opening night in Wilmington, Delaware when the show, with its ad libs, additions and changes ran until one o'clock in the morning, it was suggested that major surgery was needed and this involved cutting two verses and choruses from Leonard Sillman's number "My Cutie's Due at 2:22 Today." Sillman was appalled. Cut his material? This would bring him down to only twenty-one numbers! He slunk off, muttering, to his dressing room where he found Libby polishing her toenails and reading a book.

Libby was deeply distressed when she heard what they were doing to her friend Leonard. She wrote a twelve-page letter to the producers, synopsizing the reasons for Sillman's gloom. In it she said he was also threatening to resign from the show. It was such a good letter that Sillman's two verses and choruses were restored to him.

"Thus I discovered Libby's genius for *belles lettres*," Sillman recalls.

But Libby and Sillman were not always pals. They got into fights, so violent sometimes, that Sillman says he was tempted to forget the difference in their sexes and knock her teeth down her throat. "What stopped me was the fact that she was a lot bigger than I."

Ultimately, it was Leonard who inadvertently brought about the demise of that edition of *The Greenwich Village Follies* which closed on the road. Movie houses were beginning to book big vaudeville acts then and Sillman had the idea that two of the stars of the show, McIntyre and Heath, a pair of elderly vaudevillians, would be naturals for such a booking. He sounded them out and they gave him an okay on the idea, and suggested that he act as their manager for five percent of whatever he could get them. Within two days Leonard's contact in New York had booked the act for thirty weeks at $4,000 a week. The two old gentlemen nearly went through the ceiling with delight, and promptly gave their notice to the management of *The Greenwich Village Follies*. It had never occurred to Sillman that without McIntyre and Heath, the *Follies* would fold, and that the two old troupers could not play in the *Follies* and vaudeville at the same time. So the *Follies* closed within two weeks, and Libby refused to talk to Sillman all the way home. She showed her feelings when she attended Sillman's opening in another revue shortly afterwards called *High Low* which also featured some of the *Greenwich Village* stars and a new girl comic named Imogene Coca.

Sillman admits he was indubitably the shortest juvenile on earth, "a midget's dream of Clifton Webb" (Webb was the reigning star of light comedy and revue musicals at the time). Sillman, for his opening number, leaned against the proscenium, exhaling smoke in a sophisticated style he had copied from another revue star, Jack Buchanan, and saving most of his breath for the song he was about to sing. But when he finally opened his mouth to perform the number, he was greeted from the audience with a razzberry "so long, so loud, so obscene, that it could only come from a real expert."

"My mouth was still open," Sillman says. "I looked down into the first row of the audience. There was Miss Libby Holman in the process of winding up the longest, loudest Bronx cheer on record."

Libby had made a good impression on some of the critics and certainly on her fellow performers in the course of the run of *Greenwich Village Follies*. But she was still far from a household word along the Great White Way and 1926 was a year of endless unsuccessful, ego-destroying rounds—shows that started up but never actually made the boards, near-misses, shows that folded in a day or so—nothing seemed to work. This time, however, Libby was more convinced than she had been back in her *Garrick Gaieties* days that she had a future in show business. After a year of getting Broadway's coldest shoulders, Libby finally landed a spot with her old friend in a revue by Howard Dietz and Morrie Ryskind called *The Merry-Go-Round*.

The producer of the show was a gentleman of the old school named Richard Herndon, who, some years earlier, had enchanted New York with a revue called *Americana*, written by Robert Benchley and J. P. McAvoy. During the run of the show he developed an unknown, sad-eyed singer with a baby face and a husky voice, who made a big hit with a song called "Nobody Wants Me." The girl's name was Helen Morgan." No sooner had Sillman signed for *The Merry-Go-Round*, than he insisted that Herndon listen to a friend of his whom he described as "the greatest, most glamorous singer in the world—better than Morgan." According to Sillman, Herndon already had his cast set by then, but he agreed to hear Libby on the strength of Sillman's hyperbolic recommendations and "six solid hours of . . . pestering!"

Sillman dashed around to the English Tea Room on East 48th Street, which was then a big actors' rendezvous, and found Libby sitting at a table with Romney Brent and Sylvia Sidney. "She was still wearing her beret on top of that stork's nest of hair and she was still hugging her precious rabbit fox coat close to her. She seemed cold and forlorn, a classic picture of an actress out of work. Rather than immediately overwhelm the poor thing with the news that I had arranged an audition for her with one of Broadway's leading producers, I decided first to feint with my left. I asked her what she was doing at the moment. 'Nothing,' said she. That wasn't quite the case. She was doing something interesting—at the moment. She was smoking a pipe."

Sillman told her about the interview he had arranged with Herndon. Libby yawned. She had decided to give up the theater, she said. She was going back to college and take up law as her father had urged her. The theater was just too sordid and chancy. Sillman threw a virtual fit and went into what he described as "a large-sized tizzy" before he persuaded her to sing for Herndon.

Auditions then were often held in strange and rather offbeat places—in offices, on empty stages and even in bedrooms. In the case of Herndon, his office was busy at the moment of Libby's audition, stages weren't available, and his bedroom had been preempted. So he arranged for a hearing in the basement of the Holy Cross Church at 47th Street, while a Mass was being said upstairs. "When Libby appeared," Sillman says, "Herndon gasped. She had no makeup on. She was wearing a dress made for a lady hermit. She got up in front of Herndon and sang 'Bim Bam Beedle Bum Bay,' a number she had rendered in *The Greenwich Village Follies*. It was one of her flat days, one of her *real* flat days, which means that she was at least five tones off. The sound that came out was that of a pump organ being very feebly pumped. In desperation, I kept talking to Herndon all through her song: 'Isn't she wonderful? Isn't she fabulous? Mr. Herndon, this is *real* talent! She'll be the new Helen Morgan!'"

Sillman kept this chatter up so incessantly, he says, that he was sure Herndon never heard a note Libby sang. In any event, he signed her with the show.

Herndon gave Libby two songs. One was called "He Said Whadda Ya Say, I Said Not Today, No Sir, Not Today and Not Tonight!" The other song was a number

Dietz had written called "Hogan's Alley," described by one writer as "the wail of a corned-beef-and-cabbage Delilah." The music was by Jay Gorney. Corned beef and cabbage or not, Libby's rendition of the Dietz-Gorney number was a smash hit, and in fact was the only part of the show that got any decent critical notice. Such good word went out on Libby's blues-inspired rendition of the Dietz number that she was offered a part as the lead in an all-black revue called *Rang Tang*. The producers apparently were under the impression, as was much of the public, that Libby was at least part Negro.

The Merry-Go-Round, which included in the cast Libby's old acquaintance Loeb, who went on to fame as Jake in *The Goldbergs* series, and Frances Gershwin, sister of George, already a famous composer, ran for one hundred and thirty six performances at the Klaw Theater and then went on the road. The show marked an important juncture in Libby's career. It was the first really good critical notice she had gotten and it served as an introduction to Howard Dietz, who was delighted with her rendition of the "Hogan" number, and all the attention it had brought to him as well as to Libby.

But stardom was still a long way off for Libby. According to one writer, during the following months, Libby hung up a record "for appearing in more continuous flops than any actress of her weight and age in the United States." On the strength of her hit number in *The Merry-Go-Round*, she was called on by the powerful Florenz Ziegfeld again to play Helen Morgan's part in a second *Show Boat* company. However, this never materialized and Libby joined a troupe of what seemed to be half of the unemployed singers and chorus girls applying for the casting call of a new mammoth production called *Rainbow*. Miracle of miracles, against stiff competition Libby got the part, and a good one, with super-sad, pensive moanings, lavish costumes, and a spotlight all around.

The production, as predicted, was extravagant, a bit too extravagant. The producers gave the critics a very long seventh inning stretch. Exactly forty-five minutes elapsed as intermission between the two final acts (musicals in those days sometimes had three acts). *Rainbow* folded and died after three weeks at the Gallo Theater.

By now it was 1929, the height of the "bet a million" excitement of the bull market and the eve of the Great Crash. There seemed to be money around for anything, except in Libby's case, for hit shows. There followed an engagement with Ned Wayburn's *Gambols*, which was already on the boards and in deep trouble. The show was playing in Pittsburgh at the time and Wayburn sent his agent, Paul Yawitz, later a Broadway columnist, to escort Libby to the Smoky City. Libby was in one of her upbeat moods and according to Yawitz, made a delightful traveling companion. As she and the agent were sitting on the observation platform of the Pennsylvania Flyer speeding through the Alleghenies, Libby became excited and talkative about her feelings concerning her career.

"All my life, I wanted to push myself up to the peak of intelligence," she said.

"Her throaty voice," Yawitz later said, "was always at its best in moments of confidence. It had the strange quality of a bass violin string stretched across the mouth of a French horn."

"When I was a little girl," Libby confided to Yawitz, "I always wanted to mingle with the kids whose parents were considered smart. I had a natural repulsion to the vulgar words children pick up in alleys and instinctively I moved away when they were spoken."

She told Yawitz about her studies and her attempts to get involved in a law course as her father had urged her. But she said, "When I finally came to New York, the steam of the streets enraptured me. I forgot all about the law I intended to practice, and what good was law anyway, when you have suddenly grown up and discovered that it isn't law you wanted?

"Here I am on my way to Pittsburgh with you. I am to sing in a big show, and if it's a success it'll be great for me. I haven't had much opportunity to do all that heavy singing for what I call *my* public. But you'll see, I'll get to the top eventually!"

But this was not to be Libby's big crack at fame. *Gambols* was a terrible fiasco. It finally came to Broadway anyway, but not even Libby's husky voice could lure a paying audience to the Knickerbocker Theater. *Gambols* closed even before Libby could buy the fresh silk underwear that her part seemed to call for.

Meanwhile Libby had nearsightedly fallen into a manhole while on her way to the theater and badly damaged her knee. The injury resulted in a form of traumatic arthritis and Libby was practically paralyzed during the Broadway opening of the show, to the point where she couldn't even dress herself. The director planted her against the stage column and let her sing without the benefit of any movement. So painful was her condition that between the matinees and the evening performances she couldn't even change her costume. A doctor was summoned and he advised her to get some rest, but Libby refused to quit the show. She needed the money and she needed the attention. So the doctor sat through every performance and observed that when she sang most movingly, Libby was suffering most exquisitely. But not even that touch of pathos could save *Gambols*. It went the way of all trash and Libby Holman was again at liberty.

By now, people were beginning to talk about this seductive young woman whose throbbing notes stirred passion and pity. But the managers were busy and so, in Libby's case, were streptococci. Out of work and depressed, Libby succumbed to a septic sore throat and it was decided to take out her tonsils. Then, according to her press notices, a "miracle" happened. In removing the damaged tonsils, the surgeon was either too thorough or not thorough enough. His scalpel invaded a column of her throat and nicked a piece of flesh out. Libby even carried around, in a little jar of alcohol the pickled offending tissue. In the hospital, she told a writer from *Collier's*, she observed the difference. She began singing the moment the nurses and adjoining patients would stand for it, and she felt there was a new shade to her voice—a prolonged vibrato that underscored the low full notes.

This is another of these Holman legends about which one can only wonder. Was it a masterful piece of drama, a good press agent's inspiration, a complete fabrication, or a bit of dramatic truth? In any event, most of the friends who knew Libby in her early days, even dating back to college, tended to laugh at the tonsils story. It made good copy, but according to these old friends, Libby had that same haunting, throbbing voice as far back as her freshman year in college.

With the folding of *Gambols* Libby was out of work again, and so discouraged with Broadway that she decided she might take her dwindling savings and spend them on a train ticket to Hollywood. If Broadway wouldn't take her, maybe the burgeoning film industry might show some interest. Everybody said that talkies were soon to be the new thing, and Libby thought that her singing voice might find a place in the great Golden West. Howard Dietz, the lyricist who had been so pleased with her rendition of his song, "Hogan's Alley" in *The Merry-Go-Round*, heard that Libby was leaving town. Dietz' main job was chief publicist for MGM, and had excellent contacts with the Hollywood grapevine. At the time he was completing a new revue, largely inspired by the success of earlier intimate revues like *Garrick Gaieties* and *The Greenwich Village Follies*. The trend was away from big, lavish productions like *Rainbow*. The producer and backer was Dwight Deere Wiman, whom Libby had met in passing on her first trip to Europe. Wiman was noted for his taste and was famed for his wealth. He had a wickerwork Rolls Royce built which, according to Dietz, was the most expensive-looking car ever to appear in traffic. It was equipped with a bar, and this to Wiman, Dietz commented, was its most important equipment. His new venture, *The Little Show*, was to be a revue, but not in any respect like the rhinestone creations with huge staircases of Flo Ziegfeld or Earl Carroll, the G-string titillator. It was to be topical, artistic, and witty. Wiman and his coproducer, Tom Wetherly, had signed up comedian Fred Allen, who would set the mood of *The Little Show* along with Clifton Webb. They recruited Dietz as the lyricist and Arthur Schwartz, a composer Dietz had never worked with before, to do the music. At Dietz' suggestion, they also signed up Libby Holman who was by then well known to Dietz as well as to Fred Allen and Clifton Webb. Dietz described her at the time as a "swarthy, sloe-eyed, houri."

After getting an okay from the producer to hire Libby, Dietz found that she had already left to catch the Twentieth Century Limited to Hollywood. He took a taxi to Grand Central station and caught Libby just as she was about to board the train. He begged her to take the part in the new revue with Webb and Allen. But Libby's mind was made up. She was bound for Hollywood and she told Dietz, he says, to "go to hell." But Dietz refused to let her go that easily and according to one reporter, there "ensued a row that it took the police to quell." Finally, Dietz won out and Libby remained in New York and signed up for *The Little Show*, which was to be the turning point in her career.

5

"Moanin' Low"

This was it, the big moment, the opening curtain of the real life of Libby Holman. She was in a Broadway revue, headlining with the veteran star and Broadway darling, Clifton Webb and the bright, new hoarse-voiced comedian, Fred Allen. The music and lyrics were basically by Arthur Schwartz and Howard Dietz, the result of their first major collaboration. Jo Mielziner designed the sets. The glamorous playboy producer Dwight Deere Wiman co-produced the show. Before the revue could even try out, there was a lot of reshuffling of numbers, complaints, bickering—the usual amending and additions. Clifton Webb wasn't entirely happy with his part. He wanted a few more numbers. Up to this point, he had been largely known as a sophisticated dancer, much along the lines of the young Fred Astaire, who was wowing them on Broadway with his sister, Adele. Clifton wanted a chance to do more comedy and more acting. Dietz and Schwartz went back to their drawing board and dug up a tune that Schwartz had written for none other than Lorenz Hart, when they had both been counselors at Brandt Lake Camp, a resort for boys in the Adirondacks. Dietz liked the melody and sat down and wrote a new lyric for the song which originally was called "I Love to Lie Awake in Bed." The new title was "I Guess I'll Have to Change My Plan." It turned out to be Schwartz's first hit, although he didn't know it at the time.

The other addition demanded by Webb, who wanted to do a number with Libby Holman stressing her torch-singing talents, gave more trouble. Finally, Ralph Rainger, one of the two pianists, came up with a song that had been moldering in his trunk for some years. It had a haunting tune that fit the mood of what Webb was looking for. Dietz sensed a certain low-pitched, earthy appeal in the song and said later, "The lyric wrote itself." They titled the song "Moanin' Low."

The Little Show opened for tryouts in Asbury Park on April 30, 1929. The country was in a state of high spirits and euphoria. The market was soaring. Everybody was investing, trying to become a millionaire. But the mood was less bright with the producers and authors of *The Little Show*. Arthur Schwartz and Howard Dietz took a train which stalled en route and didn't even arrive at the theater until after the final curtain. The producers, Dwight Deere Wiman and Tom Wetherly greeted them in the lobby.

"Wiman was plastered and Wetherly had a glum face from which emerged disheartening words," Dietz recalled.

"It's just as well that you missed it," he told Dietz. "If I were you, I'd turn around and go back to New York. We'll close Saturday."

"As long as we've come all this way," Dietz said, "we might as well take in tomorrow's performance, and I'll collect the $100 you guaranteed me."

This was in reference to a standing joke between the producers and Dietz, who had at first refused to work on another revue, since he hadn't made any money from any of his previous works, which included *Dear Sir, Poppy,*

Oh, Kay! and *The Merry-Go-Round.* He finally agreed to work on the show only if the producers would guarantee him a minimum of $100 a week against a half-percent of the gross. Dietz was only half joking when he said that. He had a job at MGM that he was neglecting for the show business he loved and he was damned if he was going to continue if he couldn't make any money out of it.

Wiman, smiling a bit blearily, peeled a hundred dollar bill off a wad in his pocket. "It's the show of a century," he said, handing him the century note.

The next night the two authors watched the show with heavy hearts. It was playing to an almost empty house, but in spite of this handicap, there was a terrific hand for the three leading players, Webb, Holman, and Allen. The audience, sparse as it was, gave show-stopping hands to a comedy number called "Hammacher Schlemmer, I Love You," to "Moanin' Low" and a number by Libby also destined to become a standard, "Can't We Be Friends?" which was composed by Kay Swift, with a lyric by her husband at that time, the banker James Warburg, and added to the show at the last minute.

"All I can say," said Wetherly at the second performance, "is that what was a flop last night looks like a hit tonight."

"That's all you're allowed to say," Arthur Schwartz commented.

Dietz handed the hundred dollar bill back to Wiman. "This payment was premature," he said.

A skit had been built around the "Moanin' Low" number, a sort of apache dance in which Clifton Webb and Libby, both in dark makeup, floundered around the stage assaulting each other in various sado-masochistic poses. In those days, if you wanted to do something sexy, it was considered safer to do it in blackface and the songs of sin that Libby sang were always considered more acceptable coming from the lips of a "mulatto," than from a white lady.

The curtain went up on a stark set, designed by Jo Mielziner. It portrayed the bedroom of a Harlem prostitute. The walls were dingy and rust-streaked from ancient leaks. A tin can under the bed served as a cuspidor for the woman's clients. The bed itself was a cheap iron affair covered by a gaudy patchwork spread.

The girl entered and began to fix her make-up in the cracked mirror of the battered bureau to one side of the sparsely-furnished room. Tawny skinned—obviously a white girl in black smoke-up—wore a skirt that showed her slim, shapely legs. Opening her purse, she counted a thick roll of bills then peeled off several which she tucked into the rolled top of her stocking.

The door burst open and the man came in. He, like her, was made up as a Negro, his hair straight and slicked back with pomade. He was dressed in the height of style. This was the woman's "sweet man"—her pimp. They danced, first making suggestive gestures of love, finishing with a climax of Apache-style violence.

He sweet-talked the woman, then demanded her money. Taking the roll of bills from her pocketbook, she handed them to him. He counted the money contemptuously, then slapped the girl, throwing her around the room as though to shake additional money out of her lithe body. Finally he calmed down and started to make love to her again, running his hand up her leg until he found the hold-out roll, which he ripped from her stocking. He counted the money with a satisfied smile then threw the girl to the floor. She wept bitterly, begging him not to leave, but he exited coldly, leaving her alone with her grief.

The lights went down and a set of black drapes fell across the grim Harlem set.

Backstage, Libby quick-changed into a clinging silk gown. She stumbled uncertainly through the props. Her hands reached gropingly for support toward the scenery. She seemed unable even to recognize her dearest friends standing a dozen feet away. She stumbled and a stage attendant rushed to her, took her by the arm and guided her to her position, behind the curtain that shut off the spotlight.

Then the black drapes glided back slowly, revealing Libby, standing beneath the halo of a magenta baby spot. Her lustrous, raven-hued, tousled mop of hair shimmered in the light. She held her arms out to the audience as if to embrace them. Her low, liquid tones rolled out to the audience like dark honey laced with emery grit, as she reprised the song.

Day out, day in
I'm worrying about bad news.
I'm so afraid!
My man I'm goin' to lose.

Moanin' low
My sweet man I love him so
Though he's mean as he can be
He's the kind of a man
Needs the kind of a woman like me.

Gonna die
My sweet man should pass me by
If I die where'll he be?
He's the kind of a man
Needs the kind of a woman like me.

Don't know any reason
Why he treats me so poorly
What have I gone and done?
Makes my trouble double with his worries,
When surely I ain't deservin' of none.

Moanin' low
My sweet man is gonna go.
When he goes, Oh Lordee!
He's the kind of man
Needs the kind of a woman like me.

The song seemed made for the throaty, sexy contralto-baritone. When she finished, the audience was sweating, silent for a moment, then came a great wave of applause that almost shook down the house.

"Encore! Encore!" the cry went out.

Libby took a dozen curtain calls and the audience still demanded more. Eventually, she was too exhausted to respond any longer. Dietz himself finally strode to the front of the stage and made a plea for them to let her retire to her dressing room. And even then the audience remained begging, wildly excited, for one more taste of that haunting, honey-toned melody.

The Little Show opened on Broadway to rave reviews from the critics. Brooks Atkinson of the *Times* wrote that Libby had a voice like "a purple flame." Everywhere she was hailed as Broadway's "premier torch singer." She was interviewed by all the major papers and several nationwide magazines, and audiences flocked to hear the marvelous voice which her press agents described as "the ages-old cry of women's aching hearts, imprisoned love, and frustrated passions."

6
The Gay Life

Libby's old drama coach, Mrs. Cunningham, who had been so amazed that Libby could get any kind of a job singing, was still not absolutely thrilled by her success or impressed by her talent. She visited her backstage shortly after the opening of *The Little Show*. By that time, the former star told the *Mirror's* Arthur Mefford, she had read accounts of Libby Holman, the famous torch singer.

"I could hardly believe my eyes," Mrs. Cunningham said. "It was too impossible. I went to see the show.

"Libby had to sing, first of all, some inconsequential song, and I noticed she walked with her hands behind her back. She seemed to have forgotten all I had taught her about the use of her hands. She didn't know what to do with them. During intermission, I went around to her dressing room.

"It was nice to see the child. She seemed delighted to see me, too. She gave me an autographed photograph of herself. We were alone and this famous Libby, hurling sex at audiences night after night, became herself again.

"As she removed the skin darkening from her entire body, out cropped that olive skin of the enthusiastic little Jewish girl I used to know. Soon she was plain Elsbeth Holman."

The teacher scolded her old pupil gently. "Child, how many times have I told you what to do with your hands? When you were singing that first song, you held them behind your back."

Libby just laughed. "You're right. I have forgotten what to do with them." She made several clowning gestures, throwing her hands into various exaggerated positions. "See? I just don't know anymore. I still hope to go on the legitimate stage." In the meantime, Libby told her former teacher, she had found that she could sing in this husky voice "and I am making money out of it. That's what people want. This sexy stuff, and a low, throbbing voice."

Then, Mrs. Cunningham recounted, Libby suddenly stepped back and actually blushed. "You're not going to stay for my next song, 'Moanin' Low,' are you? I hope not, because I don't want you to. In fact, I wish you'd go home."

Mrs. Cunningham was astounded. She assured Libby that she was going to stay and hear the song. "Why don't you want me to hear it, Libby?"

"In the first place," Libby said, "it's rotten. In the second place, with you out there, I will be as nervous as a cat. You wouldn't like this sort of thing. They go crazy about it here. But you won't be proud of your little Cincinnati pupil when you hear it. I hate it myself. It's just that I can make money out of it!"

Finally Libby warned her teacher not to be shocked.

"But the warning did no good. It was far worse than I expected it to be," Mrs. Cunningham commented later. "Shocking would be putting it mildly. But I must say that Libby did it well.

"When the gigolo ran his hand up her leg in a torrid love scene and then suddenly plunged it down into her stocking and took out the money that she, as a street girl, had held, and then ran from the room, Libby ran after him. The door slammed in her face and she hurled herself against it with arms extended with despair.

"That was acting. That was worth the whole scene. That was Libby at her best."

Sidney Skolsky honored Libby with an entire column called "Behind the News," in the *Mirror*. As was the case throughout his career, Skolsky had the tendency to mix fact with legend and not all of the fact turned out to be accurate. To be fair, he gave her date of birth as May 23, 1906, no doubt accepting that figure from Libby, who by now felt it might be sagacious to shave a few years from her age before it was too late. "She is five feet, six-and-a-half inches tall. Weighs 124 pounds. Her hair is black. Her teeth are too small for her mouth. The upper two front teeth overlap. Her eyes are naturally hazel. Often, they are gray or green. They change according to her mood.

"Is impractical with her hands. She can't cook or sew. A guy would have to marry her for love.

"Has eight photographs on the wall of her dressing room. They all are pictures of Greta Garbo. She considers Garbo the greatest actress. She has a Great Dane, Rex, who is almost as big as she. She calls him 'X-Ray' in pig Latin.

"Most people believe she is snooty because she passes them by on the street. The truth of the matter is that she is very nearsighted. When singing, she can't see across the footlights. Refuses to wear glasses. Carries a lorgnette.

"Her two favorite dishes are spare ribs and cabbage and spinach with a hardboiled egg. Eats four meals a day and always says she's on a diet.

"Is a great listener. Keeps a person talking for hours. . . .

"Was the first person in this city to own a Ford Town Car. One afternoon, while speeding through Central Park, a traffic cop stopped her. 'I'm sorry, lady,' he said. 'But I'll have to pinch you.' 'If it's all the same to you,' came back Libby, 'I'd rather be tickled.'

"Arriving at a swank party, she immediately hurries over to see what's in the icebox . . . She goes in for bright color schemes in pajamas. The top part of one pair is a bright red and the trouser is a bright blue. The top part of another is a deep rose, and the trousers lavender . . .

"In *Rainbow* she had to smoke a cigar. Got to like it and says she may take it up seriously."

Actually, Libby regularly smoked one full man's cigar in public every Saturday night, usually in the company of her friend Louisa Carpenter du Pont Jenney, a transvestite millionairess—one of *the* du Ponts of Wilmington, Delaware. Some said Libby's motive was simply to give New Yorkers something to talk about—and talk they did.

Libby was a person about whom there always were a multiplicity of opinions. To Howard Dietz, she was serious, ambitious and studious—or so he told a newspaperman. "The best image I can give anyone of her," Dietz said "is to describe the way she lived, which I hope won't sound too silly. She got up around ten o'clock, and, when she was in town, usually went riding in the park. She didn't have any favorite riding companion—nothing of that sort—but I guess that anyone who was around just went with her.

"And then she was taking a course in short story writing at Columbia . . . and she took singing lessons and piano lessons. A pretty strenuous day when she was acting at night.

"After the show, she'd probably drop into some speakeasy where her friends were likely to be and have a drink or two before going home. Her friends were the people you hear about and the people just as swell that the public never hears about. She was just one of us.

"Sometimes she brought a friend with her and sometimes she didn't. What I'm getting at is that Libby was not a 'Broadway dame' as the boys say and she never had any of these gushing 'Johns' hanging around. She has always been fond of reading, and she was bookish without being 'lit'ry,' if you know what I mean. She could talk about Dreiser or Hoover, about love or war, about acting or eating, and liquor, like culture, she could take or leave alone. She was a lot of fun. I remember driving with her from New England, and in a rainstorm in a roadster without a top. We were wet all through, and she had the time of her life.

"She spent lots of money for clothes, but she didn't care a lot about dressing. I don't know what else to say but that she was vigorous, adventuresome, interesting, fond of swimming—that's it. The kind of girl that a married man liked to go swimming with."

Dietz, in the book he wrote years later called *Dancing in the Dark*, said that "No one in the theater was more discussable than Libby Holman.

"Libby became well known, too," Dietz commented, "not only for her stage manner, but for her individuality. She did outrageous things."

There were those who said that Libby was a cheapskate and others who said she was generous to the point of eccentricity. One Christmas season after her success, she gave as gifts to her friends corkscrews which were rumored to have been purchased at the cost of about ten for a dollar. But in the first week of *The Little Show*, when the cashier was passing out the very first weekly pay envelopes, a member of the cast came in and suggested that a collection should be taken up for the families of the Pathe Studio disaster in Harlem, in which ten died and twenty-two suffered horrible injuries. Four of the dead were showgirls known to Libby from other revues in which she appeared. One of the cast suggested that *The Little Show* cast contribute ten percent of its salary to the families of the dead girls. Instantly there was a subdued murmur of dissent. After all, this was the cast's first week's salary after months of rehearsal. Some of them, including Libby, had actually been living on crackers and milk toward the end. But Libby, who could always be counted on to do the unexpected, amazed the rest of them when she jumped onto a piano bench and delivered this speech, reported by Arthur Mefford in the *Daily Mirror*.

"Come on folks, let's do something grand! We've all

been up against it hard, but we're in sight of daylight now. We've managed to get along somehow, this far; we've got a job; we'll have another payday next week.

"I think we ought to give at least half of our salary to help these poor unfortunates. Personally I'm going to give all of mine!"

And with that Libby stepped down onto the stage again and, stumbling blindly as usual, she nonchalantly tossed her unopened pay envelope into the hamper which the cashier had used to distribute their pay. Then, without another word, according to a witness of this incident, Libby stalked out the stage door unescorted, and walked all the way back to her little hotel way up in the fifties because she didn't have cab or carfare.

Whatever the varied opinions about Libby's personality, there were few people who would dispute the fact that Libby knew how to have fun. She adored active sports and was anxious to devote some time every day to them, partly to keep her figure, which had a tendency to become plump if not cared for, in top condition. Her favorite sports, in addition to riding were tennis, golf, croquet, and aquaplaning.

Freddie Ziegler, a Broadway playboy who once made a tremendous bid for her favors, said, "No one could match Libby's skill as an aquaplane rider. I often saw her in the surf off Long Island. She had more nerve than most men when she rode one of the boards and went skimming along the waves behind a fast motorboat."

But Libby's leisure life involved a lot more than sun, salt spray, and horse sweat. Although she had always specialized in steamy torch numbers, Libby never actually became what you would call a sex symbol, until the success of *The Little Show*. As one writer said, "Nobody who knows the inside story disputes that—for some reason even her best friends can't explain—Libby Holman came to have the greatest over-the-footlights 'it' in show business. She received more mash notes than any other actress and more men fought to meet her or learn her telephone number."

Her close friends were always puzzled by her widespread appeal. It might have been because of the rampant sexuality of "Moanin' Low." Offstage, Libby didn't seem to have so much glamour. She dressed sloppily and wore tailored suits which she flung on herself offstage. In the language of one friend, she frequently "looked like hell." But what Libby did have in private life, even those who were not particularly friendly with her admitted, was a certain magnetism.

Lucinda Ballard, the costume designer who later married Howard Dietz, said of her, "She had what you would call 'presence.' When she was in a room, you were always aware of her and she tended to be the focus of attention without making any particular effort to do so. She didn't raise her voice or try to dominate the conversation, and always seemed relaxed and at ease. Yet even in a crowd of show business celebrities with egos as big as the Ritz, Libby somehow stood out.

"She had a certain quality which doesn't show up in photos. Her skin had extraordinary texture and while her hair often looked messy, it had a beautiful sheen. And one always noticed her eyes, a changeable greenish-hazel color which made such a startling contrast to that tawny complexion."

Though she used tan makeup in her act, Libby was, in fact, quite dark-skinned, a heritage, some said, of her Sephardic ancestry. Because of her coloring and the type of songs she sang, there was a persistent and recurring rumor that Libby was part Negro. Certainly she had a lifelong interest in black people and in their culture; in those Jazz Age days there was plenty of opportunity to acquaint oneself with the black contribution to popular music. It was considered the thing to do after the show to go up to Harlem and catch some of the Negro acts which often were not seen at all in the posher places downtown.

Following her success on Broadway, Libby was seen, according to some, almost nightly at Connie's Inn, The Yeahman, the Clam House, and other spots in Harlem, or else at Tony's, which Libby and her friends called "The

Tony's," to distinguish it from all the other speakeasies called Tony's.

With Libby on these jaunts to Harlem was a veritable female Mafia, which included, in addition to Louisa Jenney, actresses Tallulah Bankhead and Jeanne Eagels, revue star Beatrice Lillie and Marilyn Miller, the quintessential Ziegfeld girl. Libby and Louisa Jenney went to Harlem dressed in identical men's dark suits with bowler hats.

A year after Small's Paradise opened in its new location on Seventh Avenue in Harlem and became the focal spot for uptown rounders, the owner took an ad in *Variety* which said, "Word-of-mouth plugging has made Small's an all-season playground. To see the 'high hats' mingle with the native stepper is nothing unusual. Where formerly the dance floor was either all white or all black, the races mix and the atmosphere permits for no class distinctions."

A popular feature at Small's was watching the waiters dance the Charleston late at night while carrying loaded trays. It was partly the publication of Carl van Vechten's novel *Nigger Heaven*, in the mid-twenties, which describes some of the more colorful activities taking place uptown, that stimulated this rush of white trade to the best known cabarets. And the club owners and producers of the floor shows tried to give the sensation-seeking whites what they were looking for. Shake-dancing with its bumps and grinds was stepped up and more primitive and the jungle-like aspects of the entertainment were highlighted.

This all led to the establishment of a somewhat staged nightlife that was popular from about 1927 to about 1933, shortly after Repeal. Nobody in Harlem objected to the huge sums of money pouring into the local cash registers. But, in fact, most of the more lucrative joints were controlled by white hoodlums, principally the notorious Owney Madden.

Still, the somewhat romantically envisioned Harlem of van Vechten did exist, although most of the general public didn't see it. A woman named Helen Valentine staged sex circuses on 140th Street, which featured "drag parades" of homosexuals. These were popular stops for Libby and her friends, as were the tiny marijuana parlors illuminated by blue lights where white musicians often sat in with six-piece jump bands to jam. Libby and her friends would often go off the tourist route to journey to the Lafayette to hear Bessie Smith shout the blues or to the Savoy Ballroom to listen to Chick Webb's Chicks.

Most of the whites who saw nontourist Harlem in those days were in show business—singers, dancers and musicians like Libby and her friends, and people like Mae West, Anne Pennington from George White's *Scandals*, bandleader Phil Harris who picked up much of the Negro jargon that he later used in his specialty acts during these trips. The spots were unknown and hard to find, but jazzmen managed to find their way. One of the most popular features in Harlem were the breakfast dances on Sunday mornings from 7 A.M. to 11 A.M., when most of the show business people didn't have any work to do later in the day. At Small's, the Lenox Club and other all-night places, these early morning shows featured ad lib entertainment and music, sometimes from the biggest names in the business, always including Libby when she was on the scene.

But the appeal of Harlem was not just the opportunity to "go native" or "do your thing." Harlem was then, as now, the principal source for all sorts of dope and stimulants. Libby was a close acquaintance of a cocaine dealer named Yellow Charleston and marijuana was as freely available then as it is now, especially in Harlem.

One of the places Libby frequented which was particularly popular with Schwartz and Dietz, the songwriters of *The Little Show*, was a place called Pod's and Jerry's or "P and J's" to the cognoscenti. "Willie the Lion" Smith, a regularly featured piano player, described it this way: "The customers at P&J's varied from tush hogs to the biggest names on Broadway. They kept good order like they did in all Harlem places, and if a guy got too much Prohibition poison, one of the bouncers (they were *big* tush hogs) would waltz him right out onto the sidewalk. Or if a guy got fresh with another man's chick, they would just miss him for a while."

Besides Arthur Schwartz, among the others who dropped in in those days were the famous Bix Beiderbecke, Paul Whiteman (who would sit on the floor next to the piano while Willie played and drink from his own bottle of gin), Hoagy Carmichael, Eddie Condon, Artie Shaw, and Benny Goodman. The list was endless.

Dietz and Schwartz often worked on material for shows they were scoring by writing all over P & J's tablecloths while listening to the Lion play the piano.

Others whom the Lion remembered well as being regulars at P & J's were Tallulah Bankhead, Martha Raye, Helen Morgan, Lucille LeSueur (who gave up her classy name to become Joan Crawford), Belle Baker and Beatrice Lillie—all of them close friends of Libby's, particularly Tallulah and Bea Lillie.

In addition to Yellow Charleston, another frequent visitor was a man known as Black Charleston. Both of them were paid killers for the Owney Madden mob and Yellow Charleston actually was sentenced to die in the chair for stabbing one of Madden's competitors. "It wasn't hard for Yellow to do," the Lion remembers, "because he was always hopped-up on opium." But Yellow managed to die from tuberculosis before they got around to electrocuting him.

The other Charleston was a pimp with a string of four or five women. He always wore a diamond stickpin in his tie. "All of the girls in his stable were crazy about him," the Lion remembered. It is believed that Black Charleston and another pimp named Lovey Joe were the inspirations for the Clifton Webb character in *The Little Show*, while a whore named Chippie Mame, "a good-looking yellow woman," was the model for Libby's character.

But all of the nightlife was not uptown. Tony's was the place for Libby's crowd which, in addition to dancers and singers, included such literati as Heywood Broun,

Alexander Woolcott, Dorothy Parker and Howard and Betty Dietz.

Tony's was at 59 West 52nd Street. It was known to be an expensive joint, higher priced than the other clubs on the block, with the exception of the Iron Gate (which later became 21). Basically, Tony's was considered to be somewhat effete by the patrons of the other speakeasies on the street which was an easy putdown of people who not only had more money than the other clients but culture, taste, and sophistication. A lot of the Algonquin Round Table people frequented Tony's, notably Robert Benchley and Dorothy Parker.

Alec Wilder, the composer, songwriter, and arranger was also a regular and a great friend of Libby's. There were so many speakeasies on 52nd Street at one point that those people who still lived as normal residents in the brownstones along the block had to put up signs saying DO NOT RING. THIS IS A PRIVATE RESIDENCE.

Several times Libby and her band of female tosspots decided they would try to duplicate Benchley's famous feat of having a drink in every speak on 52nd Street, but they were unable to complete the job. Even Benchley could only remember what happened the time he tried it because he had taken notes.

Leonard Sillman says they all tried hard to keep Tony's a kind of secret among themselves, "their own sidestreet Parnassus." According to Sillman, Tony loved writers and actors so much he frowned at the intrusion of the mere public whenever it came prying. Sillman remembers one of the guests, "an unhappy ham who had come into the kitchen of Tony's speakeasy every night of the week and stood on his head." Tony was a student of yoga and loved to urge customers to try the exercises. This particular actor was the butt of most of the jokes at Tony's because he had "the vaselined slick good looks of Valentino but he was a hopelessly lousy actor and he knew it. So he'd stand at the bar taking a ribbing from the patrons until he'd get pitifully tanked, then he'd go into the kitchen and stand on his head for an hour or more. We called him 'Bogey' even then, though Humphrey was his first name and Hollywood was a long way away."

Sillman remembers Libby as a regular at Tony's long before her success in *The Little Show*, because among other things, "Tony had the biggest cuff in New York. He would carry a bar bill for years and never mention it. If you tried to apologize to Tony for your inability to pay, he'd invite you into the kitchen and persuade you to stand on your head for a while." (One of Libby's friends who was a notorious head-stander but who seldom attended the flashier nightspots was the actress Blanche Yurka.)

Oddly enough, in all this hectic, spicy, reckless nightlife, several of the men were noted for taking their mothers wherever they went. Clifton and his mother Maybelle were a popular couple as were Franchot Tone, another close friend of Libby's and his mother, Gertrude, "a tall, alarmingly elegant woman," as Sillman remembers her, "with snow-white hair drawn back in a knot, wearing a pince-nez." Tone brought his mother to one of the tables occupied by Sillman, Libby, Dietz and Schwartz one night and introduced her. "Gertrude Tone sat demurely down among us," Sillman says, "and proceeded to drink the lot of us under the table."

Many thought that bringing Gertrude to Tony's was a mistake, because she fell in love with the place and became the grande dame of all of its devotees. "She would join us every night," Sillman reports, "regal and lovely as a queen, and after the improper amount of boozing and badinage, it was always Gertrude, adjusting her pince-nez, who would shout 'Let's go to Harlem!'"

Another locale where Libby and other swingers played was Betty and Howard Dietz's apartment in the Village. Betty, who had "a wonderful Bostonian kind of good looks and a figure for a chorus line," but who also possessed, according to Sillman, "one of the most remarkable thinking apparatuses since the invention of the brain," ran with her husband one of the last of the old-fashioned salons. Their beautiful house on 11th Street was a way-station for such literary figures as

Alexander Woolcott, Dorothy Parker, Robert Benchley, Allen Jackson, John O'Hara, and Charles Brackett. But the show biz figures and literati came to Dietz's for more than good talk and honest booze. Howard owned one of the first sunlamps in America and it was a cherished plaything of the entire group, particularly Libby, who throughout her lifetime was obsessed with keeping the marvelous tan which almost rendered makeup unnecessary in her Negro-inspired roles.

The year 1929 was to be one of enormous contrasts for the nation and world as a whole and for Libby Holman, personally. It was the year the big stock market frenzy reached its peak, with everyone from shoeshine boys to chorus girls investing in the great bull market of Wall Street and it was the year the stock market crashed on October 24.

For Libby, too, the year started as the greatest in her career to date and ended with the first of the many great tragedies which were to afflict her life. Certainly the success of *The Little Show* got the year off to an auspicious start and by the early fall of 1929, Libby was making $2,000 a week at a time when sixty percent of the population was making less than $2,000 a year. And this was still considered a time of prosperity. Her new notoriety and enormous popularity on Broadway seemed to accelerate the hectic social life which was beginning to become a part of her pattern.

Libby, who was not known as a drinker in her earlier years, appeared to spend more time in the speakeasies, blind pigs and nightclubs of Harlem and showed strange shifts in mood which some attributed to drugs. Certainly her close friends Tallulah Bankhead and Jeanne Eagels were known users of stimulants and the trips to Harlem were often as much in search of cocaine, opium or marijuana as they were in search of musical divertissement. Cocaine, though not a drug of the masses, was as popular with show business personalities then as it is now, so much so that nobody thought it was remarkable when Cole Porter included the line *I get no kick from cocaine/Mere alcohol doesn't thrill me at all* in his popular song "I Get a Kick Out of You."

It seems almost certain from the testimony of survivors of those days that Libby and her playmates were indulging in bizarre sexual shenanigans, under the influence of stimulants and narcotics, not simply lesbianism but all sorts of trios, quartets, and exhibitions. At that time, sex circuses were a popular part of the Harlem entertainment scene.

Tallulah Bankhead, at this point had lived more of her adult life in London than she had in New York. Libby had made her acquaintance there in the '20s. At the time, Tallulah had a following of hysterical teenage girls that was said to rival Frank Sinatra's some years later. Brendan Gill in his book *Tallulah*, wrote of her: "Tallulah fell in comfortably with the tradition of bisexuality in the English theater, a state of affairs more common in the '20s there than in the United States, where the majority of people working in the theater were either strictly heterosexual or strictly homosexual and had a sort of puritan distrust of the license implied in chancing both. A tradition of bisexuality existed also in the English upper classes, which Tallulah was soon invited to move among. One of the earliest and coarsest of her bawdy stories concerned an English lord and lady to whose country house she had been asked for the weekend. Host and hostess proved equally eager to make a conquest of her, each in his/her way and concurrently, not consecutively. As one might expect, Tallulah was fascinated by the acrobatic ingenuities required to give simultaneous satisfaction to all.

Tallulah seemed to delight in taunting her audiences with generous glimpses of her slim but provocative body. A reviewer for *Theater World* who signed himself "V.H.F." once commented: "No criticism of Tallulah Bankhead's plays is complete without reference to her display of lingerie. Personally I find her more attractive in her jumper suit than without one, and I am quite willing to take her underclothes for granted. I am told, however,

Tallulah Bankhead during her extended stay in London.

that these rather feeble attempts at immodesty are for the benefit of the feminine element of the audience. Well, well, girls will be boys!"

In any event, Tallulah ended her long stay in England in 1928, returning to the States just at the time Libby's star was ascending. There again, she was an easy target for the gossip of Broadway columnists. When the news reached the papers that Miss Bankhead of the distinguished Alabama family was disporting herself outrageously in the precincts of Harlem, grave distress struck at the family manse in Alabama. A stern telegram went out from Daddy, criticizing this outrageous behavior and pointing out that it did not do her father, a distinguished member of Congress, any good to have his daughter spending so much time in Harlem. Oddly enough, the usually insouciant Tallulah seemed very distressed by the note from her father and she had her producer, Walter Wanger, explain the incident by telegram to Senator Bankhead:

> TALLULAH SHOWED ME YOUR LETTER OF FEBRUARY 14TH. I THINK IT IS SCANDALOUS THAT HER SOLE TRIP TO HARLEM SHOULD BE SO MISINTERPRETED. SHE WAS SENT THERE WITH HER DIRECTOR MR. CUKOR TO SEE CONDITIONS AS THERE WAS A HARLEM NIGHTCLUB SCENE IN HER PRESENT PICTURE. BUT AFTER A VISIT IT WAS DECIDED THAT THE ATMOSPHERE WAS TOO VULGAR . . . I REGRET EPISODE SHOULD HAVE CAUSED SUCH MISREPRESENTATION—
>
> WALTER WANGER.

Libby and the rest of Tallulah's friends thought the telegram was a hoot. As one biographer described it, "Tallulah made the Harlem nightclub scene because she felt freer uptown to do and see and say. She could also get cocaine there from a black hunchback named Money. There was good jazz and fun, smut and all varieties of sexual exhibitions which her natural curiosity impelled her, no doubt, to witness."

But Libby, Tallulah, Louisa Jenney and the others had their mellower moments, too. They often would like to sit around the piano in Connie's Place or the Hotshot Club and sing songs to one another or listen to the local entertainment. Others who often joined their group, brought by Tallulah, included Noel Coward, Cole Porter, and Billie Holiday. In fact, it was often Tallulah who bailed that legendary singer out of jail when she was locked up on drug charges in later years. Certainly Miss Bankhead was one of the sparkplugs of a group that already had more ignition than it absolutely needed.

The coterie usually started and ended its travels without any men, although there were occasional boyfriends. Clifton Webb and his mother, when they were not entertaining in the salon in their apartment, were often part of the traveling troupe.

Throughout this high-living period, Libby never failed to pay attention to her public image, and her statements to the press during interviews were often a strange mixture of fantasy and truth. Here's what she told a reporter from the old New York *World* at the height of her *Little Show* success: "I want to live to be a smart old witch who rules with an iron scepter. I never want to envy youth. I never want to be dependent.

"At fifty, sixty, seventy and eighty I want to have enough charm and fascination inside of myself to draw the admiration and love of men, to make them forget lush, young girls.

"While a girl is young and voluptuous, she can't help but be admired. She can get by on her looks. Old age is the problem.

"Here's my program: five more years of the theater. No more. I'll play bigtime dramatic roles. Right now I am coaching for *L'Aiglon* and I'm flirting with *Camille*.

"In five years I hope to have enough money saved to give me a sure income of $15,000 a year. I'll go to France and get a villa. Then I'll concentrate on the development of my mind. I want to be rich inside.

"I want at least one great love, maybe more, but NO MILLIONAIRES!

"Lastly, I'll have a child! That's a necessary part of the experience!"

7

Jeanne Eagels

Despite Libby's popularity with men and the number of them who wooed her, it is clear that during the years of her early success on the stage no man gained her serious attention.

It was at this point that Libby met Jeanne Eagels, who had become a regular visitor backstage at *The Little Show*. She and Libby's co-star Clifton Webb were old friends from their early theatrical days. Jeanne Eagels was at the time one of the most notorious and talked-about stars on Broadway. She was just finishing an eight-month suspension by Equity—the longest such sanction the newly-formed actors' group had ever given.

She was a striking blonde with haunted eyes that always seemed to be masking some hidden pain. She was fourteen years older than Libby and deeply concerned with her approaching fortieth birthday. Like Libby, she had made up a skein of yarns concerning her origins which is often hard to disentangle. According to the early biographies based on interviews she gave, she had been the daughter of a very romantic Spaniard named Aguilar, whose name in translation became "Eagle," and she had been born in aristocratic Boston. This Spanish heritage, writers were to say of her later, accounted for her stormy and overheated temperament. In fact, she was born in Kansas City, not Boston; her father was a poor carpenter, not a distinguished architect.

Jeanne grew up playing road shows all over the Midwest in a variety of parts, and lying about her age from the time she was eleven. When she was a scrawny, stage-struck child of fifteen, Jeanne toured Midwest tank towns with popular tent shows. One night she was put into the starring role when a drunken patron jumped onto the stage and beat up the lady who had been playing her part. For the next six years, she played in everything from *Little Lord Fauntleroy* to *Camille*. She got $25 a week for the job. At sixteen, she married one of the company's owners, a short, stubby man named Maurice Dubinsky by whom she had a child which she shortly afterwards turned over to his family.

Ultimately, she left the tent show and, driven by ambition, came to Broadway through a role in a musical that had played in Kansas City. The musical folded in Providence, but she managed to scrape up the money to come to New York and haunt the theatrical agencies.

She got a bit part in a Billie Burke play called *Mind the Paint Girl*, where she was spotted by Ziegfeld. She was worth glorifying and Ziegfeld knew it. He offered to make her a *Follies* girl but she turned him down. "I am a dramatic actress," she said, and that was that. She accepted jewelry and furs from a rich, old man but sent them back when she finally got a lead part in *The Crinoline Girl*. The only critic who caught her in it was one from the *Morning Telegraph*, the racetrack sheet, but he gave her a rave review and letters to important theatrical people, especially David Belasco. (Not all shows got reviewed in those days, when as many as 200 to 300 shows a year opened in New York alone.)

Belasco felt an instant rapport with the girl. "She

reminded me of a starved, little alley-cat. Beautiful—ahh! That wonderful golden head and the blue angelic eyes and the sweet mouth and the tender but firm chin and the cunning nose. But gaunt, starved, sick!

"She was a timid girl who feared no man, a girl who had been whipped by adversity until she cringed, but who faced me with hard, ambitious eyes, a girl in shabby clothes with the air of a Duse, the voice of an Earl's daughter, and the mien of an alley cat. I asked her why she wanted to be an actress, and she said something in her would never let her be anything else."

Belasco made her the star of his new show *Daddies*. But after a few months, she quit in a rage when Belasco's executive manager insisted that she go to bed with him if she wanted to keep the part.

In 1922, Jeanne was catapulted to stardom "overnight." (After only eleven years on Broadway and seven on the road.) She was cast in the pivotal role of the prostitute Miss Sadie Thompson by Sam Harris in *Rain*, the new play he was producing, based on Somerset Maugham's story "Miss Thompson." John Corbin, who gave the *Time* review, said of her, "Miss Eagels, noted as a young actress of promise since her performance in *Daddies*, rises to the requirements of this difficult role with fine loyalty to the reality of the character and with an emotional power as fiery and unbridled in effect as it is artistically restrained." The play, which was a canto against bigotry and prudery, seemed perfectly molded to Jeanne Eagels' background. "In the last scene," Corbin notes, "Miss Thompson blazes forth in her cheap finery, fierce in her hatred of 'all men.' But the missionary has committed suicide, and for that she forgives him." The play was the sensation of the season.

She was called "one of the most beautiful and brilliant actresses on the American stage." The play itself was to become a landmark of American theater. In New York and on tour it ran a solid five years, and during that period it could be fairly said that Jeanne Eagels was the most luminous star on Broadway.

Jeanne Eagels in "*Rain*."

Jeanne Eagels in 1928

Jeanne Eagels in the film "*Jealousy*," completed shortly before her death.

In the beginning she was excited by her success—she stayed up all night to watch workmen screwing the bulbs in that spelled out her stardom: JEANNE EAGELS IN RAIN. Edward Doherty, who wrote her biography, serialized in *Liberty*, claimed that Jeanne never smoked until she began to rehearse for *Rain*, and that she didn't drink whiskey and seldom drank anything until several years after the show opened. Her new stardom gave her access to social worlds which had previously been closed to her. Among her suitors was Edward Harris "Ted" Coy, a great Yale football hero, son of wealthy parents, and a Wall Street broker with what was said to be a fantastic future. Coy's rival for Jeanne's affections was Whitney Warren, Jr., son of a famous architect and a war hero who had left Groton to enlist in the French army and earned the Medaille Militaire and the Croix de Guerre.

Warren and Coy competed so heartily for her affections that it was feared at times they might actually get into a fistfight. Jeanne would worry about this, too, and sometimes would order both of them put out of the theater. Ted Coy was her age, but Warren was seven years younger and this caused a certain amount of sour commentary in the press.

The newspapers showed a great interest in the romantic life of the glamorous Broadway star and some months after the two men started courting her, a report was published of Jeanne's engagement to Whitney Warren, an announcement which was vigorously denied by Warren's somewhat aristocratic, if not snobbish, family. Jeanne had not authorized the announcement, she said, and had known nothing of it. But, she told the press, she was not engaged to anyone. She never questioned Whitney about any part he might have had in planting the story. She adopted a policy which she was later to pass along to her friend Libby:

"Never deny. Never explain. Never rush into print. Let them think anything they like, say anything they like. Say nothing—and become a legend."

In 1925, at the height of her stardom, Jeanne Eagels

married Ted Coy. They settled into a lavish estate in Ossining, New York, adjoining the estate of publisher Gerard Swope. The marriage was a disaster almost from the start. Jeanne had almost no respect for the fawning and servile young broker. She often slapped his face in public and let him alone at parties to go wandering off to speakeasies or private parties with her friends. Certainly by this time, it could be said that Jeanne Eagels had graduated from drinking "little or nothing at all" to becoming a problem drinker. Her erratic behavior and suddenly decreased span of attention were clues to those in the know that Jeanne was getting a little help from something more than liquor.

Coy, adoring and distraught, was completely unable to control her and she held him in contempt for this. Her friends and defenders claimed that Jeanne said she had injured her arm severely as a child while playing Liza in *Uncle Tom's Cabin*, and that the constant dampness on the set of *Rain* aggravated a chronic pain that she felt in this arm. She was forced to resort to pain-killing and mood-altering drugs, to keep from a lifetime of agony.

This may very well be true, but it is also the story told in the history of most drug-addicted celebrities. Certainly her greatest friends and comforters in her fits of despondency were Clifton and Maybelle Webb. The Webbs' home was an informal "Lamb's Club" where everybody came—artists, actors, writers, movie stars, opera singers, and musicians. Here one might meet in one afternoon or evening Rudolph Valentino, Marilyn Miller, opera stars Geraldine Farrar and Rosa Ponsell—anybody who was anybody. Jeanne and Clifton became known to Broadway and to each other as "the girlfriend" and "the boyfriend." Those who knew both smiled fondly but skeptically, since Webb was known to be homosexual. They truly were great friends.

Certainly in the beginning of Jeanne's career, no one could have predicted her later erratic behavior. In five years of playing Sadie Thompson, she missed only seventeen performances, most of these after she married

Coy, when she began to complain of colitis and other ailments, in addition to her chronic arm problem. Meanwhile Coy and Jeanne had such frequent tiffs that almost always one or the other was living in the otherwise unoccupied eight-room lodge-keeper's cottage on the estate. In 1926, when *Rain* returned to New York from a tour, Jeanne gave a party in Ossining, but her unsteady temperament got the best of her. In a fit of temper, she chased every guest out of her home, rushed away to New York, checked in and out of the Algonquin Hotel, and vanished while her understudy played the part. Later, she explained that she'd had another fit of illness for which she went to treatment to her beloved "Dr. Cowles." Cowles was a theatrical doctor of the time who nowadays would probably be called "Dr. Feelgood." In any event, he managed to keep Jeanne going in times of desperate chemical need and stress. The long run of *Rain* ended in 1928, due not to Jeanne's increasingly erratic behavior but rather to a squabble between Sam Harris, the producer, and the newly-formed actors' union, Equity, which was strongly backed by the great actress Blanche Yurka, then appearing on Broadway in *The Wild Duck*. Harris, like George M. Cohan and certain other producers, was determined to have nothing to do with it. Jeanne supported her producer. She felt that Equity might be all right for chorus girls and extras, but not for creative artists. Unwilling to back down, Harris closed the play but promised Jeanne he would cast her soon in another part. Meanwhile, leading organizers of Equity developed an animosity toward Jeanne which was shortly to have a profound effect on her career and her life.

The show Harris mounted for Jeanne was *Her Cardboard Lover*. Now suffering even more intensely from various aches, pains and illnesses, including sinus attacks, neuralgia, kidney disease, a throat infection, and nervous exhaustion, she showed up for rehearsals a month late, causing the cancellation of several bookings. The show opened at the Empire Theater in New York in March of 1927, and some critics thought her stage behavior erratic in a way not entirely called for in her role of a beautiful and wealthy Parisienne.

"It was a visibly nervous Miss Eagels, all fidget and misgiving, who entered shakily upon the scene," a critic for the Boston *Transcript* wrote. "There was the dim, insistent suggestion that somehow Sadie Thompson herself had got hold of the fine raiment of Madame Simone Lagorce and swaggered into the baccarat room at Hendaye, bold as her own blinding hair without, inwardly sick with panic lest she be found out. But somehow all this fell away as the play advanced. Indeed, Miss Eagles swept it away magnificently, playing several scenes with an almost fey charm and delicacy and plunging into the romp."

But the erratic behavior noted by the acute critic was to grow during the run of *Her Cardboard Lover*. In one performance, Jeanne stopped the play abruptly and ordered Leslie Howard, her leading man, to get her a drink of water. Howard looked astonished and made no move. Jeanne walked off the stage herself to get the drink while the audience waited impatiently.

When the show went on tour in Kansas City, an actor irritated Jeanne by leaving a door open after his exit, so she walked through it off the stage and back to her dressing room, leaving the rest of the cast onstage to improvise lines until the curtain came down.

Then she didn't appear for three nights in a row at a road performance in Brooklyn and completely forgot a booking in Boston. People said she had become the vanishing American actress. While there were no comments about the possibility of drugs taking a hand in all this, there were insinuations here and there in the press that alcohol was a factor. This she denied strenuously.

The show was to open in Milwaukee on a Tuesday. Jeanne didn't appear. Ticketholders were invited to come back again on Wednesday, but still no Jeanne. On Thursday she still had not come and the booking was canceled. When she finally showed up, she told the producers that she had been "ill with ptomaine poisoning," and she had certificates from twelve doctors to prove it. A representative from Equity called on her but she refused to see him. She told him she would be at the performance in St. Louis the following week. However, she never showed up. This was the last straw for Equity. On April 3, 1928, Jeanne Eagels was suspended by Equity until September 1929 and was fined $3,600—two weeks' salary. The sanction must have given great pleasure to various Equity officials with whom Jeanne had clashed during the formative years of the union but Jeanne was still an unreconstructed antiunionist.

"No group of actors for whom, with few exceptions, I have no respect, can keep me from earning a living," she stormed. "Why the whole thing is silly. Equity is an organization for the rank and file. I don't belong to the rank and file. I'm not the kind to stand in line and kick as high as the next. A creative person cannot be bound by labor rules."

But being barred by Equity meant that Jeanne was banned from every legitimate stage in America.

At first, Jeanne laughed about her banishment, and jeered at Equity and everyone connected with it. A few days later, however, she was seen to weep bitterly and say that her life was ruined "because I was sick and desperate and all alone and drank too much trying to forget my illness and my loneliness, and because I refused to see that man from Equity. I was too sick to see him. But what do they care? I'm thrown out. Lost everything. The most brutal criminals are given more consideration in our courts that Equity gave me. But I'll show them! I'll come back in eighteen months and in the meantime there's always vaudeville and movies."

Jeanne was aware, of course, that vaudeville would pay her even more than the legitimate theater and that the movies would pay more than vaudeville and it was true that shortly afterward people were pointing her out in restaurants and hotel rooms not as Jeanne Eagels, the star of *Rain* and *Her Cardboard Lover*, but as the Jeanne Eagels who had appeared with John Gilbert in *Man,*

Woman and Sin, her first film. She got more recognition for her one movie role that she had gained in her entire career on stage.

After her suspension by Equity, Jeanne went to the country estate near Ossining and took with her members of the company of *Her Cardboard Lover* who were put out of a job on her account and had neither homes nor money. Many of them lived on her largesse for weeks and she loved cooking for them and taking them to and from New York in her cars. She was booked for twenty weeks at $4,000 a week on the Keith-Albee-Orpheum circuit, and the vaudeville tour was a triumph for her. She was a headliner wherever she went and nobody seemed to care that Equity had thrust her into limbo. She drank more than ever after the shows and kept a supply of liquor in her dressing room. Friends would call for her and drink with her. They'd go places with her sometimes when she could hardly walk. It was not an uncommon sight to see her come into a room sedately walking between two men, each holding one of her arms. She'd look so serene and charming that only a few would realize that if her escorts let go of her arms, she would stagger and fall to the floor. She'd often keep on drinking and partying until seven or eight in the morning, sleep a few hours, and be ready for her vaudeville stint for the matinee.

Jeanne now had a serious problem with her reputation in show business, and the producers of the movie version of *Rain* refused to cast her, choosing Gloria Swanson instead. In June, she got a divorce from Coy, charging that he habitually beat her, although friends claimed it was more often the other way around.

Between vaudeville engagements, when she would recite bits from *Rain* and *Her Cardboard Lover*, Jeanne took to frequenting the home of the Webbs even more than she had before. She went everywhere with Clifton, and often they pretended to be brother and sister. One critic, describing her performance in a vaudeville show, said that she looked "like an excited and glorified Clifton Webb in crinoline." Jeanne laughed for days. Maybelle helped Jeanne to pick out her clothes and to furnish her rooms, but Jeanne spent her money so quickly that despite top wages she was rapidly going broke. Of course, no one knows what happened to her money during her frequent disappearances and lapses. Maybelle delighted trying to mold Jeanne's conduct toward people she wanted her to meet but Jeanne seldom took her advice.

"Who's coming tonight?" she would ask, "and how shall I act? Shall I be water? Shall I be milk? Or shall I be champagne?"

"Just be yourself," Maybelle would usually answer.

Nobody knew what that self was. When Jeanne was expected to be wild and exciting and full of fun, she would be prim, proper, and even dignified. When the guests had left she would roll on the floor laughing and shout "Oh Lord, didn't I fool them? Didn't I put on an act?"

Jeanne and Clifton were often given to playing innocuous practical jokes on theatrical friends. Once they decided to attend one of Bea Lillie's revues and when Lady Peel requested the audience to name any song and promised that she would sing it, Cliff was to rise up and demand a song which Jeanne had ascertained she had never heard of. But to Jeanne's disappointment, Webb dropped out of the joke, deciding it was a bit too cruel a prank to play on their good friend.

By this time, *The Little Show* had debuted and had become the leading musical revue on Broadway. Webb had a room in the Music Box Theater one flight up from the lobby and near producer Sam Harris's office. Every night, about a quarter of an hour before the opening, except on Sunday, Jeanne Eagels would be there. Though she had been barred by Equity, she found poignant pleasure in visiting the dressing room of her friend and it was there that Jeanne made the acquaintance of Libby Holman.

Both were instantly attracted to one another. Libby was drawn to the frail, wan, undernourished, haunted look of the older woman and probably somewhat influenced by her fame as a star and a problem child.

Jeanne, on the other hand, responded to the darker, sultry, and exotic looks of the young torch singer. They talked excitedly of Jeanne's plans to be in a new Sam Harris play that was to put her back on Broadway after Equity's ban expired, in a matter of months. She was determined that when it happened she would have Clifton's room. "I love this place," she said, looking around. "But you've got to walk down all these stairs and then down an aisle and back stage before you can get out and speak your little piece. When this room is mine—and it will be mine unless you stay here forever, damn you—I'm going to have a chute put in, so that when I'm dressed, I can slide right onto the stage."

For the first time in a long time, possibly in her whole life, Jeanne seemed to have found a relationship that made her happy. "If I'd only known Libby and people like her a long time ago," she frequently said in those days, "how different my life might have been."

Within a few weeks, the estate in Ossining was all but forgotten except for occasional visits to rest or dry out. Jeanne actually moved into Libby's new East Side apartment, and the two were seen everywhere, playing tennis, drinking, singing, dancing. They seemed never to be apart. For Libby, too, this was probably her first deep and serious relationship. So enthralled were they by one another's company that Libby all but dropped her other friends, Louisa Jenney, Tallulah Bankhead, Bea Lillie and the rest, to be with this fragile, half-wrecked blonde beauty.

Until she met Jeanne, Libby had been living with a young girl named Lisbeth White Guthrie who served as her secretary. Lisbeth's husband was a stockbroker; in later years he sued his ex-wife, claiming that she and her mother both lived in Libby's apartment and that Libby had "some strange and mysterious connection" with them. But once she took up with Jeanne, Libby found a job for her friend Lisbeth, working for Grace Moore the opera star, and Lisbeth left the apartment to settle for a while on the West Coast.

Friends in show business were aware of the intensity of Libby and Jeanne's relationship but the public hardly noticed. Despite their obvious delight in one another, however, the relationship was not terribly healthy for either. Libby, at the pinnacle of her success could be as wild, as undisciplined and as unpredictable as her blonde friend, but while Libby's star was on the rise, Jeanne's was on the wane. She had constant premonitions of death and obviously dreaded the approach of her fortieth birthday. In interviews she would often make references to times when she would be "too old to act," and have to direct. Once, after a fight with her husband, Coy, she was found drunk in her nightgown, draped over a tombstone in a neighboring graveyard in Ossining. "What's the dif'," she said as they carried her home, "we'll all wind up here someday anyway and I have a hunch in my case it won't be long now."

This melancholy mood would show up at strange times in the press. An unsigned feature in the drama section of the *Times* on March 24, 1929 was headed: "JEANNE EAGELS IN A TEARFUL MOOD." It described a situation in which Jeanne, who was making a film called *Jealousy* for Paramount's studio in Astoria remained alone on the set after the director and the rest of the company had gone. "With her elbows resting on her knees and the handkerchief still pressed against her face, Miss Eagels began to sob . . .

"Finally Miss Eagels stood up with tears running down her cheeks. She walked from the library into an adjoining set, the foyer of the apartment and there, as if offstage, she wept again. One of the assistants came and offered his services but Miss Eagels only flopped into another chair and sobbed murmuring some words about a 'possible breakdown' and 'strain.' The young man left her alone. In a few moments she arose, dry-eyed, her makeup partly washed off. With a sigh she dropped her hands to her sides and slowly walked across the wide stage —to lunch."

Two months later Jeanne sold the estate in Ossining

and its thirty adjoining acres. The amount she got for it was not disclosed. And keeping her East 58th Street apartment only for appearances, she moved fulltime into Libby's home.

Jeanne's mood shifts became even more extreme. If she was not laughing hysterically, or flitting about like a haunted golden bird, she was plunged into despondency, full of forebodings of harm and death. She tried to shake off these fits of depression as well as the pain of her various illnesses, whether psychogenic or purely biological, by frequent trips to Dr. Cowles' Park Avenue office, which was also popular with other current show business personalities who were involved in drugs. Libby, of course, was pleased to make the acquaintanceship of Dr. Cowles, who was free with his prescriptions, though at a very substantial cost.

When they were on their upswing moods, it seemed to both women that they were headed for the stratosphere—Libby just starting her career, and Jeanne positive that her role in the new Sam Harris play would take her to even greater heights. At least she felt that way on her good days. She had all sorts of plans for what she would do when her Equity sanction was lifted. She was particularly intrigued by a play called *Diana*, a drama based on the life of Isadora Duncan. This led Libby to speculate again on the possibility of doing a dramatic play with music based on the life of Josephine Baker, with whom she had been intrigued since her first trip to Europe. Aside from her fascination with Jeanne's beauty and outrageous wit, Libby was also intrigued by the great respect shown for her dramatic ability because Libby had never stopped thinking of herself as potentially a dramatic actress. For her the torch singing was only a means to an end. The two would chatter excitedly together of their plans for the future. On these up days, calls from Tallulah, Louisa Jenney, Bea Lillie, and other friends went unanswered. The only people to share the excitement of their mutual discovery were Clifton Webb and his mother.

But on her down days, Jeanne Eagels darkened the sun

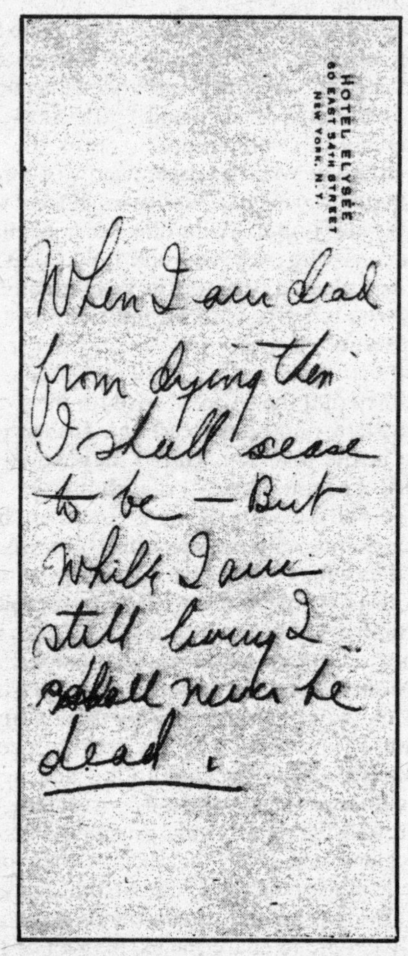
HOTEL ELYSÉE
60 EAST 54TH STREET
NEW YORK, N.Y.

When I am dead
from dying then
I shall cease
to be — But
while I am
still living I
shall never be
dead.

The note Jeanne Eagels scribbled on an envelope a few days before her death.

with her gloom. One evening, on a visit to her apartment to air it out, give it a more lived-in appearance, she brought along her secretary-companion, Christina Larson. Christina threw up the window to let in the late summer breeze and while Jeanne stood there looking out, a bird flew in, one with bright yellow wings, possibly a goldfinch, and flapped the gold wings against Jeanne's shining, blonde hair. Jeanne beat her hands at the fluttering creature in panic.

"Stina!" she cried. "Stina, I'm going to die!"

Christina laughed. She knew that Jeanne was superstitious and there was a belief that a bluebird flying in the window meant death. "But this is a golden bird," Stina said. "That doesn't mean death. It means fortune. Good luck! Love! Gold! Something nice!" She took the panicked bird and stroked its feathers, but Jeanne backed away, still frightened.

"No," she said, "it means death."

With a quick flip of her palm, Christina tossed the small golden bird into the night and tried to comfort her trembling mistress. 'It's a gold bird, Miss Eagels," she reassured the distressed actress, "not a bluebird."

"Never mind," Jeanne said. "Birds mean death, Stina. I know I'm doomed. I hope it's a spectacular death. I hope it's on the stage after the last act."

A few days later Libby's maid found, scribbled on an envelope from the Hotel Elysee an odd sentence in Jeanne's erratic and untutored handwriting: "When I am dead from dying then I shall cease to be—But while I am still living I shall never be *dead.*"

Concerned, she asked Jeanne what it meant, but her friend, with deep circles under her eyes from sleeplessness and probably drugs, simply shrugged. "Whatever you want it to," she said.

A few days later she asked to be released from the film she was making in Astoria based on a play called *The Laughing Lady*. Jeanne had not been fond of the picture from the start. She said that they'd taken a beautiful play and vulgarized it. She read the script and was disgusted with it. Finally she sent for the author, Bartlett Cormack, and with an endearing smile, gave him her suggestions for changes and asked what he thought of her ideas.

"They're terrific." Cormack said. "I think they'll strengthen the story. They shook hands and Cormack went back to his room and spent all night rewriting the scenes that she didn't like. Next day he walked into the office with the new script. Jeanne looked at him with blank eyes. "Are you the scenario writer?" she asked. She stared at him as though she'd never seen him before. "What's your name?"

"Cormack. Bartlett Cormack."

"Cormack," she said, "so nice to meet you. I'm glad you brought the script, but I want some changes made."

"What are you talking about?" Cormack asked in surprise. "I sat up all night writing the changes you suggested yesterday."

"What do you mean?" Jeanne said, outraged. "This is the first time in my life I've seen you and I asked you to do something, you say you've already done it?"

"But," Cormack protested, "I met you yesterday and you gave me your instructions."

Jeanne turned to the producer, Monte Bell. "What is he talking about now? I never saw him yesterday. I told him nothing."

Bell smiled wearily. He had dealt with Jeanne before. "Don't worry about it, Miss Eagels. We'll get the whole thing fixed up, if we have to stay up all night to make the changes."

But the next day, Jeanne came in and asked to be released from the contract. "Look, Monte," she said, "I'm very sick. My eyes are in terrible condition. It would take two weeks for the operation I need, and it might not succeed. Besides, I don't like this picture. The adaptation has been cheapened and gagged up. Can't we come to some other agreement? I want to quit movies forever. I want to go back to the stage when I'm well."

"I'll take it up with the legal department, Jeanne," Bell said. "I think we can arrange it."

She gave the producer a quick little kiss and then disappeared forever from the movie studios.

A day or so later, a story appeared in the New York *Times* stating that Jeanne Eagels has been operated on at St. Luke's Hospital for ulcers of the eyes caused by a sinus infection. The doctor assured reporters that there was no danger of blindness; Miss Eagels would be able to leave the hospital in a few days. Until then, she would be kept in a darkened room until her eyesight recovered.

The story had appeared on September 15. Jeanne's suspension by Equity had been over at the beginning of the month and she announced that she planned to be in a new play produced by Sam Harris. She left the hospital a few days later and her doctor reported that if she did not strain her eyes she would be very much improved within a week. That was on September 17. As soon as she was released from the hospital, Jeanne made her way to the dressing room at the Music Box theater to celebrate with Libby and Clifton Webb, both of whom had visited her almost every day during her brief stay at St. Luke's. Later the two women downed at least a magnum of Pol Roget and were found in each other's arms asleep the next morning by Libby's maid Felice.

Libby went early to the theater to work on some changes with Clifton Webb and author Howard Dietz. Jeanne had one of her "regular appointments" with Dr. Cowles. Christina Larson, who later said that she had had a terrible premonition in Ossining, arrived just as she was leaving the apartment, accompanied by a nurse. "I'm going to Dr. Cowles," she said, "for one of my regular treatments."

"I'm going with you," Stina decided and hurried downstairs after her.

The visit was to be at Dr. Cowles' private Park Avenue hospital at 591 Park Avenue. But Cowles had not yet arrived when they got there. They spent a few minutes chatting with the nurse, awaiting the doctor. Jeanne wore a blue frock. For someone who was usually so casual, she seemed to be extraordinarily well turned out. On her neck was a double strand of pearls with a diamond clasp. On her fingers were four rings, a square diamond in a platinum setting, a large pearl ring, the diamond-studded wedding band given to her by Edward Coy, and a plain guard ring. Stina particularly noticed the wedding ring and the guard ring, since Jeanne Eagels never wore them. A second nurse appeared and announced that the doctor was now ready. Jeanne stood up, started up the stairs, then hesitated, turned, and gave Stina her compact and lipstick to hold. Then, inexplicably, she gave Tina's hand a firm squeeze and with a smile, she was gone. Tina continued to chat with the nurse for a few minutes and then went upstairs to be with Jeanne.

She found her in a small room near the head of the stairs lying on a couch, gasping for breath. Then, even as Stina watched her, paralyzed with fright, Jeanne ceased to gasp. Her arms fell of their own weight to her side.

The headline of the New York Times next day, square in the middle of the front page said: "JEANNE EAGELS COLLAPSES, DIES IN HOSPITAL/ON VISIT TO BE TREATED FOR NERVE AILMENT."

An autopsy was ordered immediately after her death and the first announcement said that her collapse was caused by "alcoholic psychosis." On Saturday the report of the cause of Jeanne's death was amended when the city toxicologist discovered that she had died from an overdose of chloral hydrate, described as "a nerve sedative and soporific."

Others in Jeanne's crowd knew of chloral hydrate, too. It was often referred to as "knockout drops" and was the principal ingredient in the Mickey Finns administered to bring grief to obstreperous customers.

As she lay in state at the Campbell Funeral Home on 66th Street and Broadway, crowds mobbed to see her last picture, *Jealousy*, playing at the Lincoln Square Theater, almost directly opposite.

Cowles gave a statement to the press saying that chloral hydrate was a legitimate sedative. "Only proper medication was used in her case. It was all a most deplorable accident."

The papers in general were sympathetic and so were many of Jeanne's old Broadway friends who rushed to defend her. The *Sun* said, "Jeanne Eagels kept the history of her prolonged physical tragedy from the public record. Her sufferings kept her awake nights and days on end, and sometimes at the end of her endurance, she resorted to the bottle only to bring comatose sleep."

David Belasco, who had brought her to fame first in *Daddies*, defended her on ethnic grounds: "Her temperament was not her fault, but that of her Spanish-Irish inheritance."

But aside from Belasco and a few others, the only ones who showed up at the funeral home were Jeanne's fans, the audience, with the exception of Clifton and Maybelle Webb and Libby Holman. Sam Harris, who made Jeanne a star, was there, pacing the floor, angry and anguished. "There lies the greatest actress in the world," he said, "and the greatest comedienne. And where is the crowd of actresses not good enough to kiss the hem of her skirt, where are the people she's been feeding and clothing who aren't here? Who haven't even sent flowers or telegrams of sympathy? They hate her. Are they afraid of Equity? Would Equity be offended at their grief?"

Finally, dawn came and ended the all-night vigil by Libby, Clifton and Maybelle Webb, Sam Harris and Barry O'Neill, an actor thought once to have been a lover of Jeanne's. Preparations were made for the chapel services and for the train that would take her body back to "that slow little town," Kansas City, Jeanne hated so, for burial.

Libby went off by herself after the service. She disappeared and was not seen by anyone until her performance the following Tuesday.

The New York *Times* carried a memorial tribute by John D. Williams, who had directed *Rain*.

> "Miss Eagels," he wrote, "is lamented in death by everybody who really knew her and very few did. As another tragic example of one who, with all she had yet to give in the theater, not of mere representation but of high

interpretation, actually extinguished a great gift through an idealistic but unmeasured struggle for the summit of her art."

On Monday in a follow-up story, the *Times* reported that the jewels Jeanne Eagels wore at the time of her death were worth $250,000. Other papers placed the estimate even higher. But in the world of fantasy that Jeanne had inhabited, this, too, was an illusion. When her estate was probated, some time later, the value of the jewels was put at less than $5,000. The pearls were fake, though the clasp was real. Somewhat heartlessly, the *Times* reported she had three imitation pearl necklaces worth $9 and another imitation pearl necklace valued at $250. All together, Jeanne left to her mother Julia Eagels and her sister Helen a total of less than $50,000, including almost $30,000 in cash.

Libby was totally shattered but since their relationship had been conducted on a level of high discretion it was not possible for her to reveal publicly the extent of her grief. However, she disappeared from public life and all her haunts for several months following. It wasn't until May of the following year that a second medical report was quietly released. It revealed that the actress had been treating her pains with heroin, along with chloral hydrate; when she died, at age thirty-nine, there were 2.4 milligrams of heroin in her brain.

At about the same time, *Liberty* announced that it was about to run a fifteen-week serial starting at the end of the month based on Jeanne's life: "Genius, drunkard, artist and hellion, poet and devil," was the way the popular magazine described its upcoming exclusive. Jeanne's sister Helen and her mother sued to prevent publication of the article but they were unsuccessful. The writ was denied by the Supreme Court, which pointed out that it was not possible to libel a dead person.

Libby was mentioned only in an admiring paragraph or two.

8
"Body and Soul"

Libby, who had a reputation for a sunny, if capricious disposition, went into a deep blue period following the death of her friend and lover, Jeanne Eagels. Shunning her favorite haunts—Connie's, The Hotshot Club, The Tony's, she holed up in her East Side apartment, seeing only the Webbs, who shared her grief, and brought Jeanne's secretary to live with her as a household companion.

Libby's blues may have reflected the mood of the country as a whole. America was just coming out of the shock of the Great Crash of 1929, which took place only weeks after Jeanne's death. Libby hadn't made any money to speak of before 1929 and consequently she wasn't hurt by the crash. Oddly enough, the nightlife world of clubs and theater seemed at first to ignore the growing signs of the Depression—the shantytowns springing up on the outskirts of town, the breadlines. But it was to be at least another year before the depths of the Depression was really felt. In the winter of 1930 things were still roaring in New York. People still gave bathtub-gin parties.

According to sociologists Robert and Helen Lynd, "Drinking increased markedly . . . in '27 and '28 and in '30 was heavy and open. With the Depression, there seemed to be a collapse of public morals. In the winter of '29-'30 and in '30-'31, things were roaring . . . there was much drunkenness . . . there was a great increase in women's drinking . . ."

The public tried to deny the impending disaster with silly fads. Thousands of Americans were parking their sedans by half-acre roadside courses and earnestly knocking golf balls through little mouseholes and wooden barricades, over little bridges and through drainpipes in their passion for miniature golf. And the public followed with fascination the exploits of all the dashing new aviators who every week were trying some new challenge—flying the ocean one way or the other, circumnavigating the globe or flying over one or the other of the poles. Lindbergh reigned as the national hero. In 1930, a pair of flyers named Costes and Bellonta almost pushed him off the front pages when they made the first successful westward flight across the Atlantic, reversing Lindbergh's trip by taking off at Paris and landing in Long Island.

Closer to the ground, there was an epidemic of tree-sitting, which impelled thousands of publicity-crazy boys to roost in trees day and night in the hope of breaking somebody's record. And backgammon (*plus* ça *change, plus c'est la même chose*) was the rage.

Libby was coaxed out of her funk by her friends Howard and Betty Dietz, Franchot Tone and his bizarre mother, Tallulah Bankhead and Bea Lillie, who between them could make a stone gargoyle smile, and her ever faithful, sympathetic and generous friend, Louisa Jenney, who tried to cheer her up by buying her a sixteen-cylinder Rolls Royce convertible to replace the notorious flivver in which Libby had been tooling around Manhattan and Long Island. Despite the success of *The Little Show*, which ultimately ran for three hundred and thirty-one performances, Dwight Wiman, the producer, did not want to repeat the three stars, Clifton Webb, Libby Holman, and Fred Allen in a second *Little Show*. The producers wanted to build an equity around the title and were afraid the stars would quickly take control if they were featured again.

But their strategy backfired. None of the new songs by Schwartz and Dietz in the second show were successful and despite the casting of J. C. Flippen and Arlene Judge, the revue died after only sixty-three performances.

Dietz and Schwartz, however, had wisely signed the three stars of the first *Little Show* for a new revue to be called *Three's a Crowd*. Max Gordon would act as producer. Featured in the cast was a band called "The California Collegians." One of Libby's big numbers in the show was a syrupy ballad called "Something to Remember You By," which went on to become a standard. But Libby, who always had trouble knowing what to do with her hands, wanted to have some dramatic focus, someone to sing the song to, rather than directing it out to the audience in general. She picked out a tall, skinny kid, a saxophonist with "The California Collegians" and asked him to stand with his back to the audience so that she could sing the lyrics to him. "What's your name, fella?" Libby asked. "Rex Beech," the young man said, naming a popular novelist of the day.

"Come on, no kidding, what's your name?"

"Well, it's a dopey name," the young man said. "I'm kind of embarrassed by it—Fred MacMurray."

"Don't worry," Libby said. "It's a better name than Rex Beech."

But again, when the show opened in Philadelphia, it seemed to lack character. Libby was so discouraged that she got hold of the poster and rearranged the billing and pinned it to the wall of her dressing room: "Clifton Webb and Fred Allen in *Two's Company*."

Dietz sensed that something had to be done to salvage the show. There was only one outside number in it. It was

Three's a Crowd, 1930. Libby with co-stars Clifton Webb (left) and Fred Allen.

called "Body and Soul" and it was written by Johnny Green and three lyric writers. At Libby's request, Dietz touched up the lyrics a bit. But still the number didn't click. Finally, in desperation, Dietz sent for Ralph Rainger who had done such a good job on "Moanin' Low."

"He had a special feeling for this type of dark number," Dietz said.

Libby, coached by Rainger, experimented with all types of deliveries, but it was not until the last night in Philadelphia that they hit on the right way to present the song. It was given the full treatment by Hassard Short, the director. After the song was introduced by Libby during the first act with a straight but steaming delivery, it was reprised in the second part for a dance interpretation by Clifton Webb and Tamara Geva, the jazz ballet dancer who echoed Libby's offstage singing with erotic, sensational choreography.

When *Three's a Crowd* opened at the Selwyn Theater on Broadway in October 1930, "Body and Soul" was an even bigger show-stopper than "Moanin' Low" had been the year before. Libby, with the impact of her style and personality in two shows, had created four great standards which remain popular to this day: "Moanin' Low," "Can't We Be Friends?" "Something to Remember You By," and "Body and Soul." If Libby had been the Crown Princess of Broadway in 1929, in 1930 she was the Queen. And her vast critical and popular success served to pull her out of her personal depression.

The Dietzes had acquired a new house in the Village at 18 West 11th Street and again their home became the center for a sophisticated, literate, and lively crowd. Betty arranged to have the house decorated by Dorothy Rodgers, the wife of Richard Rodgers. A wall was broken through to make a huge living room, forty-four by forty, in which they entertained such luminaries from the neighborhood as Howard Lindsay and his wife Dorothy Stickney, Donald Ogden Stewart, Lawrence Langner, Morris Ernst, the lawyer, and Lucinda Ballard, who later became Dietz's second wife. Another popular neighbor was Jane Bowles, the moody and androgynous wife of novelist Paul Bowles, who seemed from the start extremely taken with Libby's dark and sultry charms.

The success of *Three's a Crowd* and the ensuing obligations for record dates, concerts, parties and the like finally brought Libby back into the party scene, although she was more likely than before to become morose and withdrawn and would occasionally disappear from a party for an hour or so, presumably to alter her mood with one drug or another. Certainly she did not break her connection with Dr. Cowles when Jeanne Eagels died.

Fred Allen, the comedian who was already married to Hoffa, his onstage sidekick, was definitely not part of the social scene inhabited by Libby and Clifton Webb. Fred was aggressively heterosexual and was put off by their offbeat activity. He wrote to a friend that the show was having enough troubles in its tryouts without having to deal with Webb on his "lavender high horse."

The Broadway crowd, ignoring the recent tragedy in her life, felt that Libby was lucky. She was marked for success and everyone gathered around, wanting to be near her, to touch her, to talk to her, to love her. But Libby, despite the recognition she had gotten as the quintessential torch singer, was not happy with the limitations of that role. She still had some interest in writing and high hopes of becoming a serious dramatic actress. For press purposes, she described the man of her dreams: "A man who has achieved something in the arts. He must be more than my match in physical vitality and artistic achievements. You can say I haven't met a soul who qualifies . . . I'll write stories, novels, poetry. There'll be a salon like Mme. Sevigne's—none of the hanging on in saloons that the alleged literati run to in New York . . . I want the sensitivity and understanding of Katherine Mansfield and the penetration of George Sand. Pretty high, wide and handsome for a blues singer? But one thing is sure anyhow. I'll never by crying my heart out over a guy that loves me and leaves me. After this 'blues' business, I'm positively immune to such silliness."

And certainly that seemed to be the case as far as men were concerned. Not only didn't she start any romances, but according to old friend Leonard Sillman, she would often turn her brilliant, biting humor on those men that attempted to win her favors. "She had a terrible quality and that was that she knew she was brilliant and she was an intellectual snob. She would find a vulnerable spot in people she knew and then she would keep hitting it. Most of the time the vulnerable spots she would find would be in people who weren't as brilliant as she was or didn't have the same humor. Then she would say, 'You poor, pathetic person, you're so stupid. You've had an education and yes, you went to school, but you had to learn by rote.'"

Sillman says Libby was in The Tony's one night, in one of her morose moods, "complaining at length about the fact that all men were beasts, wanting her not for her mind but for her body." Sillman said that when he was trouping with her in those early years she had told him that she had been a virgin until she was twenty-two, the year she appeared in *Garrick Gaieties.* At that time, she told Sillman, "The body is so beautiful that you must never destroy it or besmirch it or make it dirty, it's beautiful and we must not give it to anybody unless we really love them."

Sillman says that Libby felt that the sexual organs were in the wrong place—a man's penis should be in his throat and that the vagina should be in the throat, too, so that "when they saw each other, they could start screwing right way."

In any event, Sillman says, it was on that moody night at The Tony's that he was listening to Libby's complaints about men until he couldn't stand it any more. He finally got up and walked back to the kitchen to get some air. "At one of the tables in the kitchen, I found a young man who seemed pathetically handsome. I sat with him. He told me his name was Smith Reynolds. He did not further identify himself, but he didn't have to. The name told me all:

Smith Reynolds was the heir to the Reynolds Tobacco fortune. He was also sensitive and very well-mannered. I asked him to wait while I went out and got something for him. I came back with Libby Holman."

Part Two

Mrs. Zachary Smith Reynolds

9
The Reynolds Clan

Young Zachary Smith Reynolds—he was barely eighteen when he met Libby—came from a family deeply marked, some say cursed, by a multimillion-dollar tobacco fortune amassed by his father, the original R. J. Reynolds, Richard Joshua Reynolds, the man who realized that the big money in tobacco was not in chewing the stuff, sniffing it or making cigars out of it, as had been the principal form of tobacco consumption prior to World War I, but smoking it in little, rolled-up white tubes. Richard Joshua Reynolds' clever merchandising of Camels Cigarettes probably caused more premature deaths in America than World Wars I and II and the Civil War combined. While the Surgeon General had not started warning people back in R. J.'s day, the harmful effects of cigarettes were well-known and it was not long after people started smoking them by the handful that they became known jocularly as "coffin nails."

R. J. was a burly and bearded nineteenth-century Southerner, a great judge of the golden tobacco leaf that grew so copiously throughout the Piedmont in North and South Carolina and Virginia. By the time R. J. Reynolds had finished glamorizing the cigarette, he had amassed a fortune of $100 million, back when the dollar was worth something. He left all his money to his four children.

R. J. Reynolds himself had not exactly grown up poor. His father had a little tobacco factory in southern Virginia. Certainly, he did not know the luxury that he provided for his four children, two sons and two daughters by Catherine Smith, a secretary whom he had met when she wrote a prize essay on the pleasure of tobacco.

One of R. J.'s daughters (now Mrs. Nancy Bagley, mother of Jimmy Carter's troubled financial aide and crony, Smith Bagley) quoted her mother as saying in a family joke, "Daddy only married me to get his prize money back." (The prize money amounted to $1,000.)

R. J. Reynolds served his apprenticeship in the tobacco business on his father's Rock Spring plantation in the shadow of a peak bearing the strange name "No Business Mountain." He married Catherine Smith at the age of fifty-five. She was his junior by twenty-five years, but despite his late start, R.J. decided to set up an exemplary family and household to extend the Reynolds dynasty far into the future.

As a home base for this planned dynasty, Reynolds built an ambitious medieval-style estate-village on 1,000 acres of prime land in northwest Winston (Winston and the older Salem were not, at that time, joined into one city). To design the house, R. J. employed Charles Barton Keane, a Philadelphia architect. The estate and the planned residence would be known dynastically as "Reynolda." The fifty-room manor house, the centerpiece of the estate, was called incongruously, or perhaps with a bit of Southern wit, "the bungalow."

During some of the summer months, while construction was going on, the Reynolds family, which now included the four children, Richard, Jr., Mary, Nancy and Zachary Smith, lived in tents set up on the site. Young

Smith Reynolds, at the time that he met Libby.

R.J. Reynolds and family. Smith is on the far right.

Zachary Smith was, of course, a mere toddler when he watched with fascination as the magnfiicent sprawling building went up, complete with a charming scaled-down cottage for the girls to play house in and separate log cabins for each of the Reynolds boys. Even before Reynolda House—the bungalow—was ready for the family, other structures were built as part of Reynolda Village. This included a small church, a blacksmith's shop, a dairy barn, a horse barn, greenhouses, and residences for the army of servants who worked on the estate.

In those early months after the estate was opened, streams of distinguished political, social and business acquaintances of R. J. Reynolds came to the estate, where they were entertained at lavish barbecues by the oriental-style lakeside boathouse and concerts on the Aeolian organ in the huge living room, often performed by visiting artists of international renown. There were all sorts of amusements in those early days, dances with music by famous bands, garden parties and lavish formal balls. Unfortunately, old R. J., Sr., then sixty-eight, fell prey to an incipient heart condition only a few months after the family moved into the shining new estate and died after living there only eight months.

His widow Catherine did her best to be a good mother to the four Reynolds children and still cope with the enormous responsibilities of the huge Reynolda estate. Will Reynolds, R. J.'s brother, took over management of the Reynolds tobacco interests. But Catherine who had never been able to get used to the great wealth which surrounded her since her marriage, allowed the boys to go wild. They went to school with pockets stuffed with five and ten dollar bills, were treated like young princes of the realm, attended classes when and where they saw fit.

Zachary Smith from the beginning was smaller, less masculine, less athletic than his older brother Dick. He was also a lonely child; there were no boys of his own age on the estate and Dick was often impatient with his smaller brother. Catherine was afraid that young Smith, as he was usually called, would grow up to be a sissy because he had no male companions, so when he was four she arranged with the family of a nearby real estate broker to have their son, Abner Bailey Walker, just about the same age as Smith, become a permanent playmate of the lonely young heir. And so it was that Ab Walker, from his earliest toddling days, was the childhood and school companion of Smith Reynolds.

His mother's death when Smith Reynolds was only twelve, contributed to the boy's confusion and tendency to melancholy. The Reynolds estate was placed in trusteeship and Will Reynolds, their uncle, became the children's guardian.

In his teen years, Smith jumped, checkerboard style, through a series of swanky preparatory schools, often accompanied by his friend, Ab. But he never acquired enough credits to graduate. However from an early period he became extremely interested in aviation and began to study aeronautical engineering, geography and mathematics, as well as any other subjects that would help him to become a flyer.

Smith Reynolds' interest in aviation was probably sparked by the fascination of his brother Dick with the subject. Dick, too, had an extremely early interest in aviation and an equally early interest in drinking, women, and carousing. Before he was twenty-one he had a considerable reputation as a playboy. In 1927, when Dick was twenty-one, he made the front page headline in *The New York Times* when he disappeared from a West 51st Street nightclub with a young woman whom he said he was escorting to Grand Central to catch a train for St. Louis. The woman arrived in St. Louis alone and returned to New York. A few hours after Dick Reynolds had left the nightclub, ostensibly for Grand Central Station, his yellow Rolls Royce was found overturned in the water of Chicken Point, near Port Washington, Long Island. There was no one in the car when it was hauled from the water the next day and claimed three days later by Reynolds' chauffeur.

Eleven days after Reynolds left the nightclub, police in Nassau County received a telephone message from New York asking them to investigate a "murder in which a yellow Rolls Royce figured." The caller declined to identify himself. Dick Reynolds was in New York and on Long Island at the time, arranging to purchase Curtiss Field for the Reynolds Airways Company which he organized for the purpose. He had also been spending a lot of time up and down Broadway putting money into shows and dating chorus girls. In fact, he had come to New York five days before his mysterious disappearance to attend the opening of a musical comedy at the Waldorf Theater. It was said that he was one of the backers of this production. On September 15, the day before his jaunt to Grand Central, he gave up his rented house at Long Beach and checked into the Hotel White on Lexington Avenue and 37th Street with two friends and business associates. Earlier in the day he cashed a check for $5,000 and sent his chauffeur a little later to cash another one for $700. That afternoon, while in the City, he sent the chauffeur out to Long Beach with $130 and instructions to buy train tickets back to Winston-Salem for two servants who had accompanied him to New York. He also told the chauffeur to take the yellow Rolls Royce from the garage in Long Beach and leave it at the Mineola railroad station, where he would pick it up at 11 P.M., after a visit to the Nassau County Fair. Dick and his friend John Graham went to the fair and apparently did quite a bit of drinking, after which they drove to a place called Rothman's Roadhouse in Oyster Bay, where they drank some more and stayed till about 11 P.M. They were next spotted at the Charm Club, a speakeasy at 137 West 51st Street, where they continued to drink until six o'clock the following morning and it was sometime after this that Reynolds and the young lady took off for Grand Central for whatever reason.

On September 28, the day after the *Times* front page

story, the mystery was at least partially cleared up. Reynolds was found in a chop suey place on North Grand Boulevard in St. Louis by operatives of a private detective agency which the trustees of the Reynolds estate had put on the case. He was with a woman and another man and at first he denied that he was Reynolds at all, but later he admitted it but said he didn't know why there was such a fuss about his disappearance or that anybody cared until he read about it in the papers that morning. Reynolds claimed that he was strictly on a vacation and he had used an alias because he "did not wish to be bothered." He told the investigators that he had gone to Chicago to see the Tunney-Dempsey fight and then come to St. Louis where he spent his time at the horse track in Fairmont Park and the dog races at night. When the detectives first interviewed young Dick, he had claimed that he was actually his friend John Graham and showed Graham's license to prove it. But finally, under further questioning, he told one of the detectives, "This is getting on my nerves. Yes, I'm Reynolds." While he was stalling the detectives, the girl, described as a well-dressed pretty blonde of about twenty-three, slipped into the night and disappeared. Reynolds appeared surprised when he heard that his Rolls Royce had been found overturned in Long Island Sound and said that it must have been stolen. The man who had been sharing the chop suey with the girl and the young chap be believed to be somebody named Graham said he'd met the youngster around the racetracks and that was all he knew.

Further investigation by the Hargrave Detective Agency of St. Louis unearthed the fact that Reynolds had been living in the Claridge Hotel, impressing people by passing out "dollar tips." A woman named Miss M. Huston was also registered in the Claridge and it turned out that the woman with whom Dick had disappeared from the nightclub was named Marie Houston, but whether they were the same people could not be established. It was, however, determined that the Marie Houston from New York was "a hostess at a nightclub."

Meanwhile Carter Tiffany, vice president of Dick's company, had been deeply concerned about the disappearance of his wealthy partner and had been checking around the State Department in Washington to see if a passport had been issued to him. Tiffany said that Reynolds had been terribly impressed by a motion picture of life in the Foreign Legion and he thought it was possible that the young man had gone to France to enlist in that organization. He also checked out three or four musical comedy starlets and showgirls to see if Reynolds had disappeared with them.

Apparently, this wasn't the first time something like this had happened. "It's a habit of his to go away without telling anyone," Tiffany said. "Even when he was in school, he would slip away and spend several days, usually for sporting events."

Ultimately, Reynolds agreed to be interviewed and gave this story of his disappearance. "I just got fed up on society and the nightlife along Broadway and decided to take a little trip as a sort of vacation. There was nothing extraordinary about my taking a jaunt out of town. I can't understand what all the fuss is about. . . .

"I had been going to every nightclub along Broadway and got sick of it."

Close friends of Reynolds admitted that he was an extremely heavy drinker and tended to go on frequent similar week-long toots, accompanied by one or more flashy women, but he managed to keep his name out of the papers for the next few years and spent his time continuing to develop his interest in aviation business and helping his younger brother to learn to fly.

But less than two years after the chop suey caper, Dick Reynolds was in more serious trouble. At first he almost succeeded in concealing the affair from the press. A small item appeared in the *Times*, less than an inch in length, which said that a man named Leslie Joshua Reynolds "an American living at Grove Court, London," was to appear before a magistrate the following day on a charge of manslaughter.

"Reynolds was alleged to have been involved in an accident on Bath Road, on May 14, in which Alfred Graham of Slough received injuries from which he died in a hospital at Windsor."

For the next few days, the newspapers didn't seem to catch on that "Leslie" Joshue Reynolds was, in fact, the famous roué and tobacco heir. But by the time Dick Reynolds got to Old Bailey to face the King's Counsel, the word was out and the story moved from the shipping pages to the scandal section.

Basically the story told by Traffic Constable Waller was that Dick Reynolds, under the influence of liquor, had run down a man on a motorcycle named Arthur Graham and then driven off without stopping. The constable chased Reynolds and caught him at Chiswick, near London. When he told the young tobacco heir that he'd be charged with being drunk and with dangerous driving, Reynolds said, "If you think I am drunk, officer, you have made a big mistake." But British authorities didn't seem to think so. The police surgeon testified that Reynolds was drunk and denied Reynolds' claim that his symptoms were only due to "excitement." In fact, one officer testified that Reynolds was so drunk that he was "still suffering from the effects of drink on the morning after the accident."

On the evening of the incident, Inspector Neal of the Burnham Police stated that Reynolds had offered to take care of the matter by contributing $2,500 to get a specialist to see Graham, who was still alive but in serious condition at the hospital. But the inspector advised the young man the offer "might be construed into an admission of liability. Take my advice and consult a solicitor," the officer told Reynolds.

Reynolds and Ronald Bargate, twenty-two, who had been with him in the car at the time of the accident, said that they'd only had two or three Pimm's Number Ones. Bargate gallantly volunteered the fact that Reynolds had had a clear head and a steady hand in the game of darts which they had been playing in a pub shortly before the accident. Dick Reynolds was ultimately found guilty of manslaughter but then managed to get a mistrial declared when it was learned that the foreman of the jury had talked with one of the witnesses. But it did no good. The testimony remained the same and Reynolds, to his amazement, was sentenced to five months' imprisonment in the "Second Division" jail. He was ordered to pay the costs of the two trials.

He seemed genuinely surprised at the stiff verdict. British authorities said that they had been relatively lenient only because Reynolds had agreed to provide for Graham's widow for life "on a higher scale than her husband could have earned."

The judge had charged the jury "with regard to Reynolds' wealth, you ought not to make the slightest difference in the way you look at this case because he is very rich. If he has used some of his wealth to behave generously to the widow, he has done no more than the law would compel him to do. You will try him just as you would try a London costermonger charged with knocking somebody down through driving a cart furiously."

However, to Reynolds' relief, there was no mention of "hard labor" in the sentence. Young Dick Reynolds was taken in a prison van to Brixton Prison where he was given a flea bath and the usual khaki-colored British prison suit, decorated with broad, black arrows. The British officials said that he would only be required to do such tasks as cleaning out and washing cells and making beds.

The *Times* thought enough of this incident to devote an editorial to it.

> "What would have happened over here? . . . A serious crime would have been lost sight of in a gush of fraternity and sentimentality. The judge's duties would have consisted largely in keeping his mouth shut, as much as he would have liked to interfere in the interests of common sense and justice."

Dick Reynolds was still in Brixton scrubbing cells when his younger brother Smith managed to get himself into a jam which also led to a considerable loss of personal freedom. Down in Winston-Salem, Smith, still trying to emulate his more virile and romantic brother, decided he'd try to find out what sex was all about. He had been seeing a wealthy local young lady named Ann Cannon who was the daughter of Joseph F. Cannon, the millionaire towel manufacturer. Mr. Cannon was noted for such eccentricities as shooting out light bulbs in nightclubs, firing at pillows in hotel rooms, and fighting with his fists at the drop of a remark. So when he came upon Smith and his daughter Ann, who was two years older than the tobacco heir, between the sheets in the Cannon mansion, he routed them out at gunpoint at two o'clock in the morning, put them into an automobile and drove with them across the state line to York, South Carolina, where marriages could be performed with consummate speed and few questions. Later that morning, the mollified textile manufacturer dropped the newlyweds off in Concord, North Carolina, where they decided they would climb into Smith Reynolds' new plane that morning for a wedding trip in North Carolina and nearby states. This story also made the front page of the New York *Times*, but there was no reference to the troubles of brother Dick nor to the reasons for the somewhat precipitate matrimonial party.

Mr. Cannon's haste appeared to have been justified since a baby girl was born to Ann Cannon in May of 1930, not quite nine months after the South Carolina wedding party, and quite a few months after Smith Reynolds and Ann Cannon Reynolds had decided that their marriage was a big mistake.

10
The Courtship

Despite Leonard Sillman's story of having introduced young Smith Reynolds to her at Tony's speakeasy, Libby remembered things differently and recalled later when testifying that she had met him while in a road company tour of *The Little Show* in Baltimore. "I was going down to Florida for a vacation, the Holy Week vacation," Libby recalled, "and Mr. Reynolds came to Baltimore with a friend of his who was a friend of mine, and I met him through him and that was all I had seen of him."

It seems at least a possibility that Smith, who came from a family equally as wealthy as that of Libby's dear friend Louisa Carpenter duPont Jenney, might have known the Wilmington heiress since she was also an early aviation enthusiast. For a boy of seventeen Smith had already developed into a considerable legend. He'd been fascinated by aviation, for several years, certainly the most romantic calling open to any well-heeled young man of that day.

Smith's moody nature fit right into Libby's life style at

the time. In the midst of the most lively party, she could be counted on to sit back and brood, perhaps about the loss of her friend. At any rate, young Smith was one of those "who could make two 'glooms' blossom where but one grew before."

But love does not feed on gloom alone. Reynolds' conversation about aerial navigation and airplane mechanics bored Libby half to death. But when she appeared inattentive he would burst into tears and say he wanted to give up aviation because "a man couldn't do but one thing at a time."

"And what else is it you want to do?" Libby asked him the first time he pulled this line.

"I want to marry you and be happy beside you forever."

"Is this a proposal?" Libby said laughing. "I've only known you for two nights."

"You have to say yes—I'll die if I can't have you."

Libby, eight years his senior, smiled tolerantly and patted the overwrought boy on his head.

"I admire your taste, but I'm not planning any marriages in the near future. Why don't you finish your schooling and make something out of yourself?"

But Smith was not to be put off that easily. When Libby went down to Florida for her holiday he followed in his plane and resumed his marriage proposals there. Libby swam with him and drank with him and cuddled him—an enjoyable holiday, but she still couldn't take his marriage offer seriously. When she turned him down for the tenth time, Smith said if that was the way she felt he would take his plane and fly around the world. The next thing Libby knew he had checked out of their hotel, flown to New York, landed his amphibian in the Hudson River, had it pulled aboard the liner *Berengaria*, and sailed for England. There he unloaded his expensive plane and spent the spring months flying moodily over Europe, Africa, and the Orient. Whether it was his disappointment in love or a death wish is not certain but before he sailed he stopped in New York to apply for a berth on the

American East Indies Expedition which was to do aerial exploration work in New Guinea and Borneo. He even offered to donate his amphibian to the expedition and some of the executives were seriously considering accepting the offer even as Smith persisted in his courtship of Libby.

Smith soon got tired of zooming around Europe where he frequently was arrested for filing careless or improper flight plans and was finally grounded temporarily when he was stricken by a mastoid infection which required an operation in London. When he had recovered he returned to New York and went straight to Libby's apartment, where he again resumed his obstinate and seemingly unrequited pursuit.

Libby had a real sympathy for the motherless young man who was shy, sensitive, and somewhat inadequately sexed. She found something genuinely appealing in his oriental looks and his deeply cleft chin.

In New York, he began to hang around the various speakeasies and nightclubs frequented by Libby and her friends, accompanied by several cronies, friends from the South who had been living in New York and more or less showed him the ropes. And everybody was glad to have him around in at least one respect—about every half hour or so the young tobacco heir would signal to the waiter and buy a round for the house.

Friends who knew them both at this time said that Libby was nice to the kid and "seemed to like him for himself... didn't pay attention to his money and didn't make a play for him." Certainly the lure of a free drink or a ride in a fancy car could not have counted much with Libby in those days. She was then one of the highest paid stars on Broadway and was earning more than Reynolds got as an allowance. But in the beginning, though he was clearly infatuated with her, all he got from Libby was a smile and a wave and an occasional peck on the cheek.

It was a period when, coming out of the grief at the loss of her friend Jeanne Eagels, Libby was closer than ever to her friend Louisa and to Tallulah when she returned from England.

From the beginning Smith had told Libby that he was married and expected soon to be the father of a child but explained that the marriage would be ended soon. Already he had discussed with Ann Cannon the possibility of a split, offering her a half-million dollars for her pain.

Smith's marriage to Anne Cannon had started to go on the rocks very shortly after their nocturnal marital jaunt to South Carolina.

"She liked big parties and I liked little parties," Smith said in explanation of their difficulties. By this he no doubt meant that he was not a terribly gregarious person and felt inadequate and inferior in large gatherings, tending to skulk in corners and sigh into his drinks. Certainly he had no trouble paying for the drinks—or the parties. While still a minor he was to receive an allowance of $50,000 a year from his father's trust plus use of Reynolda and all of the various family appurtenances. According to the terms of his father's will he would inherit about $20 million when he reached the age of twenty-eight.

Libby had less time for him in New York than she had during her Florida holiday. In the first place she was busy rehearsing the new show, which was having plenty of troubles in its development, and in the second place she had mobs of friends to see and places to go when she was in New York. In spite of this he finally prevailed upon her to take a flight with him in his two-seater plane. Smith Reynolds had enough sense to know that he was at his best in the air rather than in a smoky 52nd Street or Harlem nightclub. Nobody denied that he was an experienced pilot, resourceful and courageous. Many think that Libby began to have a higher regard for him after she had seen him at the controls of the plane. They made several flights together whenever Libby could spare the time and once when she was resting between rehearsals they flew to North Carolina and Smith circled the thousand-acre family estate and pointed out the house in which he had grown up.

But when the show started tryouts on the road, Libby

had to estrange herself from his somewhat enervating company again. The agonizing grind of the day and night practicing, one night stands, and constant moving, produced in her a nerve-jangling hysteria and a fatigue which caused her practically to snub her anxious would-be lover. Smith didn't understand her obsession with work. After all he had enough money for both of them, millions, and they were all hers. It didn't seem to occur to him that she loved show business, loved the limelight, loved the adoration of the crowds and loved the kinky, offbeat amusements that seemed to go with the business.

Smith pleaded with her, "Come on, Libby, why all this worry? It isn't worth it. Just marry me. I've got enough money to last us our lifetime. You won't have to work. What's there to all this stage business anyhow?"

But his constant whining only irritated Libby, fatigued as she was from the daily grind of the show. With increasing regularity, Libby would lose her temper at the young man and then there was always a loud scene. The series of squabbles ended in a shouting, screeching argument that started in a Harlem speakeasy and ended in Libby's apartment when she ordered him to leave her house for good.

Young Reynolds took her rejection to heart. Before sunup he was down at his brother's airfield in Long Island where the amphibian was kept in its hangar. Whenever things got too much for him to bear, Smith Reynolds' instinct was for flight. Now, rejected by the only woman for whom he had ever cared, he was determined to drown his sorrows in the sin spots of the West—or die trying.

Smith flew his amphibian to the Los Angeles area, lost $10,000 or $20,000 at the gaming tables at Agua Caliente and then flew back to Reynolds with the strange idea of making peace with his wife Ann Cannon.

Ann, however, had had her fill of Smith's immaturity, his moody tantrums, and his occasional beatings. She felt that Reynolds' affections were as insubstantial as the smoke produced by one of his father's Camels. What

Smith had hoped to accomplish by this attempt is not known but it is clear that he had a desperate need for a woman's company and affection. He climbed back into his plane and began to fly haphazardly westward, behaving more and more wildly the further he got from home.

Landing in Denver late one afternoon, he went to the Brown Palace Hotel and bought a bottle of liquor from a bellhop and killed the whole thing within an hour. With his bourbon-fired courage he ventured a call to Libby in New York. She had just gotten back to her apartment, tired, worn out by tryouts and the endless arguments over revisions for *Three's a Crowd.* Zachary Smith Reynolds was probably the last person in the world she wanted to talk to. She had half a mind to hang up on him but his voice had an urgent, ominous note.

"Libby darling," he said, "I haven't been able to live without you. You're the only woman I ever cared about in my life. If you don't promise to marry me I'm going to kill myself. I really mean this. I can't go on living without you.

"I know you said you didn't want to see me anymore and I tried to go along with your wishes. I came out West here to try to forget you but I couldn't. You're all I can think of night and day. Please help me Libby. I love you."

His voice now took on a thickened mumbling quality and Libby realized that the self-destructive young heir was completely out of control and perfectly capable of fulfilling his threats. "Smith," she said, "Smith darling, don't do anything. I really do love you. I've missed you. I didn't mean it when I told you to go away. Come on back here to New York. We'll talk it over."

Mollified but still truculent, Smith hung up and agreed to sleep off his drunk and return to New York the next day. In actuality Libby was furious about having been put on the spot by his threats. She grabbed a taxi to the Webbs' house where she raved and ranted to Maybelle because she had, as she expressed it, "put herself on the spot for that damn fool kid."

When he woke up the next day Smith found that there

was trouble with the plane's manifold and the engine had to be dismantled. This delayed him for a day and a half. Then the field was socked in by spring weather, heavy rainstorms, and mud. Since most planes in those days were not equipped with instrument flying equipment, Smith had to stay grounded for still another day. By the time he managed to make it to New York, *Three's A Crowd* had opened on Broadway to smash reviews and Libby was at the pinnacle of success.

Brooks Atkinson, always a Holman fan, wrote: "Although the applause from the Selwyn may have broken hearts over at *The Second Little Show* last night, it was merited, and symptomatic of considerable real enjoyment on the part of the nabobs of New York's play set." (The second *Little Show*, it will be recalled, was Dwight Wiman's abortive attempt to cash in on the title of Libby's first hit revue without hiring the stars. It sank without a trace after sixty-three days.)

Even Libby had not anticipated such a triumph. As Arthur Mefford put it, "Her name was the toast of Broadway. In *The Little Show* she had been a hit. In this new venture, a million hits in one."

By the time Smith arrived in New York, shortly after opening night, Libby was riding high and felt she could be kind and sympathetic to her bedraggled suitor. Smith, sensing this new softness in her attitude, became even more enamored and dogged her footsteps night and day from that point on.

Libby tolerated his attentions with amused patience. She danced with him and rode with him and they resumed their nighttime tours of the hot spots downtown and up in Harlem. Reynolds, in one of his rare up-moods, was throwing around hundred dollar bills like cigarette papers. He thought nothing of spending $1,000 in one night to keep Libby happy.

And it wasn't only nightclubs they visited. There were parties on Park Avenue and in the Village where they mixed with the "creme de la creme" of society as well as the elite of New York's intelligentsia. Libby's gang,

Tallulah, Janet Reed, Franchot Tone, Bea Lillie, the Webbs and Louisa Carpenter, viewed the young North Carolinian with strained tolerance. Certainly he had not much to offer to any conversation, unless it was his money, and most of them didn't care about that.

Libby now found herself drinking more heavily to keep up with her bibulous young paramour. Reynolds drank like a teenage fraternity boy, fast and furiously, usually throwing down his first two or three drinks without a breath. Libby tried to keep up with him. Her friends said that Libby changed in that year. Formerly barely able to navigate with more than a few drinks under her belt, she now wouldn't even try to go out unless she had half a dozen. Bacardi cocktails were her favorite. The partying didn't stop when the show went on the road, either. Wherever they happened to be, whether it was Cincinnati, St. Louis or Kansas City, Libby had no trouble finding out where the action was and being accepted by the local swingers. The two became familiar as a couple now, drinking and brooding their way across the country. Nobody ever said that Libby wasn't full of surprises. Even her personal smart set was taken aback when, at a huge party at Pod's and Jerry's in Harlem paid for by Smith, they announced that they were tired of the high life and were going on the wagon for good.

"I'm taking a house out at Port Washington," Libby declared, presumably for the reason that they could be near Smith's airplane.

"I'm going to get a good rest. No more dancing, no more drinking and no more anything. I'm off this fast life stuff forever."

There was a spattering of amused, if incredulous applause and Smith Reynolds broke the pattern of his usual taciturnity to chime in. "Yes, we're off the stuff. I'm going to settle down in Port Washington, too."

"Does this mean you're getting married, my dear?" Bea Lillie asked. "How dreary."

Libby smiled sweetly, peering nearsightedly at her friend through her lorgnette. "My dear girl," she said, "*il ne faut pas exagerer.* Marriage is such a bore. We're just going to see each other and be happy. Besides, the chap is married you know."

The announcement was not taken too seriously and was greeted with laughter and a new round of drinks.

But they made good their threat, at least in the beginning. Libby leased a bungalow in Port Washington near the Sands Point beach colony and Smith helped her move in. They hadn't been there more than a week, though, before they were back at their old squabbling. Often Libby teased Smith for his lack of background, ambition, and humor. She seemed alternately to caress and fondle him and then to reject him with coldhearted sarcasm or disgust. Smith flounced off again in a huff and this didn't bother Libby one bit.

The smoke from his exhaust had hardly faded on the horizon, when Louisa Jenney pulled into port in her palatial new seventy-five-foot yacht which she had named *Three's a Crowd.* Some people said that this could be taken either as a tribute to the title of the hit show or a comment on Libby's romantic situation. In any event with the arrival of Louisa, Libby's resolve to stay off the sauce and settle down flew out the French windows of the Holman cottage at Barker's Point.

According to the neighbors, riotous parties ensued, often lasting for days at a time. But, the neighbors said, the parties were presumably innocent enough, since men were not allowed. In fact when one or two of Libby's former show business boyfriends such as Clifton Webb and Leonard Sillman showed up they were figuratively tossed out on their ears amid gales of laughter.

Smith returned after getting over his sulk, and this time brought his pal Ab Walker up from North Carolina to keep him company at the Reynolds North Shore cottage, help him work on the plane, and discuss plans for Smith's favorite project, the round-the-world flight. For the moment both of them steered clear of Libby's cottage. *Three's a Crowd* had closed for the summer after 272 performances, and Libby was footloose and fancy-free as far as work was concerned until fall, when there was talk of getting up a company for a national road tour.

Neighbors were scandalized by the behavior of Libby's gay party guests, but at the same time intrigued by the glamour and excitement Libby's crowd brought to those hitherto staid environs. Mrs. Antoinette Murdock, who had rented the bungalow to Libby, said they found it a little difficult getting used to the fact that Libby and her guests often ran around in nothing but their shorts and sometimes even less. At night, moonlight skinny-dipping was all the rage, something which had not previously been a popular nocturnal pastime in that area.

The scene became even jollier when Bea Lillie rented a cottage next door to Libby's and became a regular guest at the nightly shenanigans. In fact, Lillie's arrival as a neighbor was the catalyst that started still another cat-and-dog fight between Libby and Smith.

Lady Peel (Bea was married to Sir Robert Peel) decided to give a party for various female friends she shared with her neighbor, Libby Holman. Naturally, Smith was not invited. Smith was visiting Libby's place when the invitation was delivered. It is possible that he didn't understand the nature of the party, that his exclusion was not a personal but a sexual question. Anyway, after reading Libby's invitation, Smith slammed out of the Spanish-style cottage and drove at breakneck speed down to the airport. Peter Bonelli, the aviation instructor who had been coaching him in flying, said Smith was very upset that day. "I thought he had had another fight with Libby—he was always upset after these—and tried to kid him out of his mood. I was afraid to let him go solo, but when he insisted there was nothing else to do but let him go.

"He told me that Beatrice Lillie was trying to break up his affair with Libby, that she was throwing a party for Libby but failed to invite him, although she knew that he was staying at Libby's cottage.

"He hopped off without giving his motors more than a minute's warming up. He zoomed up off the ground crazily. I thought he was going to crash. His plane wobbled but he held her nose up, then, straight as a crow flies, he headed out into the ocean.

"He was gone for seven hours and when he returned he admitted that he had intended flying straight out until, gas exhausted, he would fall into the ocean. The least little mechanical trouble would have finished him."

It wasn't the first and only example of Smith's impetuous reactions to Libby's carrying-on. A few weeks earlier, he had come upon Louisa and Libby together on the couch in the living room. On that occasion, he did an about-face and slammed out without saying a word. He climbed into his Rolls Royce roadster and headed straight for the ocean, careening crazily across the beach and over a four-foot retaining wall into the water. When his car finally came to a stop about fifteen feet short of the beach, he fought his way to the surface and swam half a mile with all his clothes on to his yacht anchored off shore, where he sulked for two days without trying to contact Libby at all.

The neighbors were just about to write a petition either to lynch Libby or have her forcibly removed when Smith Reynolds, apparently cooled off, returned to the scene, a day or so after Lady Peel's soiree. Libby was getting tired of her nightly romps and gave him a fond welcome. Soon it was not an unusual sight to see Libby dressed in her usual colorful shorts skipping across the salt marshes with Smith in his leather-legginged flying suit, often disappearing for an hour or so in a hollow of the dunes for a hot session of whatever it was they did together. (Nobody was quite certain.) This, added to Libby's previous behavior, was shocking enough, but the nerves of the local people were completely shattered when a loud pistol shot rang out one night from the Holman cottage, followed by a thunderous shouting match which could be heard all the way out to Sands Point.

According to the story that went around afterwards, one of the neighbors managed to get up enough courage to sneak up to the cottage and peek through the undraped window, perhaps to get a glimpse of a bullet-riddled corpse. But the Peeping Tom was disappointed. He saw no dead bodies and no smashed furniture. What the peeper saw was Libby sitting in a comfortable wicker chair reading a book and eating an apple while Smith Reynolds was sprawled across from her on the studio couch, puffing philosophically on his pipe. The neighborly voyeur crept back to his friends and reported the scene, which they found completely baffling.

When Libby expressed her fear that Smith would hurt himself or somebody else with his pistol, he said, according to Libby, "Shucks, I've had guns since I was a baby." And that summer in Port Washington, where Smith rented a place not far from Libby's Spanish bungalow colony, he informed her that he "had had several notes" threatening his life.

"He told me there at Port Washington," Libby said, "that after people had called up his house and asked where he was and tried to get in touch with him, he even used to put a dummy on the top of the bed, wrapped up in newspapers and sheets, and slept under the bed.

"There were two weeks there he was so frightened he didn't know what to do. And one night he heard two persons in the front room talking and he jumped out the back window with the gun and went down about two miles for the police, and brought them back, but didn't find anybody. He never was without a gun as long as I was with him."

It is not possible to say exactly what took place that provoked the firing of the shot in the Spanish cottage. It was well known that Smith Reynolds and his companion Ab Walker both carried pistols in their hip pockets and pulled them out and waved them like cowboys at the slightest provocation. Smith had an obsession that someday he might be kidnapped and held for ransom and was always hearing strange noises in the woods or outside the house, whereupon he would run to the window or the door, his pistol in hand, often shooting out into the darkness. This was during the Depression and the very rich were deeply concerned about protecting their wealth.

Libby was terrified of firearms and begged him time and again to leave the pistol behind, or at least not to keep pulling it out and waving it about and firing. Often, after Libby ended a quarrel with the promise that she loved him and would ultimately marry him, Smith would take the pistol out, look at it fondly, and say, "Well, if anything goes wrong, I've always got the little old Mauser." Libby later told writer Ward Morehouse that Smith habitually slept with the pistol on the table at the right of the bed.

When the pair grew bored with the cottage, they turned it over to her parents, who took it for the rest of the summer. It wasn't until they moved out that the mystery of the shot in the night deepened. When Mrs. Murdock took possession of the cottage again and came to clean it up, she found a .38 caliber bullet hole in one of her antique living room tables. The bullet had passed through the table at a sixty-degree angle and lodged itself in the baseboard. The bullet holes had been puttied up and varnished over in order to hide the traces but a close examination revealed that the slug was still embedded in the moulding. These facts were not revealed until much later and gave rise to stories that Smith had actually tried to kill himself as promised when Libby again refused to marry him. Certainly the death threats were now coming more frequently and earnestly, but nobody took them very seriously. It was fashionable to say, "Those that threaten it, don't do it."

Libby left the cottage and turned it over to her parents before the end of the summer because of the return of Louisa Jenney. She came out one evening and took a walk among the dunes with Libby while Reynolds snoozed in the living room sozzled. When they returned from their stroll, Libby calmly told her young admirer that he'd have to clear out since she was leaving the very next day for an indefinite cruise on the Great Lakes with her faithful comrade Louisa, and a group of their friends.

Smith threw a tantrum when he heard the news. "What's the big idea?" he demanded. "I thought you promised to get rid of that dame when we made up before!

I've got my own yacht, anchored right offshore. If you like cruising so much, we can go in that."

Smith had never cared for Louisa Jenney, whom he had met previously when they were fellow flying enthusiasts.

"It's just going to be a big hen party," Libby told him in all innocence, "nothing but a bunch of the girls."

This explanation almost mollified Smith, until Libby teasingly warned him not to throw another tantrum. "The last time you did, you know what happened? I went out with Tallulah and Gary Cooper and, I want to tell you, Mr. Cooper is not as quiet in bed as he looks on the screen."

There is no way to verify whether Libby really did sleep with Cooper, but it was commonly believed around town that Cooper had been Tallulah's lover (as had a goodly number of the actors, actresses, reporters and taxi-drivers on Broadway). This is something of which Tallulah made no secret. And since Tallulah was not at all shy about sharing her love and even occupying the same quarters in a *ménage a trois*, it seems extremely possible that the "Splendid Splinter" may have had the Alabama bombshell and the Cincinnati torch singer in bed at the same time.

Smith was extremely jealous. He could hardly handle one lover at a time, so he was understandably miffed at Libby's confession. He stalked out fuming, jumped into the Rolls which had by now been refurbished, raced it to New York, left it parked in front of Pennsylvania Station, and jumped on a train to Winston-Salem.

Libby's hen party cruise lasted almost six weeks. She apparently had a marvelous time relaxing and getting away from things, because certainly the big party she had described to Smith failed to materialize. No Tallulah, no Blanche, no Bea Lillie. Nobody but Libby and Louisa. The seventy-five-foot yacht cruised up the Hudson into the Great Lakes and into the yacht basin at Detroit.

Smith, still fuming, finally caught up with them. Again the big dramatic scene, threats of suicide, groans of passion. Libby may have found it boring, but she was also flattered by the young man's depth of feeling for her, and his inability to function without her. Finally he calmed down and they persuaded Louisa to vacate the scene temporarily while she and Smith had a quiet little chat.

Smith told her of his lifelong ambition to fly his plane around the world, and how marvelous he thought it would be if Libby took the trip with him. Hardly believing that it would actually happen and partly to accommodate Smith's mood, Libby agreed to take the trip. First stop: Paris.

In fact, Libby, her mind ever curious, her spirit always adventurous, thought that the trip would be a lark and that she would enjoy the scene. She loved Louisa, but six weeks of her solitary company was enough. So over her friend's violent protests, Libby agreed to take the trip. Besides, Paris meant Josephine Baker, in whom Libby had always been intensely interested. She welcomed the chance to see the black dancer, now a legend in the Folies Bergère, dancing in a costume that consisted of a handful of bananas and little else.

Libby had an idea in the back of her mind. She still thought she might be able to create a stage vehicle around the life of Josephine Baker and play the part herself. After all, Baker was neither an actress, nor a particularly stylish singer and, in the States, Libby had a bigger name with producers.

She was tired of the revues that she had been gaining success in. They offered only uninteresting parts. She wanted a vehicle in which she could carry the whole show or at least appear in it from beginning to end. And she wanted a chance to use the dramatic talent she had so assiduously nursed since her college acting days.

Again, they put the plane on a boat, this time the *Aquitania*, for the trip to Europe. When they got there, Libby immediately managed to persuade Smith to sidetrack his round-the-world flight project while they checked into the hot spots of the Continent.

In Paris, Josephine Baker made the perfect hostess.

She knew every boîte in town and was delighted to see Libby again. They made the rounds of the swinging cabarets in the Pigalle and Montmartre where Libby was able to hear almost as much black jazz as had been available in Harlem. Since the war, a good many musicians like Bechet and others had discovered that blacks and black music were appreciated in France. Finally, worn out by their nightly revels, they seized a period when La Baker had a break from the Folies Bergere and tooled off to Deauville, then the "in" resort.

Smith was getting grumpy, as his cozy vacation *à deux* had again become a threesome. Deauville was then the hub of a strange little universe, what has these days become known as the "international jet set." Its enormous cream-colored casino was haunted by the likes of the Aga Khan, Lord Derby, the two Dolly Sisters (whom Libby knew from vaudeville), Alexander Woolcott, Noel Coward, Somerset Maugham, Cole Porter, Elsa Maxwell and, surprise of surprises, Bea Lillie! Bea introduced Libby to the portly Elsa, whom she described as "thirty-nine of my most intimate friends." Even George Bernard Shaw passed through during their stay.

Libby made a bigger splash than ever at the beach. She had no sooner ventured onto the white sands of the resort in what she felt was the latest word in bathing suits, purchased in Paris, when a pair of gendarmes descended on her and arrested her for "indecent exposure."

There was always a bit of mystery about that arrest, but it made for great headlines. Whether her skimpy bathing suit really bothered anybody at the liberated French resort, or whether she was the victim of a practical joke, Libby never deigned to speak of the incident. Her enemies said that she had set the whole thing up herself as a publicity stunt.

After wearing themselves out with another round of parties, swimming, aquaplaning, and gambling, the couple decided to proceed to Germany. Josephine had to get back to the Folies and Bea had an engagement in London, so Libby felt the time was right for a trip to

Berlin, where they made a triumphant tour of the *bierstubes*, and the decadent cabarets so popular in those last days of the Weimar Republic. Berliners adored transvestism, sado-masochistic entertainment, and sex circuses, all of which Libby found greatly amusing, and Smith found somewhat embarrassing. It must be remembered that, despite Smith's wealthy background, he had not really begun to move in a fast and sophisticated set until he met Libby the year earlier; he was, after all, only eighteen years old.

Exactly where they went, whom they saw, and what they did after they left Deauville is not a matter of record and Libby seldom spoke of it in later years. It is known that Reynolds found the pace of Berlin a bit wearing and not all to his taste. Finally he insisted that they return to London, where he at least knew the language.

Libby spoke excellent French, German and Italian and was happy anywhere on the Continent, but Smith frequently felt left out of the lively conversations Libby had with the Europeans, just as he had back in New York.

In London, Libby made the acquaintance of a playwright named Noel Pierce, whom she engaged to write the show based on Josephine Baker. The play was to be called *Dusk* and would use Josephine Baker's situation as a symbol of the problems of interracial romance. As often happens in these dramatizations, the final story had little to do with the actual facts of Josephine Baker's life. In the play, the dancer is married to a white man. But when he takes her home to meet his folks, they are unable and unwilling to accept her. In the end, depressed and anguished by the rejection of his wife, the husband ends his life—with a bullet in his brain.

A draft of the play was turned over to the Curtis Brown Agency in London and Libby agreed to play the role of the rejected Negress. But the British were not terribly interested in American race problems and Libby was unable to obtain backing for the play in London. Finally, Smith, who was not entirely enamored of Libby's career, offered to make a deal. If she would go back to the States and marry him, he would back the play with his own money.

There was, of course, a stumbling-block to the plan, since Smith was still married to Ann Cannon, but he promised he would be able to clear this up in a month or so and Libby agreed to return. Besides, she'd had a desperate call from Max Gordon, asking her to go into a revived road show company of *Three's a Crowd* at $5,000 a month. Libby decided to take the money and run to the States. She promised Smith that it would be her last fling on the musical stage.

As soon as they returned, Libby went on the road and Smith went down to Winston-Salem to arrange a settlement with Ann Cannon, who was as anxious to get the divorce as Smith was. Eager to get the whole thing over with, Smith offered Ann $500,000 to get out of his life. Despite the fact that she came from a family as wealthy as Smith's, Ann was very shrewd when it came to money. She insisted that, in addition to the $500,000 offer, he should give her an additional half-million for the infant daughter she had borne him eight months after their precipitate marriage.

Smith agreed to Ann's terms and persuaded her to take the little girl and fly in his plane to Nevada where she could stay at Cornelius Vanderbilt, Jr.'s dude ranch in Yerington to avoid publicity while she waited the six weeks requisite for a divorce. Ann protested that she was not feeling well. She thought she had the flu or at least a bad cold but Smith pointed out that there couldn't be a better place to rest and recuperate than in the clean mountain air of Yerington, Nevada. She agreed to go.

Just after she left Reno, Ann, not one to let dust gather on her decree, announced her engagement to Frank Brandon Smith of Charlotte, a real estate broker. They were married at about the same time that Libby and Smith Reynolds announced their marriage, in May.

Smith decided to use the six-week waiting period to take a fast trip back to Europe and straighten out some matters concerning his proposed round-the-world flight, an obsession which he had not yet given up, although his plan now was to take the trip with Ab Walker rather than with Libby. Having moved with so many successful and talented people, young Smith was determined that he would do something to make his mark in the world. Something on his own. Something not connected with Libby and her influential friends. And at a time when the papers were full of the doings of people like Lindbergh, Admiral Byrd, Wiley Post, Amelia Earhart, and other dashing aviators, Smith felt that an around-the-world flight would be just the thing to establish himself as a hero and a man.

He arranged to return to the United States when the divorce decree became final. As soon as he got back, he flew to Pittsburgh, where Libby was playing, and the two of them slipped away from the show to Monroe, Michigan and secretly filed their marriage intentions. There was a five-day wait and, the way Smith had planned it, the fifth day would be the day after the divorce decree from Ann Cannon was final. The marriage was performed by Justice Fred M. Schoepfer and, as he recalled it, there was nothing about it particularly to distinguish it from many others performed in the parlor of the Schoepfer home in Monroe. Libby gave her name as Elizabeth Holman, no occupation, and Smith as Zachary Reynolds, student. It's doubtful that, even if they had used their real names, the justice or his wife, or the neighbor who served as a witness, would have realized who they were. All the witness remembered when asked later was that they were a nice young couple who had come to the house one Sunday in an automobile, had spoken the words required of them, and left.

After the wedding, Libby had to go back to the show and finish out the tour, but already she and Smith were making plans for their future. Libby would study to become a dramatic actress and leave the world of musical theater. Smith would take courses at NYU and continue his studies in aviation. But first Smith had to return to Paris, and they agreed that as soon as Libby finished her

Smith Reynolds, at the time of his marriage to Libby.

tour, he would fly to Hong Kong, where she would join him for their honeymoon.

Meanwhile their marriage was to be kept secret. Libby told Leonard Sillman that it was essential that news of the marriage be kept from the Reynolds clan since Smith was underage. She was afraid that if word got out that he had married her the family might take some action such as changing the provisions of the trust to disinherit Smith of the $20 million he was destined to get when he was twenty-eight.

It could not be said that Libby was obsessed with money, but certainly she liked it. Sillman later claimed that it was her principal interest in life. In any event, very few people would voluntarily put such a large inheritance into jeopardy.

As soon as the Michigan marriage ceremony was completed, Smith went to New York and on December 1, 1931 sailed on the *Paris* to France to begin his planned flight to Hong Kong. In his diary he recorded his hopes of winning fame through the trip and renown as a daring and skilled aviator. He hoped to set a record for the flight from Paris to Hong Kong.

On April 2, 1932, he reached Hong Kong, apparently somewhat shy of the record. There is no report that he made aviation history.

By this time, the *Three's a Crowd* tour was over. Smith had arranged for Libby to meet him in Hong Kong when he landed. She flew from New York and took a boat to the Orient from Seattle, where she arrived on April 1. Smith had been unexpectedly delayed. The plane broke down in a place called Fort Baird, two-hundred-fifty miles from Hong Kong.

Smith came up to get her and picked her up at the Peninsula Hotel. It was the height of the Sino-Japanese War and the lobby was full of anxious-looking British and Chinese uniformed personnel but Smith seemed oblivious to the political tensions. Smilingly in the bar, he pulled from his pocket a copy of the Hong Kong colony aviation regulations and laughingly pointed to a section which stated that neither cameras nor pistols were permitted to travelers in Asia. "And then," Libby said, "he pulled a pistol out of one pocket and a camera out of the other!"

Libby looked over her shoulder at the stern, mustachioed visages that thronged the bar, smiled nervously, and suggested that Smith put away his playthings. The next day, they went down to Fort Baird and tried to get the *Savoia Marchetti* fixed, but there were serious problems and ultimately they had to leave it there. However, they had an enjoyable time in the Orient, dodging the terrors of war, eating fabulous Chinese food, and mainly being alone together, away from his or her friends. They tried smoking a little opium together but did not drink seriously until they left on the boat which was to take them to Victoria, British Columbia, from which they would proceed to New York by commercial plane.

The honeymoon had been a vast success and now, with their happy plans for the future and without the distractions of Libby's Broadway pals, they were closer than they had ever been. But on the long voyage back, Smith began to drink again and once more drifted into his morose delusions. Once, when both had left the cabin and taken different paths to the dining room they got lost. After they had searched for one another without any luck, they went separate ways to their cabin and met. For some reason, this brief separation made Smith so despondent that he pulled out his ever-present pistol and put it to his head.

Libby wanted to scream, but she felt that this would only precipitate an unfortunate action. "I decided that the only thing to do was to act calmly," she said. "So I said, 'Please Smith, be logical and put down that gun.'

"He said to me: 'How could you sit there so calmly if you love me?'

"I pushed the gun away and put my arms around him. I would always do that, and, if the pistol were to go off, the bullet would go through me, too."

What Libby didn't realize was that Smith was carrying

around a guilty secret all that time. After their wedding and on their Asian honeymoon, Smith had been an open book to her; he never in her presence had an unexpressed thought or an uncommunicated emotion. But there was a story about his trip to Europe that he didn't have the nerve to tell her.

11
Smith's Secret Love

After the marriage in Michigan, the plan had been for Libby to continue her tour and Smith to go to London and Paris to consult with Jean Assolant, the French pilot, with whom he planned to make his historic round-the-world flight. Then he and the Frenchman would proceed to Hong Kong where Libby, traveling by boat, would meet them. They could have their romantic honeymoon in the exotic Orient, far from the eyes of Broadway columnists and Libby's lady friends.

Smith took first-class accommodations on the *Paris* for his trip to London. In his absence, Smith suggested that if Libby was stuck for an escort in New York, she could always go out with his buddy Walker. Smith had instructed Walker to make himself available to her at all times. He would be staying at the Reynolds cottage out in Port Washington.

The *Paris* had no sooner tooted its farewell whistle and streamed off in a trail of farewell confetti, than Smith was in the first-class bar, up to his ears in Pol Roger. There are usually not very many good-looking young women traveling solo in the first class of major liners, but Smith had the good fortune on this trip of running into a lissome high society girl named Nancy Hoyt, a novelist and niece of famed writer Eleanor Wiley. Nancy, no mean belter herself, kept Smith company during the wee hours in the first-class bar. She was older than Smith by six or seven years, and could mother him in his dark moods. Nancy Hoyt was married at the time, but not very pleased with her husband. When she complained about his behavior, Smith took great delight in teasing her about her mate and the rest of her "high-brow friends."

It began to appear that Smith was as uncomfortable with people in his own social set as he was with Libby's Broadway crowd. Anyway, the two socialites drank away the long week of the trans-Atlantic crossing and pretty soon felt there was no need to stay in the bar all night when they could stay in one or the other of their palatial staterooms. According to Nancy, never once during the long trip did Reynolds say a word about his marriage to Libby. What he did say before the voyage was over was that he loved Nancy and was ready to marry her as soon as things could be arranged.

When they got to London, Nancy and Smith pitched one last binge at the Savoy and then parted, temporarily she thought. "I loved Smith Reynolds," she later told the press. "He was so trustworthy. He treated me like Venetian glass. We both used to drink a lot but we did try to go on the water wagon. He was wonderful."

After a honeymoon free of their usual spats Libby and Smith returned to New York and checked into the Ambassador Hotel on Park Avenue. By this time, both were so well-known that their marriage could no longer be kept secret. Libby graciously made a statement to the press. "Well, we might as well admit it now," she said, "as the newspapers have it anyway. We do not wish to give any interviews, however." Smith and Libby let it be believed that the wedding had taken place in Hawaii, instead of in Michigan. The reason for that might have been Smith's youth. By post-dating the marriage a few more months were added to the age of the bridegroom.

Following the brief, peaceful honeymoon, there were quarrels again, the result of insecurity on Smith's part, disputes about Libby's friendship with Louisa and the others, threats of suicide and the rest. Once, Smith actually went so far as to write a suicide note and a will, after Libby had rejected him with particularly biting invective.

Once they were back in New York, the old round of parties, nights in Harlem or at Tony's, all-night binges continued. Meanwhile Smith found time to see Nancy Hoyt and reassure her that his plans to marry her were still in effect. Perhaps when they got drunk he forgot that he was already married. Once, he even asked Mrs. Hoyt to elope in his plane to North Carolina.

Nancy, who knew nothing of his marriage to Libby, said, "I wouldn't do it. I thought my friends would say Nancy is marrying for money. Besides, he was seven years younger and I was fool enough to think my friends would talk."

A few days after Libby and Smith publicly acknowledged their marriage, Stanley Lindahl, the friend who had helped Libby get her first bit in the chorus of *Garrick Gaieties*, spotted her walking into Tony's with Smith and the everpresent Ab Walker. Libby appeared not to notice him. Lindahl, awed by her new-found stardom as a torch singer, and not wishing to butt in with two gentlemen he did not know, seated himself at a table some distance away, with a group of friends from the theater. They were all talking and laughing loudly, when eventually Libby halted in the midst of an animated conversation with her husband, and turned around, facing Lindahl's table.

"Oh," she said, loudly enough for them to hear her, "I thought I recognized the voice of a very dear friend just then." Libby stood up and, blindly as always, groped her way toward the sound of his voice.

Lindahl stood up and shook her hand. She insisted that

he join their party, which he subsequently did. "She looked me over queerly in that not-quite-focused stare of hers," Lindahl said later, describing the scene. "She began reproaching me for never coming to see her since she had become a success.

"I started to draw her off to one side, when she whispered: 'I'm married. I married Smith Reynolds last November,' and then led me over and introduced me to him. Ab Walker got up and left the party a few moments later.

"Reynolds was a nice, rather pathetic little sort of chap. He was thrilled when Libby told him how I had been instrumental in getting her a job in *Garrick Gaieties.*"

Lindahl actually got to spend quite a bit of time with Smith Reynolds, because Libby was constantly being called on to sit down at other tables and chat with friends who were passing through. "Reynolds, during those moments when his wife was absent, plied me with questions about Libby. He told me how madly he loved her and in almost every other sentence he kept reiterating that she was too popular, too much admired, to be content with him.

"Once Reynolds left the table for a few minutes. While he was away, some young fellow whom I didn't know by name, but who seemed well-acquainted with Libby, came over and whispered in my ear that 'Smith is dippy about Libby.' I told him that Reynolds was in good hands; that she'd make him a wonderful wife.

"Later, when Reynolds returned, I told him the same thing, but he could not be appeased. During our talk, Libby kept coming over to us and I explained that I had previously thought her success might have spoiled her.

"She just laughed and told me now that I learned otherwise I must come and visit them often.

"When she skipped away a moment later, young Reynolds turned to me and, seizing my hand between his two, said rapturously:

"'Isn't she a wonder?' Then he went on and on with his ever-recurrent plaint that she was too good for him, too popular and with too many far more handsome male admirers for him ever to hold her love.

"I told him that I didn't believe he had any cause to worry. But to tell you the truth, I did notice that Libby had changed; that she seemed overstimulated, overexcited. That is the last I saw of them. They went South shortly afterwards."

On another occasion, also in Tony's, Reynolds turned to his friend Walker for solace. "It's no use, Ab," Reynolds is said to have told him. "It's no use. Libby doesn't love me. I'm not the type of he-man she needs. Why don't you take her out once in a while and show her a good time?"

Walker looked at him curiously for a moment, then sighed, favoring his friend with his wide, white, all-American-boy smile. "Anything you say, Smith. I'm your man."

At times, Libby seemed to weary of Smith's despondency and constant nagging. But she couldn't help but be flattered at the way he worshipped her and basked in the gleam of her satiric wit and reveled in her infrequent caresses. Also, he was the only man who ever told her that she was wasting herself by catering to the gross sensual audiences which wildly applauded her "Moanin' Low" type songs. For Libby was deeply committed to getting out of the torch-singing game and into real drama.

One night at Pod's and Jerry's, Smith suddenly turned to Libby and said, "I'm sick and tired of all this, Libby. Let's go down to Winston-Salem and live for a while. We'd be somebody down there. Everybody's real folks at home. We could get a good rest. There is nothing in this sporty life. Come on, Libby, let's go!"

In the six months they had been married, Smith must have made this pitch at least a dozen times. Libby apparently had never given him the slightest hope that she'd leave Broadway for a life of rustic simplicity, so her answer on this occasion really took Smith by surprise. "All right, Smith," she replied, according to friends at their table. Libby had appeared withdrawn and subdued all night, in one of those frequent mood swings to which she was prone. "I'm ready to go anytime you say the word. I'm tired too. Sick of this." And she flung out her arm in a gesture of disdain. "Come. We're going home."

12

Life at Reynolda

Flying into Winston-Salem in 1932, the most dominant feature on the landscape, towering high above the Piedmont hills of western North Carolina, was the grandiose, twenty-two-story tower of the R. J. Reynolds Building. It was reputed to have cost $2,500,000. The money from plug chewing tobacco, cigars and, above all, Camels Cigarettes built it. From the parapet that surrounded its roof, you could look down on the one-hundred twenty-seven church spires and the homes of Winston-Salem's 80,000 inhabitants, most of whom were black.

Of those 80,000, 20,000 were employed directly by the R. J. Reynolds Tobacco Company, and at least that many more obtained their livings indirectly from the Reynolds enterprises.

On the green edges of the city, you could also discern the estates of one hundred millionaires, all of whom were white and got their money from tobacco. The parapet also commanded a view of the R. J. Reynolds High School, the R. J. Reynolds Memorial Auditorium, and the multimillion dollar remodeled Methodist church, paid for with Reynolds money.

In Winston-Salem, the name Reynolds was everything, and the tower was simply a symbol of their autocratic power. Yet the Reynoldses were generally liked by their serfs. They had a reputation for being kind to their "darkies" and certainly generous with their charity. The Reynolds estate sat in rolling green hills about four miles northwest of Winston. It had been occupied only sporadically since 1924 when Smith Reynolds' mother died, but was always kept fully staffed with servants for the occasional visit by one of the four children. There was a great flurry of excitement among the staff when word came that Smith and his new Yankee bride were coming South, presumably to stay. Walls were painted, flower gardens weeded, lawns mowed, rooms aired, and pantries and refrigerators were filled to the brim.

Once again the crown prince was to brighten the halls of the old manor and make it ring with song and mirth! Smith's older sisters, Mary Catherine and Nancy Susan, both had long since married and settled in the North. Dick, temporarily abandoning his plans to purchase Floyd Bennett Field, had bought an old freighter, had it completely refurbished as a luxury cargo yacht, and was spending his time coasting off the shore of Africa, perhaps still daydreaming about the French Foreign Legion.

The house is sequestered well off the public highway and approached by several miles of winding, pine-fringed driveway. The first sight one has is of the rambling white manor house, the so-called "bungalow" with its green, shining, gabled roof reminiscent of the old English country places Libby knew so well. It occupies a wooded knoll in the 1,000 acres of meadow and forest which compose the estate. To the south, it fronts upon the billowing expanse of green lawn where sheep once grazed. This was the number one fairway of the Reynolds' private nine-hole golf course.

The terrace on the northeast side of the house sloped

The living room of Reynolda House, as it appears now.

down to the shore of a six-acre lake with swans gliding majestically on its placid surface. On the shore of the lake was a charming boathouse with a pagoda, reminiscent of the Orient the newlyweds had so recently left. Beside it was a flower garden and the elaborate children's playhouse. Scattered gracefully along the shore were Japanese cherry trees, which had just burst into blossom when the newlyweds arrived that May.

Libby, despite her glittering nights in the sin spots of the world, loved the country. She was quick to notice, despite the lavishness of the Reynolds spread, its essential quality of calm and dignity. "I love it, Smith," she said breathlessly, putting her hand over his as the chauffeur drove Smith's Rolls Royce slowly up the pine needle-cusioned driveway. To the west, beyond the house, as originally envisioned by old R. J., stood the dairy farm, the clover meadows, the hayfields, the antique smithy, the miles of bridle paths and the private church with the private pastor. "I think you have the right idea," Libby said softly, gazing at the scenery through her ever-present lorgnette. "We can be happy here. It's so quiet. So different."

Smith smiled with pleasure at her reaction. Riding down the sun-dappled road with the May greenery blooming all around them, it seemed that all of the squabbles, bitterness and tears were over. There would be nothing, Smith felt now, except the peace of old faithful servants and good friends.

And at first the good feelings seemed to prevail. Smith's young acquaintances, of course, knew who Libby was. They'd heard her renditions of "Moanin' Low" and "Body and Soul" on the radio, and they were awed by her glamour, her celebrity, her witty grace and charm. Despite her success as a theatrical star, Libby could often subjugate her ego. She could listen and ask intelligent questions and make amusing remarks without needing to dominate the scene or to be the center of attention at all times. At first, the newlyweds even stuck to their resolve to cut down on the drinking.

Ab Walker had come back to Winston-Salem as well, and was so involved in helping to plan Smith's future trip, that he moved into Reynolda.

There were gay but quiet parties for people such as Virgina Dunklee and Charlie Hill, called C.G., a fellow flyer. Charlie dated Virginia and was the richest and most eligible bachelor in town. He was a cousin to Ann Cannon, Smith's ex-wife. Other guests were Lew McGinnis, who operated the local airport where Reynolds kept his plane and sometimes coached him in flying, and Charlie Norfleet, a local banker. There were pleasant little gatherings at the boathouse or on the north veranda overlooking the lake.

Libby had determined that she was not going to vegetate in the country. The plan was for them to spend all of the summer in the restful environs of Reynolda and in the fall to go North, to New York University. There they would arrange to take classes that would be near one another.

Although somewhat calmed down and less neurotic, Smith was obsessed with the thought that Libby would not spend enough time with him. For the summer, Libby, who was enthralled with the huge Aeolian organ, decided to learn to play it at the Winston-Salem Conservatory of Music. But as soon as Smith tried to move Libby into the real society of Winston-Salem—among the people who had been his father's friends—the real attitudes of the people of Winston-Salem began to surface. To the tobacco clan, Smith, despite his weaknesses and vagaries, was still a "good ol' boy." He was one of them. He flew a plane and carried a pistol. He came from good English-Irish stock, and belonged to the Methodist Church. Sure, he'd get into a scrape once in a while, through drinking or with women, but that was just the style of the South. Secretly, everybody laughed when they recounted the story of Smith's teenage shotgun wedding.

But the older generation could not understand for the life of them that dark, foreign-looking Yankee, and it did not take long for word to get out that Libby was Jewish.

Behind her back they referred to her as "that Yankee Jewess." This did not exactly set up friendly vibrations in a community that in those days was considered one of the centers of Ku Klux Klan activity. Only a few years before, North Carolina and the Winston-Salem area had left the ranks of the Democrats for the first time since the Civil War to vote for Hoover in an election largely dominated by the Klan's campaign against the Catholic Al Smith. The Klan was as anti-Jewish as it was anti-Catholic.

In May, Libby, perhaps unconsciously, offended many of the older set by playing tennis without stockings and smoking cigarettes while walking down the street. In the pious Methodist world of the older generation Carolinians, stockingless, cigarette-smoking females were very much frowned upon. Libby tried to win them over. She was frequently heard to say in public, "I don't see how anyone would deliberately live in New York when they could live in this marvelous Winston-Salem." But nobody believed her.

Possibly the most grating aspect of Libby's behavior, and it bothered Smith as much as anyone else, was her breezy friendliness and familiarity with the black personnel of the estate and the Negroes she would run into casually on her rare trips into town. Folks in North Carolina considered themselves "kind" to their Negroes but there was a line between kindness and social equality which Libby crossed too often. In New York she had spent half her leisure time among blacks and it could honestly be said she counted some of them among her best friends. She probably was aware of the impact of her behavior but could not control it any more than she could control her flashing wit.

Libby, used to being surrounded by throngs, even mobs of admirers, began to feel lonely after a while, and perhaps a little bored. She and Ab Walker and Smith took tours of the countryside, sometimes going as far as Greensboro or Durham, or up to Roaring Gap, where there was an attractive summer camp. But in the end, it was boring, boring. The decompression from her high-powered life was just too fast. Smith, sensing her growing impatience, got jumpy again. Pretty soon, the couple started hard drinking again. When Smith drank, he got moody and morose; when Libby drank, she got acid-tongued and restless. No one knows whether Libby brought a supply of drugs with her or had them sent, but suddenly she began to behave in a manner reminiscent of the way she acted during the height of her affair with Jeanne Eagels. She would frequently be high-spirited and gay to the point of mania and then, alternately, sluggish, moody, grouchy, and "out of it." She took to spending long periods of time sleeping off the effects of booze or drugs in the cool porch adjoining her second floor bedroom. And her restlessness seemed to be catching. All of a sudden plans for the fall season seemed less appealing. Libby desperately wanted to get back to the theater and felt that she had to have at least one chance to prove herself as a dramatic actress.

Smith, catching the tempo of Libby's changing moods, dreamed again about starting his round-the-world trip early, rather than waiting until he completed courses at NYU. They had already sent for a young mathematics tutor. As soon as he graduated, he was to come down to Reynolda and help Smith with his math. Perhaps, Smith reasoned, that would be enough. Besides, he planned to take Ab Walker with him on his round-the-world trip and Ab was much better at academic things than Smith was.

Libby, casting about for a plan, suddenly remembered a discussion she had with Leonard Sillman some months earlier. Sillman, years before, had appeared at a benefit with Libby and Blanche Yurka, in which he had imitated a great German actor named Alexander Moissi. Moissi had made his name in a Czech play called *Periphery*, which was produced in German, and Sillman had been haunted by Moissi's brilliant performance. One day it occurred to him why he was so fascinated. He realized that, in his own estimation at any rate, he would be a brilliant choice to play the lead in an English version of the play. Libby, who was still one of his best friends, would be perfect for the female lead. And Sillman's dear friend Blanche Yurka, who was of Czechoslovakian extraction, would be the ideal choice to translate the play from its original Czech.

Sillman had arranged a meeting between Blanche and Libby and told them his ideas. They both thought it might be interesting but the plan was temporarily tabled when Libby decided that she might give up the theater. Now, however, the idea seemed more appealing. She called Sillman and suggested that he and Blanche come down to Reynolda and spend a month with her to discuss the adaptation in peace and quiet and perhaps get something in shape which might interest a producer. Her agent, Walter Batchelor, thought the project might have some merit and it was suggested that he come down with his wife, Janet Reade. It would be a godsend to the bored Libby, that much was certain. They agreed to come down and spend part of June and July on the palatial estate. But a few days before they were supposed to leave, Sillman got a wire from his sister in California offering him a part in a new revue being prepared at the Pasadena Playhouse. Was Leonard interested? "I was packing for my month with the Reynoldses . . . Adapting masterpieces from the Czech in the mimosa country of North Carolina in the company of Blanche Yurka and Libby Holman was the sort of glamorous prospect I always find it infinitely difficult to slough off. But the telegram from my sister offered an infinitely more glamorous possibility—viz: a salary. There would be no money for me in *Periphery* for a long time to come, if ever, whereas *Hullaballoo* looked like steady work for a few weeks.

"I called Blanche and Libby and told them to proceed without me. I would be in California for a few weeks. When I came back from the Coast, richer and consequently happier, we could begin our collaboration in earnest. The ladies seemed disappointed but resigned."

And so the plan was left that way. Blanche and the Batchelors would go to Reynolda; Sillman would join them later. The project seemed to be a good one. The

Batchelors and Blanche loved the luxury and peace of the estate. It was an ideal place to work. They would spend hours during the morning or late afternoon reading lines, reshaping scenes, and generally trying to shape the play into a Broadway hit.

The leading role, no novelty for Libby, was that of a woman of the streets who accepts a young married architect as a client. At the crucial moment, her lover, a cabaret entertainer—the part Sillman was after—catches them in the act, flies into a rage, and kills the architect with a blow. The girl and her lover then decided to dispose of the architect's body by dumping it into the street in such a way that it would appear that the victim had fallen over some rubble and been fatally injured. They put mud on his shirt and made sure that his diamond shirt studs and a considerable amount of money are left on his person, so that people will think that it is an accident. Then Libby and her cabaret boyfriend "find" the body and notify the authorities. The dead man's wife is so impressed with their apparent kindness that she gives them the money found on her husband's body. Several Broadway people who read the play said it was "sordid and thoroughly depressing, a deep-dyed tragedy throughout." Certainly a big change from the old Harlem "vo-de-o-do."

Early in July, Blanche wrote a letter to Leonard expressing her pleasure at the assignment.

"Dear Leonard, I can't possibly tell you what you missed in this veritable paradise. The place has the serenity and the peace of heaven. I am writing this in the drawing room, and the sun is shining through the window. Libby is in the music room vocalizing. Smith is out on the lawn with the dogs. Oh, how I wish you were here."

Libby, too, was happy again, and so pleased with the creative turn her life was taking that she suggested to Smith that he invite some of his friends to a small gathering during the first week in July. Charlie Hill's twenty-first birthday might be a good occasion, she suggested, for the little group of young Winston-Salemites who approved of Libby to meet her friends from New York. Smith agreed and invitations were sent out and plans made for the party, which was to be a small and intimate one. Everything seemed cheerful, pleasant, and peaceful at Reynolda, but there were rumblings of discontent.

13

Death by a Party Unknown

In newspaper reports of massive catastrophic events, when conflicting impressions reach the international desk, occasionally the lead article is datelined "From Combined Reports." And one must resort to this tactic in any attempt to reconstruct what ensued at Charlie Hill's birthday party at Reynolda on July 5.

In the first place, the whole event seemed to be somewhat spur-of-the-moment. Most of the guests were not called until the day before, principally by Ab Walker and Libby.

On Sunday, July 3, Libby, Blanche, Walter Batchelor and Janet Reade had an after-dinner run-through of the Czech play they were adapting. Some of the language of the translation seemed stiff and awkward and they asked Smith and Ab Walker if they would like to sit in and listen and offer their comments on the use of colloquial English. Neither seemed terribly interested. Walker said he didn't see how he could be of any help since he knew "absolutely nothing about it." It appeared from his response that he had barely more sympathy for Libby's theatrical ambitions than did Smith.

Smith, after declining to help, went upstairs. Then Walker noticed him standing outside of the building in the driveway holding a small overnight bag. Ab asked him what he was doing, and he replied, according to Walker, "How about carrying me downtown?"

Walker said, "Sure."

They went in and had a few drinks, while one of the servants fetched the car. It was then about ten o'clock, and Walker drove Smith down about four miles to the center of town and asked him where he wanted to go. Smith said to the Robert E. Lee Hotel, then the only major hotel in Winston-Salem. "You can't do that," Walker said. "If you insist on going to the Robert E. Lee, suppose you let me register you in the hotel?"

Smith agreed, said Ab, and he did so. Then, Walker said, the two of them went up to the room, got some liquor, drank it, talked "the bigger part of the night," then went to bed. At the time, Ab said, he had no idea why it was that his friend was so disturbed that he left his own home and preferred to spend the night in a downtown hotel.

From other sources comes a report that whatever they did in that hotel room, it was a lot more than talk. There were loud sounds of either argument or revelry heard until the wee hours of the morning, when Smith eventually left, leaving his friend to sleep in the room until later in the day when he also returned to Reynolda.

On Sunday, the Fourth of July, Libby said she and Smith played tennis in the morning and went swimming in the pool of the estate. Then, after lunch, Libby went horseback riding and possibly for a final chat with her manager Walter Batchelor. After dinner, Blanche Yurka and Ab Walker drove the New York couple to town and put them on the train and Smith and Libby stayed on, chatting, and finally went to bed, apparently with few, if any, drinks.

Blanche and Ab Walker went to a movie in town after

dropping the Batchelors off at the station.

The guests who trooped into the palatial Reynolda living room on Tuesday, July 5, comprised a fairly typical cross-section of Winston-Salem's younger life. The party was only partially in celebration of Charlie Hill's 21st birthday. It was also to be sort of a send-off for Smith Reynolds, who planned to start his round-the-world trip in a matter of weeks. Hill's date was slim, petite, Virginia Dunklee, a lively brunette whose father owned the largest laundry in town. Another guest, invited at Libby's suggestion, was Mrs. Billie Vaught, a beautiful, blonde young widow, née Mary Louise Collier. She had been one of the most popular girls in Winston-Salem before marrying Vaught. She had been despondent and drinking heavily following her young husband's death, less than six months earlier, in a tragic fire. Since his death, she had been working in Montaldo's, a very exclusive ladies' ready-to-wear shop downtown. Jim Shepherd, the art shop proprietor, a local socialite, arrived with a male date, Billy Shaw Howell, a stranger to the crowd who was a radio salesman from Charlotte, North Carolina. Charles Norfleet, known as "Little Charlie" Norfleet, was there, son of a local millionaire and head of the trust department of the Wachovia Bank & Trust Company in Winston-Salem. And Lewin McGinnis, who ran the municipal airport where Smith kept his plane and also coached the young man in flying.

Essentially, it was a small, intimate group of Smith's friends plus Libby's friend, Blanche Yurka, who was seventeen years older than Libby and about twenty-five years older than most of the guests. C. Raymond Kramer, who had come down a few days before to tutor Smith in aeronautical mathematics, a bright Jewish kid from the Bronx who had been recommended by the head of the NYU aeronautical engineering department, was in his room. He had not been asked to join the party.

How much drinking was done at the party later became a matter of wild conjecture, with vastly conflicting opinions as to the amounts consumed by the various guests, but in any event the festivities started in the main house with a pre-prandial drink or two, after which the group sauntered down to the elegant, Oriental lake house where a home-style barbecue buffet was being served by Plummer Walker, an old Reynolds family retainer, who had come to Reynolda a month after Smith was born. She watched the proceedings with a jaundiced eye as the young guests drank, sang, gossiped, swam, and canoed in the gaily-lit boathouse. From Plummer's point of view, everyone was having a good time except Smith. Smith, Plummer said, seemed to be unhappy about Libby, who appeared to be very attracted to Mary Louise Vaught. Shortly after dinner Libby got into a contest with the young blonde widow, drinking corn whiskey shot for shot with home-brew chasers. Plummer said that Libby wanted to show Mrs. Vaught that she could "drink like a man." Smith stood in a corner, scowling.

"You know, he just liked anything to be straight," Plummer later said. "As you understand, I was here when he was a little boy. When he doesn't like things, I can tell by looking at him; he don't have to speak. I noticed down there that he didn't exactly like the way things were going."

The party members, according to Plummer were "just cutting up." Libby said to Mrs. Vaught, "Let's do something. Let's sing!" She started to climb up on a hassock.

"In some way she stumbled, a bottle of pop fell over, and she liked to have fell because she was up on a high thing. Mr. Smith looked up and I looked at him. He looked like he was disgusted. So he finally got up and went over to her and went to talking to her. What he said I don't know. I know he wasn't satisfied. He liked for things to be straight, because he was raised that way. You all know that."

That apparently was the way old family retainers saw young Smith in the background of Winston-Salem, at any rate. When asked whether Libby was "under the influence of liquor" down at the boathouse, Plummer said, "Well, she was jolly." And so was Mrs. Vaught, in Plummer's opinion.

Smith, Plummer says, "didn't seem to take on to the party, didn't seem to get into it. I offered to fix him a plate, and he said 'No, Plummer; I haven't got up an appetite yet; I will be over directly and get me something to eat.'

"Finally," Plummer said, "he did go to the table and started eating, but he didn't eat but very little because he got up and went over to speak to Miss Libby."

After the barbecue, Ab and Mary Louise Vaught changed into bathing suits and went swimming. Libby, who was resplendent in her usual garb for sporting occasions such as this, was wearing white flannel pajama bottoms and a red striped top. Nobody noticed whether she went swimming or not. This was about 8:30, and it was getting dark.

After the swim, Mary Louise Vaught disappeared for a couple of hours, apparently on an automobile ride with Jim Shepherd. Libby, too, disappeared from the scene for about forty-five minutes, between nine and ten, and then later on for a couple of hours. After her first disappearance, she came up to Ab Walker, who was still sopping wet from his swim down at the boathouse, put her arm on his shoulder and said to him, "Smith doesn't love me anymore."

Walker later said that he thought that Libby was "pretty tight" at the time. Smith, already unhappy with Libby, apparently saw this little scene. He came over and Walker thought that there was going to be an angry confrontation. Smith pulled him aside "to straighten things out about Libby," but told Walker, "Don't misunderstand me, Ab . . . I'm not blaming you."

Around ten o'clock, Ab Walker, assuming somewhat the role of the host's alter ego, suggested that everybody who was finished canoeing or swimming come on up to the house for a drink afterwards, where they could listen to some of Libby's records on the Victrola.

Between eleven and twelve, the guests sat around, had some drinks, chatted with one another, and departed.

Blanche Yurka went up to her room in the east wing and Mary Louise Vaught, too much under the weather to leave, was put to bed in one of the rooms in that wing, also.

Walker asked Smith where Libby was and Smith said, according to his young secretary, "She's probably roaming around the woods."

At about midnight, the watchman, making his rounds, saw Libby coming up through the bushes from the pool on the north side of the house. Walker met her outside. They exchanged a few words and walked into the house, where Smith met them at the door and took Libby upstairs.

Now things get really confusing. But apparently, a few minutes after they had gone upstairs, Smith returned alone in an even more dismal mood than before. Walker, since his appointment a few days earlier as official secretary and factotum to Smith, had taken to cleaning up the place and locking up the doors at night. He was doing this when Smith came down. "Plans have been changed," he told Walker. "The trip around the world is over."

Walker was surprised, but said nothing. "And you don't have to leave a door open for me. I'm going out and I'm not coming back."

He pulled his billfold from his pocket and tossed it to Walker. "Here. Do what you want with that. I won't need it."

Walker, who had been through a number of these scenes with his friend, was not impressed. He dropped the wallet on the divan and continued straightening up as Smith returned to his room where Libby was presumably already asleep. So by 12:30 there wasn't a soul awake in Reynolda except Ab Walker.

A little before 1 A.M., Blanche Yurka, who had not fallen asleep and was glancing through the script of *Periphery*, thought she heard some signs of activity downstairs in the kitchen. She heard a noise, a conversation, perhaps a squabble. She got upstairs and walked out onto the balcony that ran around the upper level of the huge living room, but there was nobody there but Walker, busily straightening up. "Isn't anyone around?" she asked. "No," Walker said, "they're all gone and I'm locking up."

Miss Yurka returned to her room, but didn't completely fall asleep. She dozed fitfully. An indefinite restlessness possessed her, perhaps a premonition. Maybe it was something in the tone of the voices she had heard. In any event, less than five minutes after she returned to bed, she heard some sounds again. This time it sounded to her like a wild shrieking. She went to the window and listened for a moment and then ran through the hallway to the west wing. Walker was still there, rearranging furniture and removing glasses and bottles. "I heard a voice," Blanche called to him. And now, even before she could complete her sentence, they could both hear the shrieking, this time wilder and louder. Walker cocked his head at the sound which was coming from the east wing where Smith and Libby were sleeping. "I'd better go up and see what's the matter," he said and ran up the stairs two at a time and disappeared into the hallway leading from the balcony into the east wing. Before he got up the stairs, Libby staggered out of the corridor, her lacy peach-colored negligee drenched with blood.

"Smith's killed himself," she said, and fell in a faint on a divan at the foot of the corridor. Walker ran down the hall to Smith's suite at the end of the corridor and there he found Smith Reynolds still in the white duck pants and blue polo shirt he'd been wearing all evening, sprawled across the bed with a gaping wound in his temple.

Walker left Smith's unconscious body on the bed and raced downstairs to the telephone, where he called the Baptist Hospital for an ambulance and then ran up the stairs again to the Reynolds room. Libby, in the interval, had apparently recovered and was sitting on the bed, holding Smith's bloody head on her shoulder. Between them they tried to carry the wounded young heir out of the room and downstairs to where the ambulance would soon be arriving. Walker took the unconscious Reynolds by the shoulders and Libby held the feet but she was either too drunk or too weak to hold on and they had proceeded only to the end of the corridor when Blanche came over and helped to carry Smith the rest of the way downstairs.

Since the ambulance had not arrived by the time they had carried Smith's bleeding body to the second floor, Walker decided it might be faster to take his friend in his own car to the hospital. He and Blanche, with some help from the distraught Libby, carried him outside, placed him in the car. Blanche sat in the back seat, trying to hold and comfort the unconscious young man while Libby sat weeping in the front seat beside Walker, who drove to the hospital, still wearing his bathing suit, as fast as the high-powered car would go.

The call to the hospital had been made at exactly 1 A.M. and Walker's car was at the emergency entrance, four miles from Reynolda by 1:10. Nurse Ethel Shore, night supervisor at the Baptist Hospital, met the car at the entrance. She got an orderly to help carry the limp body of Smith Reynolds into the elevator and up to the fifth floor operating room. Smith was fading rapidly. His blood dripped on the floor, soaked through Ab Walker's bathing suit, and covered the white tunic of the orderly.

Libby, distraught, her peach negligee unfastened and also covered with blood, was stopped at the fifth floor reception desk and barred from the gruesome scene in the operating room. Mrs. Shore pulled out a cot near the elevator and helped Libby to sit down on it and tried to wash some of the blood from her neck, chest, arms, hands and feet. Libby was still barefoot. Finally, disgusted by the appearance of the blood-soaked negligee, Mrs. Shore provided Blanche Yurka with a room in which to rest and a hospital gown and put Blanche's black robe on Libby, fastening it with safety pins and a belt.

As soon as she was sure the surgeons were taking care of Reynolds, she moved Libby to a private room on the third floor and put her to bed.

Dr. Fred Hanes, who examined Smith as soon as he was put on the operating table, said that he saw on his

The "sleeping porch" where Smith Reynolds was shot to death in 1932.

right temple a swelling "as large as a small orange, with a puncture wound in the skin in the middle of the swelling." Behind the left ear, he found another wound much smaller. The three doctors examined the two wounds to decide which was the entrance and which was the exit. Around the right temple wound they found what seemed to be slight powder burns and a blackening on the edge, which made them think this was the point of entry, since the smaller wound behind the ear was not seared or scorched but just covered with blood.

It was immediately evident to all three surgeons from the course of the bullet straight through the brain and the amount of hemorrhaging, that there was no chance that Reynolds would recover, although his heartbeat continued to be fairly steady for the first hour or so.

Meanwhile the surgeons worked over the dying heir. From the beginning it was a hopeless case. The blow had done grievous damage to the brain and the bleeding had weakened Reynolds to the point where surgery would have been impossible. As soon as he had arranged for attendants and the other doctors to do what they could for Reynolds, Dr. Johnson went to see Libby and check on her condition. He found her "highly nervous and very dazed—and rather drunk," as was Ab Walker, in the doctor's opinion.

When Smith Reynolds had been on the operating table for an hour or so, Ab Walker, still in his bathing suit, chilled, shaky and half drunk, asked to be driven back to Reynolda to change clothes. J. T. Barnes, an assistant to R. E. Lasater, one of Smith Reynolds' guardians, had come to the hospital as soon as they got news at two o'clock, and now drove Ab Walker to the estate. Walker told him, as he later recalled it, that he wanted to change clothes but he also wanted to get "the pocketbook that Smith gave him and something else."

By now, Walker was sober, though still very shaken. It was still Prohibition in a state where the law was often enforced vigorously and it may have occurred to Walker that if there was going to be a lot of police tramping about the house, it would be a good idea to get rid of the empty bottles and glasses of liquor. When he finished straightening up and recovering the wallet, which he did in the presence of Barnes—there was $80 in cash in it and a collection of cards—Walker returned to the hospital for the death watch.

At 5:25 A.M. the weary, blood-covered surgeons emerged from the operating room to announce that Reynolds was dead. Ab volunteered to bring the news to Libby, who was sleeping—or passed out—in Room 311, two floors below.

The coroner, who arrived within an hour after the death was announced, pronounced the cause of death as suicide and declared that he could find "no motive" for Reynolds to have put himself to death.

Meanwhile Dr. Johnson, who was family physician to the Reynoldses, examined Libby again and declared that no one should be permitted to see her for at least twenty-four hours. This restriction, the doctor said, was necessary because of her extremely disturbed condition. And, the doctor said, the restriction applied to members of the family as well as to outsiders. Johnson said that he had spoken to Libby and at the moment she "knew no more of the shooting than she had been told."

After being taken to the hospital, Dr. Johnson said, at the same time her husband was rushed there, she looked at him in a stunned and bewildered way and said, "But where was Smith shot?"

Despite the ruling of Coroner W. N. Dalton that Smith Reynolds had committed suicide the newspapers instantly leaped on the case and began to speculate on other possible theories. The *Daily News* said: "Three questions remain to be answered and fully backed up by evidence. They are:

"Was 'Skipper'—as young Reynolds was known to a circuit of night clubs as well as a smart social set of Glen Cove, L.I.—murdered?

"Did the impetuous tobacco princeling kill himself

because $20 million bored him?

"Did he shoot himself accidently while his torch-bearing bride from Broadway waited for him in their bedroom?"

14
The Inquest

The questions raised by the *Daily News* and other tabloids apparently bothered Forsyth County Sheriff Transou Scott also. Even before the funeral on July 8, Scott was leaking statements to the press concerning his doubts that the death of Smith Reynolds was a simple suicide, despite the pronouncements of the county coroner.

Smith Reynolds' death naturally made front-page headlines across the country and in most parts of the Western world. The drama was irresistible. The effete multimillionaire, the sexy, exotic torch singer, lavish parties, booze, weird antics, gossip—it added up to good copy, especially for the tabloids, some of which, like the *News*, even beat the sheriff in throwing up clouds of doubt and suspicion on the case. The day after the death, the papers were full of innuendo, unconfirmed suspicions and reports from "reliable sources."

The one "reliable source" that was totally unavailable

was Libby, who had been placed completely off limits by her physician.

The *News* had an interesting theory:

> *"Those who believe Reynolds may have been murdered by an assassin who invaded his estate have evolved the theory that he was terrorized by blackmailers. There is no direct evidence of this, but several suspicious circumstances have been brought to the attention of the police. One of these 'suspicious circumstances' was the appearance on July 4, the day before the murder, of a mysterious advertisement in the Twin City Sentinel, the Winston-Salem daily.*
>
> *"'Death hangs over me unless the man who was to phone me Thursday comes to my relief. No alternative. Guarantee immunity. Readers, please spread this notice. Call phone used before between 12 and 1 P.M.'*
>
> *"Strange and anonymous instructions were that the words 'Death hangs over me' be printed in large display type.*
>
> *"However," the* News *commented, "so far as is known this advertisement has not been linked with young Reynolds."*

The *News* and other papers pointed out that Smith left instructions for his airplane to be prepared for an early morning takeoff on the 7th and for it to be fueled with a large supply of gasoline. Apparently, if he had changed his mind about the round-the-world trip, he had not instructed the airport before his death.

People had trouble figuring out why a young man with his money and situation would commit suicide. It must be remembered that Smith's death took place during the depths of the Depression. It was a time when a bonus army of veterans was laying siege to Washington to get desperately needed money and food and people were living in tin shack and wood crate "Hoovervilles" on the outskirts of every city. When women and children were sleeping in the parks. When people were starving to death. For somebody with Smith Reynolds' wealth and opportunity to take his own life, in a perverse way, gave people some sense of pleasure, made them feel, perhaps, that there are worse things than being jobless, hopeless and starving.

"Certainly," the *News* said, "young Reynolds was a very envied young man. Because Libby Holman, after her stardom with Clifton Webb and Fred Allen in 'The Little Show' and 'Three's a Crowd,' was generally admitted to be the most proposed-to actress in the world."

Naturally all the articles about Smith contained sidebars about the possible disposition of his wealth, but the speculations varied wildly. One close friend said Libby would probably inherit nothing from the Reynolds millions because Smith was not yet of age when he died. Others said that she would inherit at least half of his personal property.

Smith had left a will made only months before his marriage which mentioned neither of his wives, but by North Carolina law the will was not valid in any event, since Smith still had three months to go before his 21st birthday.

The drama provided a field day for sensational journalism. The story broke on the morning of the 6th. Reporters from the AP and UP arrived in Winston-Salem before dark. By Thursday, crack reporters from the International News Service, fresh from reporting the Lindbergh kidnapping case, arrived in Winston-Salem. By the next day there were reporters from the *Evening Journal*, *The New York Times*, the Cincinnati *Post*, the Chicago *Daily News*, the New York *Daily Tribune* and the New York *Daily Mirror*. They made their headquarters at the Winston-Salem *Journal* and *Sentinel* and during the week in which the story unfolded, most of them ate and slept very little.

On Thursday, the day after Smith's death was announced, R. E. Lasater and Will (W.N.) Reynolds, Smith's two guardians, finally allowed themselves to be interviewed by the press. W. N. Reynolds said that he and Smith's two sisters "feel like it was suicide." Lasater also said all the evidence pointed toward suicide and he had no cause to doubt it.

Later that day it was announced that Stratton Coyner, an attorney for the Reynolds family, had managed to reach Dick Reynolds by cablegram at Las Palmas in the Canary Islands, off the coast of Africa. Coyner said it would be impossible for Dick Reynolds to reach Winston-Salem in time for the burial, since it would take from ten days to two weeks to make the trip.

Smith's funeral was held on July 8, at the historic Salem Cemetery. Among the pallbearers were Charlie Hill and Ab Walker. By this time, Smith's two married sisters Mary, now Mrs. Charles Babcock, and Nancy, Mrs. Henry Walker Bagley, had arrived to attend the funeral. As Dr. D. Clay Lily, who had married Smith Reynolds' father and mother years ago, read the eulogy by the graveside, Ab Walker turned pale, his knees grew weak and he collapsed, almost hitting the ground before being held up by Charlie Hill and Rev. Lily. Throughout the funeral, Libby sat with her head on the shoulder of her father, Alfred, who had arrived the previous night and was staying at Reynolda. Garbed in black, Libby was trembling with emotion. She kept her face in her hands and appeared to be weeping, but without making a sound, as her mother, who had also arrived on the previous night, comforted her.

Just before the funeral, Coroner Dalton had announced that despite his initial verdict that Smith's death was a suicide, there would be an inquest that afternoon. This move was apparently made at the instigation of Sheriff Transou Scott and Assistant Solicitor Earl McMichael. (The solicitor of Forsyth County was the equivalent of a district attorney.) Chief Solicitor Carlisle Higgins was not present during this announcement, he was busy on another major case involving the theft of carloads of R. J. Reynolds tobacco from a siding.

Mourners who had gathered at Reynolda for a private memorial service were cleared out of the house while a hastily summoned jury was sworn in and witnesses, including most of the guests at the party, were summoned. Two doctors and a half dozen nurses helped Libby, who was under the influence of what were described as "opiates," pull herself together for the early-evening inquest.

Libby then conferred at length with her father, the tall, spare lawyer from Cincinnati.

The proceedings of the first night's inquest were kept secret from the public and the press by order of the coroner and the solicitors. It was held in the sleeping porch where Smith had been found and where Libby lay half comatose on the pillows giving a sketchy account of Smith's death to the officials and the jury. In the hall outside, nurses were held in readiness to rush in if needed.

The first witness called at four o'clock that afternoon was Dr. Fred Hanes, who told how he had been called to the hospital at one o'clock in the morning. Regarding the question of the likelihood of suicide, he was asked by McMichael:

McMICHAEL: Do you have any opinion satisfactory to yourself as to the distance, from the examination you made of the temple wound, that the pistol was away from the temple at the time the shot was fired?

HANES: Yes. I should think it would be reasonable to conclude from the fact that the skin was so slightly powder burned, that the muzzle of the pistol must have been resting almost, if not quite on, th skin itself, close to it. The greater the separation from the skin, the greater the powder burn.

McMICHAEL: Up to three feet?

HANES: Yes. Until you get away to where the powder does not burn at all.

There were some questions about Hanes' return to Reynolda after having been at the hospital and the finding of the Mauser in that room at 6 A.M., but this can wait till later.

The next witness was Ab Walker and the first questions he answered concerned the length of time he had lived in Reynolda. Apparently that was only since Friday, the first of July. The next question concerned the visit of Smith and Walker to the Robert E. Lee Hotel on Sunday night, the third. Ab explained that he and Smith had been invited to participate in the reading of the play by Blanche, Libby and Batchelor but had refused. He told how Smith had suggested they go downtown at about ten o'clock.

"Smith asked me to go to the hotel with him," Ab testified, "I asked him why he had taken a room there instead of spending the night at home and he answered: 'I think I am going insane and I am going to see a doctor in the morning.'

"I asked him what made him think so and he replied: 'I believe I have done things, this or that, and Libby would tell me that it was my imagination, that I hadn't done the things that I thought I had done.'

"I laughed at all this because Smith did a lot of this kind of talking in jest, and I never believed that he was going crazy."

During this testimony Walker said that Reynolds, far from being in agreement with Libby's idea of backing her in the new Broadway play, actually had planned on leaving her and taking the round-the-world trip on his own.

"I had completed, at Smith's request, arrangements for his contemplated trip," Walker swore.

A little later, however, Ab Walker made one of the most startling and inconsistent statements of his whole testimony, when he said that he thought that his dead friend was "love-starved and a weakling."

Smith Reynolds had told him, he said, that he could never fulfill Libby's ambition to have a child, and that he had urged Libby to carry on an affair with another man. Smith told him, Ab said, that he was willing to close his eyes to any improprieties on his wife's part. He said she was young, voluptuous, physically starved for love, and

Ab Walker, lifelong companion and accused murderer of Smith Reynolds.

that he was entirely unsatisfactory as a husband, Walker added.

WALKER: . . . during the reading in the afternoon of this play, which both Smith and myself were listening to, Mrs. Reynolds was taking one part of the play and reading that, and she told me that she went to place her hand over on Smith's leg, and he moved it away, and during this time I was sitting there, I didn't know where he was exactly, but it happened that she told me he was upstairs talking to her, wanting to know why she—I don't know the words she used, but in other words, drew away from him.

McMICHAEL: I understood you to say he drew away from her?

WALKER: Yes, that's what he told her. That is what Mrs. Reynolds told me late yesterday afternoon or this morning, I don't know which, and she said that she said she didn't, that she said "I couldn't, I never could"· that he said "You either did or I am insane; I will go down and see a physician." And when we went to the hotel he never mentioned anything about this incident, but he talked about he was afraid he might be insane to me that night. We got back to the house here next morning before anybody got up, and Mrs. Reynolds told me that he told her—in fact, he went right up and waked her up and told her that he had a weakness to temptation such as this, and he promised never to leave again.

McMICHAEL: She only told you that since you have talked to Mr. Scott?

WALKER: Yes, sir.

McMICHAEL: You say you have just been here since Friday?

WALKER: Since Friday.

McMICHAEL: Had you been there since Smith had been back previous to that?

WALKER: I have been here practically every week end.

McMICHAEL: State to His Honor and the jury what Smith's conduct was in regard to drinking since he has been back.

WALKER: He practically hadn't done any. I remember right after the house party here he went strictly on the water wagon on account of his studying.

McMICHAEL: In the last week or two, since the first day of July, since you have been here, state to His Honor and the jury what the extent of Mr. Reynolds' drinking was then.

WALKER: Well, he has drank a little since then, very light.

McMICHAEL: State to His Honor and the jury what you think his condition would have been on this night.

WALKER: He was absolutely sober.

McMICHAEL: Do you know whether he had had a drink at all or not?

WALKER: Yes, sir, he had had a drink.

McMICHAEL: About what time of night was it?

WALKER: I imagine he came up to the house around ten-thirty or eleven and we fixed a drink together, which I think I left practically half of mine.

McMICHAEL: And that was the only drink he had had that night?

WALKER: We had a bottle of beer down at the barbecue, and outside of that I don't know of any other drink he had had.

McMICHAEL: When Mr. Reynolds was drinking, when he was taking a social drink with the guests, state to His Honor and the jury about how many drinks he would take in the course of an afternoon, from seven o'clock until twelve.

WALKER: Quite a few.

McMICHAEL: Then, in your opinion, one drink and a bottle of beer—he would have been what you would say practically sober?

WALKER: Yes—and his wife told me he intended leaving the party and going up and getting some sleep so he could put in a good day of studying the next day.

After this, Mc Michael asked Walker some questions about the guests at the party and the events of the evening. McMichael then led Walker to describe the departure of the guests between eleven and twelve, and the final moments of the party, to his best recollection.

WALKER: Well, Mr. Shepherd was leaving. Smith and his wife were in my room when he started upstairs and she met him in the hall and they went in my room, or he went and she followed after him. By this point there was no one in the reception room downstairs and Jim Shepherd was outside going to Walker's car which he drove home.

McMICHAEL: Where were you when he left?

WALKER: At first, I sat in the reception room and heard this talking, and then walked out with Mr. Shepherd.

McMICHAEL: Before Mr. Shepherd left, Mr. and Mrs. Reynolds had come upstairs?

WALKER: Yes, sir.

McMICHAEL: How long had they been upstairs before he left?

WALKER: They had just gone upstairs.

McMICHAEL: They were upstairs before he left?

WALKER: They left a little before Mr. Shepherd started out the door.

McMICHAEL: This is your room on this hallway, the last room on the left before you get to the balcony?

WALKER: Yes, sir.

McMICHAEL: This room we are in now was Mr. and Mrs. Reynolds' room?

WALKER: Yes, sir.

McMICHAEL: Have you any reason why Mr. and Mrs. Reynolds would have gone in your room—do you know of any reason?

WALKER: No sir.

McMICHAEL: Was she in the habit of going in your room?

WALKER: No, sir. The early part of the evening Mr.

Reynolds and myself—he was in my room talking to me. We had planned this trip around the world which we were going to try and do next spring in record time, and there was a globe in my room which he was looking at and telling me the difficulty in the thing, while I was dressing; and Mrs. Reynolds came in the room then and I went on in the bath room and finished dressing, and I don't know whether Mr. Reynolds started in my room to look at the globe or not. It is the only globe in the house.

McMICHAEL: How could you tell by listening to the voices from the reception room that they were in your room?

WALKER: I saw them go in, and I could hear them very plainly, although I couldn't understand what they were saying, that they were in my room all the time.

McMICHAEL: You could see them go in your room from downstairs?

WALKER: Yes, sir. In the reception room we always used the sofa on the far side—magazines, mail and everything placed on that table.

McMICHAEL: Did Mr. Reynolds come back downstairs again?

WALKER: Yes, sir.

McMICHAEL: How long after they were in your room did he come down?

WALKER: Mrs. Reynolds started to her room, and he followed her on down there, and Mrs. Reynolds [said] to me that he said—this was this morning she told me this—she said he told her to go on to sleep, he wanted to go downstairs and talk to me. But I think so much conversation between Mr. Reynolds and myself could be explained. I had gone to work for him the past Monday and was in his employment.

McMICHAEL: After they came in here, then he came back downstairs?

WALKER: Yes, sir.

McMICHAEL: How long did you all stay down there?

WALKER: He sat down there for some time and talked to me.

McMICHAEL: Then what happened, what did he do? Was Mr. Reynolds disturbed at that time?

WALKER: What do you mean by disturbed?

McMICHAEL: Was there anything about his conduct or demeanor, his manner, his talk, his speech?

WALKER: Mr. Reynolds at all times, regardless of the situation, was practically the same; whether he was worried or happy, you never could tell by his reaction.

McMICHAEL: Then there was nothing in his manner in any way that would put you on notice of anything out of the ordinary in his manner?

WALKER: No, sir.

McMICHAEL: Then when he started upstairs the last time, what time was it then?

WALKER: Well, that was within ten minutes of the shooting, the last time.

McMICHAEL: What did he say to you when he left?

WALKER: When he left he said something—"You needn't bother about leaving a door unlocked..... I am coming back downstairs but I am going out and I won't be back." The part I can't get straight in my mind, the order of it, this last talk before he went upstairs; I can't remember straight the interval. He talked to me previously about the same thing, and then the last time, which we were interrupted, I remember, and he had given me his wallet and I had placed it beside the cushion, and someone walked in, but I can't get that straight.

McMICHAEL: He gave you the wallet, then, before all of the guests had left?

WALKER: Yes, sir.

McMICHAEL: Instead of just as he had come up the steps the last time?

WALKER: Yes, sir.

McMICHAEL: What did he say to you when he gave you the wallet?

WALKER: He told me—he said "You can have that," in such a manner that I took it to mean I hadn't been paid for my week, and that was my pay, which I tried to joke off with him, saying, "Thanks," and tossing it around.

McMICHAEL: Then when he started up the steps, did he say anything to you about closing the house?

WALKER: No, but in the past few nights I had always locked up the house.

McMICHAEL: What did you do this night?

WALKER: I proceeded to do the same thing.

McMICHAEL: How long were you in locking up the house?

WALKER: Much longer than usual, being as I was waiting for Mr. Reynolds' return. I didn't want him to find me sitting there waiting for him, and I continued to take time and kill time locking up the house.

McMICHAEL: How long would you say you were down there before you heard any commotion, after he came upstairs?

WALKER: Ten minutes, I would say.

McMICHAEL: Then what did you hear?

WALKER: I heard Miss Yurka calling for me. She was coming from the west end of the house.

McMICHAEL: You didn't hear a shot?

WALKER: I heard what I thought at first was a shot, but it went through my mind "That is not loud enough for a pistol shot."

McMICHAEL: Did you hear a woman scream?

WALKER: Miss Yurka called me and said she heard someone scream, and immediately after that I heard someone scream.

Walker then told how he had found Smith on the bed and how he and Blanche and Libby had carried the body downstairs. He described the position of the body across the bed, the feet hanging off on the window side. McMichael asked him if he had seen the gun.

WALKER: No, sir. I never did see the gun. . . .

McMichael then asked Walker what Libby had told him about her side of the story.

WALKER: I asked her to tell me exactly all she knew about it, this morning. She said she was sleeping out here, but I had the impression previously she was in her own bed, but she told me she was out here, and she waked, at the same time hearing a pistol shot and Smith crying "Lib," and at that he fell right across her.

McMICHAEL: Did she say which side of the bed he was standing on when he was shot?

WALKER: No, but it seems like the only place he could have been standing was on this side of the bed.

McMICHAEL: And he fell face forward across the bed?

WALKER: Yes, I imagine that's the way it was.

McMICHAEL: That is what she told you this morning?

WALKER: Yes.

McMICHAEL: Then when you were over at the hospital you talked to Maginness and J. T. Barnes?

WALKER: I didn't talk to Maginness in the hospital.

McMICHAEL: You talked to Barnes in the hospital?

WALKER: Barnes and myself drove back out here to the house.

McMICHAEL: What statement did you make to Barnes over there about how it happened, do you recall?

WALKER: Well, Barnes insisted to know something, and I told him as little as possible, I remember.

McMICHAEL: Why did you do that?

WALKER: I didn't see any need of telling Mr. Barnes all the details.

McMICHAEL: You told him that you thought Mr. Reynolds shot himself?

WALKER: Oh, yes.

McMICHAEL: At that time you had not talked to Mrs. Reynolds at all?

WALKER: No, sir.

McMICHAEL: Except she said Smith shot himself?

WALKER: Yes, and in the previous conversation he had practically said he was going to do so.

McMICHAEL: When was that conversation?
WALKER: When we were together downstairs.
McMICHAEL: You hadn't told us about that.
WALKER: I was only answering questions. I told my story to Mr. Scott today.
McMICHAEL: What did he say downstairs he was going to do in regard to shooting himself?
WALKER: He said "Walker, our trip is off around the world." I said "What do you mean?" He said "I am going out and end it all tonight."
McMICHAEL: Is that the statement you gave Mr. Scott before?
WALKER: Practically the same.
McMICHAEL: Didn't you tell Mr. Scott that when he threw you the wallet he said "You needn't leave a door unlocked; I am leaving and I'm not coming back'"?
WALKER: Yes, sir, he also said that.
McMICHAEL: Then he didn't say anything about going upstairs and shooting himself?
WALKER: No, sir, he left the whole impression—Smith, I always took every word he told me to be absolutely the truth, that he was going to do that, and when he said he was going upstairs and was coming back downstairs, I felt perfectly confident he was coming downstairs.
McMICHAEL: And from his manner and talk you were confident he was fixing to leave?
WALKER: Yes, sir.
McMICHAEL: And that was the reason you were waiting, killing time, to try and stop him.
WALKER: Exactly.
McMICHAEL: Why did you think, then, he was going to come up here to kill himself?
WALKER: I didn't think he was coming up here to kill himself. When I knew that he had shot himself, from my conversation there wasn't but one thing in my mind, that he had committed suicide, from this conversation with him.

McMICHAEL: What was the reason for being so anxious to get back over to the house after you were over at the hospital?

WALKER: Well, I wanted to get the wallet and remove the whiskey glasses and things before anybody got in the house. I never came back to the room. Mr. Wharton and Mr. Warnken and J. T. Barnes were with me everywhere I went in the house, and I wanted to get out of the bathing suit.

McMICHAEL: Did you make the statement at the hospital you wanted to see what was in the wallet and that there was something more you must do before you got to the house?

WALKER: No, sir. Mr. Wharton was with me when I opened the wallet. I wanted to see the wallet, and then they advised me not to remove anything that might be in the wallet, and that there wasn't anything in there but cards, and Mr. Wharton removed the cards with me.

McMICHAEL: You talked to Mr. Lasater over at the hospital?

WALKER: Yes, sir.

McMICHAEL: What was the reason you said you were afraid the police would search your room?

WALKER: I didn't say that, as I remember.

McMICHAEL: Didn't you say that to Mr. Lasater?

WALKER: No, I said the door was wide open and there was no telling who would enter the house. I didn't tell Mr. Lasater that whiskey glasses and whiskey were sitting around and I wanted to remove that, but that was the idea of going back to the house, to remove that.

McMICHAEL: You came back over here twice, didn't you?

WALKER: No, sir, only once.

McMICHAEL: Didn't you come back and then Mr. Warnken carried you over to the hospital?

WALKER: I drove Mrs. Reynolds' car back here and asked Mr. Warnken to have the back of the car cleaned up, and Mr. Warnken drove me back to the hospital.

McMICHAEL: You came back next time with Mr. Barnes.

WALKER: No, Barnes was with me when I came in Mrs. Reynolds' car, and Barnes went back in Mr. Warnken's car with me.

McMICHAEL: How did you come back the second time?

WALKER: I didn't come back the second time until next morning, after everybody was here.

McMICHAEL: You did come back the second time?

WALKER: Yes, next morning when everybody was in the house.

McMICHAEL: That was around six o'clock, was it?

WALKER: That was fully an hour or two hours after I left the hospital.

McMICHAEL: You were here when the sheriff came?

WALKER: Yes, sir.

McMICHAEL: He got here before six?

WALKER: Mr. and Mrs. Dunn took me from the hospital to my home, and I changed clothes. I laid down on the bed for a while and changed clothes and came back out to Reynolda.

McMICHAEL: Did they bring you back?

WALKER: No, I drove my mother's car and had Mr. Wharton, I believe, to send my mother's car back.

While he was at home changing clothes, his father asked one question: "Son, is there any reason to believe that they suspect you of being involved in this case?" and Walker had replied, "No, Daddy, it was just a case of suicide."

McMICHAEL: When you got back the last time, whenever that was, Mr. Warnken said something about it being peculiar that they couldn't find the gun. What statement did you make then?

WALKER: No one said anything to me, as I remember.

McMICHAEL: Do you remember making any statement about the gun at all to Mr. Wharton or Mr. Warnken?

WALKER: No, sir. I remember saying this, that my theory of the shooting was this, that when Mr. Reynolds went in my room it was with the intention of getting the gun that was in the table between my beds, but if that is the gun it wasn't the gun that was in my room. But next morning, when I was with Mr. Scott, I noticed that gun was not in my room, and I come to the conclusion Smith had gotten the gun that was in between my beds.

McMICHAEL: I will ask you if you didn't make this statement to Mr. Warnken, or to Mr. Lasater and Mr. Warnken, when he said, "It's funny we can't find the gun," you made the statement, "It's in the room."

WALKER: I don't remember that.

McMICHAEL: Do you deny that you made that statement?

WALKER: I don't remember any discussion about the gun except the gun that we discussed in my room.

McMICHAEL: Do you deny that you made that statement?

WALKER: Everything is sort of hazy on that point.

McMICHAEL: You were sober?

WALKER: Yes, sir.

McMICHAEL: Hadn't had but half a drink the whole night?

WALKER: I would naturally be sober; this was entirely all night and next morning.

McMICHAEL: You will call this the right door to the sleeping porch (indicating door on east end of sleeping porch, opening into bedroom). You went in the right door and saw Mr. Reynolds on the bed. You came out, went downstairs and phoned, came back and went through the same door, picked him up and carried him out of that door?

WALKER: Yes, sir.

McMICHAEL: And you used the right door every time?

WALKER: Yes, sir.

McMICHAEL: You don't recall at any time seeing the gun anywhere?

WALKER: No, sir.

McMICHAEL: Mr. Reynolds was very jealous about his wife?

WALKER: As far as reason for being jealous, I don't know.

McMICHAEL: I didn't ask you whether he had cause. I said he was exceedingly jealous about his wife.

WALKER: I don't know. He was scared of their happiness.

McMICHAEL: Will you answer the question as to whether or not he was jealous?

WALKER: I don't know.

McMICHAEL: Had anything ever passed between you and Mr. Reynolds in regard to intimacies with his wife?

WALKER: No.

McMICHAEL: Except this one time when he said he didn't accuse you of being intimate with her?

WALKER: Yes, sir.

McMICHAEL: Haven't you repeatedly made the statement to people here since this occurred that he was jealous of Mrs. Reynolds?

WALKER: I have said this—jealousy, to my mind, is interpreting another man being involved in it. That I didn't believe, that he thought there was any other man involved in the woman's life, but he was scared that there was going to be something.

McMICHAEL: Do you say, then, that he was suspicious of her?

WALKER: No, sir.

McMICHAEL: What do you mean when you say he thought something would become involved?

WALKER: I mean he was looking into the future of the thing. The reason I say this is because in the conversation we had in the hotel he said, "Well, even if we do go, this winter I would be from eight o'clock in the morning all day in school, and she wouldn't get away from the theater until probably one o'clock, and we would never see each other." And he was afraid something was going to break up this happiness of his.

McMICHAEL: Did Mr. Reynolds have any opposition or was he opposed to Mrs. Reynolds remaining on the stage?

WALKER: No, sir. Mrs. Reynolds had asked if he didn't want her to give up the stage, and he said, "By no means," and also in this conversation in the hotel he told me it was the last thing he would ever want her to do; that if she would ask him to give aviation up he would be terribly hurt but would do it, and it would be the same thing with her.

McMICHAEL: In this conversation in the hotel—you related that to Mr. Scott as well as you remember it?"

WALKER: Yes, sir.

McMICHAEL: And you never said a word about him being in school all day and her being on the stage half the night?

WALKER: I thought I told that. I don't remember.

McMICHAEL: You never mentioned a word about him saying he was insane or that he ought to see a doctor?

WALKER: I don't remember whether I told all that or not.

McMICHAEL: Did you tell anything about that?

WALKER: I don't remember. I thought I did, thought I told him the whole story of the night.

Even that early in the case, it soon became clear McMichael and Sheriff Scott who were more or less a team in the prosecution, were working on a theory that Ab and Libby were somehow involved in Smith's death. Certainly a strong element in their suspicions had been the discovery in Ab's room of Libby's bedroom slippers next to his bed and what was described as her sweater hanging in the bathroom. The "sweater," which was described as red and striped, sounds more like the top of the pajamas Libby had been wearing that night. McMichael picked up this line of questioning.

McMICHAEL: You never mentioned a word to Mr. Scott about Mr. and Mrs. Reynolds being in your room until after Mr. Scott showed you Mrs. Reynolds' bedroom slippers under your bed?

WALKER: I thought I told him the story then about seeing Mr. and Mrs. Reynolds go in the room.

McMICHAEL: I will ask you, after talking with Mr. Scott on the porch downstairs about two or three hours later, after being carried upstairs in Dick's room, he asked you where was Mrs. Reynolds at the time Smith threw you the pocketbook, and you told him you didn't know—is that right?

WALKER: I didn't.

McMICHAEL: Three minutes later, after that conversation, after being carried in your room, and after seeing Mrs. Reynolds' bedroom slippers beside your bed, and her sweater in your bathroom you said this: "By the way, about five minutes before Smith and his wife went to their room last night, they were both in my room, and those slippers are hers." Did you say that to him?

WALKER: Yes, sir.

McMICHAEL: And when told that you had just said you were downstairs looking up, you said, "I was, but I heard their voices, and recognized them."

WALKER: Well, there is no conflict between that and the first one. At the time I was talking to Mr. Reynolds I didn't know where Mrs. Reynolds was.

McMICHAEL: But you hadn't mentioned to Mr. Scott in your first conversation anything about them being in your bedroom, had you?

WALKER: I don't know; I thought I had.

McMICHAEL: Or had you in your second conversation, until he carried you in your own room?

WALKER: I don't know; that is the first I knew about it if I hadn't.

McMICHAEL: Do you deny that you hadn't?

WALKER: I don't know. I can't place what I told him. We went in part of the things, didn't go straight through it, came back here at one interview and that conversation at another interview, it wasn't straight through, and I don't remember which interview it was.

McMICHAEL: Did you say this: "Well, the whole truth of the matter is Smith just thought too much of that woman"?

WALKER: Yes, sir.

It is clear that from the time the sheriff arrived early on the morning of the 6th, until the afternoon of the 8th when the inquest took place, Scott and his chief investigator, his brother Guy Scott, had been busy gathering up a certain amount of evidence and a great amount of gossip and innuendo, much of which served as the basis for questions during the inquest. It must be remembered that the inquest was not in any sense an adversary proceeding; it was not a trial; there were no defendants and there was nobody to represent the witnessess, although Libby's father was present, listening intently to all the questions. The line of questioning, however, went far beyond the normal range in a courtroom proceeding and much of the questioning would have been objected to by defense counsel in an actual trial.

Scott had apparently talked to an unidentified informant who had made certain statements concerning Walker's conversation after Smith's death.

McMICHAEL: Did you say later that there was something about this affair you couldn't tell and that you would carry to your grave?

WALKER: That I said, but it was in a state of mind—I am willing to answer any question you ask as truthfully as I can.

McMICHAEL: Why did you make that statement at that time?

WALKER: I have no idea why I made that statement. There were personal things that were said in that thing that would have no bearing on this, but I will answer any question you ask me.

McMICHAEL: You knew Mr. Scott was an officer of the law?

WALKER: Yes, sir.

McMICHAEL: Doing his duty, investigating this affair?

WALKER: Yes, sir.

McMICHAEL: Trying to get at the truth of the matter?

WALKER: Yes, sir, and I gave him all the truth I possibly could.

McMICHAEL: You didn't think for a minute that Mr. Reynolds had carried his wife in your room to show her—

WALKER: She followed him in the room; he went in first.

McMICHAEL: That he asked her to come in your room to show her her bedroom slippers under your bed?

WALKER: No, sir.

McMICHAEL: She wasn't in the habit of leaving her bedroom slippers in your room?

WALKER: No, sir.

McMICHAEL: Nor her sweater in your bathroom?

WALKER: No, sir.

McMICHAEL: Had she been wearing that sweater that night?

WALKER: I don't know.

McMICHAEL: Can you give us any reason at all why, if she was in there with her husband, she should leave her bedroom slippers in your room, under your bed?

WALKER: I have no idea. Mrs. Reynolds was very tight.

McMICHAEL: Mr. Reynolds wasn't?

WALKER: No, sir.

McMICHAEL: He could have picked her bedroom slippers up and carried them out?

WALKER: That doesn't sound like Mr. Reynolds, to pick up—

McMICHAEL: Didn't he look after his wife when she would get drunk, as best he could?

WALKER: That was the first time I have ever seen her drunk.

McMICHAEL: I ask you if it isn't generally reported

and if you don't know that since she has been here she has stayed drunk practically all the time?

WALKER: No, sir, it is not true.

McMICHAEL: She drank all the time?

WALKER: No, sir.

McMICHAEL: Day and night?

WALKER: No, sir. She worked practically ten hours a day, in the morning at the piano with Mr. Vardell, in the afternoon with Miss Yurka at dramatics.

McMICHAEL: Will you say now why you made the statement that there was something you would "carry to your grave"?

WALKER: I don't know. You have to remember in that interview with Mr. Scott I had been up all night, collapsed at the hospital and had been carried away from there, and the interview with him was practically two hours after I had left my home.

McMICHAEL: What was on your mind, with a man trying to find the truth, that you would make that statement?

WALKER: I don't know, sir.

McMICHAEL: Have you any explanation to offer to the jury now as to why you made it?

WALKER: No, sir.

McMICHAEL: What was it you didn't want to tell?

WALKER: I can't think of anything I would refuse to tell now or then. I don't know why I said that.

McMICHAEL: Since making that statement on Wednesday morning, you have had many conversations with Mrs. Reynolds?

WALKER: Several conversations.

McMICHAEL: And at each of these conversations you all have discussed this affair?

WALKER: No, sir, only twice.

McMICHAEL: When was that?

WALKER: It was last night and this morning, and which we called in—I went down and called Mr. Will [W. N. Reynolds, Smith's uncle and guardian] in the first time she had talked anything about it; and I rode in town and had a talk with Mr. Will this morning, and he said during this afternoon he would like to talk to her if she would be in better shape, and I went in this morning to tell her that.

McMICHAEL: What was it, when you were over at the hospital, you wanted to tell Mr. Lasater that you didn't tell him?

WALKER: I don't remember anything I wanted to tell him that I didn't tell him.

McMICHAEL: Didn't you tell him over there you wanted to make a statement to him?

WALKER: I went out and talked with him twice for quite a while and told him everything I knew about the thing. I thought, being as he was one of the guardians, he should know everything. I called him out myself to tell him everything I knew about it.

(At this point McMichael asked him apparently non-sequitur questions which figure later in certain discoveries made by the author in researching this case.)

McMichael went back to questioning about the night Walker and Smith had spent at the Robert E. Lee Hotel.

McMICHAEL: At the hotel that Sunday night, did you ask Smith why he wanted to spend the night down there?

WALKER: I never asked Smith anything pertaining to his life or anything. If he wanted to tell me I was perfectly willing to listen.

McMICHAEL: You didn't interrogate him at all?

WALKER: I mean after the conversation had started I asked him some questions.

McMICHAEL: After your conversation down there, did he ever tell you why he went to the hotel to spend the night?

WALKER: Yes, sir, he said he was insane; he said he was going to see a doctor in the morning.

McMICHAEL: Well, was he insane?
WALKER: Not to my knowledge.
McMICHAEL: This is the first time you have told a soul about this?
WALKER: Yes, sir.

McMichael abandoned this line of questioning but returned to it the following day, when he carefully went over all of the ground concerning the stay at the Robert E. Lee again, and succeeded in eliciting some new information.

McMICHAEL: Do you remember what room was assigned to you?
WALKER: It was on the ninth floor.
McMICHAEL: Did you and he spend the night there together?
WALKER: Yes, sir.
McMICHAEL: Did he ever make any explanation to you that night as to why he wanted to leave home and his guests and go down and register at a hotel?
WALKER: He told me: "I am insane. I am going to see a doctor in the morning."
McMICHAEL: Didn't you ask him why he couldn't see a doctor from the house here, as well as starting twelve hours ahead of time and going to the hotel?
WALKER: No, sir.
McMICHAEL: He told you he was insane?
WALKER: Yes, sir.
McMICHAEL: Had he ever made that statement to you before?
WALKER: No, sir.
McMICHAEL: You didn't observe anything unusual about his condition?
WALKER: No, sir.
McMICHAEL: He hadn't drunk anything except that one highball?
WALKER: I don't know. He had a bottle of Scotch.
McMICHAEL: Before he said that about being insane?

WALKER: That was in the conversation in the room.

McMICHAEL: Had you had some more drinks?

WALKER: He had a bottle of Scotch with him.

McMICHAEL: That was after you took some Scotch down there at the hotel?

WALKER: Yes, after we were sitting there talking.

McMICHAEL: You had had how many?

WALKER: I don't imagine we had one when he told me that, hadn't finished one.

McMICHAEL: You didn't see anything out of the ordinary with Mr. Reynolds' conversations or his actions from the time you finished your drink here and got in the car and drove down to the hotel?

WALKER: Not about Mr. Reynolds.

McMICHAEL: Did you about anybody else?

WALKER: Mrs. Reynolds, when I saw her she looked like she might have been angry.

McMICHAEL: You were downstairs and she was upstairs?

WALKER: I was in the reception room. She came on down, walking very fast, and she walked straight on down there, and didn't speak.

McMICHAEL: Did she walk by you?

WALKER: She walked through the room I was in.

McMICHAEL: And never spoke?

WALKER: Yes, sir.

McMICHAEL: You judged by the speed with which she passed and the fact that she didn't speak that she was angry?

WALKER: Yes, sir.

McMICHAEL: You hadn't done anything to make her angry?

WALKER: No, sir.

McMICHAEL: And so far as you know, none of the other guests had?

WALKER: No, sir.

McMICHAEL: Mr. Reynolds was up there, and came down from the direction of that room up there after she had come down and passed you?

WALKER: Yes, sir.

McMICHAEL: Didn't you say anything to her?

WALKER: No, sir.

McMICHAEL: Mr. Reynolds didn't seem to be angry when he came down?

WALKER: No, sir. I don't know whether Mrs. Reynolds was angry, but I just presumed that from—

McMICHAEL: He said he was going crazy—what was his language?

WALKER: After we got to the room, I said, "Why are you staying here?"

McMICHAEL: If you could ask him after you got to the room; why couldn't you ask him before he got there why he was going?

WALKER: I don't know, sir.

The more Walker talked, the more contradictions he seemed to get himself into, as though he were backing up and trying to fill in his footprints. It was obvious to McMichael that if there was a weak link in "the defense" (though there was as yet neither a defense nor a prosecution) it was Walker.

McMichael ascertained that Walker himself had a gun and kept it in a drawer in his bedside table. "I looked in there once before, and I remember seeing it there, but next morning, when I was there with Mr. Scott I saw the gun wasn't there. I think it was a German Luger," he testified.

McMICHAEL: Up until you saw that gun today, you thought Mr. Reynolds had killed himself with the gun [normally kept] in your room?

WALKER: Yes, sir.

McMICHAEL: You thought that was what he and his wife went in the room to get?

WALKER: What I thought he went in to get.

McMICHAEL: You only saw him go in your room at the time he and his wife were together?

WALKER: Yes, sir, except the early part of the night before we went down to the barbecue.

McMICHAEL: You were in there then?

WALKER: Yes, sir.
McMICHAEL: And he didn't get the gun at that time?
WALKER: No, sir.

If the reports were true that both Smith and Ab Walker carried pistols in their hip pockets all the time and were shooting them off at random in the bushes at suspected intruders, it seems strange that Walker did not know that the pistol was a Mauser and not a Luger. Also there is considerable mystery about the location of Walker's missing pistol; it never turned up.

McMICHAEL: Mr. Walker, if Dr. Johnson, Dr. Hanes, Mr. Lasater, Mr. Barner, and the rest of them swear you were practically drunk, what do you say about that?
WALKER: No, sir. I was far from even being drunk. I think any of the house guests, from Miss Yurka who was dead sober, all those at the last part of the party, would say that I was practically dead sober.
McMICHAEL: Well, you were almost drunk when you were talking with the sheriff the next morning after six o'clock?
WALKER: No, sir.
McMICHAEL: You were just as sober as you are now?
WALKER: Yes, sir.
McMICHAEL: Yet you can't remember the things and the times you told the sheriff, and what you told him?
WALKER: No, sir, I don't remember the exact time.

McMichael dismissed Ab Walker after a few more routine questions, and the room fell into a dramatic silence as Libby, still shaken and semi-comatose, was called to the stand.

15
Libby's Version

For her appearance at the inquest, Libby was dressed in a stunning white pleated negligee, her lustrous black hair tied back with a matching ribbon. McMichael asked a few questions concerning Libby's activities at Reynolda until Monday, then led her up to what everybody was waiting to hear—the widow's version of the tragedy.

Despite her weakened condition, she answered the assistant solicitor's questions in a reasonable and coherent fashion until McMichael got to the heart of the matter. Then she launched the first bombshell of what was to be a long day of surprises.

McMICHAEL: On last Tuesday, Tuesday of this week, did you spend the entire day here?

LIBBY: I spent the entire day here, but I don't remember—I was asking Miss Yurka this afternoon if we worked together, because I don't remember that day at all since the time I woke up.

McMICHAEL: You don't remember Tuesday at all?

LIBBY: No.

McMICHAEL: You don't remember anything you did?

LIBBY: No, I don't know if I took a piano lesson. I usually took a piano lesson from Mr. Vardell.

McMICHAEL: Do you remember what you did on Monday previously?

LIBBY: Yes, that was the Fourth of July. I remember everything I did.

After some further questions, McMichael went back to the question of Libby's memory.

McMICHAEL: You remember distinctly and clearly what took place on Monday?

LIBBY: Yes.

Asked if she could in any way account for Smith's strange mood on the fourth, Libby recalled that Reynolds during part of the reading was seated in a chair near the lounge where Libby was listening to a portion of the play being read by Blanche Yurka.

"I put my head on Smith's knee," Libby said, "because he was sensitive and I wanted to show him by every gesture that I did love him. He drew his knee away."

A few minutes later, Smith went up to his room and Libby rushed to join him. She asked him what the matter was and she testified that he replied: "'You shrank from me!'"

"No, darling, I didn't shrink from you," she said.

"'Libby,'" she quoted Smith as saying, "'if you did not shrink from me, I must be crazy. I see things that are not true and I make you unhappy.'"

"We used to have arguments about his saying he made me unhappy, because it wasn't true." Libby testified. "And that day he repeated, 'I know I am going crazy and I'll have to get my head examined.'"

She added that before he left with Ab for the Robert E. Lee Hotel that evening, they had consumed at least a half bottle of whiskey while talking "about different things."

McMICHAEL: You do not remember anything that took place on Tuesday?

LIBBY: I don't remember anything that happened Tuesday or anything that happened the next day.

McMICHAEL: You were feeling all right when you went to bed Monday night?

LIBBY: Yes.

McMICHAEL: You do not recall getting up, waking up, Tuesday?

LIBBY: No, I don't remember any of that day. The last thing I remember is Monday night.

McMICHAEL: So that you have no recollection at all of anything that happened after you went to bed Monday night until when?

LIBBY: The last thing I remember, and it is just a flash, is hearing my name called and looking up and seeing Smith with the revolver at his head, and then a shot, and after that I don't remember anything.

McMICHAEL: And that is the only recollection that you have from Monday night. Then what other event since then do you first remember distinctly, with the exception of that flash?

LIBBY: I remember being here.

McMICHAEL: When was that, do you recall?

LIBBY: I don't know what day it was.

McMICHAEL: How many days prior to today—was it yesterday or the day before?

LIBBY: It seems like yesterday—yesterday you arrived, didn't you? [Speaking to her father] I remember before you arrived because I remember them saying that you all were coming, but it is all a blur, that whole—after that.

McMICHAEL: Can you account in any way for the fact that you do not remember anything that took place on Tuesday?

LIBBY: No.

McMICHAEL: You didn't take any medicine of any kind on Monday?

LIBBY: No, I don't think so. I never do. I usually get up and go downstairs and practice the piano, and I have a lesson and we have lunch usually, and then we go out under the trees and work, but I don't remember any of it. Miss Yurka was telling me what we were working on this afternoon, what we were doing that afternoon.

McMICHAEL: You didn't drink anything on Monday?

LIBBY: No.

McMICHAEL: Or Monday night?

LIBBY: No.

McMICHAEL: So then there was nothing unusual about the day Monday at all?

LIBBY: No.

McMICHAEL: No accident happened to you?

LIBBY: No.

McMICHAEL: And the only recollection you have of Tuesday is a flash of your husband with the pistol?

LIBBY: That is the only clear thing.

McMICHAEL: Do you recall where you were?

LIBBY: Not clearly, but I am so used to sleeping on the sleeping porch, I sort of imagine I was sleeping out there.

McMICHAEL: You have no clear recollection as to where you were or who you saw that day?

LIBBY: No.

After some questions about the party plans, McMichael returned to the question of Libby's relationship with Smith.

McMICHAEL: You and your husband never had any differences?

LIBBY: We were terribly happy.

McMICHAEL: You never had had any differences at all—I mean by that, you never had had any disputes?

LIBBY: No, no big ones at all.

McMICHAEL: So far as you know, he was happy?

LIBBY: I know he was.

McMICHAEL: Do you know about a pistol being in the house?

LIBBY: Yes.

McMICHAEL: Where was it kept, if you know?

LIBBY: Well, usually it was kept on the right hand side of the bed on the sleeping porch. There were two little marble tables. I used to sleep on the left hand side and Smith on the right hand side, and I would have the water over there, and he kept that pistol there because we had been hearing footsteps and he was always worried, so he would either get up at the window with the pistol or else he would go downstairs and find the night watchman. Several times we heard them, and the pistol was kept right there.

McMICHAEL: Do you recall where it was Monday night?

LIBBY: No, I don't remember whether it was there or not.

McMICHAEL: You don't remember whether it was in its usual place on Monday night or not?

LIBBY: No, I don't know.

McMICHAEL: The only recollection you have at all of Tuesday was that blur, and you think it was, perhaps, in the bedroom?

LIBBY: Yes. I think it was out in the sleeping porch.

McMICHAEL: Do you recall any words that were spoken?

LIBBY: That's all I remember, "Libby," that name.

McMICHAEL: That is your name?

LIBBY: Yes.

McMICHAEL: Do you recall who spoke the name?

LIBBY: Well, I recognized it as Smith.

McMICHAEL: Do you remember hearing a shot?

LIBBY: I remember the pistol to his head and the shot, I can't hear the shot now, but I remember—I don't know what it was; it was just—oh, I don't know; it was just like a crash.

McMICHAEL: Do you remember, then, anything after that?

The gun that ended the life of Smith Reynolds.

LIBBY: No, I do not.
McMICHAEL: Where were you the next clear recollection you have?
LIBBY: I was in this room.
McMICHAEL: You think that was the day before your father came?
LIBBY: I think it was.
McMICHAEL: Did you talk to Mr. Walker about what had happened?
LIBBY: I couldn't remember and I was trying to piece it together. I did try to ask him what had happened, but whatever he told me I couldn't remember.
McMICHAEL: Where did Mr. Walker stay here in the house?
LIBBY: He stayed in Smith's old room, which was right opposite here.
McMICHAEL: That was the room Smith used to occupy before you were married and when he used to make his home here?
LIBBY: Yes.
McMICHAEL: Do you know about your bedroom slippers being in Mr. Walker's room?
LIBBY: No.
McMICHAEL: You have no recollection of taking them in there at all?
LIBBY: No, but Ab told me when we went upstairs he knew Smith and I went in that room, but I don't remember it.
McMICHAEL: When did he tell you that?
LIBBY: I don't know whether he told me today or yesterday.
McMICHAEL: You don't have any recollection of anything in the room?
LIBBY: No.
McMICHAEL: Do you have a recollection of anything more on Tuesday?
LIBBY: No.
McMICHAEL: You don't know how your sweater came to be in his room, in the bathroom adjoining his

room, if it were there?

LIBBY: No.

Then after some further questions concerning Libby's background and a reaffirmation of her statement that she couldn't remember anything, McMichael switched the line of questioning and produced another bombshell.

McMICHAEL: Has your health been good all of your life?

LIBBY: Yes.

McMICHAEL: You have been strong?

LIBBY: Yes.

McMICHAEL: Otherwise than the shock, is your health good now, so far as you know?

LIBBY: I don't know.

McMICHAEL: I regret to ask you this question, but it may be material. Are you pregnant at this time?

LIBBY: I don't know yet. If I am it is recent.

McMICHAEL: It is recent and you don't know it?

LIBBY: Well, I have had one symptom.

McMICHAEL: You have passed one of your periods?

LIBBY: Yes.

McMICHAEL: How long past, please?

LIBBY: From June 25th.

16

Damaging Evidence

At this point, if Blanche Yurka had been directing the drama, it would have been the end of Act One. But the sheriff and solicitor were anxious to press on. The evening was getting late and Libby was visibly fading, so they elected to call only one more witness before adjourning, Blanche Yurka. (Earlier, in the press she had been identified as "Blanche Yeager.")

It was apparent that few people in Winston-Salem or in fact on the staff of most of the tabloid journals were aware of Blanche's distinguished career, which included playing Queen Gertrude to John Barrymore's memorable Hamlet. After establishing her identity, McMichael went to work again trying to establish a motive for the possible slaying of Smith Reynolds by Libby.

McMICHAEL: Did Mrs. Reynolds at any time talk to you in any manner about any jealousy of Smith Reynolds?

YURKA: None at all.

McMICHAEL: You never have seen it exhibited at all since you have been here?

YURKA: I saw nothing but the most beautiful companionship I have ever witnessed.

McMICHAEL: On both sides?

YURKA: On both sides. In fact, I made the statement in a letter to a family I had seldom seen two young people who seemed to have such a community of interests.

McMICHAEL: You noticed nothing in the conduct of Mr. or Mrs. Reynolds that would lead you to believe there was any dissension between them?

YURKA: None whatever.

McMICHAEL: Neither Tuesday night, nor Monday night, nor any night since you have been here?

YURKA: Not any night since I have been here. If I may be allowed to expand a little, I was particularly impressed with Mr. Reynolds' geniality and friendliness on the day preceding his death. He had been a little reserved and I felt that I didn't know him, but that day I played golf with him and sat and chatted with him about two hours prior to going to bed, and felt he was more relaxed then he had been at any time since I had been down here, and I was very glad.

McMICHAEL: Since you have been here, state to His Honor and the jury what Mr. Reynolds' condition has been in regard to drinking.

YURKA: I have seen nothing but the most casual social drinking, people having a highball before dinner.

McMICHAEL: I am talking about Mr. Reynolds.

YURKA: That applies to Mr. Reynolds as well.

It was clear that if McMichael was going to make a case, it was not going to be on the basis of Blanche Yurka's testimony.

McMICHAEL: When you were down at the boathouse, what did the party have to drink down there?

YURKA: Well, there was beer being drunk. I remember that because I had asked for it, and just a casual amount of drinking.

McMICHAEL: Was there anybody on the party that night that was under the influence of whiskey?

YURKA: I should say no, to the best of my knowledge.

McMICHAEL: Were you down at the float at the time Mrs. Reynolds put her arms around Mr. Walker?

YURKA: No.

McMICHAEL: You didn't see that?

YURKA: No.

McMICHAEL: Were you out in a canoe during the evening?

YURKA: Yes, out in a canoe twenty-five or thirty minutes.

McMICHAEL: You didn't hear Mrs. Reynolds carry Mr. Reynolds over and ask Mr. Walker if she had kissed him?

YURKA: No, I didn't witness anything of the sort.

McMICHAEL: You haven't heard anything about that since?

YURKA: I think somebody mentioned it as having been discussed. I think you, perhaps, Mr. Holman.

McMICHAEL: Who did Mr. Holman say had told him about it?

YURKA: I can't recall.

McMICHAEL: Did he say Mrs. Reynolds had told him?

YURKA: I frankly can't recall.

MR. HOLMAN: Are you sure it was I?

YURKA: No, I am not even sure of that, Mr. Holman.

This exchange with Alfred Holman indicated what possibly had not been known before, that Blanche, prior to going on the stand, had apparently had some discussion with Alfred Holman. McMichael continued his questioning and continued getting what seemed at the least a sanitized version of the events of the evening of July 5th.

McMICHAEL: Who came up to the house together—did you come up with Mrs. Reynolds?

YURKA: I came up, as I recall it now, being very

careful—I think I came up with Mr. Norfleet and Mr. C. G. Hill who had been with me in the canoe.

McMICHAEL: So far as you know, nothing unpleasant had happened down at the boathouse between Mr. and Mrs. Reynolds?

YURKA: Nothing that I saw. I felt it was a particularly genial event.

McMICHAEL: Did you notice anything out of the ordinary Tuesday night or Tuesday, about Mrs. Reynolds?

YURKA: Absolutely nothing.

McMICHAEL: Just her normal self, as far as you could tell?

YURKA: Yes, a very charming hostess.

McMichael tried to establish something about Libby's absence but Blanche said she couldn't recall anything about Smith hunting for Libby during the evening at the boathouse. She did admit that when she and the other guests got to the reception room about half past nine, Libby was not present.

McMICHAEL: Do you have any idea where she was?

YURKA: No, I simply presumed she had been away in some other part of the house with some other members of the party.

McMICHAEL: Will you tell us who was absent from the party?

YURKA: I can't tell you that because the names of the people are not terribly familiar to me. I believe I can tell you who was present in the drawing room. Miss Virginia Dunklee, Mr. Hill, Mr. Walker, myself, Mr. Reynolds. I am not sure about Mr. Maginness; he was there part of the time but I am not sure whether he was there the entire time I was there.

McMICHAEL: How about Mr. Shepherd?

YURKA: I believe he was there.

McMICHAEL: How about Mrs. William Vaught, Mary Louise Collier?

YURKA: I don't recall her being there.
McMICHAEL: She was the only lady that had a bathing suit on?
YURKA: Yes, as nearly as I recall, she was not in the drawing room with us.
McMICHAEL: At no time in the two hours?
YURKA: No, in fact, I think I can be positive about that.
McMICHAEL: So Mrs. Reynolds still had not come in when you retired?
YURKA: I don't know whether she had come in, whether she had retired—I gave it no thought.
McMICHAEL: You didn't think she would retire and leave all the guests downstairs?
YURKA: I frankly didn't give it any thought. I am in the habit of retiring before anybody else, and when I find myself getting sleepy, I excuse myself and go to bed.
McMICHAEL: She is not in the habit of retiring and leaving the guests downstairs?
YURKA: No.
McMICHAEL: It didn't disturb you, the fact that for the two hours you were in the reception room you didn't see her?
YURKA: No, I never gave it a thought.
McMICHAEL: In fact, during the whole evening you saw nothing that would attract your attention, no detail of any kind that might raise a question in your mind about anything?
YURKA: No, none whatever.

McMichael now rehearsed the story of the carrying of Smith down the hall, down the stairs and to the car, with insistent emphasis on the quantity of blood and where it fell during the proceedings. Obviously there was something about this that disturbed the prosecutor's office and the sheriff.

McMICHAEL: When you got to the hospital you stayed with Mrs. Reynolds?

YURKA: Yes.

McMICHAEL: Did you discuss how this thing happened?

YURKA: No. Mrs. Reynolds was in no condition to discuss it; she was frightfully hysterical.

McMICHAEL: Did you discover the odor of alcohol on her at that time?

YURKA: No.

McMICHAEL: Could you tell that she had been drinking?

YURKA: No.

McMICHAEL: You can tell when people have been drinking?

YURKA: I think I can. I have seen as many as most people, unfortunately.

McMICHAEL: If she had been drinking you could have told it?

YURKA: I am sure of it.

She wasn't any more helpful when describing Walker's situation in regard to drunkenness.

McMICHAEL: What was Mr. Walker's condition in regard to drinking?

YURKA: He seemed quite sober to me. He sat in the drawing room with Mr. Reynolds and the rest of us and discussed casual affairs in a perfectly friendly way. I saw no evidence of drinking.

At this point Blanche, as though to ring down the curtain on act two of one of her classic tragedies, produced a bombshell of her own.

YURKA: I don't know whether this is of any interest—in fact, I think it will be of very great interest to you—but about Friday or Saturday—I am not accurate at all—Mr. Reynolds, we were all standing reading the family Bible, and Mr. Reynolds at the end of it picked up a pen and wrote what seemed to me a curious thing.

McMICHAEL: The date of birth of Zachary Smith Reynolds was written in the Bible before?

YURKA: Yes, sir.

McMICHAEL: Where did he get the pen?

YURKA: It was lying on the table; we were all grouped around the table.

McMICHAEL: Where was the Bible?

YURKA: On the long refectory table.

McMICHAEL: Downstairs in the reception room?

YURKA: Yes, in the reception room.

McMICHAEL: He wrote in there what?

YURKA: As nearly as I can remember, something to the effect: "and died of old age shortly thereafter." And Mrs. Reynolds was very shocked and hurt at it, and I saw her face change and heard her say, "Smith, I don't think you should have done that."

McMICHAEL: You just thought he was playing?

YURKA: Yes, I thought it was a joke in bad taste. It is only in looking back at it that it seemed to be a rather quaint form of joke.

The jury rustled like aspen leaves in the wind over the implication of Blanche's statement that Smith had indicated a strong death wish so shortly before his demise.

McMichael quickly changed the subject, trying desperately to establish that Libby had been lying about drawing a blank all day Tuesday.

McMICHAEL: As a matter of corroborating what Mrs. Reynolds said about it, what did she tell you this morning or yesterday as to what her recollection was about how it happened?

YURKA: Well, I have been rather careful—not careful, but I have been rather loath to question Mrs. Reynolds, because she was in a frightfully hysterical state, and it seemed almost inhuman to open the matter up with her, so that I didn't discuss it, never opened the subject at all.

McMICHAEL: She did with you, didn't she?

YURKA: Sometime within the last day, I am not perfectly accurate about when it was, she said—I am trying to think what she said exactly—I don't believe I have ever heard her relate to me the procedure of events.

McMICHAEL: What I want to get, as a matter of corroborating her and Mr. Walker, is what she said and anything about what happened Tuesday night before she came upstairs.

YURKA: No, she said nothing whatever about that.

McMICHAEL: Did she say anything about what happened over at the hospital, did she discuss that with you at all?

YURKA: No.

McMichael tried another tack.

McMICHAEL: Have you discussed this since it happened with Mr. Walker?

YURKA: No, I have not. I have frankly preferred not to get involved in the discussion. I knew what my relation to the situation was, knew exactly what had happened, and thought it might be a little easier for me if I didn't become involved. The thing that happened was seemingly so clear to me, that Mr. Reynolds had committed suicide on, to me, some utterly unexplainable impulse, and I frankly felt that it would be easier for me if I didn't make any inquiries, so I can say quite honestly that I have not.

McMICHAEL: You four were the only ones here in the house at that time.

YURKA: Yes.

McMICHAEL: I believe there was one person sleeping, the tutor, instructor?

YURKA: That I couldn't tell you.

McMICHAEL: You mean to say that although you and Mr. Walker have been here in the house since then, that you all haven't discussed how it happened or what occurred?

YURKA: Well, I haven't, no.

McMichael returned again to the question of the blood. It was now clear that what bothered the sheriff and McMichael was the fact that no blood had been found on the corridor or on the stairs between Smith's room and the outside, yet copious blood had been found in the car and in the hospital. But Blanche indicated that it was very possible that the blood had clotted while they were carrying Smith downstairs and that besides, much of it had been absorbed by Libby's negligee and Smith's bathing suit.

McMichael then returned to the question of Mary Louise Vaught and her absence during those crucial hours.

McMICHAEL: You said that in the time you all were sitting in the library, Mrs. Vaught was not in there with you?

YURKA: That is my recollection.

McMICHAEL: I will ask you if you don't know Mrs. Vaught was up here in the room at the head of the steps, dead drunk?

YURKA: I certainly don't know that.

McMICHAEL: Didn't you see them carry her up there and put her to bed?

YURKA: No.

McMICHAEL: You are quite positive neither Mrs. Reynolds nor Mr. Walker were drinking in excess?

YURKA: I am positive about Mr. Walker. Mrs. Reynolds, at the time I saw her down at the boathouse, was certainly not drinking.

McMICHAEL: You saw her again on the way to the hospital?

YURKA: Yes.

McMICHAEL: You say then she was not under the influence of liquor?

YURKA: I should say she was not. She was under the influence of terrified emotion and highly hysterical.

McMichael concluded the day's proceedings with some unsuccessful questions concerning any knowledge Blanche might have about why Libby's sweater and slippers were found in Walker's room, but got no further with that than he had with the questions about drunkenness. It was now getting dark and it was clear that Libby and even some of the jurors were getting exhausted. Reluctantly, McMichael called a halt to the proceedings with one more question, a question relating to the whole prosecution theory of the case and one that has not been made public until now. But this should await a further exposure of the prosecution's case. The hearing was adjourned until nine o'clock the following morning.

And now the prosecutor, as though frustrated by the enforced secrecy of the inquest proceedings, had a bombshell of his own. Ab Walker, he announced, was to be held in the county jail pending the end of the inquest as a material witness and Libby Reynolds was to be regarded as in arrest in quarters at Reynolda.

Frustrated newsmen who had been barred from the first day's hearing raced to the State Capitol in Raleigh and got a court decision that a coroner's inquest had to be public and so, from that point on, the inquest was open to the press. But it appears that all of the transcripts of the first day's hearing were not made available and newspapermen had to make do with informal reports from the various witnesses they could reach. Not all of the testimony made it into the papers that day, particularly Libby's statement that she might be pregnant, which certainly would have appeared well up in the story had it been known.

Small-town politics had already entered the picture. All of the county officials, to some extent, were beholden to the Reynolds family for their jobs. Sheriff Scott and assistant Solicitor McMichael apparently got it fixed in their head that the Reynolds family would be pleased to see the "Yankee Jewess" get what was coming to her. They didn't for one moment believe her story of blacking out and there was much gossip about the town concerning

Libby and Ab Walker, none of it confirmed. Scott and McMichael paved the way for their case by leaking damaging gossip and innuendoes to the press, including the statement that Smith's wound in the right temple was highly suspicious, since Smith was left-handed.

After the first day's hearing, Solicitor Higgins was asked whether it had been determined whether Smith was right or left-handed. He said that the question had not yet been asked. Higgins seemed to have a dim view of McMichael and Scott's zealous pursuit of a murder theory.

When Smith's sisters, Mary and Nancy, heard that Ab Walker was being held in the Forsyth County Jail, they made a strong protest and Walker, whom they had known since he was a little boy, was allowed to spend the night in the Robert E. Lee Hotel under guard.

Meanwhile in the county jail and in the cars in which he was taken back and forth, Ab Walker had placed a bit too much trust in some of the deputy sheriffs, some of his friends, who instantly ran to Sheriff Scott with his remarks.

He told a friend named Walter Critz that there was a secret about the case that he would "carry to his grave," and he told one of the deputies, "I don't care what happens to me, I just hope that Libby isn't hurt."

The statements were reported to the sheriff and used as the basis for attacks on Walker's credibility.

Libby, at Reynolda, was also kept under tight security and was not allowed to speak to anyone except for her father and then only in the presence of a deputy sheriff. Although this restriction was undoubtedly illegal, Holman did not make an issue of it at the time.

Because of the presence of the newsmen as a result of the court decision, the second day's hearings were held in the spacious reception room of the Reynolds mansion.

Libby emerged from the bedroom where she had been confined since Thursday, supported by her mother and her sister Marion. Her eyes were swollen from weeping and her deep tan and black hair were accentuated by the white silk of her negligee. Libby sank into a chair directly opposite her father, cast a quick frightened glance at the strange faces of the jurymen and the reporters grouped around, and began to sob in the low throaty voice which made her so famous.

Carlisle Higgins took charge of the questioning that day and was considerably less aggressive than his cohort McMichael. Despite this, Libby's testimony was constantly broken up by bursts of sobbing, during which her mother pressed smelling salts on her, while Marion, who was weeping herself, pressed her hands sympathetically.

The first witness, W. E. Fulcher, night watchman on the estate, told the court that just around the time that he was to make his midnight check, the dog began to bark and he went out to investigate. He found Libby walking up the road from the lake toward the kitchen end of the house. He thought she was drunk. Fulcher said, "She had a mighty curious walk to me. She walked one short step and a long one, stepping this way and then that way."

HIGGINS: What did you do then?

FULCHER: I went out and took the dog by the chain. She came walking up toward me. I said, "The dog won't bite you," and the dog stood up on his back feet—he was as tall as she was—and she sort of grinned and walked up beside me and put her arms around him. I said, "You will get your clothes dirty." She looked up at me and went over and sat down on the runningboard of the car.

Libby stumbled around a bit, Fulcher said, and then Smith, who had heard the disturbance, came out and met her. Meanwhile, Ab Walker called from the direction of the kitchen. Smith came out of the house and took Libby by the arm and Libby, Fulcher said, "kind of looked up at him and smiled." And the two of them walked back onto the porch.

Between 12:30 and 1:00, Fulcher said, he heard what sounded like a shot, but he didn't pay much attention to it. "Very often boys around here—they had a little .22

automatic and they would stand in the door and they would shoot around. I thought it was something like that. Didn't pay any attention to it."

McMichael took over the questioning and asked if Fulcher thought that either Libby or Walker was drunk. Fulcher said he couldn't say about Walker, but as for Libby, "She walked mighty funny; walked like I used to walk when I drank a whole lot."

Asked how Libby was dressed, Fulcher said she was still wearing her white pants and the red striped top. Fulcher also was questioned about the search for the gun. Fulcher didn't realize anything had happened to Smith Reynolds until the ambulance arrived. It apparently had passed Ab Walker's car somewhere on the road. Fulcher, who was unaware of what had happened, met the ambulance driver, who said he had gotten a hurried call to come out to Reynolda. Fulcher said, "There ain't nothing wrong; Smith has just gone to town, I reckon. The car is gone." "Well," said the attendant, "that is a pretty way to do, call us out here and don't need us." And he slammed back into the ambulance and took off. But Fulcher now, looking around the room and noticing that the doors were all open, got worried and phoned Stewart Warnken, the estate superintendent. Warnken came right over and, with Fulcher, they made a search of the house. They came into the porch room: "I had my flashlight in my hand and had it turned on," Fulcher explained. ". . . he [Warnken] looked in and I stuck my head in. I said 'Good night, look at the blood on the bed.' And I went all along, all over the floor. Warnken said, 'You can look at it, I don't want to see it.'"

Fulcher meanwhile, his flashlight in hand, walked all around the bed, looking at the bloodstains, trying to figure out their origin. He told the prosecutor that he had looked all around the floor at the bloodstains with his flashlight and that the light in the room was also on.

"Did you see any pistol?" McMichael asked.

"No, sir," Fulcher answered.

Much was made of this later, but it should be pointed out that at this point Fulcher had no reason to be looking for a pistol, since he had no idea why the bloodstains were on the bed and the floor.

Walker was put back on the stand and McMichael led him over his original testimony, trying to find some discrepancies. He found a few details which Walker had neglected to tell about the day before but nothing of deep significance.

Walker testified that he and Jim Shepherd had finished putting Mary Louise Vaught to bed upstairs and they heard the dog barking at Libby outside. "Mrs. Vaught was very much under the influence of whiskey, wasn't she?" McMichael asked.

"Yes, sir," Walker replied.

"And so was Mrs. Reynolds?"

"Yes, sir. Mrs. Reynolds was not as much though, as Mrs. Vaught."

"Who else in the party was under the influence of whiskey?"

"Those I remember were the only two people who seemed to be."

Next Warnken took the stand and told the court that after having gone through the room with Fulcher, Deputy Sheriff A. T. Barnes came up and told him what had happened and they went to the sleeping porch a second time, this time at Barnes' suggestion to see if the gun could be found.

"Did you find it?" McMichael asked.

"No, sir, we didn't see it," Warnken said.

Shortly after this, Warnken said, Ab Walker returned from the hospital. "We came on upstairs and Ab went in his room and changed his clothes."

Having taken another look in the room, Barnes, Warnken and C. A. Wharton, one of the groundskeepers on the estate who had also arrived, went downstairs to the reception hall, leaving Ab alone on the second story. After Walker had changed clothes, he asked Barnes to drive him back to the hospital. Wharton went along.

"When was the statement made by you or Barnes, if any, that it was peculiar that you couldn't find the gun?"

McMichael asked.

"I don't recall that that statement was made," Warnken answered. "But on the way back to the hospital with Barnes and Ab Walker, Barnes inquired, 'I wonder where the gun was.'"

"What did Walker say?" McMichael asked.

"Walker said the gun was up here in the room."

This was a telling point for McMichael because it established that after several searches nobody had seen the gun but that Ab Walker had certainly had an opportunity to get into the sleeping porch and replace it if he had, perhaps, removed it earlier.

Sometime later, after dropping Ab Walker off at the hospital, Warnken returned and when Dr. Fred Hanes and Deputy Sheriff Barnes got back, the three men made another search of the room. At this point, Smith's guardian, R. E. Lasater, had arrived and he joined them.

"Did you find the gun that time?" McMichael asked.

"Yes, sir," Warnken said.

On further questioning, he indicated that the gun was found on the rug in one corner, lying at an absolute right angle to the rug, with the barrel parallel to one side and the grip to the other. By this time it was daylight—about 6 A.M.—and the gun was clearly visible.

After finding the gun, Warnken said, they continued to look around the house, trying to piece together the events of the evening. Downstairs, they found a half-gallon jar of moonshine about half full and a bottle with "what looked like a little gin in it." Also, Warnken said, they made another find. There were two pieces of clothing on the downstairs sofa.

"What were they?" McMichael asked.

"Two pieces of white clothing, one of them possibly a pair of pajama pants," Warnken said. "I picked them up, put them on the edge of the sofa."

It now began to appear that Libby's clothes were found scattered everyplace in the mansion except in the room she shared with Smith Reynolds.

A. C. Wharton, the groundskeeper, was put on the

A veiled Libby at the Wentworth courthouse. Holding her hand is her father.

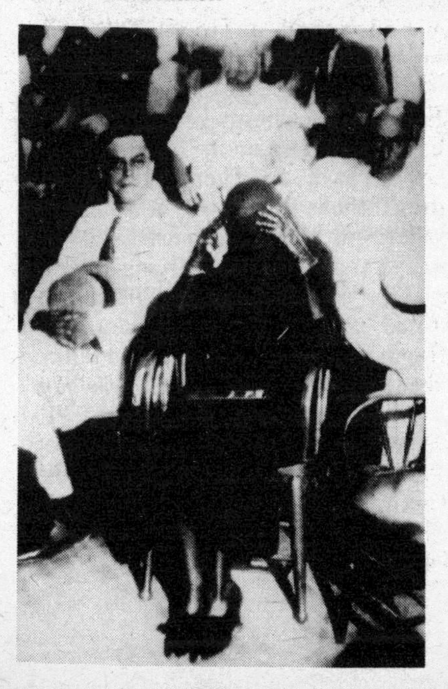

stand next and established that he was the one who actually found the gun.

"Did you have any trouble locating the gun the last time you were in there?" McMichael asked.

"I stepped on it as I went in . . . I said, 'Here it is.'"

"Do you have an opinion satisfactory to yourself as to whether or not that gun was there in that position at the time you and Mr. Barnes searched that room?" McMichael asked.

"I don't think it was there," Wharton said.

But what they did find, he testified, were some smears of blood on the doorjamb leading to the bathroom of the Reynolds suite and inside the bathroom door. One of the jurors, when shown the actual bloodstains, seemed quite curious. "Do you think," he asked, "that the doorjamb has tried to be washed off?" "Yes, sir," Wharton said, "since I was in here that morning."

"It was very distinct then?" the juror asked.

"Yes, sir."

"What sort of smear was it?"

"It looked like somebody's hands or a towel. There was a towel I think hanging here behind the door with quite a little blood on it."

Sheriff Scott testified that when he arrived about seven o'clock, he found the pistol lying up on the bedside shelf. Apparently at least several of the searchers had handled the pistol before, putting it there. Since everybody at that point was assuming that Smith had committed suicide, presumably nobody gave thought to preserving fingerprints on the gun. The empty cartridge from the automatic, Scott testified, was found behind one of the french doors. Some fragments of the steel-jacketed bullet were found on the bed. But the bullet itself was not located.

"The only place we could find where the main part of the bullet left the room," Scott said, "was a hole in the screen here on this south side of the porch."

"How high from the floor?" McMichael asked.

"About six and a half feet."

My Girl has turned me down. Good bye forever
Give My love to Mary, Virginia
Nancy Dick etc. Good bye
cruel world. Smith

A portion of Smith Reynolds' "will," written when he was 16, presented as evidence of his "suicide complex."

McMichael, who had been working out a murder theory with Scott, asked one of the key questions. "Sheriff, could a man five feet, eleven inches tall, standing on the right side of the bed, at the foot, facing the foot, with a bullet entering here, taking this line of flight, entering his right temple and exiting two inches behind his ear here—could a man standing in that position and a bullet fired that way, have punctured that hole in that screen?"

"Not if he was standing in an upright position," Scott said.

"Do you have any opinion satisfactory to yourself, had a man been standing on the south side of the bed facing the head, and had fired a gun into his right temple, whether or not a piece of the shell that went through his brain could have gotten in that position on the bed?" McMichael asked.

"No, sir. In my opinion it could not have."

"Have you an opinion satisfactory to yourself as to how that bullet got on that bed?"

"By this piece of steel being found here where it was," Scott said, "in the center of the bed within six inches of the head of the bed, would indicate to me that the shot was fired at that side of the bed, on the north side of the bed."

"At the head or the foot?"

"In my opinion, it would be nearer the head than the foot," Scott answered.

At the time, apparently neither the sheriff nor his deputy noticed a peculiar dent in the heavy iron enameled antique headboard.

Scott then testified to the story that Ab Walker had told of Smith's suicide and explained how he had gotten his bathing suit all bloody.

"I asked him where the bathing suit was and he said it was over in his room..... I said let's go over and look at the bathing suit. We went over there and when we walked in the room there was a pair of bedroom slippers sitting about middle ways beside the bed..... The bathroom door was open and inside of the bathroom was a striped sweater, a woman's sweater, just a light sweater. Walker said, 'By the way, I forgot to tell you that about five minutes before Smith and his wife went to their room, they were in my room,' and I said to him, 'You told me you were downstairs locking up when Smith came up.' He said, 'Well, I was but I heard their voices and recognized them.' I said to him, 'You also said that you didn't know where Mrs. Reynolds was when Smith came upstairs,' and he didn't make any reply to that, except he said, 'Well, the truth of the matter is, Smith thought too much of that woman.'"

Blanche Yurka was called to the stand again to describe the carrying out of the body. She gave a touching bit of evidence in Libby's favor. Libby, she said, still hysterical and distraught over the death of her husband, had asked Blanche to see if she could go to the room and get his shirt or his passport. "She said she wanted something that he had had next to his body, something that touched him."

Deputy Barnes' wife, who was on the scene now, went up to the room and brought out a logbook of his and Libby said, "No, that is not it." Finally Blanche went up and brought back one of Smith's slippers.

"While you were up there did you go in the bathroom?" McMichael asked.

"I went in the bathroom, yes."

"Did you wash any blood off the doorjamb in there?"

"Oh, no, sir."

"Did you see any there?"

"No, sir."

Now McMichael read Blanche the family Bible in which she had previously testified, Smith had made his notation several days before. McMichael read the entry. "'Zachary Smith Reynolds was born on Sunday morning, November 30, 1911, at ten minutes after five o'clock'—this is shown in the old ink, isn't it?"

"Yes."

"Added to that in a different handwriting: 'but he died of old age shortly thereafter.' That is the entry you are talking about?"

"Yes, sir."

This, too, had to be helpful to Libby as it supported her statement that he had been morose and suicidally inclined for some time.

Kramer, the tutor who had slept through the entire affair, was put on the stand, and had nothing much to contribute except for one point. He was asked by Coroner Dalton, "Do you know whether he was left-handed or right-handed?"

"He used to write with his right hand," Kramer replied.

"Did you play golf with him?"

"No, I don't play golf."

"Tennis?"

"I can't play tennis; I have a sore foot."

Disgusted with the tutor's athletic incompetence, McMichael had Kramer step down and called Libby to the stand. Solicitor Higgins, in attendance this session, whispered in McMichael's ear and took over the questioning. He led Libby over the ground of her first meeting with Smith Reynolds, their courtship, marriage, and honeymoon.

HIGGINS: Do you know whether he ever talked to any lawyers in New York about the divorce [from Ann Cannon]?

LIBBY: I know that he used to go to Joe Babcock, Charlie Babcock's brother. He said he had gone down to see Joe Babcock and wanted to make a will, and that he said, "There is no use for you to make a will; you are not twenty-one years old."

HIGGINS: Did you and he talk about a will?

LIBBY: I never talked about a will. He wanted to, but I said, "Why make a will? Please don't talk about anything like that." He said, "Suppose something happened to me in an airplane?" I said, "They told you you are a minor; why bother about making a will? It would be only a scrap of paper." He said, "In North Carolina you would never have any right to my estate." I said, "That's fine. I hope that is exactly what happens, so we can work out our own jobs and get out of the curse of that money." I didn't want him to talk about it. I hated all that. He knew it.

Libby broke down in tears for a moment at this recollection. Her mother and sister comforted her until she could testify again.

After she recuperated, Higgins led her carefully through the rest of her narrative, up to the point where she seemed to have lost her memory on Tuesday. He asked her if she could recall anything as yet.

"I don't remember the party. I don't remember canoeing on the lake. That one memory of the flash is the only thing.

"The only picture I have in my mind is Smith standing over me on the sleeping porch.

"First he called my name and then there was a flash and then that crash of the universe—just like everything falling around me. And that feeling of his head in my arms and the warm blood."

Libby broke off at this point to tell some of the things that had led her husband to brood about the unhappiness of their married life in recent months. She was worn out by this time and was about to be excused by the solicitor, when she suddenly remembered to produce two notes which she said she found the day before, among her husband's papers. She said that as far as she could tell, they had been written when he was in his teens. She was submitting the notes at this point, she explained, to show how the thought of suicide had often been on his mind even before he met her.

One note, dated June, 1927, when he was fifteen years old, was written at Woodberry Forest, Virginia, where he went to a preparatory school.

> "My girl has turned me down. Goodbye forever. Goodbye, cruel world!"

The other appeared to be a humorous "will" drawn up while Smith was still in prep school, but nevertheless gave further evidence of his morbid obsessions.

In an obviously drunken handwriting, scrawled on the back of an envelope, were these words:

> "I will my car to Ab, if he finishes it. My honor to Nancy. My money to Dick. My reputation to Virginia. My good looks to Mary (she needs it).
>
> "P.S. Hope you don't feel hurt about this will.
>
> "P.S. You think that I'm tite, but I'm not."

The word "tight" had first been written spelled correctly, but crossed out.

Libby said that after she had refused to have him draw up a will, Smith had urged her to keep these scraps of paper for her own protection.

She had been telling this in a dull tone, but in an extremely rapid fire delivery. The words seemed to tumble over themselves so quickly the stenographer had trouble keeping up with her. Now having delivered a minor Niagara of express-train verbiage, Libby seemed exhausted again.

She slumped into her chair once more, covered her face with her hand for a moment, and then, as though determined to show the court that she would reveal the whole truth—hold nothing back—she told of a scene that shocked the staid Southern jurors and almost surely disturbed the image they preferred to keep of their dashing young aviator-princeling. Again speaking at word-tumbling speed, she addressed the jury.

"Smith told me—on Sunday night, after we had gone to bed—and it happened on Monday, too—that he couldn't love me in a physical sense.

"It worried him so much. I tried to comfort him. He said: 'I've been reading in books and doctors say, too, that women can't be happy in our kind of marriage. I want you to have an affair with another man.'

"I said I would never do such a thing and he said: 'Then I'll do something to break up and ruin our marriage.'

"I said: 'That's only a small part of our love. The rest of our love is so great and so big—"

At this point, Libby began sobbing and shaking. When she finally recovered, Higgins asked gently, "That was the first time he said anything about breaking up your marriage?"

"That," Libby answered, "was the first time he said definitely he was going to break up our marriage. I told him: 'Whatever you do, I'm going to do it too. If you do anything to yourself, I'm going to do it, too.'

"I said, 'I'll never leave you.'"

She said that Smith told her, "You're a roaring success but despite that no one is more thoughtful than you. It's not humanly possible for you to give up the theater and your friends and come here to Winston-Salem and be really happy. . . . The only way for you to be happy is for me to get out of your life."

She replied, "Never, never will I leave you unless you think our marriage wasn't a success."

"He was so worried about my happiness, and all the time I was happy!" she went on. "I just wanted to save him from any danger from himself. That's true, God knows; that's true!"

All together, Libby's testimony took more than two hours and left her completely exhausted. She practically had to be carried from the stand. But those in Winston-Salem who didn't like or didn't trust Libby pointed out that of course she was an actress and was capable of simulating any emotion necessary for the occasion.

Certainly the press and probably the jurors were moved by Libby's dramatic recital. But there was some surprising and damaging evidence to come that afternoon.

Ethel Shore, the night supervisor, was put on the stand and she explained how she had washed the blood off Libby and changed her from the blood-soaked peach negligee into Blanche Yurka's black wrapper, then led her downstairs to the private room on the third floor where she could await news of her husband.

Ab Walker, she said, had insisted on coming into the room also, over her objections, to talk to Libby.

McMICHAEL: Did they ask Miss Jenkins [the other nurse] to leave?
SHORE: They asked Miss Jenkins, didn't ask me.
McMICHAEL: Miss Jenkins came out to where you were at the desk?
SHORE: Yes.
McMICHAEL: Did you all hear a commotion in the room or some noise?
SHORE: Yes, sir.
McMICHAEL: What did you hear?
SHORE: It sounded like someone had fallen on the floor.
McMICHAEL: Did you go to the room?
SHORE: Yes, sir.
McMICHAEL: What did you find?
SHORE: I found them both on the floor.
McMICHAEL: State to His Honor and the jury the condition of her apparel then.
SHORE: She had on a kimono.
McMICHAEL: Was it open or closed?
SHORE: It was closed: her knees and legs were exposed.

Ruby Jenkins, who was in charge of the third floor, followed Nurse Shore to the stand. She gave more details of this scene.

McMICHAEL: Were you in the room where Mrs. Reynolds was with Mr. Walker?
JENKINS: Yes, sir.
McMICHAEL: What did he say to you?
JENKINS: He asked me to leave the room, that he wanted to talk to Mrs. Reynolds alone.
McMICHAEL: Did you hear anything said in there?
JENKINS: I did not hear it in there, but I was almost out of the room, and I hadn't closed the door, and he told

her not to talk.

McMICHAEL: Can you give me the exact words he used?

JENKINS: I can give them to you as near as I can. He said, "Don't talk; don't say anything." We were all trying to get her to be quiet. He said, "Don't say anything to anybody."

McMICHAEL: Did you go back in the room?

JENKINS: Yes, I did.

McMICHAEL: What was the occasion of your going back—why did you go back?

JENKINS: Well, it is the usual thing when we admit new patients like that, to watch out after them, and she was smoking, both she and Mr. Walker, and I was told by Miss Shore to watch them very closely, and I did.

McMICHAEL: Did you hear any noise in the room?

JENKINS: I heard them when they fell off the bed.

McMICHAEL: Did you go in the room soon after?

JENKINS: Yes, before they got up.

McMICHAEL: Describe to the coroner and the jury what the conditions were in the room when you got in there.

JENKINS: Both of them were on the floor. Mr. Walker was on the bottom, and they were both trying to get to their feet when I came in.

McMICHAEL: How long after you heard the fall did you get in the room?

JENKINS: Just immediately. I was right there at the desk.

McMICHAEL: Did you hear any conversation between them when you went in there?

JENKINS: No, I didn't.

McMICHAEL: At the time Mrs. Reynolds occupied that room she had on a black and white—

JENKINS: Yes, sir, she had that on [referring to Blanche's black negligee] and I took that off and put on one of the hospital robes.

McMICHAEL: What did you do with this?

JENKINS: I think Mrs. Shore hung that up. I didn't see that anymore.

McMICHAEL: Was anyone else in the room when Mr. Walker first asked you to go out?

JENKINS: No, sir.

McMICHAEL: Did you comply with his request and leave the room?

JENKINS: I said, "Can't you talk to her, with me in here? I don't want to leave her in here." He said, "No, I would prefer you go out."

McMICHAEL: How many times did he request you to leave?

JENKINS: Twice. I went out once and came back in, and he asked me again.

McMICHAEL: How long after you went out the first time at his request until you came back?

JENKINS: Five or ten minutes.

McMICHAEL: Then what did he say with respect to your leaving the room again?

JENKINS: Mrs. Reynolds kept saying, "Oh, my baby, my baby!" like that; and he said, "What do you mean by that?" And when he said that, he said, "Will you please go out of the room?" And when I got to the door Mrs. Reynolds said, "Don't you know that I am going to have a baby?"

By the time this testimony was passed through the lurid filters of the tabloid newspapers covering the case the next day, there were implications added that Ab was actually kissing Libby on the floor, that they were practically in *flagrante delicto* and that they were nearly undressed. And this version of the nurse's testimony became more or less history. In fact, Libby, as the nurses testified, had been pinned into her gown and still was. And Ab was still in his bathing suit. These were the days when bathing suits had tops and bottoms. In fact, Arthur Mefford, who wrote the longest series of stories on the case, by September 9th, put it this way:

Both were lying on the floor, her clothing was awry. They had their arms around each other, and Ab was kissing her.

Possibly Mefford got hold of some source of information other than the transcript, since there is nothing in the transcript about embracing or kissing.

Questioned about the incident, Ab said that he had sat down at the foot of the high hospital bed and suddenly felt faint and fell to the floor. He wasn't aware, he said, that Libby had toppled after him, possibly in an attempt to get him to his feet. In any event, according to Ab, that's all there was to it.

But considering the state of inebriation in which they both appeared to be, according to the testimony, and the precarious awkwardness of hospital beds, it is possible there is some truth to his statement. He had been seen to faint at the funeral two days later.

There was testimony about the smudges of blood found on the door and the towel and Sheriff Scott announced that he had sawed out a segment of the doorjamb and sent it to a fingerprint expert in another city for examination.

Warnken and other witnesses who had known Reynolds all his life were put on the stand briefly and were asked whether they thought he had "an inferiority complex." They were all positive that he did not and that he was a sterling, splendid, courageous and virile young man.

Sheriff Scott said a lab report had come back on the fingerprints found on the doorjamb, but they were so smudged it could not be told whether they were made by a man or a woman, let alone be identified as those of any specific person.

Raymond Kramer, called back, repeated that he'd gone to bed early, heard nothing, didn't even know that Smith was dead until ten o'clock the following morning. He did say that when he arrived at the house after a jaunt to town the evening of Smith's death, his employer ran out and looked at him strangely, as though he were waiting for him.

"Do you want me?" Kramer asked Reynolds. "No," his employer answered. "I was just waiting for someone. . . ."

[Later two Winston-Salem citizens told Sheriff Scott that an unidentified motorist had asked for directions to Reynolda several hours before the shooting.]

All the testimony was in by 6:29 P.M. that night and the jury retired to the courtroom downtown, followed by several hundred curiosity-seekers, to make its decision. More than five hours later the jury came out and announced to the waiting press and the anxious crowd that Z. Smith Reynolds had come to his death from a bullet fired by a person or persons unknown.

17

Facing The Grand Jury

The inconclusive verdict of the coroner's inquest—neither suicide nor murder—released both Ab and Libby from custody, but it also left the status of the case open to the possibility that a grand jury, if it believed the situation warranted it, could take action. Still in her mourning black, quaking with sobs, Libby Holman, her father, mother, and sister fought their way through a crowd of photographers and newsmen to Winston-Salem station the day after the verdict was announced.

Mr. Holman told reporters that he was convinced that the death was a suicide and he thought that some of the "horrible" suspicions created by the inquest were disgraceful.

But the train bearing the Holman family back to Cincinnati had hardly cleared out of the station before Sheriff Scott was bombarding the press with further doubts. He said that he intended to call handwriting experts to check on whether the curious entry in the Reynolds Family Bible had really been written by Smith.

"So far as I and my office are concerned," the sheriff said, "the investigation is not closed. No case is closed as long as it remains an unsolved mystery. But I am not in a position to give any statement in what particular way the investigation will be conducted."

He refused to comment on the coroner's jury decision. But Solicitor Higgins seemed perfectly satisfied. "The coroner's jury, composed of honorable men, had heard all the testimony and considered it carefully. They are satisfied, and according to their verdict they do not know how Smith Reynolds met his death.

"At this time we have no additional information. We've presented to the coroner's jury all the evidence we had, and unless something additional is discovered I know of no reason why the solicitor's office will make any further move in this case.

"However, the grand jury, acting on their own initiative have the right to make an investigation and submit a presentment if in their judgment such action seems proper. Under North Carolina law, the solicitor has no right to appear before the grand jury in any case. If the grand jury should call for the records in this matter, I would consider it my duty to present them. Thus far they have not done so."

The press was full for the next few weeks of statements sometimes attributed to Transou Scott, sometimes to McMichael and sometimes to various mysterious unconfirmed sources—all tending to keep alive the sheriff's theory that Smith Reynolds had been murdered. Transou Scott told the press there were still many mystifying aspects of the case which convinced him that it was not a simple suicide.

He was bothered by the time sequence of the trip to the hospital. Walker reportedly phoned for the ambulance at 1 A.M., but without waiting for it to arrive, he drove to the hospital and arrived at 1:10. Scott pointed out that in the brief ten minute interval between the time the telephone call for the ambulance was made and his arrival at the hospital, Walker had to get up to the sleeping porch, carry

Libby being met at the train station in Cincinnati by her father Alfred and sister Marion after Smith's death.

his wounded friend to the garage, get him into the car and drive him to the hospital.

Scott himself drove from the house to the hospital at the rate of forty miles per hour and the trip took seven minutes. He also found something very suspicious about the fact that though there was blood near the bed, in the car, and in the hospital, there was none in the corridors. And despite plenty of testimony to the effect that Reynolds was right-handed, Scott kept reiterating his suspicion that in fact Smith was a lefty. But probably the biggest discrepancy, in the sheriff's mind, was the location of the bullet hole in the screen and the fact that the bullet itself had not been found.

Almost every day the sheriff had a new story to keep press speculation alive. He was going to find two witnesses who'd been asking for the house. He was looking into the possibility that Reynolds may have been shot by an outsider. Scott told reporter Fulton Lewis that he had two witnesses who claimed that Libby had discussed with them the next day the events of the fatal birthday party at Reynolda. "The alleged new evidence is considered by the State as vital in refutation of the famous memory lapse story by the Broadway singer," Lewis wrote. Like much of Scott's much-touted evidence, the witnesses never materialized.

Scott said he had been trying to assemble all possible information about the recent past of Reynolds and Libby in New York. He was handicapped by the fact that North Carolina did not provide an adequate appropriation for such investigations and so he did not have the budget to check every disturbing detail.

The sheriff implied that he was awaiting the arrival of Smith's brother Dick, who was expected back from the Canary Islands any day, and that he might be able to get some funds from the Reynolds family to continue his investigation. Two days later, Scott let drop the fact that Libby's white pajamas were found under a pillow on the davenport in the reception room at Reynolda. The presence of the pajamas was unexplained and Scott said he didn't know yet what bearing they would have on the case. A few days later he told the press that he had received a telephone call from a Captain George Maisie, claiming to have positive knowledge of a plot a year or more ago by New York gangs to come to Winston-Salem and put Zachary Smith Reynolds "on the spot."

"Captain Maisie" left his name and a telephone number with a request that the sheriff call him long distance in New York if he was interested in the information. He said he would come to Winston-Salem to assist in any investigation. But when Scott checked out the information, he was told there was no such phone number and that there was no Captain Maisie in the Police Department.

Another day Scott got press attention with the story of a letter he had received from a man who described himself as an astrologist. This man, whose name the sheriff withheld, said he went into a trance and while in this trance, saw a man drive up to the Reynolds home in a car with either a New York or New Jersey license plate. The man entered the house, he said, and shot Smith Reynolds. He fled immediately, the astrologer stated in his letter. The astrologist wrote that he had been in numerous trances and all events depicted while he was in this condition in the past had come true.

This was only one of dozens of crank letters that arrived in Scott's office every day. The conscientious sheriff tried to check out each one that was not completely in the realm of a fantasy.

Meanwhile, when the papers were not full of innuendoes from the sheriff, they were full of defenses of Libby, some of them two-edged, originating among her friends on Broadway.

"Libby never cared about another man," one of her friends declared.

Another told of the passionate devotion of Smith Reynolds to his Broadway bride. "He was not just batting around nightclubs, flirting with the town beauties when he met Libby," this friend said.

"He was a perfectly normal young man but simply didn't know love until he met Libby, which was when he was seventeen or eighteen. After he fell in love with her, he never looked at another woman."

Mrs. Cunningham was reached and had her own ideas about the case. "Poor little Libby. I do not for an instant believe that she had any hand in her husband's death. She always was a sweet little girl. She came from a fine, decent family. All this sex stuff, I don't approve of it. Even though it is purely professional. Sooner or later, it seems to overtake you and you must suffer.

"That is what I believe happened to Libby in this case. Her husband was so very young, and I understand always was a peculiar sort of boy. Libby, to him, represented sex. He had become attracted to her in her superficial role of a voluptuous girl, radiating sex. Something the real Libby was not. He did not know the genuine Libby Holman!"

Her friends also were certain that Libby had not been after Smith's money and was not concerned about the possibility then being discussed in the newspapers that she would not inherit any of it. "Libby has made $100,000 or so herself, and she isn't the kind of person who wants to buy yachts," another friend said.

Martin Sommers in the *Daily News* said that Libby's true Broadway friends "rushed to defend the Jewish singer they so much admire from the ugly specter of scandal, which reared its head after gossips on the Broadway fringes got through tearing her character to pieces at delicatessen seances . . .

"Naturally the fringes didn't spare the slain $15 million cigarette princeling and the passionate artiste who, 'Moanin' Low,' reached the highest pedestal of Broadway fame overnight.

"As a result of the fringes' seances there is the story told that both twenty-year-old Reynolds and his mate were abnormal people, there is the story that colored blood flowed in Libby's veins, there is the story that Smith Reynolds had a suicide mania and tried to end it all about every night or so.

"All these stories sound pretty silly to Tallulah Bankhead. Bankhead, the flaming Alabaman, now of Hollywood, Ernest (Tommy) Thomson, the scenario writer; Walter Batchelor, former agent of Libby and his wife Janet Reade; Franchot Tone, the actor; Mrs. Louisa du Pont Carpenter Jenney—in fact to all the friends who foregathered with Libby and Smith at Tony's and knew them best....

"Other true friends of Libby Holman went further in her defense. They said the intimation that she might have shot her wealthy husband is disproved on the face of it because she is so nearsighted she couldn't possibly hit anything if she did shoot...."

Meanwhile, Libby Holman's father announced that his daughter had gone into seclusion to escape "the morbidly curious," and made a statement denouncing the "politically ambitious" motives of North Carolina authorities. "She hopes that by seclusion she may recover her sanity and health, conceivably overcome by the grief over the loss of her loved one and by the horrors to which she had been submitted in an inquisition equalled only by those of the Middle Ages."

This statement was included in a telegram addressed to Forsyth County authorities. It read in part, "Mrs. Smith Reynolds has not disappeared and is available any time the cause of justice demands and her shattered mind and nerves permit....

"The plain physical facts surrounding the death of Mr. Reynolds, that without one word of human testimony incontrovertibly established his self-destruction, sought now to be overcome by zealous functionaries, such zeal must be attributed to self-seeking motives ignoring every canon of decency and right and humanism and justice....

"If the State of North Carolina, through these functionaries, ignores the obvious proof of self-destruction, seeking now to overcome it by garbled human testimony which was dictated by State counsel before the coroner's jury with no right accorded to counsel for the involved parties to cross-examine, despite which that jury by its verdict still primarily held that it was self-destruction, though confused by ex parte evidence which necessarily prompted the verdict that was rendered, then that great State is guilty of an injustice equal only by that of ancient times and the barbarous Middle Ages. Command me whenever you believe Mrs. Reynolds' presence in Winston is necessary."

But Transou Scott stuck to his guns. "It is my duty," Scott said, "by virtue of the office I hold to ascertain if possible the party or parties who caused Smith Reynolds' death."

He pointed out that a new grand jury would be impaneled in August and he hoped to have them reopen the question of the death of Smith Reynolds.

Following Libby's release after the inquest, Transou Scott spent his time scurrying all over the state tracing down rumors, mystery witnesses, and elusive lab reports, accompanied frequently by his brother and chief deputy, Guy Scott. He and Earl McMichael would take turns issuing veiled and often unattributable statements to the press, but Carlisle Higgins, the solicitor, stayed discreetly off stage.

Finally, despite their failure to produce any new evidence, and over the objection of Higgins, Scott and McMichael persuaded the grand jury to begin an investigation into the death of Smith Reynolds.

Judge A. M. Stack charged the jury to look into the Reynolds case "without fear or favor."

"It is hard for a solicitor to convict the rich," the jurist said from his bench. "'Big Ikes' beat the law all too frequently and the law gives them every advantage.

"Those who do not fear the law know it is feebly enforced; that crimes are not revealed; that they can leave the state. If you know any offense that has been committed in this county, it is your duty to bring forth a presentment."

A signed transcript of the inquest was presented as evidence to a jury sworn in on August 3. The only actual witnesses to appear before the jury were Transou Scott and Stewart Warnken. The testimony, of course, was secret. The jury adjourned for the evening. They listened to Scott and Warnken the next day and that afternoon issued a presentment charging that Libby Reynolds and Ab Walker "on or about the sixth day of July, 1932, with force and arms, did unlawfully, wilfully, feloniously, premeditatedly, of their malice aforethought murdered Z. Smith Reynolds."

It was a charge of first degree murder, punishable by death in the electric chair. It was announced that the defendants would be held without bail for the next criminal term of the court which was to be on October 3, unless the governor declared a special term.

The grand jury issued its presentment at 3:50 of the afternoon of the fourth, and by five o'clock Ab Walker was in jail without bail. But Libby, ill and under the protection of her family, somewhere in Ohio, presumably, was nowhere to be found. Her father, when informed of the indictment said, "My daughter is absolutely innocent.

"This is a terrible and unexpected thing. Libby told the truth at the investigation in Winston-Salem. She can prove every word she said.

"I am still my daughter's attorney. This in itself proclaims her innocence of any crime. The first thing a person guilty of such a heinous crime would have done would have been to engage prominent attorneys. She'd made no move at any time to do such a thing. She had no need to.

"Another point which proclaims her innocence is that she asked a member of the Reynolds family [W. N. Reynolds] to act as executor of the estate.

"This is a frameup and a terrible injustice to an innocent young woman."

Holman said he would not surrender his daughter to Forsyth County officials or disclose her whereabouts because she was "in seclusion in the country and under the care of a doctor and a nurse." But he assured Forsyth County officials that Libby would appear as desired at the proper time and he took a train immediately to Winston-Salem to see if he could get bond for his daughter.

A newspaper located Dick Reynolds in Rio de Janeiro, which he had reached from the Canary Islands in his ship *Harpoon*, en route to Winston-Salem. Informed that Libby and Ab had been indicted on murder charges, Richard's face, according to a reporter, "became pale." He said:

"Because I do not know the whole story, I am not going to form any opinion as to the cause of Smith's death.

"Naturally I will insist on the sternest punishment for the miscreant, if I find my brother was the victim of a foul deed."

This flowery locution is the language reported by the Universal Press Service.

Newsmen followed Alfred Holman onto the train at Cincinnati and interviewed him on his way to Winston-Salem. In the club car, he told the AP, "If I had any thought that she had anything whatsoever to do with the slaying of this boy, I would, with tears in my eyes, be the first to ask that she be punished."

Asked where she was, he simply said that she was not in Delaware as it had been rumored and was not in New York or California. When asked if she was still in Ohio, he replied, "I'd rather not answer that."

As it turned out, Libby's closest and dearest friend Louisa Carpenter Jenney had arrived by automobile at Libby's sister's home in Wyoming, Ohio a week after the inquest. On August 4, just as the grand jury was issuing its presentment, Libby was informed by her doctor that she was, as she suspected, pregnant. Louisa bundled her friend into her trusty Rolls Royce and they headed out of Wyoming, leaving word that they were en route to New York. This news reached the sheriff and he sent a man north to wait for Libby, but she never got there.

Back in Winston-Salem, Scott was in a veritable frenzy over his inability to lay hands on Libby. Ab Walker was sitting things out in the county jail where the sheriff assured the public that he was getting "no special treatment" other than the fact that his meals were being catered by the Robert E. Lee Hotel. Scott learned that Libby had gone to Wilmington, but he was a little late in getting notice to the Wilmington, Delaware sheriff. He sent him a cable saying

> I HAVE INFORMATION THAT SHE IS WITH MRS. LOUISA D. A. JENNEY OF MONT SHANNON [MONTCHANIN], DELAWARE. PLEASE CAUSE THE ARREST OF MRS. REYNOLDS AND WIRE ME."

Of course it is possible that in view of Mrs. Jenney's social prominence in that area, the Wilmington sheriff might not have been terribly anxious to disturb that lady just to please North Carolina authorities.

Alfred Holman, who told the court that his own health had been seriously affected by the tragic events that had befallen his daughter, assured the authorities, through his local attorneys, that his daughter would surrender "within a very few days." He explained that he was only hoping to spare Libby the discomfort of an arduous journey in her present condition. "She is still suffering from shock and is an expectant mother."

This caused another flurry in Winston-Salem. People began guessing who would inherit Smith Reynolds' estate, which was estimated at between $15 and $20 million. Legal experts said that if the child really was Smith's, then it would be entitled to a large share of his inheritance, possibly to be split with the two-year-old daughter that he had by Ann Cannon. However, people wondered how Libby's testimony that her husband was impotent would affect the court's belief in the legitimacy of the child. Naturally, gossip started instantly that the child might, in fact, be Ab Walker's, rather than Smith's. Of course, this could not be possible unless Ab and Libby had had an affair much prior to the date of Smith Reynolds' death just a month earlier.

While in Winston-Salem, Alfred Holman had engaged

Ben Polikoff, a tough, jut-jawed lawyer, one of the three or four Jewish attorneys practicing in the area. A spate of interest was stirred up by the arrival of the famous criminal lawyer, Samuel Liebowitz. The press descended on him with questions about the Reynolds-Holman case, but Liebowitz said that he had not been retained by Holman but was en route to Atlanta to see his client, Al Capone, and had only dropped in at the request of friends of Libby's that he knew from Broadway.

He did have lunch with Alfred Holman, however, and it is believed he gave him some good, hard advice about criminal procedure. After all, Holman was basically a securities and bond attorney.

The next day, Walker was freed on $25,000 bond and Alfred Holman assured newspapermen that his daughter would arrive within a day or so and give herself up.

Apparently on the advice of Liebowitz and the local attorney, Polikoff, Holman announced that he had engaged William Graves, a prominent attorney in Winston-Salem and former solicitor of Forsyth County, to direct Libby's defense. Liebowitz, with his keen eye for tactics, had pointed out to Holman that it was bad enough that Libby herself was Jewish, but for her to have a Jewish attorney was definitely not to her advantage.

Meanwhile, Graves and Polikoff ascertained that Libby didn't have to turn herself in in Winston-Salem, but could in fact show up at any county courthouse in North Carolina. To avoid publicity, and perhaps get away from the influence of Assistant Solicitor McMichael and Sheriff Scott, they elected to have Libby turn herself in in the small town of Wentworth, about fifty miles northeast of Winston-Salem. Wentworth was an almost deserted, former tobacco boom town. It had not seen as much excitement since the Civil War. It was, as one newspaper said, "the first tank town Libby Holman ever played or expected to play."

Libby arrived at Reidsville, the nearest railroad station to Wentworth, on August 9, dashed from the train into a car with drawn blinds and fled into the shelter of the Old

Reid Tavern. She rested for about an hour and then showed up at the courthouse in complete head-to-toe mourning, with a black veil hiding her face. Knowing that for miles around the country folk would be attracted to the area, ladies of the district church had slapped together a hastily built soft drink stand. "The Negroes came early and brought their pickaninnies," Gilbert Swan, an NEA writer, commented. "The scene found them, with mountain men and five-gallon-hatted farmers, closing in from all directions."

By two o'clock space in the tiny village was at a premium, Libby, almost invisible under her funereal black garb, dashed through the crowds accompanied by her father, Polikoff and Graves. The $25,000 bond was paid and accepted by Guy Scott, who was in Wentworth representing his brother, Transou.

Libby left the courthouse as quickly as she had arrived and despite the pleas of dozens of news photographers on the scene for the event, refused to raise the copious veil that concealed her features. Before she could be stopped by newsmen, Libby stepped, with the two lawyers, into the waiting limousine and sped out of sight. The car proceeded nine miles back to the hotel in Reidsville, where Libby spent the night.

The newspapers called it "another spectacular dash into seclusion." AP reported: "The former Broadway blues singer called on all her knowledge of theatrical effects, of swift changes of roles and costumes for the setting of her 2 P.M. dash to a retreat, such as she has occupied since the inquest. . . ."

But by this time even the national press was unfriendly to Libby. "Today," the AP reported, "mourning was not in evidence as the young widow, flanked by two young men, appeared in the lobby of a hotel here, and after making sure there was 'nobody around,' hurriedly entered a large sedan and sped away into the darkness.

"Instead of yesterday's somber black gown and heavy veil, Libby today wore a snappy sports outfit of tan, with a comparatively short skirt and a matched sweater closely molded to her figure. Yesterday's small black hat gave way to a light-colored beret. The veil was gone too, but in its place were heavily rimmed dark glasses."

The *Times* made it look even worse for Libby. They quoted the night clerk as saying, "She skipped across the hotel lobby and bounced into the waiting automobile. She gave the appearance of a young college girl instead of a widow under bond on a charge of slaying her husband."

Meanwhile, in London, Nancy Hoyt, the girl Smith had been romancing aboard the oceanliner, said that she had gone to London to blot out the memory of her love for Smith Reynolds. "I didn't even hear he had married until April. The last I heard from him was a letter at the end of last March. I never meant to give him up, but I didn't want to be a laughingstock."

Experts on Forsyth County court procedure estimated that the trial would probably be held around October 3. Without waiting, Libby returned to Montchanin to pass the time with Louisa Jenney. There she found the tranquility she so greatly needed. She read innumerable books and newspapers and theatrical reviews and took long walks through the cool and fragrant woods. And, of course, she knitted baby clothes.

On the advice of lawyers, she didn't see any reporters for the next two months, but she spoke constantly over the telephone to New York friends such as Tallulah, Bea Lillie, and Clifton Webb. In fact, Webb came to Montchanin for weekend visits several times, as did Walter Batchelor and Noel Pierce, the playwright. One reporter, Ward Morehouse, was able to see her toward the end of Libby's stay. "The most frequent caller at the Jenney country place," Morehouse observed, "was the hulking, hard-jawed, Benet Polikoff, Jewish North Carolinian by birth, who did, so far as I could make out, a lot of work and a lot of running around..... He was in charge of her case until the hiring of four defense attorneys [from Graves' firm] who represent the young widow today. They are all North Carolinians, a shrewd move, of course. An attorney from the outside—from

New York, say—would find in the event of a trial that a jury of Carolina tobacco planters can be unbelievably stubborn."

Meanwhile, Polikoff was busy trying to round up friends and witnesses who would testify on Libby's behalf. He went to New York by plane and train and, Morehouse said, "wore out considerable shoeleather in making the rounds of Broadway, digging up witnesses—theatrical personages, particularly—to take down to Winston-Salem . . . He went to 21 and to Tony's, to the Central Park Casino . . . He talked to the people that really count for something in the Broadway district." And he apparently found plenty of prominent young people who said they would not only go down to testify for Libby, but would even pay their own expenses. Two of these were young men who were at Reynolda as ushers for the elaborate wedding of Henry Walker Bagley of Atlanta to Smith's sister, Nancy.

But Polikoff also found some opposition. "Some of those whom he'd been told were Libby's most loyal friends were strangely unresponsive. Sure, they would do anything for Libby that they could. But—well, there was 'the Reynolds side.' And they didn't care to jeopardize friendship that existed between them and the Reynoldses. One young man who for years swore allegiance to Libby took to his heels—to California I think—to avoid making a possible appearance in a Winston-Salem courtroom."

Meanwhile Libby said she was keeping her plans for the future in abeyance until the outcome of the trial. Offers for her services had begun to come in already. Lee Shubert offered her a starring role in a show called *Americana* at $2,000 a week to do just one song a night. Libby laughed. Not that she wasn't pleased," Morehouse noted. "She's a working girl and there's to be a child to support, and she'll be needing a job. But—well there's the trifling matter of having to become a mother . . . If I were Mr. Dietz and Mr. Schwartz, I'd begin getting some songs ready right now."

Meanwhile both sides in the notorious case were

grinding out information for the gossip mills. Sheriff Scott told intimates, who in turn told the press, that he had evidence that Libby had tried to force Smith to make a new will providing for her future. Hangers-on in the lobby of the Forsyth County courthouse told New York writer Gilbert Swan, "Yes, we think it's right likely that Smith Reynolds killed himself. But what we want to know is, *what drove him to it*?" Scott told Swan, but not for attribution, that he was going to get key "mystery evidence" from a high official of the Reynolds Corporation. Also, he said, "there will be an old Negro servant" with other secret evidence. And, said Scott, there will be a section from "a certain door" which was sent to a fingerprint expert in Roanoke, Virginia, with results that are "highly interesting." And a "certain sketch" made by a draftsman on the coroner's jury, which was rumored to tell an interesting story of the movements that night of the major and minor characters.

But the wise heads at the courthouse pointed out that the whole story would certainly never be told because even if the witnesses would tell it, rules of evidence would block it. All of the Broadway and pre-wedding incidents, for instance, would probably never find their way into the testimony, although they might actually have a bearing on the tragedy.

However, the defense also managed to score a few points in the pre-trial skirmishing. Jim Graves told the press that he had received an anonymous letter from Charleston, South Carolina which claimed that the writer had "seen the tobacco heir commit suicide on the morning of July 6."

The writer of the letter signed it merely "An eye witness," and claimed to have seen Reynolds place a revolver to his head three times before pulling the trigger and inflicting a fatal wound. The letter said that Libby was "too drunk to know what was going on." Graves said that he would like to communicate with this writer but did not know how this was possible because there was no signature on the communication. He said the handwriting was "apparently that of a woman."

Word reached Winston-Salem that Dick Reynolds had now reached Trinidad and hoped soon to arrive in Winston-Salem. In the adjoining column of the *New York Times* was the description of a case in which a Captain W. N. Lancaster was being tried for the murder of a man named Hayden Clark. Lancaster had lost the love of an Australian aviatrix named Mrs. Jessie M. Keith-Miller to Clark. They were sharing a room together when Clark either committed suicide or was murdered by a bullet through his head. Clark's skull was produced as evidence in the case. An expert named Arthur H. Hamilton was produced to testify on the path of the bullet. Hamilton said there was every indication of suicide and "nothing in the world to give the slightest indication of homicide."

He testified that when the muzzle of a gun is held loosely against the head, powder marks generally show on the surface. When the muzzle is held tightly, the powder gases force flesh aside and leave powder and gas marks on the inner tissue, and a large swelling at the point of entry. The latter action, the doctor explained, was known as "ballooning." The autopsy in Clark's case had specified finding a balloon condition.

"Suicide," Hamilton said, "is indicated in cases where a pistol is held closely to the head in a sealed contact."

There is no way that Libby's attorneys could have avoided reading this article in the very next column at the top of the page to Libby's story. It offered a welcome parallel. The testimony of Dr. Hanes mentioned a "swelling as big as an orange" on Smith's head when he was brought to the hospital.

Meanwhile, newspapers were having a busy time reporting Libby's apparently merry life on the Eastern Shore with Louisa Jenney. The *Times* reported that she had taken "a mysterious speedboat trip" with two other women across the bay. One, according to a watchman, was Louisa and the other was an unidentified blond. "The hurried trip," the *Times* said, "took the young widow to the head of Chesapeake Bay and through the Chesapeake and Delaware Canal.

"The authorities thought it might be possible that Mrs. Reynolds might have gone to Pioneer Point, hoping to find rest and peace when her Oakington refuge had been discovered."

So numerous and potentially damaging were these constant reports of Libby's seemingly callous mourning period, that Polikoff and Graves felt compelled to issue a statement on the subject. The lawyers, the *Times* said, "emphatically denied reports that Mrs. Reynolds had been indulging in such strenuous sports as tennis and swimming or had been on shopping trips to Baltimore. They said she was taking such light exercise as her physician recommended, but was doing nothing that would impair her health." Polikoff and Graves added that they hoped that Libby would be strong enough to stand trial in October.

Meanwhile Dick Reynolds was adding to the furor by sending periodic bulletins north of his suspicions. Before he left Trinidad, he said, "I refuse to believe he committed suicide. He had more sense than to make a bad job of shooting himself with a Mauser pistol. I must clear up the mystery and make sure his memory gets a square deal."

On August 14, the *Sunday News* came out with an article by Lowell Limpus which finally openly stated the thought that had been in many minds since Libby's indictment: "CAN THE SOUTH GIVE LIBBY A FAIR TRIAL?" the article was headed. "*Nation Hopes Her Treatment Will Help Dim the Memory of the Leo Frank Case.*" The Frank case, which has since been immortalized in several books, films and television shows, had taken place in Georgia not quite twenty years earlier. Leo Frank, the Jewish owner of a Georgia textiles factory, had been lynched on suspicion of having raped one of his employees. The case had often been cited as an example of mob psychology and Southern antisemitism, led by Ku Klux Klan elements. Limpus wrote:

Down in the Deep South, they are preparing to try Libby Holman Reynolds for the murder of her husband. Columns have been recently devoted to the Broadway beauty and the millionaire youth who gave her his name, but one essential point seems to have been generally overlooked. That point is the probable effect of Libby's race and background on the stern Southerners who will sit in judgment on her.

Libby Holman is a New York Jewess in their eyes.

And North Carolina is in the Deep South; Ku Klux country with rebel antecedents where neither Hebrew blood nor Yankee ancestry is regarded as an asset. The question is whether Libby can secure a fair trial in such a community.

Feeling here is beneath the surface.

It was first noted by reporters who covered the story. They declare that there was a whispered undercurrent against "that girl from New York," amid the crowds that gathered on the streetcorners of Winston-Salem after the crime. It calls to mind the same whisperings that ran through Atlanta streets when Leo Frank was first placed under arrest for the murder of Mary Phagan.

Frank's trial developed into a legal lynching.

The eyes of the nation will watch Libby Holman with an unspoken question in the background:

"Will Libby get a fair deal?"

Her friends and family are already worried by that query. The Rialto buzzes with reports that the Broadway torch singer is being "railroaded."

Limpus pointed out that Alfred Holman's frank statements concerning the attitude of Forsyth County authorities—he had gone so far at one point of accusing Scott of seeking "political advantage" in the prosecution—had caused deep resentment not only from officials but among the public there. As soon as Libby was indicted, Limpus wrote, "public sentiment promptly crystallized in favor of Walker, the hometown boy, and against the girl from New York and her father." Two days after the indictment, Limpus noted, talk was so strong that the local paper found it necessary to plead editorially for public patience with Mr. Holman.

> "Not even the statements given to the press by the distressed and excited father of Mrs. Reynolds should prejudice any official or citizen against either of the defendants in this case," ran the editorial. "Alfred Holman is more to be pitied than condemned, for he is fighting for his child . . ."
>
> "The courts of North Carolina," Limpus concluded, "are to be given the opportunity of eradicating and in measure the blot on the robes of Southern justice left by that sensational trial and the lynching which was its sequel in the Frank case, known as 'Georgia's sin.'"

But the question remained open, and one that could have serious consequences for Libby.

Meanwhile the Reynolds clan was using friendly newspapers to sanitize the reputation of the dead man, who had been well-slandered by the tabloid press. In most articles he was characterized as "queer, effeminate, an alcoholic, suicidal and a bit crazy." Some of these innuendoes may have had more than a seed of truth in them but they did not sit very well with the surviving family.

18
Judgment

Dick Reynolds finally arrived in Winston-Salem on August 24. He exacerbated the local hostility to Libby by telling newspapermen in a brief statement in the towering R. J. Reynolds office building in the presence of Transou Scott and others:

"In view of all the facts available at this time, I believe my brother's death was murder." He added that he based his belief on a transcript of the testimony at the coroner's inquest.

"If it is I want to see justice done," he said.

"I do not think Smith was of a temperament that would allow him to commit suicide."

Asked if he intended to employ private counsel, Reynolds said that he felt that the local authorities were fully capable of seeing that justice was done.

A reporter asked Dick if he had known Libby before her marriage and he answered that they had met twice, but only in the company of Smith.

Certainly the Reynoldses had a somewhat rosy view of

their bright-eyed boy. It is probably true that Smith had been maligned in the press. On the other hand, the Reynolds family's views seem wide-eyed, to say the least.

"I can't find anybody," his brother Dick said, "who will tell me that Smith ever once mentioned suicide. Libby and Ab are the only persons who say that he talked of it.

"Smith had everything to live for. He was healthy in body and he had a good mind. It's true that he was a bit reserved, but I never thought he was given to moods.

"Smith was not much of a drinker," Dick said. "I never saw him drunk even once. He wasn't a big spender. Why we used to kid him a bit about being Scotch. The accounts of the estate prove how careful he was with money."

And they did. The tabulations showed not only that Smith was careful with money, but that Libby never got a cent from him and paid her own way on the honeymoon trip and at all other times. In fact, Smith never actually was given the $50,000 a year to which he was entitled and was somewhat noted as a tightwad except for the period when he was following Libby around the nightclubs of New York.

Dick took the opportunity to remark on this.

"Yes, he'd go to nightclubs. That was chiefly after he met Libby. He'd go to whatever nightclub she was singing in, but it was only to see her." (Actually, Libby was not performing in nightclubs at the time, but Dick had been away from Broadway for some time.)

What concerned Dick and his uncle Will was the possibility of family disgrace if it turned out that Smith had committed suicide. They seemed to accept the fact that he hadn't been murdered but preferred that the world believe that his death had been an accident.

"Maybe," Dick theorized, "he and Libby had an argument. There might have been a scuffle and a struggle for the gun. It might very well have been discharged unintentionally.

"Suppose Libby is telling the truth as far as she can honestly recall what had happened. Perhaps she was so intoxicated that she doesn't recollect a struggle for the gun and during that struggle it exploded.

"I feel very certain that Ab knows what occurred. I would like to know what he meant when he said there is something about this case he will carry to his grave. If he would tell all he knows I am sure it would go a long way to dissolve the mystery.

"Why doesn't Ab talk if he has nothing to fear? If Libby does remember what happened, why doesn't she tell us about it?"

But in his heart, Dick Reynolds did not believe Libby's story of drawing a blank.

"She was cold sober all day Tuesday and for part of that evening. She was sober when she returned from the hospital Wednesday morning, and she was sober all that day," Dick reasoned.

"Yet she can't tell us what took place from the time she arose in the moring right through to the moment when my brother was shot.... This doesn't sound reasonable to me."

Dick also made an effort to clear up impressions made by his earlier statements when he first heard of his brother's death.

"I have never said that my brother was murdered," he said. (Actually, he *did* say so in his first press interviews.) "In the only statement I have made up to now I stated that I did not believe Smith killed himself *intentionally*. He was not a suicide. I am just as convinced of this now as I was then."

Uncle Will, who was not only the guardian of the Reynolds boys but Chairman of the Executive Committee of the R. J. Reynolds Corporation, gave an interview to the *Journal's* Cowan in his office on the 22nd floor of the R. J. Reynolds Building. He, too, followed the family line:

"We don't for one minute think the boy killed himself. If his finger accidentally pulled the trigger of that gun, then it was an accident and nothing else."

He gave Cowan the surprising news that he had gotten the news of Smith's death when he was away from the city in Ohio, and on the train he had taken back to Winston-Salem, he had encountered none other than Libby's father Alfred. He and Libby's father had both spoken to her about the case, trying to find out what had actually happened.

"Mr. Holman and I tried to get her to refresh her recollections," Will Reynolds recalled. "Her father kept asking her to try hard to remember some more. It was no use.

"The next day young Walker came to see me. He had been telling Smith's sisters that there was something about this affair that he couldn't tell anyone in the world except me.

"I sat and listened to him. He went over the whole thing. Everything he told me I already knew. He had discussed all of it with the sisters, my nieces, and they had told me. I kept waiting for him to disclose to me what it was that he couldn't tell anyone except me.

"When he stopped talking I hadn't heard anything new. So I said to him:

"'What is there about this affair that you said you couldn't reveal to anybody except to me?'

"'Why Mr. Will,' he replied, 'Libby was dead drunk that night.'

"That's the last thing on earth I thought he was going to say! Everybody *knew* that Libby was drunk that night. I had heard that from a dozen people. It was no secret.

"'Hell,' I replied, 'there isn't a person in Winston-Salem that doesn't know that. You're not telling me anything. And what is there about that which is so terrible a secret that you couldn't have told it to anyone but me?'

"That's all I could get out of him. Libby had been drunk that night. Now I don't believe that is what he had in mind at all when he made the remark. For some reason he must have changed his mind about telling me. I am certain that Ab knows what did happen that night and that he intended to tell me of this when he talked to Smith's sisters."

Mr. Will also denied he had ever heard the well-circulated stories of Smith's suicidal tendencies.

"When did Smith develop this suicidal mania that Libby talks so much about?

"I talked to his first wife, Ann Cannon. He never mentioned suicide to her. He never spoke of suicide to his brother Dick or to any of his sisters.

"I can't find anybody except Walker and Libby who will tell me that my nephew ever threatened to take his life.

"I can't imagine any reason he would have to do so. He was a normal boy. He was a quiet boy—a studious boy.

"The picture that has been painted of him in the press is all wrong. He was not a rounder. He was not a spendthrift. He wasn't a heavy drinker."

The official family line was solid. Asked whether the family planned its own investigation, Reynolds assured Cowan:

"So far as I know, Mr. Cowan," Will said, "and I am in a position to know, no private investigators have been retained and none will be. We think the authorities here are capable of conducting any investigation themselves."

On the day of Dick's arrival, at midnight, in a scene like something out of a gothic horror movie, Smith Reynolds' body was exhumed and an autopsy was performed by Coroner W. N. Dalton, assisted by four Winston-Salem physicians and surgeons. The point of the autopsy was to find out where the fatal bullet entered Reynolds' head, where it came out, and to find out whether the weapon was fired at contact with the head, or from a distance. It would appear that the coroner had also read the article about the death of Haden Clarke. Results of the autopsy, however, were not released until more than a week later. They only confirmed the evidence given by Dr. Hanes. It is not certain that Richard Reynolds was even informed of the results.

While waiting for a trial date to be set, Ab stayed at his family's home on Country Club Road in Winston-Salem and Libby stayed at Louisa Jenney's at Montchanin, outside of Wilmington, where a relay of guards kept her free from the news-hungry press. The only one who got an interview in those weeks following the indictment was Ward Morehouse. She told the Broadway reporter she intended to make a bold and desperate fight "for the sake of her unborn baby—to clear herself in the murder of her millionaire husband . . ."

"I didn't shoot Smith," she told Morehouse. "God in Heaven knows that. The Reynolds family know it in their hearts. I loved Smith as I never loved anyone before or ever will again. The fullest and richest hours of my life were spent with that dear boy. . . .

"If Smith had really known that I was going to have a child, the whole terrible thing might never have happened. . . . My baby will be named Smith, of course. Boy or girl, that's to be the name."

Morehouse asked where she planned to have the baby. "I don't know," Libby said. "Not Cincinnati—not the South. Maybe in France. I feel like a man without a country." She paused and repeated the thought half to herself. ". . . a man without a country. But tell Broadway I'm not weakening; that it's my fight and I'm game. That I can take it."

Others didn't agree in this opinion. Arthur Mefford said that many of Libby's friends said that the strain would be too much. "She is bound to break," certain friends said.

Yet the whole theatrical world seemed to rally to her defense. Within two weeks after she had left Reynolda, Blanche Yurka was in the theatrical colony at Provincetown, Massachusetts, raising funds for Libby's trial.

Her attorneys, experts all, and expensive ones, were well aware of the charges of prejudice in Winston-Salem and knew them to be true. On September 16, they filed a motion to have the trial moved to Surrey County, in North Carolina, though it is difficult to see how this would have been of any substantive aid. Libby, in Winston-Salem, was still fighting not only prejudice against being a Yankee, a show business person and a Jew, but the opinion of most locals that she had somehow trapped Smith Reynolds into marrying her because of his money.

"It will be hard to convince most people that I married Smith because I loved him. There were times when I pleaded with him to get himself disinherited," Libby told Morehouse. "I told him we could get along and he knew it.

"During my married life I paid my own way. I saw nothing of any Reynolds money. Why I had—much more money than Smith had—much more. I paid my own bills, paid for my clothes. I made a lot of money on the stage.

"I guess it's a good thing. This trial will take every penny I can scrape up. I'll have a child to support and I'll go back on the stage. That's the only thing I know how to do."

The anti-Semitic suspicions refused to die. One reporter, after a chat with Transou Scott, gave his impression in a veiled statement. "It was suggested that the fact that Libby might be of the faith which ignored the founder of Christian beliefs, may have provided the impetus to carry out an oft repeated threat to commit suicide." The reporter did not identify the person who "suggested" that Smith might have actually killed himself because he found out he was married to a Jew, but in most cases, leaked statements against Libby could be traced either to Scott or McMichael.

A will that Smith Reynolds had made before he married Libby was found and filed for probate, despite the questionable legality, in view of his age. The will had been drawn up in August of 1931. According to the terms of the will, which did not mention Libby, his money was to be divided by his brother and sisters after the payment of certain specific bequests of $50,000 each. One was to Ab Walker. Two more were to Ann, his first wife and the child that he had had by her. But hardly anybody took the will seriously. Not only was Smith underage, but he would not even be entitled to get his money until he was twenty-eight. The main issue, lawyers pointed out, was the question of Libby's child. If she had an infant within ten months of the death of Smith Reynolds, the will would be invalid as the will would tend, in effect, to disinherit that child. But if Ab Walker or Libby Holman were convicted in any part in Reynolds' death, under North Carolina law, they were not entitled to inherit anything.

Libby, asked what she thought about all this, said that she was "not worrying about wills."

Transou Scott, still assiduously digging away for the evidence to send Libby to the chair, announced that he found an eighteen-inch saucer-shaped bloodstain under Ab Walker's bed. The portion of the rug containing the stain was cut out and analyzed by a chemist, but all the analysis showed was that it was human blood. Scott said he didn't find it until he had moved the bed as part of his routine search some time after the inquest.

The sheriff gave out the theory that the stain had been created when the gun, temporarily removed from the scene of Smith's death, was hidden under Ab's bed. But Scott's critics pointed out that the stain could just as well have been created by Ab's bloodstained bathing suit, when he dropped it on the floor after changing on his return from the hospital.

Two, it was discovered, could play the game of leaking evidence and soon Joseph Cowan of the *Journal* was the source of a veritable barrage of material favorable to Libby and Ab. One of the most appealing of these bits of evidence to the general public was the series of love notes written to Libby by Smith months before his death, replete with lush prose and undying declarations of love.

"All my life is a well of loneliness," Smith wrote, "only broken for a short precious moment by you."

It is doubtful that Reynolds, who was not excessively given to reading novels, was aware that *Well of Loneliness* by Radcliffe Hall, was a well-known romance on the subject of Lesbianism, considered shocking in its time.

In another letter he wrote, "Every minute that I am separated from you is a minute wasted, a minute out of my life. It is not worth the saving of a few paltry dollars or of flying in a lousy plane—to be away from you for long periods like this." The letter was written less than two months before Smith died.

These letters, Joseph Cowan reasoned, would seriously damage the State's strategy to charge that Smith made Libby his wife only because she threatened to sue for breach of promise. The revelation of the letters, Cowan theorized, would change the State's case against Libby. "Instead of saying Smith never loved Libby, they'll shift to the idea that he didn't love her at the time of his death.

"The theory now will be that Smith lost his love for Libby after his last trip to New York. That was a four-day visit the week before the tragedy.

"While in New York he learned, they'll say, that Libby had deceived him."

What the State was getting at was the suspicion that Libby became Ab's lover while Smith was away. But Ab had not been in Winston-Salem at that time. He had, as he testified at the inquest, been working at a mill in Elkin, North Carolina, and while it is possible that he could have made the trip of several hours each way for a fast rendezvous, it is unlikely that he could have accomplished this without anybody noticing the movements of either party to this putative love affair.

Cowan, who was obviously being fed by Graves and Polikoff to defuse the State's offense by shooting it down in advance, revealed another probable scenario of the prosecution.

"Branding Ab's story that Libby and Smith were together in his bedroom a few minutes before Smith was shot as a lie, the State will declare that only Libby was in that room. She went in there and took off her clothes and lay down on Ab's bed.

"So Smith walks in and sees her like that in Ab's room and the battle is on again. Libby goes to the sleeping porch and gets Smith's gun. Dead drunk, she waits for him to come in.

"Drunk as she was, far from his equal in size and

strength, nearsighted, Libby got that gun against his head and pulled the trigger. He crumpled to the floor, the State will say, and Libby picked him up and put him on the bed . . .

"She runs down the hall hysterical, as Ab, summoned by Blanche Yurka, rushes toward her. The gun is still in her hand. She tells Ab Smith has been shot. He runs in and sees it's so.

"Then he goes back to Libby. He's madly in love with her or something. Remember, there's no evidence of any of this. We're just supposing with the State. He grabs the gun and throws it under the bed in his own room. That's how the blood got on his rug. The gun was bloody."

So according to Cowan's scenario of the prosecution's case, Ab had to race back from the hospital, get that gun and put it back in the room where it was supposed to be. The prosecution presumes that's what he meant when he said he had to get back to Reynolda before the police searched his room.

Cowan, after outlining this estimate of the prosecution's case, asked would you convict anyone on this story? But Cowan's articles were not published in Winston-Salem and that was where the trial was going to take place.

Perhaps somebody did read them though, because only about ten days after the article appeared, attorneys for Will Reynolds, Smith's guardian, revealed that he had written to Solicitor Carlisle Higgins that the Reynolds family would not oppose the dropping of murder charges against Libby and Ab if the prosecuting officer felt he had insufficient evidence to seek a conviction.

Simultaneously, the Reynolds family's attorneys, Manley, Hendren & Womble, announced at a press conference that after two months' study of the case, they had been unable to find sufficient evidence to justify them in advising the family to join in prosecution of the indictments. Will Reynolds hedged this statement however by expressing the opinion in his letter that he thought that Smith was mentally so constituted that he did not believe his death was a suicide. The Reynolds attorneys' statement was cautious:

> "Something like two months ago we were retained by members of the family of Smith Reynolds to investigate the circumstances surrounding his death, with a view of advising with members of his family as to their joining with the State in the prosecution of the pending indictments.
>
> "This matter has received very careful and thorough attention, with the result that we have been unable to discover evidence which in our opinion would justify us in advising the family to join in the prosecution of the indictment, and we have so informed the members of the family."

Legal experts felt that in view of the family letter, it was very likely that Solicitor Higgins, who had never been too crazy about the State's chances anyway, would *nolle prosequi.* This meant that he would drop the indictment for lack of evidence. Polikoff, when reached by reporters, said that he wouldn't be surprised if Libby mightn't refuse to accept *nol. pros.* since she would very much like the chance to clear herself in a full-scale trial.

Discussing the letter, Polikoff, speaking with William Graves, said, "I am not surprised. I felt that when Mr. Reynolds had investigated the evidence, his fairmindedness would cause him to write such a letter.

Higgins himself said that he would "take plenty of time" to consider the letter.

"I have taken no action in the case," Higgins said. "I'll make up my own mind, regardless of who wants this or that done."

Libby confirmed Polikoff's opinion the next day in a telephone interview. "I want this accusation against me cleared permanently, not temporarily. I am entitled to complete exoneration." Polikoff had told her of the request of the Reynolds family that the cases be dropped without trial, but Libby said, "I don't want that. I won't stand for it. It isn't justice. I am innocent, and they know it."

"Then you want me to demand a trial?" Polikoff asked.

"That's exactly what I want," Libby said, "and nothing less."

Some people thought that the Reynolds family action was finally triggered by their discovery of several cable messages sent by Smith Reynolds to Libby in which he spoke several times of suicide. One cable sent to Libby from Paris on January 24, 1931, when she was touring with the show, said:

> WHY RETURN NOW? MEET YOU LATER—BUT SUICIDE IS PREFERABLE. THIS IS THE LAST CABLE. GOODBYE. LOVE.

On that same day Reynolds sent this letter to Libby:

> Darling Angel,
>
> I would gladly come home if you were not going on with the show. I'll gladly give up this trip or anything I have to devote all my time to you, if you would do the same for me.
>
> If I get to the point where I cannot stand it without you another minute—well, there's the old Mauser with a few cartridges in it.
>
> I guess I've had my inning. It's time another team went to bat.

It's not clear how the Reynolds family got hold of these letters, but it is most likely that the energetic defense team of Polikoff and Graves dug them up and turned them over to the family.

Cowan theorized that the State would, in fact *nol. pros;* "with leave," which meant that they would have the freedom to open the case up again if further evidence was discovered.

"Every effort will then be made to get Ab Walker to tell the whole story of what happened that night at Reynolda, if there really be any more to tell. If evidence is given to the

State by Ab, then the first-degree murder indictment against Libby will be revived and he will take the stand for the prosecution.

"Now it may be that Walker hasn't concealed anything. But the Reynolds family doesn't believe this.

"Will Reynolds and his nephew, Dick, repeatedly stated as you know, that Ab could clear up the mystery if he told the truth."

The reporter pointed out that the Reynolds family had all along had a soft spot for Ab and felt that he had somehow been victimized in the case but was not in any way guilty. "He was indicted," the Reynolds family believed, "because he was at Reynolda that night and wide awake at the time of the tragedy."

Will Reynolds confirmed Cowan's opinion. "No one of Smith's family," he said, "has ever had the slightest doubt about Ab Walker's innocence. We have always been certain that he had nothing to do with Smith's death."

Regardless of what action Higgins planned to take, it was made clear that Transou Scott did not intend to relinquish his investigation. He was like a man obsessed. He said the only way he would stop investigating the case was if the solicitor gave him an out and out order to do so. He told reporters that he was convinced that the entire truth had not been secured and he would continue to look for it as long as he was sheriff.

The fact that every theory he had come up with was blasted by contradictory evidence, did nothing to cool Scott's enthusiasm.

There was much speculation after the Reynolds family made its views public. The words were couched very carefully. At one point, Will Reynolds' statement said simply that there was no "conclusive" proof of murder. There was no expression of sympathy or confidence in Libby. One paper reported, "It is known that the Reynolds tobacco dynasty is bringing powerful pressure on Higgins to drop the indictments on Wednesday to obviate the baring of Libby's and Smith's private lives before a jury."

Meanwhile, Higgins announced that there would be no room on the trial docket, in any event, before November 21.

On November 15, in answer to a petition to Carlisle Higgins, Judge A. M. Stack, announced that a *nolle prosequi* be entered in the records in the Libby Holman case.

"Mr. Clerk," the judge said, hammering his gavel, "let the defendants be discharged and their bonds be released."

In the *Times,* the news of Libby's release was carried on the amusement page next to a review of a concert by Jascha Heifetz.

19

Libby in Limbo

Libby was pleased, of course, to be relieved of the enormous strain of facing the electric chair for the murder of her husband. But she didn't think that she should be grateful. The decision to *nol. pros.* the case "with leave" left her under the sword of Damocles. The prosecution could keep probing indefinitely. The statute of limitations never runs out on murder. And there would be a shadow over her forever, she felt. She would have preferred knowing that the State of North Carolina had no case *whatsoever* or else a complete trial and vindication by a not guilty verdict. However, her lawyers advised her that there was no way that she could force the State to move against her with a trial. So, reluctantly, she accepted the inconclusive decision of the State.

By this time, she was in the fifth month of her pregnancy and her mind was directed toward the forthcoming birth of her child. As soon as it became clear that Libby was not to be tried or found guilty for the murder of her husband, the question of the disposition of Smith's estate came to the forefront.

Libby, who had reputedly paid a million dollars to her defense team, was nearly broke. The word was that the Reynolds family would agree to her getting a share of Smith's estate, but nothing like the $15 to $20 million that it was reportedly worth. The matter was still in contention on January 11 when Libby gave birth to a three and a half pound baby boy at the *Lying-In Hospital* in Philadelphia. The undersized child was immediately put into an incubator. But, the doctors said, he was "healthy and normal for a premature baby." Libby was reported to be doing "very nicely."

Amidst the enormous publicity, much of it hostile, that Libby had received, there was a fear that somebody might try to kidnap or otherwise harm the new Reynolds heir. He and his incubator were immediately placed in a maximum security room where hospital authorities said "nobody could reach him without an acetylene torch."

Libby, her mother, and Louisa Jenney occupied adjoining rooms to the baby in the seventh floor suite of the hospital, pending the child's release from the incubator. Federal authorities described as "rubbish" a report that Department of Justice agents had been assigned to guard the former actress and her child.

During the period that the child was being retained in the incubator, Libby was not allowed to see or touch him, which upset her enormously. Two weeks after the birth of her child, Libby was reported to be under "special hospital treatment" for a "nervous breakdown." The information was revealed to the press by Louisa Jenney. The following day her doctor said that she was "exceptionally fine" and if it were not for her desire to stay constantly near her fifteen-day-old son, she could "leave the hospital tomorrow." He denied that she was being treated for a nervous breakdown but he admitted "special treatment" was given her to "safeguard against the

The first photo of Libby and her infant son, taken March 28, 1933 as they left Pennsylvania Hospital in Philadelphia.

possibility of a collapse in view of the strain of the months preceding her entrance."

But Libby improved rapidly and within a few days was allowed to visit her twenty-day-old son, as yet unnamed, in his incubator room. Meanwhile, Libby announced through her father that she would challenge the illegal will that Smith Reynolds had made before he married her.

On March twentieth, Libby finally displayed her two-and-a-half-month old baby, now a healthy seven pounds. Libby proudly showed off her child, surrounded by visitors in the solarium atop the hospital. Two photographers, bizarrely garbed in hooded cloaks to prevent germ infections, were there to record the historic occasion. The photographers were asked to don medicated robes and were then sprayed with disinfectant to protect the infant.

Libby told the press that the "young man," as she called him, more than compensated for all her trials and suffering. With Louisa Jenney at her side, Libby said, "When my baby shall no longer need my entire attention, then it will be time to see about my return to the stage.

"I have found as satisfying a happiness in caring and planning for him as I ever expect to find in life."

She looked up and smiled. She was clad in a black, red, and white crepe gown and was wearing no makeup. Her eyes, under straight black brows, glowed softly. "My first sight of this baby was a moment of ecstasy unlike any other in my life," Libby told the reporters. "Though small, he was the most perfect and adorable thing I had ever seen.

"Since that day, his astounding rapid growth has been my constant source of delight. No measurement, no ounce of gain in weight, has escaped my notice. Now—at seven pounds—he looks like a giant to me, a fair, blue-eyed giant of a child, wiser and more understanding and lovable than any creature on earth."

Reporters tried to ask about her suit to overturn Smith's will, but she turned off the question.

"Here in a hospital I have seen and heard so much

Libby's parents, Mr. and Mrs. Alfred Holman, photographed in 1933 at the time of the birth of Libby's son.

suffering, tragedy and frustration, poverty and privation, that in comparison my own experiences have taken on a less somber hue."

She was asked about Smith, and she said that he was "a courageous and ambitious airman." She said that her "fondest dream" would be realized if her baby would become an aviator.

Meanwhile Ann, Smith's ex-wife, was making plenty of trouble. Despite the fact that Smith had previously made a deal with her and settled a half a million on his child, she insisted that the infant be given a full share of his estate and there were plenty of lawyers that agreed that this should be done. Ann's claim was that her divorce was not legal because, she said, she was in a drugged, ill and incompetent condition when Smith took her to Nevada in 1932.

Libby said that as far as she was concerned, she'd settle for a pittance and the whole estate could be given to charity. Nobody took this very seriously.

As she began to feel better, recuperating from whatever the condition had been that she was treated for in the hospital, she let word leak out that she might consider a return to the theater.

She leased an estate in Watch Hill, Rhode Island and let it be known that she might be available in the fall to play a part in a new intimate revue similar to *The Little Show*.

Any report of Libby's activities, whether it was of her plans for a comeback in the theater or her dispute over the will, contained a rehash of the death of Smith Reynolds, and, as Libby predicted, usually included the somewhat ominous statement that the charges had been dropped "for lack of evidence." She kept her promise to name the child after her late husband, or at least in part. The boy was named Christopher Smith Reynolds and in the newspapers of the time was constantly referred to as "the $20 million baby."

But the press items concerning Libby's return to the stage seemed largely self-serving. No concrete big-time offers actually surfaced and there was a feeling that Libby was regarded as box-office poison because of her scandal. Of course, her old friends Tallulah, Clifton and the rest stayed loyal to her, as did Dietz, who was working on a show that he felt would be perfect for Libby.

At Watch Hill, Libby tried to stay out of the path of scandal and if she was up to any of her old shenanigans, it was under the cover of highly guarded privacy. An armed guard of fourteen, "fit retinue for a prince," one newspaper said, helped to insure her privacy. The whole country was still mindful of the fate of Charles Lindbergh's infant son who had been kidnapped and killed only the year before, and whose kidnapper had not yet been apprehended.

She kept to herself in Rhode Island and did not belong to the exclusive Misquamicut Gold Club or appear at its dances, although she might readily enough have joined the Sidney Scotts of Wilmington who were close friends of Louisa Jenney. Her telephones were not listed and her servants, whom she paid generously, would not talk. The cottage had a beach of its own so she didn't have to go to the public one with her infant son. Despite this, rumors were spread that Libby had been seen drinking and carousing at nearby Narranganset Pier and in Newport, but there was no documentation of these allegations, and Libby mostly was seen with her enormous, spotted Great Dane, X-Ray, going to the local stores where she was known among business people as a good spender. The dog filled her station wagon and tended to protect her from unwelcome attention.

She made an occasional appearance on Broadway, once for the opening of *As Thousands Cheer,* which starred her old friends Clifton Webb and Marilyn Miller. But she stayed on in the summer community even when all of the vacation residents had left, and made only occasional forays to the city, once appearing at the swank Mayfair Club at a black-tie affair. Guests at Libby's table included Louis Bromfield, the author, Marilyn Miller, Helen Broderick, and Coleen Moore, the actresses, Lita

Grey Chaplin, Charlie Chaplin's first wife, Georges Carpentier, the boxer and others, all dressed in black tie and evening gown, but Libby and her escorts (unidentified) wore only street clothes.

That winter the Smith Reynolds case got another round in the press when it was revealed that Ab Walker had been receiving threatening notes in Winston-Salem concerning his involvement with the Reynolds case. "We know you killed Smith Reynolds. You are on the spot. Your every move is being watched," the note to Walker said, and it demanded that he place $1,500 in a coal chute in twenty, five and one-dollar bills.

Walker, guarded by federal officers and deputies from Sheriff Scott's office, placed a decoy package in a coal chute in a small town near Winston-Salem, as ordered. But nobody showed up.

A few months later, it was revealed that Libby had also received several extortion letters threatening her life unless she paid "several thousand dollars." According to the *Philadelphia Record*, the notes were delivered to Louisa Jenney's Montchanin estate. R. George Harvey, head of the FBI office in the area, said that the sender of the missives wanted the payoff money to "stay away from you," and warned that Libby would be killed unless she complied. Libby turned the letters over to federal authorities instantly. Later that summer when the word of the threat leaked out, it spurred a rash of curiosity-seekers to Libby's perfomances in summer stock.

Libby's name also appeared in the paper when she was allowed by the court to purchase Smith's prized airplane, despite the fact that the estate was still deeply enmeshed in a legal dispute between the Reynolds family and Smith's ex-wife. She paid $1,500 for it.

That spring Libby with her son had moved to Montchanin to live with Louisa. She took a course in drama at Jasper Deeter's Playhouse in Hedgerow, Pennsylvania. Her debut in the part of Pura in an imported play called *Spring in Autumn,* a drama in which Blanche Yurka once stood on her head, caused a great uproar in Rose Valley. State troopers with motorcycles, Sam Browne belts and what theater critic Robert Garland called "hard, un-Hedgerow faces," guarded the exits and entrances. Dozens of photographers were on the spot also to cover the event.

But despite the enormous crowd of curiosity seekers, when the curtain rose and revealed Libby on stage in the part of Pura, the maid, the audience sat on its hands. There was not a single clap of applause. It was Garland's theory that the playgoers had not recognized her. "For traveling the Tobacco Road that has brought her to Rose Valley on her courageous trek back to Broadway, Libby Holman is not the Libby Holman Broadway used to know."

At the end of the play the audience, apparently now aware that the quiet, understated, black-clad maid was indeed the fabulous, sexy torch singer of Broadway, gave Libby six or seven curtain calls. The play, however, was only summer stock and at best, a limited success. But that August Libby got better news.

Arthur Schwartz had written tunes for an operetta called *Revenge With Music,* based on a story by Alarcon called *The Three-Cornered Hat.* He asked his partner Arthur Dietz to write the lyrics. The two of them, aware that Libby was anxious to get out of the sticks and back to Broadway, recruited her for the starring role. Dietz later regretted it. "She was miscast," he said. "She had been taking singing lessons and it seemed to spoil her voice. She lost her ability to project lyrics so that every word was understood."

Dietz asked a British theatrical producer what he thought of *Revenge With Music* when it opened and he said, "It's dire!" Nevertheless the show, which also starred Charles Winninger, Rex O'Malley and Ilka Chase, ran 158 performances, and had in it two memorable songs, "You and the Night and the Music," and "If There is Someone Lovelier Than You."

After the show closed, many theorized that perhaps Libby should have stuck to musical comedy where she was at home and taken a part in Leonard Sillman's new revue, *New Faces,* but then, Sillman pointed out, one could hardly call Libby a "new face" on Broadway.

She did find some time to party on occasion. Howard Dietz remained a trusted and loyal friend of Libby's and they socialized quite a bit together, but from the beginning there was nothing personal. He understood that Libby's taste was strictly for extremely young and pretty men.

Anyway, Howard was doing pretty well for himself. He had recently divorced the lovely Betty, and married Tanis Guinness, tall, beautiful, charming—and *only* an heiress to the Guinness breweries fortune. They soon bought a mansion in Sands Point near Libby's old North Shore digs and began entertaining everybody from Alexander Woolcott to Randolph Churchill. Between them, the Dietzes knew *everybody.*

Once at a party in Sands Point, Libby made the acquaintance of a gorgeous blond seventeen-year-old prep school boy. Unfortunately the young fellow wasn't much used to champagne—not in the quantities being sluiced down by the merry guests that hot Long Island night. At the end of the party, the young man, swaying in the summer breeze like a Jamaica Bay cattail, offered to drive Libby to Dietz's place, where she was staying that weekend. Never known for her caution, Libby agreed.

After two unscheduled stops to permit the preppy to whoop up some excess champagne in the bushes, they finally made it to Howard's place where the young chap nearly collapsed on the lawn.

"Why don't you stay in one of the spare rooms?" Libby asked solicitously.

"Oh no," the young man protested, "I don't want to cause a scandal." Libby laughed so hard she had to sit down before she fell down.

"Don't worry about that, fella," she said when she could catch her breath. "I promise not to tell anyone that drinking made you sick."

Libby, in those years in limbo, hardly had a choice,

except to return to show business. She as yet had not received a nickel from the estate of her wealthy husband, and its disposition was still being fought tooth and nail by Smith's ex-wife Ann and her father.

In November 1934 Libby's attorneys, on behalf of the infant Christopher, laid claim to the entire estate, now evaluated at $25 million, contending that Christopher was the sole heir to the money. Actually, Libby's lawyers did this largely to get some sort of decision in the long-standing legal squabble. Mary, Nancy and Dick answered Libby's suit with a counteroffer, suggesting that Smith's two children split $15 million of their father's estate, that Libby be personally given $750,000, and that the remainder be used to establish a Smith Reynolds Foundation for benevolent, charitable purposes.

From the beginning, Libby had suggested that the estate be turned over to charity, and she readily agreed to this proposal by the Reynolds family. But Ann Cannon refused to share the estate. She and her aging father were still extremely bitter. They continued to insist that Libby's marriage was not legal, that little Christopher was a bastard. According to the claim filed by the Cannon family, Ann had been extremely ill when she was in Nevada and was running a temperature of 104°. Ann claimed that she had been given morphine to ease her pain and that she was as unaware of what was happening when she signed the divorce papers as Libby had been when Smith was shot.

Ann also made it clear that if she had to go to court to fight for her share of the inheritance, she would drag every bit of gossip and innuendo about Libby's marriage to Smith Reynolds into court. And while Will Reynolds and Dick seemed sure that Smith had been nothing short of an Eagle Scout prior to his meeting with Libby, Nancy and Mary, Smith's sisters, were well aware that many of Smith's activities after meeting Libby would be best left unrevealed to the public for the sake of the not entirely unclouded Reynolds family reputation.

They let it be known that if Ann Cannon insisted on

dragging the Reynolds name through the mud, they would see to it that she got none of the money at all.

Libby kept a low profile in the matter, making no statements about her wishes concerning the will, and leaving the fight largely in the hands of the Reynoldses. But still needing money to live on, she accepted a nightclub engagement at the Versailles, a former speak-easy in New York.

Critic Richard Manson said, "Libby Holman has spent so much time on the front pages that many of us have forgotten this was the young lady who skyrocketed to fame some years ago by doing strange things with a song called 'Moanin' Low.'" Manson said that Libby was "ogled and applauded" by the first-night audience. It was becoming increasingly clear that Libby's biggest value was that of a scandal celebrity, rather than a distinguished performer.

Libby did her best to fight off this identification. She stipulated in all interviews that there would be no discussion of any of the Reynolds phase of her life. Her personal representative told reporters, "The kid's out. Cigarettes are out. The money's out. Winston-Salem, North Carolina, is off the map as far as you're concerned. Those are the conditions on which she'll see you."

Reporter Michel Mok agreed to these terms but there was no way of keeping him from slipping an innuendo into the story:

> "The cloth of gold evening gown, high in front, waist-low in back, the blue-black hair curled low over the ears, the curious brick-dust makeup, the deep rose polish on the nails of her amazingly long, prehensile fingers, are doubtless intended to produce an exotic effect.
>
> It doesn't quite come off. She looked pained, her smile was forced, when she made her first appearance to scattering applause and craning of women's necks.
>
> It takes no mindreader to see that she understands why the champagne buyers have come. They are not here in the cause of Art. They are simply a politely dressed, curious mob . . .

> Her face is a twisted mask of obviously genuine unhappiness as she sings, while the audience continues chattering, laughing, eating, drinking...
>
> It's the same voice with the agonized top-wails, the sudden startling drops to an almost rasping bass. But the singer has changed. She's self-conscious, a bit stiff, a trifle apologetic....

Later, discussing her act and her apparent discomfort, she told the reporter somewhat wistfully, "After all, it doesn't matter much...just so I keep working...just so I'm not forgotten.... Singing satisfies me, though it isn't what I want to do eventually. It's my ambition to become a good dramatic actress."

It was rumored that Libby got $10,000 for her two-week stint. Out of this money, Libby pointed out, 60 percent went to her agents, her accompanist, her arranger, her personal representative and her secretary and a lot of the remainder went for traveling expenses, since she was taking the act on the road.

That summer she went to Kennebunkport, Maine, to appear in a show called *Accent on Youth,* and again the newspaper publicity devoted itself largely to the guards around young Christopher and her concern that he might be kidnapped.

In March of 1935, the squabble over Smith's millions seemed settled to the satisfaction of both parties. By now the actual amount of the estate had ballooned to $27,975,000, according to the court records. The surrogate decreed that Libby would receive $750,000 for herself and that after the deduction of taxes, the remainder of Smith's estate would be divided, with 25 percent going to Christopher, two years old by that time, 37½ percent to Ann and 37½ percent to Dick, Mary, and Nancy. Smith's brothers and sisters stipulated that their share would be used for charitable purposes.

Unfortunately, Libby would have to live by her wits until 1939, since the terms of R. J. Reynolds' will specified that his children could not touch the principal of his estate until each had reached the age of twenty-eight. So, despite the fact that she was reputed to be one of the richest people in show business, for the next four years Libby would have to sing for her supper.

It was an indication of the kind of material Ann Cannon Reynolds threatened to release, that her share came to almost $10 million, whereas Libby's, in trust for Christopher, was $6,250,000. But, to be fair, the court deducted from Ann's share the $1 million that Smith settled upon her in their predivorce agreement.

Despite this generous settlement, the Cannon family again filed an appeal. Wiseacres along the Rialto pointed out that if Ann Cannon could claim that she'd been divorced under duress, certainly Smith Reynolds, had he been alive, could have claimed that he'd been married under even more duress. Three days later, the court threw out Ann's appeal. The newspapers hailed the decision as a victory, though somewhat clouded, for Libby.

The fact was that she got a rough deal out of it. As the legitimate widow of Smith Reynolds, she was awarded less than a million, but she *was* made executrix of her son's trust fund.

Now the speculation about Libby in the public press started all over again. What would she do with her new-found wealth? Would she quit show business now that she had the money? Would she quit singing? Would she remarry?

Libby in the five years since her husband's death, had maintained a more discreet and lower profile in her private life than previously. Any sign of frivolity on her part was instantly seized on by the press as a sign of her callous indifference. "To read the newspapers," Libby told her old friend Ward Morehouse, "you'd think I'm never out of El Morocco . . ." The fact was, Libby insisted, that she was working harder than ever. In 1937 Libby had the honor of being hired for a one-night stand at Grosvenor House in London on the occasion of the coronation of George VI, who succeeded his brother, Edward VIII, after the latter had relinquished the crown in order to marry Mrs. Wallis Simpson. In honor of the

Libby at Palm Beach in 1936.

occasion, Libby agreed for the moment to relinquish her dramatic ambition and fall back on her undoubted talent as a torch singer. On her program were such standards as "There's a Lull in My Life," "Funny Valentine" and, of course, "Moanin' Low." She had suggested Cole Porter's "Love for Sale," which she had succeeded in making a standard part of her repertoire, but the Royal Family turned thumbs down on the suggestive lyrics. She took with her on the trip to London Clifton Webb, Stina Larson, her secretary, and Mimi Durant, a socialite acquaintance who often filled in as a companion for Libby when Louisa Jenney was not on the scene.

On the trip back on the *Normandie,* Jack Doyle, who was known as "The Singing Pugilist" and "The Irish Thrush"—a notorious publicity-seeker—let it be known that he had met "a beautiful young brunette American widow who is a millionaire with a fortune in tobacco," and intended to marry her. Libby, reached via ship-to-shore phone by a New York newspaper editor said, "God forbid." When she got to New York and was questioned on the story, she said, "Jack Doyle is an opportunist. It was a cheap trick to get publicity." "The Irish Thrush" sheepishly admitted his hoax: "Damn it all, she's no criterion of publicity. I'm marrying somebody bigger than Miss Holman—bigger than she ever will be . . ." Doyle claimed that some reporter had gotten tobacco mixed up with automobiles and that maybe he was talking about one of the heiresses to the Dodge fortune. Interviewed in his cabin when the ship arrived, he said that he supposed that the rumors started when people saw him together with Libby on the ship. Reporters told him that Libby said she never even met him. He professed great surprise and then, with exaggerated chivalry said, "Well, then she's right; I guess I never saw her." Anyway, Doyle never married either Libby or Mrs. Dodge, in fact had trouble even being admitted to the country when he was stopped at Ellis Island because of problems with his visa. But his actions were an indication of the sort of trouble Libby was beginning to have from hangers-on and opportunists.

A Broadway columnist commented,

> "No celebrity extant suffers so much from phonies, moochers, and spurious anonymities who attach themselves to her train as the husky-voiced torch singer, who has just returned from an appearance in London, which return voyagers to the Coronation describe as a raving sucess. Part of Miss Holman's susceptibility to characters who are about as authentic currency as Confederate shinplasters is the circumstance that she is so near-sighted that half the time she doesn't know who is seated at her table. A contributing factor also is that she is as generous with her personality as the day is long and as imposed on by every ringer who can manage to insinuate himself into the photographic scene with her. She recently encountered a near-celebrity who asked her to dance in a London nightclub and in no time, the photographers had established a romance of Tristan and Isolde proportions. The fact was that she had never seen him before or since the brief moment when a photographer's flash exploded and then didn't know his name. Libby is not exactly the naive type, but when it comes to publicity-seekers at her expense, she is definitely in the victim classification."

But that fall, she really did meet a Lothario who fulfilled the romantic speculations of the columnists and this time he was for real—Phillips Holmes, a brilliant and handsome twenty-three-year-old actor and producer, who was the son of Taylor Holmes, a veteran character actor of stage and screen. The gossips loved it. Young Holmes was a veritable Adonis and the fact that he was so much younger than Libby evoked memories and new gossip of the Reynolda affair, just when it seemed that the scandal had died down. In fact, the reverse was true. A new scandal was being born.

Part Three

Libby

20

Mrs. Ralph Holmes

In 1938, after bush-jumping the country in concerts and nightclubs, Libby, through the good offices of her friend Clifton Webb, finally got another break on Broadway in a musical called *You Never Know*. Co-starred with her in addition to Clifton Webb was the Mexican bombshell, Lupe Velez. In the small world in which Libby circulated, Lupe was well known too. In Hollywood, she was one of the favorite dates of Howard Dietz, who was then between wives.

Both Phillips Holmes, her new boyfriend, and Libby were deeply involved political liberals. Libby was active in raising money for the embattled Lincoln Brigade, then fighting Franco's Falangists unsuccessfully in Spain. Franco, it was clear, was winning with the active military support of the Nazis and Italian Fascists. Hitler had shocked the British by indicating moves to incorporate parts of Austria and Czechoslovakia into his domain. Anthony Eden, in a serious policy dispute over appeasing the Germans, resigned and turned the government over to Neville Chamberlain.

Young Holmes felt that the world was soon coming to a crisis and that Americans should show more support for the embattled British. Like Smith Reynolds, Holmes had been a flyer all his life. Now, with Libby's reluctant approval, he decided it was necessary to display his commitment to democracy by enlisting, as so many other idealistic young Americans had done, in the Royal Canadian Air Force. Trained pilots were at a premium in those days and Phillips Holmes' application was accepted instantly. Within weeks, he was assigned to London as a flight instructor.

By this time, Libby and Phillips had been seeing one another on a regular basis for almost a year. Phillips Holmes resembled Libby's late husband in another respect. He was extremely jealous and insecure. All the time he was overseas in England, he and Libby were burning up the international telephone wires with long passionate calls—one of them reportedly an hour and a half long.

To make sure that Libby did not stray in his absence, he suggested that she spend her time with his brother Ralph, also a pilot, and two years younger, whom Libby had met shortly after she had met Phillips. Ralph was an actor, too, though not a very successful one, and even more handsome than his older brother. Phillips Holmes theorized that his brother's presence at Libby's side would remind people around Broadway that she was his (Phillips') bride-to-be and not available for another attachment.

That spring, Libby surprised the gossip columnists, most of her friends and Taylor Holmes by slipping off to Washington, D. C., to marry Ralph Holmes, twelve years her junior. Most of the newspaper articles describing the marriage gave more space to the rehash of Smith Reynolds' death than they did to Libby's career.

After a brief honeymoon in Florida, where Libby was appearing in a nightclub, the newlyweds returned to the estate Libby had recently acquired, on Merrie Brook Lane, between Greenwich and Stamford, Connecticut.

Again gossips were busy analyzing Libby's motives for buying the Connecticut estate. Many people felt that it was because Smith's sister Mary, now Mrs. Charles Babcock, had an estate nearby.

In spite of the show of support for Libby the Reynolds family made during the battle with Ann Cannon for Smith's money, once the will was settled, they avoided her as though she were a black widow spider.

Libby, though extremely gregarious, was never a social climber. Anyway, the Babcocks were not so highly regarded by the "old money" families of Connecticut themselves. But what Libby wanted was recognition for her young son, now nicknamed "Topper." Word was out among her friends that Mary Babcock had strong doubts that the child was actually Smith's. It is possible that she also resented having had to split Smith's money with Libby's boy.

Be that as it may, Libby seemed deliriously happy ensconced in her new estate which she dubbed "Tree-tops," with her young and handsome new husband—so happy that she told a reporter she doubted that she could put her heart and soul into singing torch numbers about unrequited love any more.

"We're both too much in love to do any 'moanin' low,'" she said. "When you look at us, you're looking at the two happiest people in the world."

In fact, the reporter noted, Libby didn't seem to want to talk about anything but Ralph.

"We get along so well, there just isn't anything to say," she said. "We're just a couple of people in love, and I don't suppose that would interest anybody."

Her career?

"Oh, it will go on. My husband comes from a long line of theatrical folk, and he won't mind."

As was the case with Smith, Broadway whisperers hinted that Ralph might be homosexual. "He's too beautiful to be straight," Clifton Webb once said, wistfully. But nobody knew anything about Ralph's sexual preferences for a fact. Author Robert LaGuardia in his book *Monty,* did describe Ralph Holmes as a "depressive homosexual."

Whatever his preferences, Libby was crazy about Ralph, and so was seven-year-old Topper, who until then had been spending most of his time at Louisa's place in Delaware while Libby toured with nightclub acts and concerts. But now the young tobacco heir moved into Treetops with Ralph and his mother to enjoy for the first time in his young life something like a normal family existence.

As usual, a pair of muscular guards had been hired to watch the gate and repel all invaders.

A few months later, on November 11, 1939, on what would have been Smith Reynolds' twenty-eighth birthday, Libby finally took possession of the $750,000 due her from her husband's estate and the six-odd million Christopher had inherited. Against that amount, Libby submitted bills for $436,944.33 which she had spent in the "support, maintenance, education and recreation" of Christopher during the seven years of his life.

Meanwhile, handsome young Ralph Holmes, who was just getting used to being the husband of a wealth heiress, got some unexpected fan mail—from the Selective Service System. He was young, he was healthy, he was childless, he was a perfect candidate for the United States Army. Holmes put in for a deferment on the ground that he had to support his wife but the news of Libby's inheritance put a pretty quick stop to that. Nevertheless, through one technicality or another, Holmes was able to get a series of deferments until 1941. When it was certain he could no longer avoid the draft, Ralph followed in his brother's footsteps and enlisted in the Royal Canadian Air Force. Only a few months after his enlistment, while he was still training in Canada, Ralph received the shocking news that his brother Phillips, Libby's former fiance, had been killed in a training flight out of Brooklands Field, near London.

Ralph, who had up to this point been somewhat of a reluctant combatant, felt an enormous sense of guilt about the death of his brother and immediately volunteered for overseas duty in the Battle of Britain. Friends of Libby and Ralph could only speculate as to what feelings the couple must have felt over Phillips' premature demise.

As if to compensate, Ralph volunteered for repeated combat missions as a bombadier over Germany, and Libby, on the home front, worked energetically for the USO and other service-related causes, putting her show business ambitions for the moment on a back burner. In 1942, while Ralph was still overseas, Libby made the acquaintance of a young, black folk singer named Josh White, through Max Gordon, producer of *Three's a Crowd,* who now was operating a nightclub called the Village Vanguard. Libby was immediately enchanted by Josh White's music, which seemed to her gutsier and more real than the Tin Pan Alley torch numbers she had been accustomed to singing. These were songs with roots in the chain gangs, whore houses and blind pigs that were part of the black experience. They were what she thought of as "earth songs."

Libby soon became deeply involved with Josh White's career, advising him, working with him, and studying with him the origins of many of the songs that became part of his repertoire, some of which he learned from the famous blues singer "Blind Lemon" Jefferson, whom White had served as a companion and guide person when in his teens. Libby adored the songs Josh was to make his own: "Move on the Outskirts of Town," "Evilhearted Man," "House of the Rising Sun." She was particularly pleased with his rendition of "Strange Fruit," based on Lillian Smith's book about bigotry and prejudice in the Deep South.

As a gesture to national solidarity, Libby and Josh put together an act which they polished by touring college campuses around the country. When she felt it was properly in shape, Libby volunteered to take the act on a USO tour at her own expense. But the big brass were unimpressed by Libby and Josh's ethnic repertoire. "No

Mr. and Mrs. Ralph Holmes in Bermuda, 1940.

HAVA
CIGA

soap," the ruling board of the United Service Organization said. "We don't handle mixed acts." Furious, Libby took her case to her friend Tallulah, an ardent liberal like Libby and also an extremely influential supporter of the Democratic Party. "We don't have to take that shit, Libby," Tallulah told her friend. "We'll take this damn thing right to Eleanor Roosevelt!"

True to her word, Tallulah carried the message of Libby's problem to the First Lady, who asked Libby about it when the two of them appeared on the platform of a benefit in Harlem. "Come on down and see me at the White House," she said, and apparently Mrs. Franklin Roosevelt gave it her best shot.

"She was tirelessly trying to get us overseas," Libby recalled. "It seems every day I'd get a letter from her reporting her efforts. When she didn't succeed, she invited us down to the President's last inauguration."

But even the President's wife could not prevail against the bigotry then prevalent in the military establishment. It's hard to remember what attitudes were like then. When Libby took her show with Josh White on the road, the headline on Earl Wilson's story in the Post was "LIBBY HOLMAN TO SING WITH NEGRO GUITARIST." In the article Wilson mused about the fact that Libby was bothering to sing at all, in view of all the money she had; but Libby had a ready explanation. "If you're an artist," she said, "you have to give."

Besides, she said, she had to do something to take her mind off the daily dangers of her husband's bombing missions in Europe. Still, when she unveiled the act, now brought to a fine state of polish, at a nightclub called La Vie Parisienne, dressed in a simple shirtwaist and a long skirt designed by her friend Mainbocher, and sang the racy lyrics of some of the "earth songs" she and Josh had dug up:

I got a man
He's big and tall
Moves his hips
Like a cannon ball...

the gossips could not help but speculate what her relationship with Josh White was. But in any event the act was a tremendous success. Libby, of course, was forced to sing her standards—"Something to Remember Me By," "Body and Soul" and "Moanin' Low." But increasingly, she wanted to dissociate herself from these songs and get into more serious work. Unfortunately, in the opinion even of a lot of her closest friends, her greatest talent still was for the torch number and she often overreached herself in her other efforts. For a time, she even talked of studying for the opera.

Finally, through her friend Bobby Lewis, also a friend of Tallulah, she came across a vehicle that seemed perfect—serious, dramatic, symbolic, with a lot of atonal and definitely not torchy music. The play, *Mexican Mural,* written by Ramon Naya, was set in a carnival in Vera Cruz and dealt in dramatic terms with religion, superstition and the poverty and desperation of the Mexican people. The social message was heavy and appealed to Libby's basic ideology. Bobby Lewis, the director, had come out of the Group Theater, one of the most leftish and controversial groups of the thirties, in which Libby's friend Franchot Tone had been one of the leading actors. Other famous alumni of the Group Theater include Lee J. Cobb, John Garfield, Elia Kazan, and Clifford Odets.

Unfortunately, Broadway was not interested in such a dire and gloomy theme, so the play had to be produced way off Broadway, actually on East 42nd Street in a tiny auditorium on the 50th floor of the Chanin Building. Despite the obscure location of his drama, Lewis' excellent reputation was able to attract a talented cast of unknown actors, including Kevin McCarthy and his new wife Augusta Dabney, Mira Rostova, a talented Russian refugee actress about Libby's age, and a brilliant and delicately handsome twenty-two-year-old leading man who was gaining a reputation as one of the brightest of the new school of actors—Montgomery Clift.

From the very beginning there was great empathy

between the singer and the youthful male star of the show. There seemed to be a current passing between Libby and Montgomery Clift, who was absolutely fascinated by Libby's dramatic past. Despite the fact that she was now approaching forty, Libby still moved with the grace of a Persian cat and had a presence that could even dominate such a group of personalities as this. Although she was still married to Ralph Holmes, who was then tirelessly shuttling his bomber back and forth from England to the Continent, Libby could not resist at least a flirtation with the dazzlingly handsome and extremely intelligent young actor.

In the beginning, the romance was all in the glances they exchanged and a certain body language which was easily read by the others in the cast of the play, all of whom found the incipient drama between the actor and the torch singer infinitely more interesting than the play they were acting in. Once or twice, Libby made a tentative move toward developing the relationship by suggesting they have drinks together during some of the rehearsal breaks and Clift would answer what apparently was then the truth: "I only drink milk."

When she was not on stage herself, Libby was noticed by several members of the cast standing at the back of the house chain-smoking Camels and watching every move Monty made on the stage. According to Robert Lewis, the atmosphere in the tiny auditorium became "sensual as hell. I'd organized all sorts of improvisation to free the actors physically since there was constant movement on the stage. I had everybody hugging and clutching each other; during breaks there was much gliding into dark corners. As opening night got closer, I could feel excitement and tension building up."

According to Lewis, it was not only Libby who was fascinated by young Clift. "Everybody was in love with him. He was absolutely mesmerizing in the show, and offstage he was like Pan, an enchanter. Everybody clustered around him and talked and took photographs. But he refused to play favorites. One afternoon, he might sit with Libby and light her cigarettes, another evening he'd go with Kevin and Augusta for dinner, but much of the time he spent with Mira Rostova and I think that ticked Libby most of all. Libby was used to having her way around men, and yet here was this Mira Rostova, with her woebegone little face out of a Kathe Kollwitz drawing—you know, *haunted*—who was monopolizing Monty." Because the fact was that Mira seemed equally fascinated by the young star. She began calling him "my comrade," and anybody could see she had an enormous crush on him.

Monty obviously took great delight in the rivalry between the two older women, but he also was fascinated by Kevin McCarthy's beautiful wife Augusta, with whom he flirted outrageously.

The play finally opened in April 1942 and seemed to baffle the critics. Brooks Atkinson wrote: *"Mexican Mural* is a strange, wild, evocative sketch of an undisciplined civilization. Some of the acting is excellent, especially Montgomery Clift's superlative portrait of a brooding, beaten youth who cannot endure the coarseness of his environment."

A lot of important theatrical people liked the play quite well. Tennessee Williams said he still thinks it is one of the great evenings he spent in the theater. Despite the fact that it attracted packed houses, the dark, expressionistic play ran for only three performances, but to Libby it was worth all the money she lost in backing it to meet the young actor who was to become the most important man in her life.

Monty's and Libby's mutual attraction existed on many levels. Intellectually, they spoke the same language and would spend hours shopping in Brentano's for books on all sorts of subjects. Politically, also, they saw eye to eye, both being considerably to the left of center. What was between them sexually was hard to say. In those days, Clift worked very hard at preserving the public image of being a heterosexual; even Kevin McCarthy and Augusta Dabney, who became his closest friends after *Mexican Mural,* were not aware for years that Monty was bisexual.

In the beginning they saw each other only occasionally.

Monty was living with his mother on Park Avenue. Libby, who had taken an apartment on East 69th Street, was still married to Ralph Holmes, but this did not exactly keep her sequestered either in the East Side apartment or at Treetops. She spent a lot of time with Topper, who was growing into a tall, gangly, good-looking boy with an uncanny resemblance to his father.

From the beginning it could be seen that there was a special rapport between Libby and Clift. Augusta Dabney recalled once seeing them together: "They were moving toward her car, bodies close and swaying, arms linked. They were talking softly to each other with total concentration, and when I got near them, they ignored me—and they seemed to be speaking in a language I could not understand."

But Monty had that effect on a lot of people, and he seemed to be equally close to Mira Rostova, who later became his full-time dramatic coach and close friend. However, with Rostova there was only a maternal relationship and never anything sexual.

Of course, Libby and Clift had something in common that the others were not part of—this was their intense interest in drugs; they exchanged constant expert information—where to get them, what new drugs were on the market, what the effects were of the various chemicals they took into their systems. But much of this developed later.

Though he had a following among theatrical cognoscenti, Monty was far from a star. Shortly after *Mexican Mural* closed, however, he was cast as the young boy in Thornton Wilder's *Skin of Our Teeth,* where he made the acquaintance of Libby's old and good friend, Tallulah Bankhead. Libby immediately tried to involve Monty in the gang that she and Tallulah ran with but Monty was wary of the overpowering Alabaman. Still, he liked her, and Tallulah, who was taking out her temperament on everyone in the cast, soon found that there was nobody in the play who would talk to her except Monty. Monty had, of course, heard all the stories about Tallulah, how she turned her servants into alcoholics, tore her clothes off in front of strange men, and had gay "caddies" around to service her. He told Libby once that he was actually afraid Tallulah might rape him sometime. But Tallulah told her friend that she thought of Monty as "a nice, sweet boy," but had absolutely no designs on him as a lover. Libby smiled sweetly. "Darling, you'd be all over him like a tarantula if he'd even give you a tumble," she said.

"Well, how is he, darling? You must know," Tallulah asked mischievously.

Libby shrugged noncommittally. "If you want to play with him, pop into his dressing room and find out for yourself sometime."

During the run of the play, Monty fell quite ill with dysentery which had plagued him in a severe form for many years. He often went on the stage so doped up with various medications he almost fell off the apron. The powerful opiate painkillers Monty took would often make him drowsy so to counteract them, he would take amphetamines or other uppers such as Ritalin. His pockets were always full of these stimulants, which he would hand out as though they were penny candies. Libby introduced him to Powders, a large drugstore on Madison Avenue, where the two would often go and emerge with shopping baskets full of goodies.

On weekends, Clift usually went to Treetops to sleep off the effects of illness, fatigue, drugs and booze, although it often would turn out that he and Libby would get even more bombed. Libby's place had become headquarters for an endless parade of guests and hangers-on, most of them talented and interesting, some just leeches. The weekend crowds usually consisted of Kevin McCarthy, Augusta, Monty and others, seldom Mira Rostova. Libby at the time was probably better known in New York and more of a star than Monty, and was constantly mentioned in the columns, but never as a companion of Clift. A columnist who squired Libby around the town one evening said that he discovered that she wore "three different and more costly fur wraps. The first, a simple mink, she discarded at the Colony, in favor of something ermine, which she wore to the theater and as far as Monte Carlo, where she picked up a flock of wonderful sables, some of them I thought alive. Her maid kept going ahead and planting them in case she got tired of what she was at the moment wearing."

Certainly Libby, now that she had inherited her share of the Reynolds money and controlled that of her son Topper, was living the life of the super-wealthy. She actually had solid gold bathroom fixtures and doorknobs in the house at Treetops and guests sometimes would playfully unscrew the knobs and throw them around like tennis balls. But even then, her use of wealth seemed almost a put-on, as though to show her disdain for money. On the floor of one of the bathrooms was a white mink bathmat. "What is money for, if not to have fun with?" Libby said.

Her tendency toward sardonic and often biting humor sometimes would get her in trouble. The public was fascinated with her image but never certain what had really happened at Reynolda, a subject which was gossiped about behind her back even then, ten years after the event. Once, chatting with Earl Wilson in the Barbary Room, he referred to somebody they both didn't like. "She said, 'Why don't we kill him?'" Wilson reported soberly. Friends who were there said Libby meant the whole thing as a joke on herself because of all the innuendoes constantly directed at her, but the press seemed never to lose an opportunity to take a dig and theatrical producers began to see her as a jinx at the box office.

Although she didn't need the money anymore, Libby always liked to keep working. In 1943 she staged a stunning nightclub act using the material she had been learning from Josh White at La Vie Parisienne. The act got rave reviews. Dorothy Kilgallen called it "the best forty-five minutes of entertainment in New York." Malcolm Johnson in the *Sun* wrote, "We never dreamed that we'd ever hear any white person sing these songs in the electrifying way this new, this more dynamic Libby Holman sings them."

The result was not only a mob scene during Libby's solo appearance each night, but a rush of musical connoisseurs and intellectuals, who were part of Libby's following. These included Leonard Bernstein, Alfred Wallenstein, Nathan Milstein, and others. Libby was delighted to be the center of attention again and to have a chance to try out her ideas about these new kinds of songs. "Whether you'd say that I sing them colored or white or just Libby Holman, I don't know, but it's getting away from the Tin Pan Alley slickness of the torch songs I used to sing," Libby said.

Despite these glowing reviews and all the favorable publicity, when Howard Dietz produced his next musical, *Sadie Thompson,* based on *Rain,* the play in which Libby's dear friend Jeanne Eagels had achieved immortality, he did not seek her out for the title role. It is probable he was discouraged by producers from taking a chance on her. Instead, he tried to get Ethel Merman for the part, but there was a falling-out over Merman's attempt to get her husband included as a lyricist, which, after all, was Howard's forte, and a young, relatively unknown actress, sister of the famous striptease dancer Gypsy Rose Lee, June Havoc, was cast in the role. The show ran only sixty performances and produced no memorable numbers.

Libby continued to correspond sporadically with her husband Ralph, who had transferred from the Royal Canadian Air Force to the United States Air Force, but there was unquestionably a loosening of bonds. Friends close to Libby felt that she could not accept the new found independence in her husband, who was maturing rapidly in the pressure-cooker of the European war. Ralph had also grown nervous and somewhat despondent under the onus of more than three years in combat and when he was finally discharged in 1945 and moved back into Treetops, he no longer seemed to fit in with the sharp, fast theatrical crowd in which Libby moved. He was even thinking of leaving the theater entirely. It was clear to both Libby and Ralph that the honeymoon was over and they agreed to separate. Ralph left Treetops after staying there only two weeks and moved into a sublet apartment at 340 East 66th Street, not far from Libby's townhouse. They consulted Ben Polikoff and had a friendly but legal agreement to separate. Plans for a divorce were discussed, but nothing final was decided.

Shortly after their meeting at Polikoff's office, Libby got word that her father was ill in Cincinnati, and flew out to see if she could be of any help. After spending some time with her ailing parent, Libby flew back to New York on Tuesday, November 20. That evening, Libby Holman's husband Ralph was found dead in his apartment. An empty bottle of sleeping tablets was beside his partly clad body, which was grotesquely swollen. It was believed the body had been in the overheated apartment for more than eight days.

The newspapers could be excused perhaps if they sought to link the tragic deaths of Libby's two husbands. The *Post* led the story like this: "Death under unusual circumstances has claimed a second husband of torch-singer Libby Holman." The following paragraph naturally contained a rehash of the death of Smith Reynolds and the murder charge which had been filed against the singer and "Al Williams." The error on the part of the writer of the story, Betsy Lewis, was typical of the distortions that pursued Libby through those years, and which became incorporated in the stories about Libby and repeated when reporters would pull out the clippings for reference in later stories. These distortions tended to be repeated and enlarged. Nowhere in the clippings did it ever say that Smith committed suicide, only that the charges were "dropped for lack of evidence."

Police stated that Holmes had been drinking and that they believed that the mixture of booze and barbiturates might have "caused visceral congestion leading to death." Earl Wilson, the *Post*'s gossip columnist, said that when he talked to Libby and Ralph a month earlier, just after

Ralph had returned, Holmes was talking about going into politics in Connecticut and Libby "was interested in a more serious type of musical comedy, combining ballet and drama."

Polikoff was quick to reach the press the next morning, pointing out that Libby and Holmes had already separated "amicably," trying to head off the speculation that the young veteran had committed suicide out of despair over his split-up from Libby. Polikoff told the newspapers that Ralph had had trouble sleeping and regularly took sleeping tablets. He pointed out that no note had been found in the apartment. "Who discovered Holmes' body," the *Daily News* said, in a shirt-tail to the interview with Polikoff, "was still a mystery yesterday."

Charles Lieberman of the Medical Examiner's Office told the *News* that according to a preliminary report, Libby found the body.

Libby was not available for comment. She had fled, as she did so often in times of trouble, to Montchanin and the comforting arms of Louisa Jenney. Friends and newspeople who phoned were simply told that Miss Holman was "not available." Monty called several times and finally contented himself with a telegram: 'LIBBY YOU KNOW WHERE TO FIND ME IF YOU NEED ME."

21

Topper

For the moment, Topper was the only man in Libby's life, and with Ralph's death she poured even more attention on her growing young son. She took him with her now on road tours and often gave him little chores to do in the theater. Young Topper was beginning to show a real interest in stage managing and set building, although not particularly attracted to the dramatic arts.

When Libby was doing summer stock, Topper would travel with her to the various summer theaters in New England. If she remained at a theater for any length of time, Topper would be entered in a nearby camp so she could visit him frequently. After Ralph's death, he became almost her constant date, beside her at dances, cocktail parties and the political meetings with which she had become increasingly involved.

A few months after Ralph's death, Libby revealed what she had in mind when she said she was interested in a "more serious" type of musical drama. She was backing and planned to appear as the star in *The Beggar's Opera.*

Secretly, Libby had been taking serious singing lessons for more than five years. But the thought of anybody with all Libby's money appearing in something called *The Beggar's Opera* struck many commentators as comical. The *American Weekly* took Libby's announcement as an opportunity not only to rehash the Reynolds case but to tie it to an obscure news item, an accounting in orphan's court in Baltimore, of how Libby had actually spent the money from the Reynolds estate.

PERSONAL EXPENSES

Clothing	$ 2,500
Schools, including dancing and skating	2,500
Governess	2,400
Trained Nurse	3,000
Doctor and medical supplies	4,000
Dentist, oculist, attorney, other professional services	5,000
Charitable contributions	7,000
Christmas and birthday gifts, parties, amusements, etc.	5,000
Toys, books, etc	2,000
Traveling, recreation, vacation	10,000
Pets	1,000

HOUSEHOLD EXPENSES

Guards (three)	$ 6,300
Dogs (three Great Danes)	1,200
Cook	1,500
Chauffeur	1,800
Housekeeper and secretary	3,000
Maids (two)	2,160
Butler	1,800
Laundress	1,090
Rent	12,000
Food for household	8,000
Uniforms for servants	1,200
Storage (two cars)	900
Depreciation on cars	900

Upkeep, servicing and repair of cars.............	2,000
Replacement of household furnishings, linens, curtains, etc....................................	4,000
Care of furnace, ash removal, etc.................	750
Laundry, dry cleaning, carpet cleaning, etc...	2,500
Heat, light, water, gas, electricity, etc..	4,500

The item for rent was lopped off in 1944 after the court had authorized a payment of $300,000 from the estate for a house which Libby had built near Stamford, Conn., at a reputed cost of $435,183. Elimination of two or three other entries brought the yearly expense account down to $83,333.28.

The article was accompanied by a fanciful illustration of what Topper would look like on a fishing trip. It pictured a skinny kid sitting on rocks at the edge of a brook, surrounded by an army of servants. Three machine-gun toting armed guards were at the top of the picture, accompanied by huge Great Danes. A maid in uniform held a can of bait on a silver tray, while a fastidious butler impaled a wriggling worm on the youngster's hook.

Libby's devotion to the rich little boy, the article was careful to point out, "is intensely strong."

"The main reason she is so anxious to have Broadway at her feet once more is that she wants her boy to be proud of her."

Regardless of her ambitions, the *Beggar's Opera* project never quite took fire. A newspaper reported that she had bowed out of it "because she considered her part too small."

Meanwhile, after a decent period of mourning, Libby and Monty began to associate with one another much more openly, after having kept low profiles during her marriage to Holmes. Friends were confused because Clift was simultaneously having his first serious and overt romance with another man. But, at the same time, he was said to be seeing and sleeping with several women besides Libby!

"Monty used to brag a little about his affairs with women in his own discreet way," Kevin McCarthy commented. "He made innuendoes that he had done pretty well with them."

In his biography of Clift, Robert LaGuardia gives this analysis:

"The question of Monty and Libby Holman is a touchy one: there was much talk at the time [the 1940's]. Some of this talk came from Monty himself. Libby Holman is dead now, and what lives on is a series of impressions, rather than facts. Undeniably, she was sexually and emotionally attracted to sensitive, homosexual men like Monty. . . ."

Observing them during the long weekends at Treetops, Kevin McCarthy was certain that there was some actual sexual involvement between Libby and Monty, despite the fact that she was fourteen years his senior.

"She was a robust, intelligent woman, but hardly attractive," LaGuardia comments, "her face was riddled with premature wrinkles. Billy [a friend of Monty's] shuddered to think of them, because the idea of this young god in bed with an unattractive older woman seemed repulsive. Monty told one male lover that he and Libby had "wild scenes" with marijuana and pep pills.

Libby at the time was strung out. The suicide of Ralph Holmes on top of the murder scandal had affected her sensitivity and poise. Maureen Stapleton recalls a marvelous dinner at Treetops, at which Libby just sat at the table drinking, not touching a bite of the exquisite food. "She didn't know most of the dinner guests and she didn't care to know them. She was almost like a female Jay Gatsby, surrounded by her own wealth—maids, butlers . . . yet uninvolved." Others remember her drinking heavily, and there was much talk—but only *talk*—of drugs. She may or may not have introduced Monty to heavier drugs than he was then taking. A few years later, Janet Cohen saw Monty and Libby coming out of a movie theater laughing, joking, and taking swigs of liquor out of a liquor bottle half-hidden in a brown paper bag."

Soon, Monty was spending so much time at Libby's

place that he had a special little room—called "Monty's room"—which was treated like a shrine and always kept in readiness. Brooks Clift, Monty's brother, says that Monty established a close and loving relationship with young Topper, that they would go for long walks on the estate and spend hours talking quietly in the library about the meaning of life, drama, philosophy and art.

In 1947 Libby, who had been working with Josh White in her nightclub acts and concerts for six years, broke off their professional relationship. Libby said that Josh could not perform with her any longer because of "previous commitments." There is very little information as to just exactly what her personal relationship with White was, but in any event he introduced her to Gerald Cook, a handsome young black pianist who had studied with the famous Nadia Boulanger. Libby later said that she had also made the change because she needed the fuller background of a piano, as opposed to Josh White's twangy and moody guitar.

But Libby no longer wanted to be out on the road all the time. She was content to spend long months at Treetops with her son, practicing voice and piano. Besides, her health was finally beginning to give in from the enormous demands she had made on it, by chain-smoking, endless drinking, and insidious chemical experimentation. In 1947 she revealed to Frank Coniff that she had had to go on a strict ulcer diet. "The ulcers are bad enough," she said, "but the diet is worse. You get milk, milk, milk and then more milk. Being a mother and an entertainer affects my psychosomatic condition or something."

So, for the moment at least, Libby concentrated more on being a mother. She took Topper with her on the Queen Mary for a five-week vacation to Europe and French Morocco. More than ever, he became the center of her life. They worked the summer theaters, Libby as a performer and Topper as a stagehand. She visited him often at Putney School in Vermont and stood by like any proud mother when, in June of 1949, seventeen-year-old

Libby and son "Topper" arriving in New York aboard *Queen Mary* in 1948.

Topper, chairman of Putney's student council, graduated near the top of his class. At school the enthusiastic youngster introduced her to Steve Wasserman, his best friend, son of William Stix Wasserman, a financier from New York and Philadelphia. Steve's father owned part of the famed Cerro Gordo gold mine in the mountains of California and the boys thought it would be fun for the summer to go and work in the mine and perhaps get in some mountain climbing. Libby, who was readying herself for a trip to Europe, during which she planned to set up a concert tour, ascertained from the Wassermans that the boys would be in good hands and well supervised and happily gave consent for her young son's first independent summer.

On August 11, the sheriff's office in Lone Pine, California, where the Cerro Gordo Mine was located, made a frantic call to the Holman estate in Stamford and then to the New York apartment on East 61st Street, but was unable to reach her. He explained to Libby's secretary that he had urgent news and had to get in touch with Libby who was then in Paris. The secretary said she would contact her as soon as she could. "Please do," the sheriff said, "those two boys went out to climb Mt. Whitney last Saturday with two days' rations. It's Tuesday now, and they're not back. We're afraid they're in serious trouble."

The sheriff's fears were too soon confirmed. Steve Wasserman and Christopher Smith Reynolds, after assuring local acquaintances that they were experienced climbers and already "climbed some of the highest peaks in the Swiss Alps," had set out to climb the east face of 14,496-foot Mount Whitney, at that time the tallest peak in the United States. When the two young men were two days overdue, a posse of local mountaineers was organized to make a search. Wasserman's car, a 1940 Plymouth, was soon found at the base of the mountain. A plane joined the searchers and dropped tools and equipment to the search team, working itself through the difficult terrain. Two days later the snow-covered, frozen body of seventeen-year-old Steve Wasserman was found in a crevasse high on the jagged east face of the mountain. But the mountaineers combing the snow for Christopher Reynolds failed to find him before nightfall. Earlier searchers had reported sighting two bodies through binoculars, but only Wasserman's was found. It was placed in a casket, but could not be brought down from the mountain until the following day. The slope was too treacherous for searchers to dare a night descent. Mountain-wise posse members speculated that Christopher Reynolds had either dropped to his death in some other gash on the mountain's rock face, or fell with Wasserman and by some exceedingly long chance, landed in the soft snow, survived, and was wandering on the mountain. The report that her son was lost was cabled to Libby Holman when she was finally located in France and she made arrangements to return by the first available plane.

An Air Force rescue team with walkie-talkie radios was summoned to join the hunt for Reynolds to provide the communications sorely lacking during the week-long search. Mr. Wasserman, who arrived with his wife soon after their son vanished, said he had tried to talk Stephen into going to Europe that summer.

"But he told me he wanted to come out here with Chris to work in a gold mine and have a shot at climbing a mountain," the boy's father said.

Members of the Sierra Club, all experienced mountain climbers assisting in the search, said that young Reynolds and Wasserman should not ever have attempted to climb the precipitous east face of the mountain without others.

"That's a job for no less than five climbers together," said a veteran member. "I climbed the Matterhorn in the Swiss Alps, and I understand these two young fellows climbed it, too. Shucks, the Matterhorn is a molehill compared to Mt. Whitney's east face."

On August 15, while Libby was still en route from France, Christopher Smith Reynolds' body was found in a deep crevasse about 700 feet from the summit of Mt.

Whitney. He had come close to succeeding in the difficult climb, but not close enough. His body was lowered by ropes to the 11,500-foot level where Wasserman's body had been discovered earlier. Ray Gorin, one of the Sierra Club hikers, said an 80-foot nylon rope trailed from Reynolds' body. There was a ten-foot length around Wasserman's waist.

Gorin conjectured that the two lads were within 300 feet of the top, when one of them fell.

"I would guess they fell maybe 400 feet before Reynolds stuck and was held by the crevice," Gorin said. "The rope couldn't take the strain of Wasserman's body. It snapped and Wasserman fell perhaps 1,500 feet more."

Libby transferred at New York for a transcontinental plane to Los Angeles and then flew the 230 miles from the West Coast city, arriving the afternoon that Chris was found. During the airport stop in Los Angeles, when Libby was changing planes, one of the men accompanying Libby Holman swung a valise at news photographer George Hullibarger. The blow knocked the photographer's glasses off and hit his camera. Hullibarger retaliated with one punch, then police stepped in and Miss Holman and her companions took off for Lone Pine. Needless to say, the incident did nothing to enhance Libby's public image. Furthermore, there was immediate speculation over the fact that Christopher Smith Reynolds had died such a conveniently short time before he was to inherit all of his $6.5 million estate. But it was impossible to connect Libby to the tragedy, since she had been some 7,000 miles away when it occurred, and had not, in the first place, even known of his plans to climb the mountain.

"Make-believe tragedy in Libby Holman's torch songs brought her fame, and real life tragedy has brought her a fortune of several million dollars," was the way the *Daily News* put it, in speculating that Libby would almost surely inherit Christopher's trust fund.

Monty Clift had been at Libby's home almost constantly during the previous year, before having to go to Hollywood, and that summer they had arranged to meet in Paris while Libby prepared the itinerary for her European tour. But Monty was called to Rome to do publicity for his new picture, *Red River,* and he left, promising that they would get together in a week or so, when he got word that Topper had been killed on Mount Whitney. Clift, without even consulting Paramount Studios, took the first plane and flew back to New York to be with Libby.

Libby didn't want to see anyone during those first weeks after Christopher's death. She drank herself into a stupor almost every day, blaming herself for the tragedy, feeling she should have seen to it that he was better chaperoned.

She began to feel that she carried with her the kiss of death, and certainly that sentiment was understandable. Christopher's was the fifth in a series of fatalities involving people Libby had loved dearly at one time or another in her life: first Jeanne Eagels, about whom only a few close friends really knew, then Smith, about whom the whole world knew, then Phillips who died obscurely in a wartime crash, then Ralph, lying obscenely purple and swollen eight days' dead from an overdose of drugs in a sublet apartment, and now Christopher, the person who was dearer to her than life itself, who ended frozen in a crevice high in the Sierra Nevadas.

When Monty called and tried to see her, she would send him away angrily. "Don't get near me, Monty. I'm poison, can't you see it? I mean nothing but death. Stay away. Something terrible will happen to you." But Monty tried to laugh away her fears. "You'll be fine, Libby. You're strong. You're fantastic. Now shut up! Take this." And he would hold out a tranquilizer or a sedative, hoping it would bring her out of her grim mood.

A month later the newspapers had a chance to drag the whole case through the linotype again when the courts awarded Libby Smith's entire estate.

"Real-life Tragedy Makes Millionaire of Libby," was the way the *Post* headed the story. The new money made

Libby suspicious and shy of people. Now she had an increasing fear that everyone was after her money. "Her mail was extraordinary," Gerald Cook, her accompanist, said, "everybody asking for a handout."

Not that Libby was stingy with her money—but she had her own idea of charity. She established the Christopher Reynolds foundation with some of the money and one of the first grants went to Martin Luther King, Jr., who was then a young minister in Georgia. The grant enabled King to go to India and study with Gandhi, where he first learned the techniques of nonviolence. King and his wife Coretta became close friends of Libby.

The drinking Libby did after Christopher's death soon caught up with her. Her ulcer started tearing her insides apart again, causing her to double up in pain after only one glass of wine. She cut down on the liquor and tried to combat depression by practicing Zen. She would spend hours a day meditating and then would come bursting out of her silence with questions she had been thinking about while sitting there, about Korea, about Truman and the atom bomb, and why was Gloria Vanderbilt so beautiful. She'd clutch her head in despair at times at her inability to answer these questions. "I'm such a stupe!" she'd say after each failure to come up with an answer.

22

Monty

After Christopher's death, Monty and Libby grew even closer. Monty was still in something of a funk over the breakup of his romance with Elizabeth Taylor. Soon Clift was practically living at Treetops, at least when he was in the New York area, and so were his closest friends, the McCarthys and others of Clift's group—friends that dated back to *Mexican Mural.* "I remember her, brown as a berry but very emaciated," Augusta Dabney told Clift's biographer, Patricia Bosworth. "She would smoke cigarette after cigarette through paper filters. On Sunday afternoon, Monty and Libby could frequently be seen floating on rubber mattresses in her pool, often in the nude. Libby never stopped gazing at Monty. It was a look of adoration, mingled with desire and love. And as often as not, Monty would return the look."

"It was a little embarrassing to watch," another friend reported.

Her relationship with Clift was unique and symbiotic. Like few of her other friends, Clift could love her and yet accept her need for varied and bizarre sexual relationships, although no one knew what they did together in bed. He was away much of the time and felt that he could not demand sexual loyalty, nor did he want it, for with his tolerance came her acceptance of his many partners, and in the fifties these seemed to be increasingly male homosexuals.

Although he had jealously guarded his heterosexual image in the early years of his movie career, Monty seemed no longer to care what people thought of his sexual preferences and openly roved a group of homosexual bars then popular near Third Avenue which were called "the Bird Circuit," catering to the most totally committed out-of-the-closet gay cruisers. As Monty's behavior became more outlandish it was increasingly obvious to Libby that he needed comfort and assurance. She was the all-forgiving mother. Even some of his closest and longest lasting homosexual relationships began to fall apart. Robert LaGuardia reported the experience of one friend identified only as "Rick."

Monty had invited his long-time lover to a house he had rented in Ogunquit, Maine, to be near Libby who had a house in Kennebunkport, and his psychiatrist, Dr. William Siverberg, a controversial analyst who specialized in treating homosexuals and drug addicts.

"The night I got up there, Monty was drinking and carrying on, and higher than I had ever seen him before," Rick recalled. "I didn't know much about pills, but I figured he had downed something else besides liquor. We took off our clothes and went to bed. Suddenly Monty started slapping me around. He got his belt and started beating me. I was frightened. Nothing like this had ever happened before. I ran out of his bedroom into another and locked the door. Monty pounded on it. The next morning, he was crying and asked me why I had locked the door on him. I told him and he said he couldn't remember a thing."

A lover Monty picked up on the beach that summer said of him, "Monty was so sadistic that I just couldn't put

Montgomery Clift at the start of his Hollywood career.

up with it. I only saw him at big parties and we got very drunk. When we did get it on, I'd wake up in the morning all battered and bruised. He was rough and overly dominant. He threw me around like a toothpick. When he kissed you, he kissed you so it hurt. One time I came away with a bloody mouth. But he was so beautiful and so physical that I didn't dare object. His eyes were like green crystals. When you looked at them, it was looking into diamonds. Sometimes they were glazed over, and I guess he was on uppers, but in those days I didn't know anything about them or their effects."

It was common knowledge that Clift was not well-endowed sexually. Along the gay grapevine he was referred to as "Princess Tiny Meat." Whether the size of his sexual equipment had anything to do with his sadistic tendencies is a matter of speculation.

These blackouts such as the one described by Rick were becoming a regular part of Monty's pattern. All of his regular friends, however, knew that always during the night in which such scenes would take place there was an obligatory trip to the bathroom where Monty would take a downer, usually Demerol. It was the synergistic effect of the drug and alcohol that put Monty out. And these incidents happened too often to be considered completely accidental. It was obvious that Monty wanted to cut himself off, at least temporarily, from life.

Even the intimate little family dinners Monty would give at his apartment or at Libby's became increasingly pathetic and only his closest friends really were able to handle his self-destructive behavior.

Roddy McDowell, one of his closest friends and Marge Stengel, his regular secretary, as well as a few others besides Libby, such as Kevin and Augusta, Arthur Miller, Maureen Stapleton, or Truman Capote would gather for dinners and watch while Monty, who would start the evening apparently perfectly sober, would take trips to the bathroom and suddenly come out dazed and obviously stoned. He would begin to slur his words. He'd get up to put on a new record, walk across the room and fall on his face with a thud. Friends would just sit there, moodily finishing their expensive food. They knew he wanted to be left where he was. Conversation would go on as if nothing happened. After about a half hour lying on the floor, Monty would get up and go to his bedroom which he kept completely sealed off from the light—a replica of oblivion. Guests would continue their dinner and go home on their own, but it must have been depressing. Monty used to call this sealed-off, darkened bedroom his "coffin." Sometimes he'd be asleep in it when his guests arrived. They would understand and just go ahead without him.

Monty, in the fifties considered one of the most brilliant and up-and-coming young actors in America, made many new friends in those years. These included the woman whom Libby had idolized since her first days in the theater, and whose pictures had always adorned her dressing room—Greta Garbo—and Thornton Wilder, who had written *Skin of Our Teeth.* It was Monty also who brought Inge Morath and Arthur Miller, who later became her husband, into their intimate circle.

One night Monty gave one of his intimate dinners for Garbo. Libby, Wilder, Miller, the McCarthys and George Schlee, the businessman whom everybody assumed to be the film star's lover, were present. With insensitive cruelty, Schlee, to whom Libby was a novelty and a curiosity, kept questioning and baiting her all through the dinner about the mysterious death of Smith Reynolds, asking details of the inquest and "what really happened," until Libby's face was livid with anger. Only Garbo, sensing the embarrassment of everybody at the table, grunted to her escort, "Shut up," and to the relief of the company Schlee did as he was asked.

Libby, like many outspoken liberals of the theater world, had her troubles in the fifties with the House Unamerican Activities Committee. She was named along with hundreds of others suspected of being "pinkos" or "comsymps." Fortunately, she did not depend on films or television for her living, so she found the charges less than onerous, though she involved herself furiously in defense of some of her friends named by the zealous McCarthy era Red-hunters.

Libby made something of a salon out of the Treetops estate. Every spring she would give a lavish party for the viewing of the million daffodils she had planted on the estate's expansive lawns. "It was a spectacular sight," Kevin McCarthy remembers. "The daffodils seemed to flood and shine and ripple across the hill opposite the house."

After she had recuperated from Christopher's death, she continued to host large, impressive, and tasteful luncheons and dinners. Monty would be at the head of the table acting as co-host. The finest French wines were spilled on her linen damask table cloths and choice fresh fruit was crushed indiscriminately into the Persian rugs. The place began to attract a crowd much different from Libby's usual intellectual set—male models, chorus boys, "male hustlers, some of them, let's face it," an interior decorator friend of Libby's told Bosworth. "They were loud and bombed out of their minds by the end of the meal."

Libby, often apparently under the influence of drugs, with her mind a million miles away, didn't seem to know or care who came to the parties anymore. "There was a lot of running around on the lawn nude, falling into the pool, and getting stoned on pot," one "friend" said. "All of that seems pretty tame now."

Not all of the visitors were unintellectual, but a very high percentage were gay, among them Allen Ginsberg and Peter Orlofsky. Paul Bowles and his wife Jane were visitors at Treetops almost as often as Monty, more often in fact as Monty was called away frequently on movie business. They more or less made their home at the Connecticut estate whenever they were in America. Libby had met Bowles during her trip to Morocco with Christopher and both were very close to her—especially Jane, who was commonly believed to be her lover. Despite Paul Bowles' fine literary reputation, the couple was almost completely broke and grateful for her hospitality.

Jane, a good-looking, sardonic and highstrung writer, it turned out, was going slowly insane. She was as close to Monty as she was to Libby, and they used to drink together and discuss with one another why they were allowing themselves to go down the drain with alcohol. "We drink to suppress our panic," Monty would say, and the drunken pair would fall onto the lawn laughing. Often, when she was drunk, Jane would admit that she was in love with Libby. And Monty would laugh and say, "But so am I."

One female friend of Libby's said, "She seemed to reserve the best part of herself for women." Then, describing her own affair with the torch singer, she said, "Libby is tender, compassionate, generous—enormously sensual with all her close women friends. With men for the most part, she acted like a ball-breaker."

Not all of the people invited to Libby's estate were crazy about Monty's habits. During the last years, shortly after his completion of the award-winning *A Place in the Sun,* Monty began to mix his liquor with barbiturates and would often pass out suddenly or draw blanks for long periods of time and even when he was simply drunk, his behavior was often revolting at the dinner table and elsewhere. "Monty acted like a spoiled brat around Libby—I couldn't stand him," designer Oliver Smith said. And Libby's nephew, David Holman, told Patricia Bosworth that Monty was always acting "silly—so babyish, hugging, kissing, biting you sometimes, and often falling down drunk."

At the lavish opening-night party Libby gave for Jane Bowles' play, *In the Summer House,* for which she put up the money, one guest said, "Montgomery Clift was in the kitchen, necking with Libby. They were being very lovey-dovey right in front of Judith Anderson and Roger L. Stevens."

It was at this party that a guest went upstairs and used the famous powder room, the one with the gold faucets, and the mink bathmat. "I walked into their bedroom and I got the feeling that Monty and Libby must have very kinky sex. Everything seemed erotic and faintly decadent—the low lights, the slippery white satin sheets on the bed, the overpowering fragrance of Jungle Gardenia perfume. And then I saw this huge bottle of Seconal on the bedroom table. It must have contained a hundred pills—the prescription on it read 'Libby Holman Reynolds.'"

When they couldn't stand the crowd of near-strangers at Treetops, Libby and Monty would often run off to the newly-discovered Amagansett area of Long Island. There they would try to dry out, taking long bike rides or strolling on the beach, both making a valiant attempt to taper off. A local painter said he used to see them holding hands and running through the dunes. "They were cold sober and quite morose," he observed.

In the spring of 1952 Monty went out to Hollywood for the Academy Awards. He was given a good chance of winning for his role in *A Place in the Sun.* While there he stayed with his good friends, Fred and Jeanne Greene, as he usually did. But he was deeply disappointed. *A Place in the Sun* won awards for Best Director, Best Screenplay, Best Camera Work, Best Film Editing, Best Scoring and Best Costumes, but Humphrey Bogart had won the award for Best Actor for his performance in *The African Queen.* Monty decided to go right back to New York where "people were normal," a peculiar view, coming from him. He asked the Greenes to go with him and help him decorate the new duplex he had rented on East 61st Street, near Libby.

They agreed to do so and spent what Jeanne Greene later called "an utterly exhausting summer, emotionally and physically." A lot of fights and clashes between Monty's idea of decoration and the Greenes'. Monty insisted that the *sine qua non* of his new apartment would be a fourteen-foot-long medicine cabinet in the bathroom. Fred felt this would be ridiculous. There would be no way to fill such a cabinet. Monty told him not to worry. And as soon as Greene had finished it, even before he had moved into the apartment, he had filled the enormous cabinet with its mirrors and louvered doors from wall to wall with a veritable pharmacopeia of chemical crutches. There were pain relievers such as Darvon, antibiotics such as terramycin; anticonvulsants, antidepressants, tranquilizers, paragoric, decongestants, antispasmodics, antinauseants, muscle relaxants, and every sleeping pill known to God, man, and pharmacists.

Everybody stayed in Libby Holman's brownstone apartment half a block away during the construction, but Libby herself stayed at Treetops for most of the summer, leaving the furniture in the city apartment draped in white dust-covers. Jeanne Greene described the mood for Pat Bosworth. "We'd sit in one tiny patch of her living room, drinking brandy and listening to a Sinatra record. But the atmosphere was vaguely creepy because Libby didn't approve of us. She was jealous and suspicious of my relationship with Monty, and she thought Fred was too inexperienced to renovate a brownstone." When she came to the city occasionally, it seemed to Jeanne, that Libby was always sneaking up and trying to eavesdrop on her conversations with Monty.

"We'd be out in her garden in the evening, and suddenly this figure would emerge and hover in the background and then disappear, and Monty would stop what he was saying to me and go off with her."

Jeanne, who was obviously not a fan of Libby's, felt that she kept Monty on a long leash. She described a scene where she and Monty were sitting on a couch in Libby's apartment listening to Frank Sinatra's rendition of "I've Got the World on a String"—one of Monty and Libby's favorite records. "Suddenly this figure," Jeanne recalled, "half-hidden by a great bunch of flowers—appears in the doorway. It was Libby unexpectedly home from the country. Monty got very clutched. He crawled over to her on his hands and knees and started telling her how gorgeous and wonderful she was. It was a frightening image."

Once in a while, Jeanne reported, Monty would suddenly turn to her without apparent motivation and tell her to take a walk around the corner. "Get a cup of coffee," he would say, "I have a gangster coming over." At the time Jeanne wasn't certain what he meant but years later a Harlem drug-runner admitted that he had supplied Monty, Judy Garland, and Libby Holman with pills on a wholesale basis. "A couple of months I'd deliver Clift a roll of pills—that's a thousand pills—Seconals, Tuinals, and Doriden, which wasn't even on the market yet. A roll of pills cost $450 in 1955—today (1965) it would cost a thousand."

Libby, under the influence of alcohol and drugs, did not behave as grossly as Monty. She was the first to realize however that she was ruining her health and her life, and that it was time to dry out and come to grips with life. Besides, drinking had become very painful since her insides were being eaten away by ulcers.

She would take herself off to various expensive drying-out institutions from time to time in an attempt to straighten out but when she was back with Monty it wasn't long before she would fall off the wagon again. Still she certainly knew every detail of the drying-out routine. By 1954 she managed to have given up, for the moment not only liquor but cigarettes which she had formerly smoked at the rate of three to four packs a day.

It was four years after Topper's death before Libby felt straightened out again, in good health and off booze and drugs.

As a symbol of her new life she adopted two boys, Timothy, nine, and Anthony, seven. Their privacy was closely guarded and no information was given out at the time of the adoption or later as to who the boys were, how she came to adopt them, or how, since she was unmarried, she was able to under the code of that period. Monty was able to establish a warm, semi-parental rapport with the youngsters, who saw him somewhat as another child. But Libby tried to keep Monty, in his worst moods, which were increasingly frequent, away from the children. Even his good friends the McCarthys did not like to have Clift around her kids in his drunken condition. But Libby accepted him with all his faults and treated him, in fact, like one more of her children. Once at a Treetops dinner, Monty got drunk and kept resting his face in the soup plate. Libby would jerk him up by the collar, wipe his face with a damask napkin, remove the plate and continue talking to her friends as though nothing had happened. As part of her rehabilitation, she felt that she would like to give a concert performance of the songs she had learned with Josh White and sung so often with Gerald Cook's accompaniment.

Feeling healthy, limber, and in top form again, Libby began to work harder on polishing the act, with an eye to bringing it back to Broadway. They had hardly started rehearsing when, as though prompted by some macabre press agent, Ab Walker died in Winston-Salem after a year's unspecified illness. Walker had gone to Texas shortly after the incident at Reynolda and had served as a real estate agent down there, taking out time to serve in World War II, where he saw extensive and distinguished combat service in the Army in the Philippines.

To judge by the obits that made the New York papers, his involvement, now referred to as "the mysterious murder" of Smith Reynolds, was the only notable feature of Walker's life. Mercifully, none of the newspapers asked Libby for her comment on Ab's death.

At her own expense, she booked a limited run of the concert at the Bijou theater. Richard Watts, critic of the *Post,* explained what Libby meant by the term "sin songs" in the title of her show. "They . . . are songs in which the singer is chiefly very unhappy because she is being badly treated by an unworthy lover in what appears to be a fairly illicit romance." Commenting on her performance he said, "That she is a singer with a strikingly individual style and considerable distinction is, of course I am sure, known by everyone. And it is my impression that she has lost none of the style or the distinction since she last appeared on Broadway, which is quite a few years ago."

As had become standard in Libby's case, each of the stories describing her act gave roughly half of the space to the description of the show and the rest to the rehash of her gloomy past. "Libby Holman's private life has given her a right to sing the blues," is the way *Time* headed its reprise. J. P. Shanley, an interviewer for the *New York Times,* asked Libby outright if she thought her career had been altered by the tragedies that had marked her life. Libby answered: "My professional life has been going a certain way, and no matter what happened to me, I think it would have taken the same turn. I may have acquired another dimension, but my course would have been the same. I'm really of the Maude Adams school. Private life is one thing, and professional another."

Exhausted by the show, which kept her on stage for a solid hour and forty-five minutes, and a little peeved at the snide reviews, Libby decided to gather up her troublesome ward Montgomery Clift and go down for a real wing-ding fling in wild and sinful pre-Castro Havana. The chances that either of them could stay off drugs or booze in that playful paradise were roughly equal to those of a frozen daiquiri in Dante's Inferno. Libby's guts were torn and riddled with God-knows-what agonizing disorders. Monty had already been told by Silverberg and other doctors that if he continued taking drugs and drinking the way he was doing, he could not possibly live another five years.

What drove these two brilliant and agonized creatures to such a suicidal mission is known only to God and possibly their psychiatrists—or perhaps no one.

Havana in those final years of Batista was like a city invented by Jean Genêt. Any vice, any perversion, any sin one could desire, was available for a price—and not a very high one, at that. One could watch in a group while the legendary "Superman" mounted an endless series of women of every color, shape and age. One could go on to a sex circus and see women mounted by ponies, mules, Great Danes, and monkies. One could lounge back and smoke opium or marijuana or inject any variety of drugs, all of them available at rock-bottom prices, while women with educated vaginas picked stacks of coins off the corner of the table or squirted a hard-boiled egg out of their vulvas into a bowl of urine half-way across the room. Round-robins, trios, quartets, and daisy chains of every sexual persuasion were available, as were children of any age. There was a girl who could inhale smoke from a cigar into her vagina and puff it out in smoke rings.

This was not, of course, the typical life of the average Habañero—but it was what tourists like Libby and Monty came down for. A woman called Magda Vasquez Bello told Bosworth about seeing the couple every day either on the beach or in the gift shop of the hotel.

"Libby Holman was a middle-aged woman, informally dressed, not too well-groomed, and always giving the impression of being slightly high—perhaps on dope. Montgomery Clift was always somewhat loud, not well-mannered, and like Libby seemed to be more or less high on dope. Their relationship seemed a happy one, but . . . there was something wrong and not healthy somewhere.

"They laughed a lot in a stupid, rather childish way. They argued from time to time. Monty's table manners were obnoxious. He was anything but the timid, sensitive person he gave the impression of being in his films. She looked very much the part of a tough cookie, and must have had him 'under her spell.'"

The closeness of their relationship was baffling even to her closest friends. Libby's lifelong addiction to the sun had left her with a dried-out, prematurely wrinkled face. But no matter how much Libby ate and drank, she managed to keep her figure lithe and supple. To some people, one of the most remarkable aspects of her concert at the Bijou was the way in which she was able to take her bows with her head almost sweeping the ground. Even her enemies—and she had many—admitted that she had a magnificent figure as she passed the fifty-year mark.

Monty in the mid-fifties seemed to reach a barrier in his career. He did not work in films for years, nor did he take on any stage roles. He spent most of his time at Treetops or on various cruising jaunts to well-known homosexual resorts. Ned Smith, a friend of his, felt that Libby was somehow behind this lack of productivity. He dropped into Clift's duplex apartment on East 61st Street one night and, unable to restrain himself, Smith just asked Clift point-blank, "What is all this talk about you and Libby Holman?"

"He was very arrogant," Smith said, "as well he should have been—it was none of my business what he did with his life. 'I'm having an affair with Libby Holman,' he told me definitely. 'Is it any business of yours?'

"'No, it isn't,' I said, 'except I think you'd want a younger girl.'"

Monty stared at him with those huge, pellucid eyes and didn't answer. Ned changed the subject abruptly.

One of the few people besides Libby who remained friendly with Monty despite his puzzling and often gross idiosyncracies was Elizabeth Taylor, with whom he had always remained close, even after her various marriages.

When Liz came to New York she usually moved into Monty's duplex with her children while Clift slept half a block away at Libby's.

Friends observed that despite certain long-lasting homosexual relationships, Monty's deepest and most complex friendships were with women, in particular, Liz Taylor, his drama coach Mira Rostova, and Libby. "I don't understand it," he once told his friend Bill Le Massena. "I love men in bed but I really love women."

Not all of Monty's women friends necessarily cared for one another. Libby, purely a product of Broadway, the stage and the literary milieu, did not get along with Liz Taylor, whom she thought of as a somewhat shallow glamour girl. But still they maintained a surface friendship. In 1955, during those times that Liz was staying at Monty's apartment, she had already decided to end her marriage to Michael Wilding and began her somewhat incongruous romance with producer Michael Todd. Clift had even been present when Todd presented

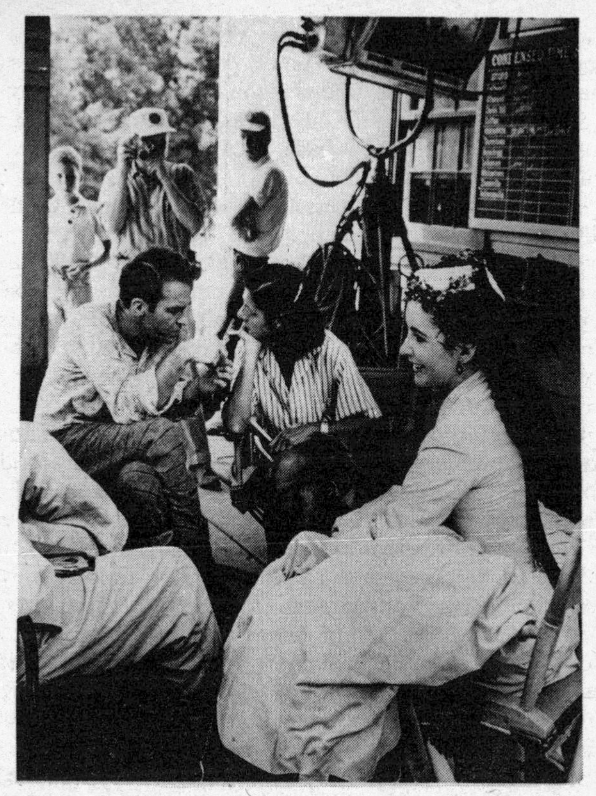

Monty and Libby chat while Liz Taylor rests on the set of *Raintree County* in 1956.

Liz with a huge pearl ring which was to be his pre-engagement present. "You'll get your real engagement ring soon," he told Taylor as they drove from Kennedy airport to the city in a chaffeur driven but battered sedan Monty had hired so that the press wouldn't recognize them.

Despite their differences, at Monty's insistence, Libby allowed Todd to give Liz her "real" engagement ring, a huge diamond worth in the vicinity of $100,000, at Treetops, where they could be guaranteed privacy. The presentation took place before Monty and Libby but as Todd and Liz left about midnight, Taylor found that she couldn't fit her glove over the huge stone. Disgusted, she stripped both gloves off and threw them on the sofa. Libby saved them. Years later, after her death, friends going through her estate found the tiny pair of white kid gloves at Treetops, stuffed in an envelope marked "L. Taylor gloves, 1956."

It was Taylor who persuaded Clift finally to go back to work and he accepted a role in *Raintree County* only because she was to appear in it. He wasn't at all convinced it would be a good picture, but he enjoyed the chance to work with Liz Taylor, which he had wanted to do ever since *A Place in the Sun.* It was to be a big-budget picture for Metro—$5 million, a lot of money in those days—and Monty was to get $300,000, plus top billing. Besides the chance to work with Taylor, the film offered him a chance to recoup his finances which had reached zero point after his years of inaction.

Libby was not fond of the Coast and decided to stay in New York while Monty made the picture. Monty stayed in a rented house, rather than with friends, as he had in the past. He worked hard on the picture despite his lack of faith in it. It was a Civil War epic which he described as "a soap opera with elephantitis." Still, in order to justify his enormous fee, Monty for once was trying to stay straight, at least for the duration of the picture, using drugs and booze as little as possible.

On Saturday, May 12, during the filming, Elizabeth

Taylor called Monty in the early afternoon to make sure he was going to attend an intimate dinner party she planned to hold that night. Monty, who had been caught in the marital problems of the Wildings, who were still living together, was not anxious to go and told her that he didn't think he had the strength to make it and besides, he had already dismissed his chauffeur. (After a series of increasingly close calls caused by his erratic driving, Clift had finally been persuaded to hire somebody to drive him about before he killed himself.) But Taylor insisted and in the end Clift, never able to resist her, agreed to come.

The party was being held in the Wildings' house in the Benedict Canyon hills, and was reached through a treacherous maze of twisting narrow roads. It was, as Liz had promised, a simple dinner party. Kevin McCarthy and Rock Hudson were there. Monty, true to his regimen, was sober when he arrived and carefully avoided liquor, taking only a few sips of wine during the evening.

It was a quiet party, one might have even said a dull one. Liz served lukewarm rosé, Michael Wilding lay back on his couch, sedated for a problem he was having with his back. Kevin, who had to catch a plane in the morning, said he was leaving and Monty, who didn't know the area very well, suggested that he would follow along behind Kevin until he found his way through the treacherous Benedict Canyon hills. Kevin started out in the direction of the airport and as he came to the first sharp turn, he saw Monty coming up very fast behind him. Familiar with his friend's habits, he thought perhaps Monty was trying to play a joke, to nudge him from behind with his car. But it seemed that Monty was coming too close for comfort. Kevin decided to speed up a bit and get some space between his and Clift's car, which seemed to be almost on top of him. He wondered if Monty was having one of his blackouts again.

"I got frightened," he told Patricia Bosworth, "and spurted ahead so he wouldn't bump me. We both made the next turn but the next one was treacherous. We were careening now, swerving and screeching through the darkness. Behind me, I saw Monty's car lights weave from one side of the road to the other and then I heard a terrible crash." He saw a cloud of dust in his rearview mirror and concerned, stopped the car and ran back. He found Monty's car crumpled like an accordion against a telephone pole.

"The motor was making a horrendous noise," Kevin remembered. "I was afraid the car would catch fire so I reached in and turned off the ignition. And I didn't see him. I thought, 'Holy shit! He's been thrown out of the car!'"

Kevin recreated the scene for LaGuardia:

"It was as dark as hell. There was nothing. I turned my car around and shone my lights into his car and saw that he had been in the car all the time... under the dashboard. That's why the motor was running. Apparently his ass was squashed on the accelerator. Gas was leaking. The car would have gone up in flames. I thought he was dead. I thought he was gone. You've never seen such a mess. Blood all over the place. I didn't attempt to move him. Everything might have been broken, his neck, his back. From what I could see in the light of my car, it looked like the whole head had been pulled apart. I was frantic... it was horrifying. I remember thinking, 'It's all over... he's dead... the movie's over!' I was confused."

McCarthy didn't want to leave the scene because if a car came down the road too fast, it would smash into Monty's car and if he were alive, he would surely be killed then. He went to one of the nearby unfinished houses and looked for a phone but couldn't find one so he got back in his car and drove like crazy back to the Wildings'. Michael Wilding came to the door.

Kevin was shaking. "Monty's had a terrible accident. He hit a telephone pole!"

Wilding just laughed. He thought that Kevin had returned to play a sick joke, but after a few seconds, he realized that it was serious. He and McCarthy started out for the scene of the accident. They tried to keep Elizabeth from following but she fought them like a tiger. "I'm going to Monty!" she screamed and raced down the hill. Liz reached the car even before the two men. She squeezed through the door and crawled over the seat and crouched down, cradling Clift's head in her lap. He moaned and then started to choke. He made a motion toward his throat. Some of his teeth had been knocked out by the impact. Two front teeth were lodged in his throat.

"I'll never forget what Liz did," McCarthy said. "She stuck her fingers down his throat and pulled out those teeth. Otherwise he would have choked to death."

The doctor finally arrived. It took him half an hour to get Monty out of the car and he later said, "It was a miracle he lived. He was bleeding like a stuck pig. He had heavy lacerations on the left side of his face. His nose was broken, as was his sinus cavity—it was crushed. His jaw on both sides was crushed as well. He also had a severe cerebral concussion."

When McCarthy saw him later that night, he said that his friend looked, "like a David Levine cartoon."

"His face had ballooned to six times its normal size. He was propped up in bed, unable to speak because his jaw was wired." Elizabeth, Michael and McCarthy stayed in the hospital until Monty was put under heavy sedation and they were assured by the doctors that there would be no permanent damage.

The accident naturally made the late news radio and television shows and was spread all over the papers the next morning, along with shocking wire service photos of the wreck. The biggest worry seemed to be whether Clift would be scarred by the accident and unable to finish the movie. A few days later the MGM press department released a bulletin predicting that the film would only be held up for a few weeks at the most.

Libby came out as soon as she heard about the accident and was horrified by Monty's condition. She told him that he looked like hell and he should rest for at least several months, not just the "weeks" predicted by the studio, if he was to get his looks and health back. This surprised Monty, because MGM executives were coming in and telling him that he looked marvelous.

Clift was released from the hospital after two weeks and went back to the apartment he had rented on Sunset Boulevard. Libby went with him. He was still obviously in terrible condition. Somewhere he'd gotten his own supply of pills and started to drink again, too. His secretary, Marge Stengel, had flown out to the Coast and was staying in the house with them. He kept saying through his wired teeth that he had to finish *Raintree County*, no matter what.

His friends and his brother Bill Clift who had also come out to help him were shocked at his statement and were firmly against any such commitment. But Libby was the most vehement. She begged him to come back to Treetops and recuperate there and to forget any ideas about going to work. She promised to get nurses to look after him and see to it that he had peace for at least the couple of months that he needed to properly recuperate. And he wouldn't have to put up with studio bigwigs coming by every day or so to check up on the condition of his face.

"You must make up your mind," Libby said to him. "I'm going to take charge, and you are not to go back to this meaningless film. Let them collect on their insurance."

It was clear to Libby that if Monty went back too soon, he would imperil both his health and his career. But the MGM executives were frantic, and not to disappoint them, Monty ignored Libby's advice and decided that he would finish the picture after the wires were taken out of his jaw. This time Libby really got furious. She felt that Monty had ignored the advice of a loving friend and allowed himself to be influenced by strangers.

"If he's going to be so foolish as to go back to work now, there is nothing more I can do," Libby said angrily. "I can only help him if he'd be sensible." And she packed her bags and went back to Connecticut.

It turned out that Libby's hunch that the MGM Studio

was using Clift carelessly was absolutely right. Somehow he made it through the picture on pills, booze and tremendous nervous energy. While Monty was still in a practically invalid condition, they sent a mob of reporters to see him and to interview the entire company. The reporters came back with juicy stories about an actor who was "hell-bent on self-destruction."

By the time the company got back from location in Kentucky to Hollywood for the final scenes of the picture, every gossip column in Tinsel Town had something to say about Monty's behavior on the set. Most of the stories portrayed Monty as a pathologically disturbed character. Few took into account that on this occasion it was necessary for him to take the pills in order to finish the film.

In spite of the fact that Libby had left Hollywood piqued at his refusal to let her help, her invitation for him to recuperate at Treetops when the film was over was still open.

Monty returned to New York about a week after the completion of the picture. He was completely shaken up psychologically by the accident, and was convinced that his looks had completely been ruined. It was true that his face was not the same, but there was nothing grotesque about it. It was now a normal face, without some of the spectacularly beautiful planes that had attracted so much attention before. He had perhaps more character now. But as far as the press and the rest of the world was concerned, Monty's glamour was gone. He felt so bad about himself and so unattractive that he didn't even think sex with any gender was possible. It didn't cheer him up too much either that the picture was a bomb and even he himself considered it "a monumental bore."

He realized that the audience would go to see the picture principally to guess which scenes were taken before and which scenes were taken after the accident. But despite his apprehension, he was quickly cast again for the part of Noah Ackerman, a sensitive Jewish war hero in *The Young Lions.*

While studying the script, he lived with Libby at Treetops. He'd pass the whole afternoon mumbling the lines and making notes on the script while his favorite records, Fitzgerald and Sinatra, boomed through the mansion in the hi-fi. Generally he would leave the Connecticut estate only to go into New York to work with his physical therapist or to see his mother.

Somehow, despite his self-doubts, his drugs and his liquor, he managed to get over to Europe and do a really impressive job on the picture, directed by Edward Dmytryk, who had also directed *Raintree.*

He had barely returned from the shooting when he got word on March 23, 1958 that Mike Todd had been killed in a plane crash. He flew out to Chicago to attend the funeral but at the last minute couldn't face the frightening mobs of curious fans and hung back and watched from a distance.

Less than two weeks after Todd's death, replete with black tie and ruffled tuxedo shirt, he went to the New York premiere of *The Young Lions* at the Paramount Theater with Libby Holman on his arm. He was keenly aware that everybody was anxious to see how he looked after the accident. Sure enough, as soon as he made his first appearance on the screen a girl in the balcony stood up, screamed and fainted. And throughout the audience, there were shocked murmurs of "Is *that* him?"

He and Libby went to the studio party at the Waldorf afterward with his co-star Hope Lange and Don Murray, her husband. He happily sat there receiving sincere congratulations from actors like Paul Newman and actresses like Anne Bancroft, Geraldine Page, and Marilyn Monroe. He was absolutely elated by their reaction. But after the party when he and Libby went with Hope Lange and Don Murray to Reuben's for a nightcap and to read the reviews, came the letdown. The *Times* said, "Clift's performance was strangely hollow and lacklustre as the sensitive Jew. He acts throughout the picture as if he were in a glassy-eyed daze. . . ."

Clift tried to lighten the depression of the group by

joking about the review, but it was clear that he was shattered. Later, everybody went back to Libby's apartment. The publicist John Springer wandered with Monty through Libby's antique-filled living room, hung with pictures of her friends, Clifton Webb, Greta Garbo, Tallulah Bankhead, Josh White, and Bea Lillie. Libby mixed drinks for the crowd but she seemed tired and worried about Monty. The atmosphere was thick with tension and nobody seemed able to think of anything to say. After a long, agonizing silence, Monty began to cry. "Noah was the best performance of my life," he sobbed, "I couldn't have given more of myself. I'll never be able to do it again. Never."

Actually not all the reviews were so dire and many of them were in fact quite favorable. But after that night, Monty could not be consoled.

Libby was still a close friend to Monty, but she began to feel neglected as he turned increasingly to new friends for comfort. Nancy Walker became one of his closest chums and confidants, as did Myrna Loy. It was always a mother-figure that he was looking for. Libby in the meantime was also busy with her own friends, particularly the Bowleses.

The relationship with the couple, both writers, was considered distinctly odd by most who observed it. In the summer of 1958, Libby decided to take one more crack at serious theater by backing and appearing in a musical version of the Federico Garcia Lorca play *Yerma,* adapted by Paul Bowles. She persuaded the Metropolitan Opera star Rose Bampton to appear in it also and planned to try the musical out for its world premiere in July at Denver University.

Roger Stevens was to be co-sponsor. Critics from New York went out to cover the opening of the haunting, weird and mystical show. The *Herald Tribune* said of Libby, "Miss Holman appears to advantage when singing but displays uncertainty in her acting. She got off to a slow, stiff start in act one, but warmed to the job as the show went on."

But the critics, after praising Rose Bampton's voice, Libby's acting, some aspects of Bowles' writing, said that the show would need plenty of work if it ever expected to reach Broadway. *Yerma* was allowed to die a decent death out of town.

Shortly before she started working on the play, Libby had had a serious fright when eleven-year-old Timothy, one of her adopted sons, was seriously injured in a scooter accident. Timothy and a friend, Richard Dennis, were being towed up a hill on a scooter which resembled a sled on wheels. The rope attached to the towing automobile broke and the scooter plunged down the hill and hit a tree. As a result of the accident, attention was focused on Libby's lifestyle and the fact that though she was an adoptive mother, she was not married. She was told in no uncertain terms that if she did not straighten out her life, her children might be taken away from her.

Marrying Monty, of course, would have solved nothing, even had he been willing. Somewhere Libby made the acquaintance of a Jewish artist named Louis Schanker, approximately her own age, a vigorous, bereted, somewhat eccentric but absolutely straight little man. And early in the summer of 1959, she announced to everybody's astonishment that she planned to marry him.

She and Schanker must have had some sort of understanding, because neither her engagement, nor her very quiet marriage some months later, prevented her from seeing Monty from time to time.

When he was making *The Misfits* some months later near Reno, Nevada, Libby came out to offer her support. But Monty was nervous and troubled and they fought almost constantly in his room at the Mapes Hotel. Libby would cue him on his lines and tease him unmercifully about the fact that through drugs and liquor, he was gradually losing his memory. Monty was going downhill more rapidly than ever and was sadly aware of it. But still he continued working in a desultory fashion.

On a Thursday evening in September of that year, Libby and Schanker were strolling back to her townhouse half a block away from Monty's, after an evening in the theater, when they saw fire engines on the next block.

Libby, who always had an almost psychic intuition where Monty was concerned, suddenly was positive that it was his house that was blazing. She was right. She raced down the street, dragging the puffing Schanker behind her, but by the time she got to the scene, firemen had already extinguished the blaze. Libby approached one of the firefighters and introduced herself. "I'm Mr. Clift's closest friend," she said. "Please let us through."

And they did. Inside the house she found that the vestibule and a good part of the first floor had been completely gutted by the fire. There was choking smoke filling the hallways. Libby raced to the second floor, where Monty's apartment was, with Schanker trailing along behind her. She called out to him. Soon she heard an answering shout from the bedroom. When she groped her way to it, she found Monty and his current boyfriend sitting up in bed, coughing mildly from the smoke. Aside from a slight throat irritation, Monty assured her, they were fine.

It seemed that painters, redecorating the hallway, had set off the fire with their acetylene torches. Monty and his friend had been trapped in their room and were only able to get out when firemen reached them by hoisting a ladder from the roof of an adjoining building to Monty's roof and rescuing the two men from the skylight. As soon as the fire was out, Monty and his boyfriend groped through the wreckage of the stairwell and crawled back into bed, where Libby and Louis saw them.

The papers the next day ran the story on the front page and described Monty's friend only as "an unidentified male companion."

Schanker was disgusted with the scene. He had no patience for homosexuality or bizarre behavior, although some people said in his artistic clothes and ever present beret and cigar, he was a fairly Bohemian figure himself.

After Libby married Schanker they spent their time divided between Libby's home in Connecticut, the estate she had acquired on the South Shore of Long Island, and the apartment in New York.

Schanker, always described after his marriage to Libby in the press, as "an artist whose work is in permanent collections at the Met, the Modern Museum and the Whitney," was not exactly a household word in the art world. But he continued working on his large, lively abstracts, and huge ceramics. "He is also known for his colored woodcuts and sculptures," Libby told the *Post*'s Sally Hammond on the occasion of a UNICEF benefit performance that she gave in 1965 at the UN's Hammarskjold Auditorium.

"I was so pleased when UNICEF won the Nobel Peace Prize," she told the reporter. "Aside from next week's concert, they asked me to tour Europe for International Cooperation Year. I said I'd adore to. I consider UNICEF one of the most important facets of the UN."

The honor of appearing for UNICEF was considerable, since the only other artist who had ever performed there was the great cellist Pablo Casals.

> "Today Libby Holman is nearing sixty," Hammond observed, "and her raven-black hair is mostly gray. But her once pouty and provocative mouth is apt to be smiling easily or talking heatedly about her concern for peace and civil rights.
>
> "Pursuing their artistic aims separately, the Schankers lead a wonderfully varied life. They summer in East Hampton at their Japanese beach house and throw at least one smashing soiree a season, inviting the artists and writers colony."

Libby told the reporter that at her home base in Stamford, she had been quite active politically and that four days a week she worked for six or eight hours with Gerald Cook, "the urbane Negro pianist," who had been her musical partner since 1947. Oddly, there was no mention of the adopted children, who were then respectively twenty and eighteen years of age, in the interview, which described her life patterns and naturally rehashed the tragedies that had afflicted her through the years.

At the same time that Libby was rehearsing for her UNICEF appearance in New York, a portrait of Zachary Smith Reynolds was unveiled at Wake Forest College, in Winston-Salem, to which his brothers and sisters had given the bulk of the money from the Smith Reynolds Foundation. The article describing the dedication delicately skirted the question of the manner of Smith's death. The president of Wake Forest, Harold W. Tribble, said only, "Matching his daring spirit that took him in fragile planes above the clouds was the unselfish spirit of his sisters and brothers in dedicating their inheritance from his estate to the establishment of a philanthropic foundation in his name." The Z. Smith Reynolds Foundation, as it was called was conceived of as "an adventure into the field of Christian higher education."

The following year Libby made a recording for Evergreen Records with seven of her torch songs on one side and seven of her earth songs on the other.

But while Libby seemed to have settled down, more in pain than ever from her raddled ulcerated viscera, by 1965 Monty had not worked in films for three and a half years.

In 1966 Elizabeth Taylor persuaded Raoul Levy to give him a part as a repressed homosexual Southern colonel in Carson McCullers' *Reflections in a Golden Eye*. In 1959, she had insisted that he be cast opposite her in *Suddenly, Last Summer*. He had also made a spy picture for Levy called *The Defector* in Europe, a total bomb. All Monty could say about it was "Nothing went right. I have never had such a bad time in my life."

He returned to the States depressed, sicker than ever, and desperately lonely. In the past few years he had become more and more openly homosexual but had gone through a painful series of unsuccessful affairs. Meanwhile Clift was getting so irresponsible that he could not be trusted to look after himself. Finally his psychiatrist suggested that he hire a companion who was discreet, sympathetic and strong enough to cope with Monty's various problems, but who wouldn't behave like a nurse or a jailer. A young black man named Lorenzo James was found to handle the job. He was a graduate both of Howard University and the Parsons School of Design. He had tried acting and singing for several years without much success. Between jobs, he would work as a male nurse, taking care of heart attack victims and other convalescent cases.

By this time, most of Clift's friends had abandoned him. Lorenzo James, in an attempt to cheer him up, tried to get some of them to visit again. Nancy Walker and his old friend Bill Le Massena came, but Thornton Wilder, fed up with his drunkenness, refused. Kevin was busy working; and many other old friends didn't seem to have the time. Even Libby preferred only to have telephone contact with him.

On Friday night, July 22, 1966, Monty seemed to drift off into his usual nightly drugged stupor, quite late. That Saturday morning, Lorenzo James tried to wake him. "I was watching television at 5 A.M. Then I went to check on Mr. Clift because he had a habit of falling asleep with his glasses on and also because he hadn't been feeling well."

When he went to Clift's bedroom, James found the door locked. He thought this was unusual, since Monty never locked his door. He rapped repeatedly, trying to get some response from the bedroom. When he didn't get an answer, he tried to break the door down, but it was too solid. He finally had to run down into the garden, get a ladder, and climb into the bedroom window. He found Monty lying naked and dead on his kingsized bed—with his glasses on.

There seemed to be a lot of confusion about the cause of his death. The autopsy report indicated that there was no evidence of foul play or suicide and the *Times* obituary on the following day quoted the Medical Examiner as saying, "Mr. Clift died of occlusive coronary artery disease." Earlier, his own doctor estimated that Clift had succumbed to "convulsions due to alcoholism." Nobody ever explained why Monty locked his bedroom door that night.

In any event, it is a fair observation that Montgomery Clift's death was the longest suicide on record.

It was cloudy on the day of Montgomery Clift's private funeral service in St. James Church. Only one hundred fifty people attended by invitation, but outside several hundred fans, many of them tourists and housewives, stood near the church entrance and watched the arrival of such invited celebrities as Lauren Bacall, Nancy Walker, Dore Schary—and Libby Holman. Not present were Elizabeth Taylor, in London, Kevin McCarthy, who was out of town in a play, Roddy McDowell in Hollywood, and Myrna Loy, also in Hollywood. Libby sat in the back of the chapel. On either side were her two grown adopted sons, Timothy and Anthony. Her face, dried and wrinkled by her perpetual obsession with the sun, looked ancient. Her usually cheerful face looked agonized and her expression did not change throughout the service. She seemed frozen and gray as she emerged from the church. The small crowd of celebrity watchers had no idea who she was. Louis Schanker was not with her and Libby did not go with the small group of mourners to the Friends Cemetery in Brooklyn's Prospect Park where Monty was buried.

It seemed that Libby's heart, dealt one last and staggering blow, had finally broken.

23
The Curtain Falls

On June 22, 1971, just short of five years after the death of Montgomery Clift, the following item appeared in *The New York Times:*

LIBBY HOLMAN IS DEAD AT 65;
"TORCH" SINGER OF HIT MUSICALS

Famed for "Moanin' Low" and "Body and Soul"—Cleared of First Husband's Murder

STAMFORD, Conn., June 21—Mrs. Libby Holman Reynolds Schanker, widow of a Reynolds tobacco heir, and famous on Broadway in the early 1930's as Libby Holman, the blues singer, died here on Friday. She was 65 years old.

Miss Holman was already dead when she was brought to Stamford Hospital from her showplace in Merribrooke Lane, in North Stamford. An autopsy was performed, but neither the local medical examiner, Dr. Sadat Ozcomfort, nor the state medical examiner, Dr. Elliott Gross, specified the cause of death. The police were not called.

Miss Holman is survived by her husband, Louis Schanker, an artist. The body was sent to an undisclosed place in New York for private burial.

In the years following Monty's death, Libby had kept up a semblance of her old gregariousness. She never entirely stopped working though friends said she just was never the same.

There'd been periodic grim reminders that time was passing—and passing cruelly. Five months after Monty's death, Clifton Webb, who had been in Hollywood for some time and gained fame for his "Mr. Belvedere" films, died of a heart attack. He had been ill since May, after undergoing abdominal surgery.

Just before Christmas of 1968, Tallulah Bankhead, who had been ill with pneumonia complicated by emphysema, died after an attack of the Asian flu that was so prevalent at that time. Although Tallulah reportedly had a good deal of money when she passed away, her funeral expenses were reported to have been covered by Louisa Jenney. She was buried in Rock Hall, Maryland, not far from Louisa's home.

An article about Libby in *Newsday* chose to look at the sunny side of things.

"The 62-year-old singer finds life these days pretty much the opposite of dreary, thanks. It's filled with travel between the four houses she and her husband keep up, constant work on her huge repertory of material and a sprinkling of weekend cocktail parties. She herself put it recently with a quick glance around the East Hampton summer house that has become a local showplace: 'The moment of my career I have enjoyed the most is the present.'"

She told the reporter that she was restricting her concerts to four or five a year, simply because: "I've done a whole lot of singing in my time."

She was in fact about to do a concert in East Hampton the following night, which was the occasion for the interview.

"I'll do what I call Libby Holman's grab-bag of musical comedy, because people want that. But I also plan to sing several songs based on speeches and put to music by my arranger and accompanist, Gerald Cook. They're all speeches on civil rights and women's rights that a former slave named Sojourner Truth made around the country in the early 1800's. I'm not trying to stand on any soapbox or put across any messages, though. If there's any message at all, it's simply the great salty humor and the fact that it's wonderful that a woman could write these speeches even before the Civil War broke out.

"When I sing, the thing I want to do is establish communication with the audience. I look for a dramatic possibility or a comedy situation in a song, something that gives a vignette of life or tells a story. I let that song get into the marrow of my bones. I want it to be so much a part of me that if I died while singing, rigor mortis wouldn't set in until I finished every last word of it."

The following year, Libby gave another concert for the benefit of the United Nations Association but devoted to her interest in civil rights. The concert was dedicated to the memory of her good friend Dr. Martin Luther King, Jr., who had been assassinated a month before. A UPI reporter reminded Libby of the statement she had made to an interviewer in the years before. *"'I never want to envy youth. At fifty, sixty, seventy or eighty I want to have enough charm and fascination inside myself to draw admiration and love . . . I want to be rich inside.'"*

"The words still stand," Libby said. "I like being where I am. I've had hardships, heartbreaks. I would not want to go back again. And one more thing," she said as the reporter left, "I wish they'd quit calling me legendary. It sounds like I'm dead."

Libby's obituary in the *Times* was followed by a long, biographical summary of Libby's life, leaving out none of the high spots or the low spots. Louis Schanker at first told reporters that Libby had passed out while walking on the grounds of the estate inspecting her magnificent display of daffodils and had been found by a household employee.

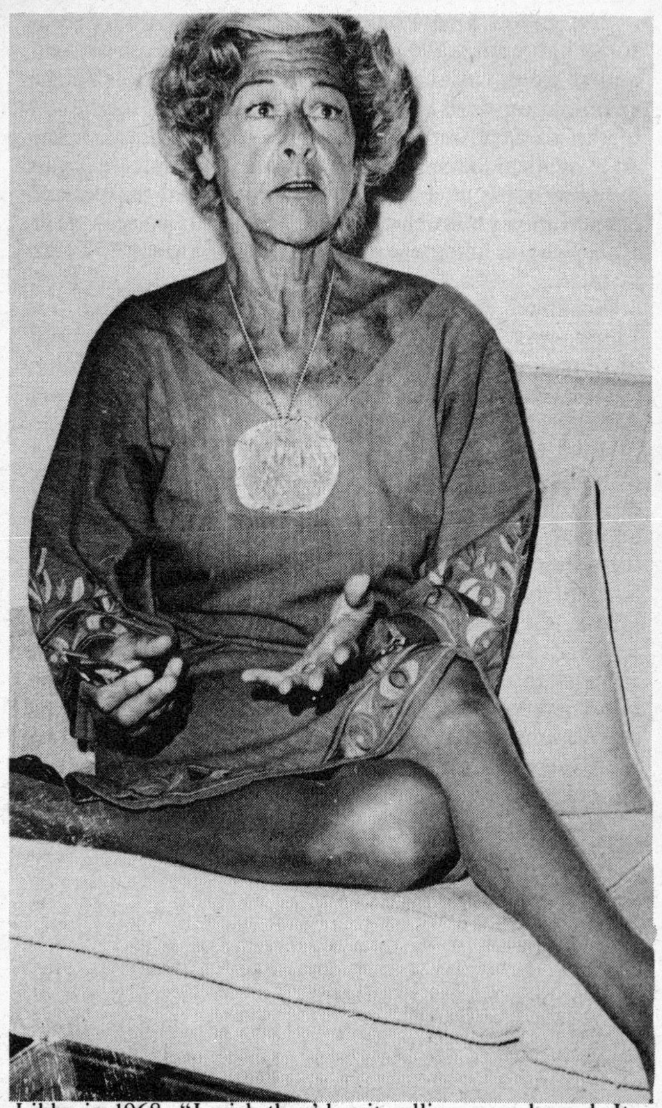

Libby in 1968. "I wish they'd quit calling me a legend. It sounds like you're dead."

Dr. Elliott Gross, state examiner, said that an autopsy had been made before Libby was hastily cremated, and it would be several days before the results of the examination were known. Three weeks later, the results of the autopsy were made public. Libby Schanker, the state medical examiner determined, was a suicide. Once the news was out, Louis Schanker admitted that he had found Libby's body clad in a bikini on the front seat of her Rolls Royce limousine in the garage of their 112-acre farm.

Schanker drove the car to Stamford Hospital, but Libby was dead on arrival. The medical examiner attributed death to acute carbon monoxide poisoning.

The headline in the Winston-Salem paper read: "LIBBY HOLMAN, REYNOLDS' WIFE, IS DEAD."

Libby left an estate of almost $12 million, about double the inheritance she had gotten from the Reynolds family. She left a million dollar trust to each of her two adopted sons, about a million and some property, including the Rolls Royce she died in, to Schanker, $72,000 to Jane Bowles of Tangiers, Morocco, $25,000 to Gerald Cook, $50,000 to the Zen Studies Society, a number of $50,000 bequests to friends and servants, and the rest to the Christopher Reynolds Foundation. She had already made several bequests to the Putney School in Vermont in memory of her son and the science building there was named for him. Boston University was given her papers and costumes.

The glory and the agony were over.

Afterword

When I first planned to do this book, I followed the usual work routine in these matters. I checked the library, the clippings, the morgues of the big newspapers and various books that had been written including mention of Libby's life. I came away with the idea for what seemed to be a great book, the story of a veritable Dragon Lady who killed at least one husband and possibly more, drove lovers to suicide and in some way or another caused the dramatic and untimely death of everyone close to her.

It was all there in the clips, though the case had been left open. It seemed a magnificent opportunity. I would go to Winston-Salem, dig into the original records of the case, find out how the Reynolds family had been blackmailed into interfering with the prosecution of Libby for the murder of Smith Reynolds, and have the satisfaction of wrapping up almost single handed a crime almost fifty years old.

The presentation I made for the story was impressive. It had everything—fast planes, fancy cars, hijinks in high society, dope, beautiful women, orgies—the works. When I contracted to do the book, the first step obviously was to go to the scene of the crime. But once in Winston-Salem, I found I had to readjust my thinking completely.

The first shock came at the offices of the newspaper, the Winston-Salem *Sentinel-Journal*. I went there certain I would find all of the local color, the stories that never made the wire services or the national papers, the intimate portraits of the local participants. I found—nothing. With a straight face, the librarian told me that the entire file on the death of Smith Reynolds must have disappeared somewhere. I found it hard to believe, and still do. The biggest story that had ever happened in Winston-Salem, and nothing in the newspaper file!

Using the date of the crime as a point of reference, I went to microfilms of the newspaper in the library and assembled a passable file. But it was apparent that even at the time of the incident, the local papers were sitting on the story. They actually gave it less coverage than the New York papers. I looked up the names of all the principals, trying to find someone still alive who could give me a first-hand view of what happened, but everybody was either dead, or missing, had changed their names, or had left that part of the world. Smith was dead, Ab Walker was dead, Blanche Yurka was dead, Libby Holman was dead. So, as far as I could tell, was everyone who attended that fatal party in July 1932.

There were a few bright notes. Reynolda was still maintained much as it was in 1932, but as a museum. I drove the four and a half miles out of Winston-Salem to the still impressive and well kept estate. I had a strange sense of *déja vu.* I had read so many descriptions of the place, seen pictures, analyzed diagrams until I knew it by heart. And it was much as I had envisioned it. If anything, I was a bit surprised at the exquisite tastefulness of the furnishings and decor. I had expected something a bit flashier, a bit more nouveau riche.

After a quick glance around, I told one of the guides why I was there. She was a woman old enough to remember the case. But she took on a hunted look as soon as I brought up the story. "We're not supposed to talk about that. We've been told if we discuss the Smith Reynolds case, we might be fired," the woman said. A conspiracy of silence after all these years!

She was friendly enough, though, and encouraged me to stroll about the house and satisfy my curiosity. I went up the stairs and looked over the balcony where Libby had cried out. I walked down the corridor toward the wing of the building in which I knew Libby's room had been with its adjoining sleeping porch. There was a door with a plush rope across and a "No admittance" sign. I looked around. There were no guides or guards. I unhooked the rope and opened the door; it was not locked.

The room was much as I had imagined it, but unlike some of the diagrams. It was larger than it appeared in the diagram. The bathroom discussed in the case was at the far end of the room to my right as I came in. In front of me was one of the two french doors going onto the sleeping porch. The bed where Smith Reynolds had suffered his fatal gunshot wound was now replaced by twin beds, but otherwise the room was much the same. I could not see any hole in the screen where the bullet had emerged. Apparently some maintenance had been done. I backed out quietly, feeling I had gained at least some idea of the atmosphere in which the incident took place.

I had no sooner replaced the hook than a pleasant young man, one of the assistant guides, appeared in the hall and asked if he could help me. He must not have seen me emerging from the room. I explained to him why I was visiting Reynolda and he seemed astonished. "All they ever told us here is that Smith Reynolds died in this house—and that we're not supposed to talk about it."

I told him that the room with the plush rope was the one in which he had been shot and he seemed surprised and interested. He asked me if I would like to see it. I couldn't very well tell him that I'd already been inside, in the face of this Southern hospitality. So I allowed him to unhook the rope again and lead me in. It seemed pointless, but I went over the story for his amusement and interest. When I finished my brief recital, he stood for a moment, bemused. "There's some interesting things about this room you might not know," he said. "Would you like to see the secret chamber?"

A secret chamber? Would I!

"You see that mirror there?" He pointed to a large antique mirror on the rear wall of the main bedroom. "Well, if you just pull on this little brass ring like this—" He tugged on a small ring in the corner of the mirror and the whole glassworks rolled back to reveal a closet big enough to be a maid's room.

"Another thing," he said. "See there in the corner, that little door. That's the safe. Every bedroom in this house has a little safe like that in the closet."

I nodded and took a note. I pointed toward the other door. "That must be the bathroom then."

"Yes." He showed me to it, and opened the door which had a matching mirror on it. "And of course you know that that other door [he pointed to a door on the far side of the opulent bedroom] connects to the next bedroom."

I had been over every drawing, every sketch, every description of Reynolda and no reporter, policeman or prosecutor had ever mentioned that there was a door connecting Smith Reynolds' room to the next bedroom.

The polite young man ushered me out and said he hoped he'd have a chance to read the book someday. I thanked him and said I was sure he would be interested and left. It was the first break that I had.

Back in town, I returned to the Winston-Salem library and went over the material there again. I saw at least a glimmer of light. There was a memorandum in what they call the "vertical file" of the library—a file containing folders with all the pertinent material on certain events. That folder at least was there, and in it I found a memo concerning an interview with Carlisle Higgins, that was apparently never published. The interesting thing about the interview was that it had been given in 1971, just after

Libby's death. The article mentioned that Higgins went on to become a North Carolina Supreme Court judge. I had looked up the name of every principal in the case in the local phone book and asked newsmen at the Winston-Salem *Citizen News* if they knew of any survivors, but nobody did. Most could barely remember the case. Carlisle Higgins, if he were alive, would have to be in his eighties, and if he had become a Supreme Court judge it was more likely that he was living around Raleigh, the state capital, than Winston-Salem.

I ran back to my hotel and called Raleigh information. It was one of those moments that make reporting so satisfying. "Why yes, sir," the information operator said. "Would that be *Judge* Carlisle Higgins you are looking for? And do you wish his office or his home number?"

He was there! He was almost surely alive, unless something had happened to him since the directory came out.

I called his home and the phone was answered by a cultivated soft voice with a hint of a Southern accent. It was Higgins himself. "Why sure, Mr. Machlin," he said when I had explained my mission. "I'll be glad to talk to you about the Reynolds case anytime. You just name it. Come down to the office and we could have a cup of coffee or some lunch."

Raleigh is a good three-hour drive from Winston-Salem and it was already six in the evening. I arranged to have lunch with Higgins on the following day.

He met me in the sleek, modern offices of the law firm to which he is now a consultant. He was a white-haired, thin-faced, rather slightly built gentleman with a firm, dry handshake and a cautious smile. He was, I learned, eighty-seven years old.

I started by asking him if he knew where I could find a transcript of the case. I had already been to the courthouses in Winston-Salem and in Raleigh. There were no records available. They, too, had disappeared.

"Well," the judge said, "I've got one right here."

And it was there in a brown manila envelope on his

desk. Obviously he had prepared himself for the visit. I asked if I could look at it and take some notes, and he agreed that I could do so after we'd had our chat. "Perhaps I could Xerox some pages?"

"You look like an honest young man, Mr. Machlin," Higgins said. "Why don't you just take it with you and bring it back when you're finished?"

Suddenly the gates of heaven were opening!

"That transcript, of course, Mr. Machlin, is partial. By that I mean to say there's quite a few pages missing."

"Oh?" I asked. "What happened to the missing pages?"

"I honestly don't know, Mr. Machlin. I never took a single page out of that transcript and I don't know who did. I had a number of folks here who saw that record. I realize that any one of them could have removed some of it."

"Where can I find a complete copy?"

"I don't believe that there is a complete copy anywhere," the judge said.

Since I had gone more carefully over the clippings after my initial reading, I had begun to form a few theories of my own. It seemed to me that McMichael and Transou Scott had been leaning very hard on the case and that Higgins had gone along only reluctantly. I asked him about this.

Higgins was a model of Southern courtliness and polite evasiveness, while being sure to score his points. "McMichael was a fine fella," Higgins said. "He was . . . well, he liked publicity—liked to see his name in the paper. Liked to hear himself quoted, and he talked freely."

"One has the impression," I said, "now that I've seen almost all of the clippings, that someone on the prosecution side—either the sheriff or McMichael—was feeding daily information to the press, not all of it factual . . ."

"I think that's true," Higgins said. "You don't see *me* quoted anywhere there, do you?"

We went over the case some more and I asked some questions, most of which confirmed material already available in a documented form. I asked Higgins to sum up his view of the case.

"There's no question about it. That girl was innocent. There was no case."

"Well, what about all those things that Scott was talking about? The bullet hole in the screen? The fact that Smith was left-handed? Those seem the strongest factual points."

"All untrue. Left-handed? Scott just made that up. There is not one shred of evidence that Smith was left-handed. He was right-handed. As for the bullet, you know we found it, don't you?"

I was surprised. Everything that had been written about the case indicated that the bullet had never been found.

"Yes, I was up there with Guy Scott, that's the sheriff's brother and he was the chief deputy and chief investigator of the case, with an expert I had brought down from the FBI. We went over the ground and we looked at the headboard of the bed, which was a massive iron antique contraption, with all sorts of cloverleaf designs on it, covered with green enamel. We found a place in the left side of the headboard, facing the wall, where the iron was dented and the enamel was chipped away. Following that line, it was clear to see that Reynolds had stood at the foot of the bed just as Mrs. Reynolds had described it. The bullet had hit the headboard and scattered parts of the metal jacket on the pillow where they were found and then, had passed through the window. We went outside and, taking a transit line to estimate its path of flight, and figuring that it had been slowed up and tumbling after hitting the end of the bed, we found it resting on a leaf in the garden less than a hundred feet from the house. I've got the bullet somewhere in my home in a little box. I can find it for you, if you like, but I'll have to do some digging."

After almost fifty years, this was the first report of the bullet being found. So there went most of Transou Scott's case.

"Another thing that makes it clear that it was suicide," Higgins said [nothing here about an accident], "was that bullet wound. The gun was pressed so tight to Smith's head that practically all of the powder burns were inside the wound. I never knew of a case where a man shot himself with a pistol where he didn't press it right against his head. But I've never known anybody to do that when they shot another person."

Higgins also told me that during the trial Will Reynolds had come to him and said that since he knew the county did not have the money to press a full investigation, the Reynolds family would pay for any expense the county incurred in its inquiry. Higgins said that he called J. Edgar Hoover, who was a friend of his, and had him recommend an FBI man who came down and worked with the Reynolds family's law firm, completely checking out the evidence and coming up with the recommendation that the charges be dropped.

"What about that night that Ab Walker and Smith Reynolds spent, the Sunday before his death, at the Robert E. Lee Hotel?"

"I'll tell you about that. There was something that never got into print. Guy Scott and I found out about it together. We went up to that hotel and they told us those boys had some bad women up there. All that night, they were drinking and carousing. We even found the bootlegger who supplied them with the liquor. They had ordered two quarts of Scotch and must have drunk it all during that night. That's probably why the poor boy was incapable the following night, after what he'd been up to. Guy Scott'll bear me out on this, too."

Guy Scott would bear him out? Then he was alive? "You mean Scott is available? Can I talk to him?"

"Why, sure. Let me write out a note to him. He lives right over beyond that little airport north of Winston-Salem. I don't know the exact address." The judge pulled out a sheet of office stationary and wrote me out a note by hand to the brother of Transou Scott.

I called Scott as soon as I left the judge's office and again was surprised when a deep voice with a mountain brogue answered. It was Guy Scott and he said he'd be glad to see me whenever I wanted to come out.

His house was on a small road, just off old Route 311, past a local airport outside Winston-Salem. I managed to find my way to the old road and asked directions to the airport. It was not until I was actually passing the parked plan that I noticed the name of the airport, "The Zachary Smith Reynolds Airport." Nobody out there referred to it by that name; they just called it "the airport."

Guy Scott unlocked the door of his small, ranch-style home in a run-down suburb of Winston-Salem, two miles north of the Smith Reynolds Airport. I had always thought it was only city folks who locked their doors. I asked him about that.

"Oh, you got to watch out, out here," Scott said. "There's a lot of them rogues about these days. You've got to watch out for them."

He was a fairly tall, stoop-shouldered man with the weathered face of a lifelong outdoorsman. After his brother left office, he told me, he had succeeded him in the office of sheriff for a while and then retired to work as a private detective, chasing down fugitives and runaways. He seemed friendly and open and didn't even ask to see the Judge's letter until I offered it. He offered me no drinks and I saw that the coffee table in his small, neat living room was covered with evangelical Christian literature, so I assumed it would be better not to ask for alcoholic refreshment.

The interview was fairly short. I had most of the facts down and I just needed certain details from him. I went over the question of the bullet.

"Why sure, me and the Judge found it." In his version Scott took a somewhat larger part in actually finding it than in the Judge's but the story was about the same. "I just found where the bullet made a little nick between the screen and the window frame." Everybody else said there had been a hole in the screen, and that they examined the wires around the hole, and that they were fresh, but Scott remembered it as having gone between the screen frame and the window frame—sideways.

"I found it out in the garden there, just layin' on a leaf. It didn't even punch through the leaf, it was so spent by that time."

"Then that explains why the bullet went in the direction it did?"

Scott shrugged. "I suppose so."

"And what about Ab Walker and Smith in the hotel room?"

"Them boys was just havin' some fun. Wasn't nothin' queer about neither one of them. Had a couple of bad girls in there all night."

"Well, then, do you agree with Carlisle Higgins that the whole case should have been dropped?"

"No, indeed! That girl was guilty sure as Christ was born."

"Well, what was the motive?"

"Money! Money was the motive. He was one of the richest boys in the world. Don't you know that?"

"But how could she get the money if Smith wasn't old enough to write a will?"

"Well, maybe they were drunk and figured that they would just settle for half his personal property. . . ."

"Why do you think that the case was dropped?"

"There was a lot of people that did not want it tried. . . . They were in the family."

"Why do you think they didn't want it tried?"

"They were afraid that maybe Ab Walker done it in place of her. He would. He would of done anything that she'da wanted him to. Libby Holman and Ab Walker were seen in the hotel together more than once. The Robert E. Lee, and other places she wanted to go—the Reynolds family had a place up there in Yosemite, somewhere and they went there together too. And all around New York. They were lovers all right.

"And that woman that was with her," he continued, "that actress. She'da done just about anything for Libby too. She was washin' her back and combin' her hair and doing everything for her."

[Obviously Scott was not aware that Blanche Yurka was one of America's most distinguished actresses, but had the impression that she was Libby's personal maid.]

"She shot him or shot at him, close to him, once the time they were up there in Yellowstone. This was produced at the grand jury hearing, in which they returned a true bill of indictment. But somebody removed that from the court house. Nobody knows where it's at. You see, they was enough pressure, they was enough money behind, if it was used, to have this file removed after they had satisfied their selves that it would not be put on trial. That would be an easy matter for any lawyer. Polikoff could have done it.

"Then after the grand jury *nol pros*'ed the case, they just let it drag on and on, one grand jury after another, till everybody just forgot about it. It was pressure from the family."

"But what do *you* think happened in the case?" I asked finally.

"Ab and Libby done it. *The whole thing was cocked and primed by them Jews up in New York.* All them people she brought down with her."

A querulous voice sounded from one of the back rooms. "I'll have to go now, Mr. Machlin. That's my wife. She's feeling poorly and we have to go up to the old folks' home to see her mother."

And that was the end of the interview, but it was enough. After all these years of speculation as to why Scott and McMichael pushed so hard for Libby's indictment, it was there, clear as a mountain stream, prejudice from the start, anti-Semitism as had been alleged. A crusty old sheriff, a hardbacked Baptist, and a politically ambitious assistant solicitor. They had lynched Libby's reputation as surely as Leo Frank had been lynched in Georgia seventeen years before Smith

Reynolds was found dying in his bedroom with a bullet through his head.

For Libby never actually recovered from the blow of that scandal which haunted her career through her life and eventually ended her stardom.

Guy Scott, like his brother, had nothing to offer but rumors and innuendo. Not one of his charges of complicity or romance between Ab and Libby were ever proved. It seems likely that if Libby and Ab really were prancing about the streets of Winston-Salem, racing around summer resorts and consorting in automobiles, Transou Scott would have been able to come up with at least one witness. He produced none.

On the Jewish matter, I got further confirmation when I began to read in my motel room that night the transcript given to me by Judge Higgins. In it I found some questions that had been asked either in the secret session of the coroner's jury or had for some reason been left out by almost all of the newsmen who reported the case.

There on page 41 of the transcript, I saw the questions, seemingly dragged in out of the clear blue North Carolina sky, which proved that prejudice was a major inspiration for the prosecution's case.

McMICHAEL: Did you know Mrs. Reynolds was a Jewess?

WALKER: No, sir.

McMICHAEL: When did you find it out?

WALKER: I never knew she was a Jewess.

Up to this point it is not certain that any of the jurors knew that Libby was Jewish, either, although people close to the family were aware of it. If they didn't know it before, though, they knew it now, right in the first hour of the inquest.

McMICHAEL: Did Smith know it?

WALKER: I don't know, sir.

McMICHAEL: Did you ever hear Smith Reynolds

express his opinion or make any statement in regard to people of the Hebrew race?

WALKER: No, sir.

McMICHAEL: Did you know he had a very peculiar opinion about them?

WALKER: No, sir.

McMICHAEL: On Sunday night, when he talked to you at the hotel, didn't he tell you he had just learned that Mrs. Reynolds was a Jewess?

WALKER: No, sir.

McMICHAEL: At no time since you have known Mrs. Reynolds, has she ever said she was a Jewess?

WALKER: No, sir.

The prosecution was working on a number of theories on the crime, and apparently one of them was that Smith Reynolds was so upset by the discovery that his wife was Jewish that he wanted to call the marriage off and that for this reason Libby killed him.

McMichael didn't let the questioning go with that. When he had Blanche Yurka on the stand, we find him pursuing it again in the testimony.

McMICHAEL: Do you know whether or not Mrs. Reynolds is a Jewess?

YURKA: I don't know.

McMICHAEL: Had you ever heard it said that she is?

YURKA: I was completely unaware of the fact until you mentioned it.

Later on, on page 149 of the transcript, I found that he was still pursuing this question.

McMICHAEL: I believe you said, although you had known her for six years, you never heard it intimated before yesterday that she was a Jewess?

YURKA: No, sir.

McMICHAEL: Do you know now she is a Jewess?

YURKA: Well, having met her father and mother—I

didn't know she was a Jewess until I met her father and mother the other day. I give it no importance.

So Guy Scott's statement is amply confirmed in the record. And why not? The South at that time and particularly North Carolina was a hotbed of Ku Klux Klan activity. There was apprehension about Roosevelt, who was running for President at that moment and rumored to be a Jew named "Rosenfeld."

Only a few years after Libby's inquest, America's first nationwide convention of anti-Semites was held not many miles away in Asheville, North Carolina. Among the honored delegates was William Randolph Hearst, owner of the *Mirror* and several other papers which took a decidedly anti-Holman point of view.

A sociologist named John Higham, studying the subject of anti-Semitism in America, noted that it was deeply ingrained in the agrarian tradition—and cropped up most frequently in times of crisis—such as the Great Depression, at its nadir at the time of Smith Reynolds' death. Higham found anti-Semitic fervor "most widespread and in many cases most intense in small-town cultures of the South. . . . Southerners were more inbred than were Northerners and were therefore more concerned with the purity of their Anglo-Saxon heritage. Religious fundamentalism, another force that encouraged anti-Semitism, was more widespread in the South than the North."

According to William J. Robertson, most Southern Methodists and Baptists were advised by their spiritual leaders that the Jews were "Christ killers." However, the feeling was most prevalent among farmers and people of rural background. Guy Scott told me he and his brother were raised on bottom-land farms and were not allowed to leave home by their parents until they were twenty-one.

Having discovered this, I expected to find that the Reynoldses were anti-Semitic, but I found that at the time of the trial they had been interviewed by at least one reporter on the question of Libby's Jewish background.

Will said: "About that Jewish question, I'm terribly sorry to see it brought into the case. I was shocked when I was told that Mr. McMichael the assistant state solicitor had asked those questions of two of the witnesses.

"Of course the family knew Libby was Jewish. Smith told me that himself. He remarked that maybe it would do the Reynolds blood a lot of good to have a Jewish mixture in it. I agreed with him.

"Some of the dearest friends I have are Jewish. I have a keen admiration for them. As a race, they don't make any finer people."

Certainly an unequivocal statement and lacking the hedging and lip-service often seen in the "some-of-my-best-friends-are-Jews" type of response to the question of anti-Semitism.

There was other evidence, too, of how deeply Will Reynolds took this. On the night that he heard about McMichael's questioning, he turned pale with anger at the dinner table. A guest who was in his home at the time said, "He didn't eat another bite. He got up and walked the floor. He was so greatly upset, he actually became ill . . . I never saw Mr. Reynolds so angry in his life. 'That's a damnable outrage!' Mr. Reynolds shouted."

Dick Reynolds, too, said that he was well aware of Libby's background. "I knew Libby was a Jewess," he said. "It never made any difference to me or anyone in my family. If you can think of any finer type of blood to have in you, I wish you'd tell me what it is."

After I had talked to Scott and read the transcript, I called Higgins to check a few points. I asked him outright if he thought that the fact that Libby was Jewish had anything to do with the prosecution.

"I'm certain it did," the Judge said, "but I was determined that there would be no repetition in my area of the notorious Leo Frank case."

One of the problems that would have arisen if Scott and McMichael had actually been forced to take Libby to trial, of course, is that all of their innuendoes and vague theories would have been thrown out. The case in any event would have been run by Higgins who would not allow such questions to be brought up in the first place.

"Do you think it is possible that Guy or Transou Scott themselves were members of the Klan?" I asked the Judge.

Higgins stammered a bit, for the first time in any of my conversations with him. "I...I couldn't answer that question. I had nothing to do with the Klan, and I wouldn't want to venture an opinion about that."

"I understand in those days a lot of people belonged to the Klan because it was socially and politically desirable."

"I think that's true," the Judge said.

"Certainly some law enforcement people..."

"Oh, a good many," Higgins affirmed. "I saw a good many that I suspected...."

So it is out after all these years. Libby's reputation was strangled for life by the prejudices of a Southern sheriff. As the years went on and the story was repeated in rehash after rehash, even some of Libby's friends came to believe it.

Leonard Sillman, who claimed to be one of her closest friends early in her career, told me he was convinced that Libby had been involved in the death of her husband "for the money. She would do anything for money," he said. I must say that he is the only person who said that about her. Also, it must be pointed out, that Sillman knew absolutely nothing about the actual circumstances of the incident, except what he read in the newspapers, which was highly tinted. Libby never discussed the matter with any of her friends, as far as I know.

Sillman's was a mine of faulty memories. He put the blame squarely on Libby for the death of Phillips Holmes and his brother Ralph. The way he told it, Libby had told Phillips that she was leaving him and Phillips had gone right up to Canada and crashed his plane. In fact, it was several years later and in England. He also said that Ralph, after an argument with Libby on his return home, had gone back to his hotel room and jumped out of the window. The fact, amply documented, was that he had been dead in his subleased apartment from drugs for eight days before he was found, though it is still a mystery exactly who found him.

But once the evil legend started, it just tended to expand in all directions.

Lucinda Ballard, Howard Dietz' present wife, who came to know Libby well in later years, was also convinced that Libby was guilty. She, too, could only know of the case from what she read in the papers. Of course, the papers through the years augmented and repeated Transou Scott's contentions. Pretty soon it became part of the legend that Libby was found hugging and kissing and even having sexual intercourse on the floor of the hospital room, although the testimony made it clear that she was pinned into her negligee, that Walker was still wearing his bathing suit, and that the two nurses who testified had seen no sign of intimacy.

Also it became part of the legend that just before Smith was shot, Libby and Ab were seen coming up from the swimming pool together. There was no such testimony and furthermore nobody seems to have ever even seen Libby in a bathing suit that night. At least, nobody was certain of it.

Walker appeared from the other direction when Libby reappeared after her disappearance, according to the watchman.

So if Smith Reynolds committed suicide, we have to answer a few embarrassing questions:

1. Is it reasonable to believe that Libby actually blacked out for that entire long period?
2. Why was Ab Walker's testimony so confusing and contradictory?
3. Was there something funny about the gun not being found immediately? Judge Higgins thought it was not mysterious at all, that the gun had been found quicker than the testimony indicated, but a reexamination of the text didn't support the Judge's impression.

Several scenarios are possible under the circumstances. Going over the evidence a number of times, I found some interesting points:

A. Libby's bedroom slippers were found under Ab Walker's bed. But when she arrived at the hospital she was barefoot, although she presumably had come immediately from her bedroom after finding her husband dead.

B. Though Ab said that he had spent the time just before the shooting cleaning up and had come back later to clear up the glasses and take care of closing the doors, the fact is that the doors were open and the liquor was still there later on when the police arrived, as were Libby's garments in his room and her pajamas downstairs. If Ab was to serve as a valet as well as a secretary, he certainly would have done a poor job.

Basically what intrigued me is the fact that Libby was missing for such a long period during the party but that during that period all of the guests, including Ab Walker, were accounted for, with the exception of Mary Lou Vaught, who was presumably so drunk she couldn't move, or so some witnesses said.

People in North Carolina at that time were not very familiar with the kind of drugs available among the habitues of Broadway. There is ample evidence from Libby's friend Tallulah Bankhead and others that from the time of *Three's a Crowd* on, she indulged a great deal in drugs in combination with liquor, a practice which we now know frequently leads to total blackouts, and sometimes to death.

It is my opinion that Libby, already drunk and upset over her public quarrel with Smith, took a few downers and passed out somewhere on the grounds during a large part of the party. You will remember that Fulcher, the watchman, said that when she returned she had a grass stain on her knee.

Now we shall construct a schedule of the moments surrounding the death of Smith Reynolds.

According to the watchman, Libby came up from the

direction of the lake about 12:30 and Smith took her by the arm and ushered her inside. A half hour later, Ab Walker testified, he was cleaning up downstairs, when Blanche Yurka called his attention to the noises from Libby and Smith's bedroom. By 1:10 Smith was in the hospital.

When the police arrived, what did they find? Libby's white lounging pajamas on the couch downstairs. The red jersey top that she wore under them, which was mistakenly referred to as a "sweater," was found on Ab's bathroom floor. A pair of bedroom slippers belonging to Libby—*bedroom slippers,* not sandals or shoes—were found under Ab's bed. And, unknown to anyone until now, there was a connecting door between Ab's room and Smith and Libby's bedroom.

It is my theory that Ab and Libby were pals but had not been alone together nor had they had sex prior to that night. Both were drinking heavily and Libby was unhappy with her husband. The only people who testified that Smith had suggested they should have an affair were Ab and Libby themselves. I don't believe this. I also don't believe that there were any girls in the Robert E. Lee Hotel room with Ab and Smith. I am suspicious of the fact that the only thing that Judge Carlisle Higgins and Guy Scott agreed on was this point, about which no evidence was ever produced, although it would have been of use to the prosecution to show that Smith was not, in fact, impotent as of the night before his death.

It is my opinion that Judge Higgins, a kindly, courtly and fastidious gentleman of the Old South, has taken it upon himself to help protect the reputation of a defenseless dead son of a powerful family. There is nothing illegal about this, or even shameful.

There seems to be a general pattern of protecting the name of the Reynolds family, and of Smith Reynolds in particular. The parts that were missing from the transcript—no matter who removed them—were the parts that dealt exactly with Smith's impotence and other embarrassing aspects of his behavior. Of course, it's not possible to know what all was said, since these pages, as I have said, were missing, but some of the testimony was later reported by witnesses.

Getting back to Ab and Libby on that fatal night, I think that Libby was in something of a stupor, totally "stoned." Remember the testimony of Fulcher, the night watchman, that she just kind of "smiled" when he spoke to her, but didn't say a word?

Libby sat down on the couch and started to take off her pajamas. Smith went upstairs, disgusted with her overall behavior. Libby went upstairs half-clothed and looked into Ab's room. Ab was also drunk. There was some sexual suggestion going on; perhaps Smith *had* said that he wanted them to have an affair, but how impotent could he be, since he had succeeded in making her pregnant only a month earlier? He had also made his other wife pregnant. If he had this sexual problem, it must have been of short duration.

Now I think that either they invited Smith to join them in bed, or Smith came in through the adjoining bathroom and saw them. In any event, I do believe that Smith was a deeply disturbed boy with heavy suicidal tendencies and it wouldn't have taken much to set him off.

Perhaps Libby was just sitting there in the nude and Ab in his bathing suit. It is well known that Libby thought nothing of sitting around in the nude in her dressing room or any place else, when she felt like it. Anyway, I think Smith went back to their room and shot himself. Libby, by now naked, heard the shot and ran into the other room. She tried to stanch the blood with a towel, unsuccessfully. Ab, who had followed her into the room, was in a funk also. Remember they were both drunk and Libby was also out on drugs. The frightened couple decided that they had to cover up the situation somehow. They took the gun and hid it, possibly downstairs, possibly in Ab's room. What they were covering up was whatever it was they had been doing in Ab's room prior to the suicide. Ab thought it would be a good idea to go downstairs while Libby got into her negligee and then came out and shouted for help. He went downstairs and fumbled around among the ashtrays and glasses while Libby slipped into her peach negligee.

Blanche, who had heard the noise of the shot or perhaps Ab and Libby's discussions of what they had found, emerged from her room when she heard Libby shouting that she'd found her husband dead.

Ab's later confusions and inconsistencies all had to do with their awkward drunken effort to cover the evidence up at first. Remember, he said he had to get back from the hospital to clean up and close the doors. But he didn't close the doors. He didn't find Libby's pajamas downstairs and he didn't get rid of the liquor. And though both swore they were sober, serious authorities, like all of the doctors that saw them, thought they were drunk beyond belief.

Well, it's a theory. It doesn't account for Libby's slippers being found under Ab's bed, but since there were so many other inaccuracies, let's assume for the moment that the police and the jurors didn't know the difference between slippers and Libby's somewhat stylish casual footgear. When she heard the shot, she ran from Ab's bed to her own room, leaving the slippers behind and by that time she was too upset and excited to go back and get the footgear so she left her room barefoot.

Another hypothesis: Libby, Ab and Smith went into the house together. Ab went to his room. Libby started to fool around with Smith trying to arouse his possibly dormant sexual appetite. She took off her pajamas down on the couch; but Smith, unwilling, unable, or embarrassed at this semi-public display stalked off to their room. Libby followed, took off the rest of her clothes, dropping the red striped jersey on the bathroom floor, and put on her peach negligee and slippers. After more loud discussion with Smith (what Blanche heard) she went to Ab's adjoining bedroom, possibly inviting Smith to form a threesome or to be a voyeur, or possibly going alone to talk with or make love to Ab.

Smith, despondent and confused, returned to their

room, if he hadn't remained there all along, and shot himself. Libby and Ab, startled by the shot ran into the bedroom, leaving her slippers behind, and running past the discarded red jersey on the bathroom floor. There are plenty of scenarios that can be written, and at this stage nobody to say what is the correct version.

I do not believe, as has been suggested in the legend through the years, that either Smith or Ab were homosexual. Again, if they had been, there would have been enough eager testimony to the fact. Ab was never seen in the company of gay young men and in his later life, when he went to Corpus Christi, Texas, he married and lived an absolutely straight life. Despite the innuendoes in the tabloid press even before the death of Smith saying that he was of "doubtful gender" and "queer," there is no evidence that he ever showed any interest in other men except Ab, and Ab had been enlisted as his companion from boyhood. On the contrary, Smith seemed to spend a awful lot of time chasing women, including Ann Cannon and the forlorn novelist, Nancy Hoyt.

It is possible he may have had some transitory periods of impotence because of the enormous amount of drinking he had done, but since he was barely twenty, not being able to get an erection might have seemed to him a tremendous affliction, and possibly one he had never encountered before.

At first I seriously considered the possibility that Topper, the child Libby bore eight months after Smith's death, was actually the child of Ab Walker, but a look at the photographs of the boy shows him not only to look like his father but to bear an uncanny resemblance to him. At first the news that Topper was born prematurely might be thought to contribute to the theory that Ab could have been the father. But in that case, Libby would have had to be certain that she had been impregnated in that one night of sexual intercourse, in order to testify as she did.

As to Smith's attack on Libby for being cold and frigid or at least very capricious in her sexual demands, her later history indicates that she was that way, and probably did not like ordinary straight sex with a man.

I think another version of the scenario above may be that Smith was in some way persuaded to take part in a threesome with Libby and Ab. It seems apparent from her relationship with Tallulah and others that Libby was fond of this. Lucinda Ballard said that she finally broke off her friendship with Libby because Libby suggested to her ex-husband such arrangements and Lucinda did not approve.

To sum up the good and the bad of it; on the negative side, Libby was a heavy drinker, a pathological user of drugs, a person of bizarre sexual appetites, a woman seldom capable of constancy in love, a person capable of maliciously using a sarcastic and pungent wit.

On the positive side; she was brilliant, intellectual, generous, funny, kind to her friends and enormously talented—and she did *not* murder her husband.

Let's give her credit too, for being a dedicated pioneer of black rights and a major contributor to that cause.

It would be right if Libby were remembered for her devastating voice and smoldering presence, her generosity and humor—what Libby called "scattering my smallesse"—rather than for the vicious trumped-up murder case that haunted her to the end of her days.

Index